*This appeared to be
her only chance
to live the life
for which she'd taken
that desperate risk.*

However grand his rank or handsome his face or splendid his physique, this was still a man, she told herself. Though he hid his eyes, she knew he was mentally taking off her clothes and liked what he saw. She felt rather than saw the slight tension in his posture: the alertness of the predator when it marks his prey.

A harem slave would be tearing off her garments about now.

Zoe knew she could not entice him in that way. Not here, at any rate. Not now. She must appeal to him from mind to mind. It must be business. The way men did it.

Or at least it must seem so.

By Loretta Chase

Don't Tempt Me
Your Scandalous Ways
Not Quite A Lady
The Last Hellion
Lord of Scoundrels
Captives of the Night
The Lion's Daughter

LORETTA CHASE

Don't Tempt Me

A V O N

An Imprint of HarperCollins*Publishers*

This is a work of fiction. Names, characters, places, and incidents are products of the author's imagination or are used fictitiously and are not to be construed as real. Any resemblance to actual events, locales, organizations, or persons, living or dead, is entirely coincidental.

AVON BOOKS
An Imprint of HarperCollins*Publishers*
10 East 53rd Street
New York, New York 10022-5299

Copyright © 2009 by Loretta Chekani
Excerpts from *Memoirs of a Scandalous Red Dress* copyright © 2009 by Elizabeth Boyle; *Lord of the Night* copyright © 1993 by Susan Wiggs; *Don't Tempt Me* copyright © 2009 by Loretta Chekani; *Destined for an Early Grave* copyright © 2009 by Jeaniene Frost
ISBN 978-0-06-163266-2
www.avonromance.com

First Avon Books paperback printing: July 2009

Avon Trademark Reg. U.S. Pat. Off. and in Other Countries, Marca Registrada, Hecho en U.S.A.
HarperCollins® is a registered trademark of HarperCollins Publishers.

Printed in the U.S.A.

10 9 8 7 6 5 4 3 2

Acknowledgments

Thanks to:

Myretta Robens for pointing the way to the fabulous diamond ring.

Sue Stewart for aid in carriage crashing.

Sherrie Holmes for assorted search and rescue missions.

And, as always, family and friends: with special thanks to Walter, Nancy, Susan, and, yes, my sisters.

Prologue

Northamptonshire, England
Spring 1799

Yesterday, when they buried his parents, the sun shone.

Today, too, was incongruously sunny, cruelly bright and cheerful and hopeful, the birds singing and the first spring flowers blooming.

Ten-year-old Lord Lucien de Grey hid from the sun and the world's horrible happiness.

His older brother Gerard found him, a ball of misery curled up in one of the numerous small passages of the old house their parents had loved. It had been a favorite of the Dukes of Marchmont since it was built, centuries earlier.

Gerard, three years older than Lucien, had become the tenth Duke of Marchmont.

"Don't think about them," he said. "That only makes it worse."

"I wasn't!" Lucien shouted. "You don't know anything! I hate you!"

The battle quickly escalated from words to blows. They fought, that day and in the following days, over everything and nothing. Family members and tutors intervened, but no one liked to chastise two grieving boys, no matter how appalling their behavior.

They broke furniture and crockery. They broke a window and knocked the head off a statue their grandfather had brought back from Greece. So it went on for weeks.

Then one day their father's great friend Lord Lexham appeared.

The two families had spent summers together. For a long time every summer, it had seemed as though yet another Lexham baby had arrived. By the time the fatal fever struck Lucien's parents, Lexham's brood appeared to have settled at eight: three boys and five girls, with the last child named Zoe Octavia.

Lord Lexham was one of the three guardians the Duke of Marchmont had appointed in his will to look after his sons.

Lexham was the only one who took an active hand.

His hand was active, indeed.

He hauled first Gerard then Lucien into their father's study and gave them each a birching, and no light one, either.

"Ordinarily I do not believe in corporal punishment," he said afterward, "but you pair are hard cases. One must get your attention first."

No one—*no one*—had ever whipped them.

And yet, strangely, it was a relief.

It certainly got their full attention.

"We had better find something for you to do," he said.

He found a great deal for them to do. He put them on a punishing course of study and exercise. It proved a powerful antidote to angry misery and brooding.

And then, as the bright spring warmed into summer, another antidote to sorrow entered Lucien's life. Once again they traveled to Lexham's country house. This time Lucien finally became personally acquainted with the catastrophe-waiting-to-happen that was Zoe Octavia. She was five years old.

Zoe Octavia Lexham hated rules even more than Lucien did, and broke them more than he did. This was no small accomplishment, considering how much harder it was for girls to break rules.

She ran away. Constantly.

She'd done it for the first time, he discovered, when she was four years old. She did it several times during that first summer after he'd met her and did not stop doing it in the years thereafter. She was the problem child. Her tendency to bolt at every opportunity was only one of the problems.

She rode horses she wasn't supposed to ride. She played with children she oughtn't to associate with. She was too often found in places where a nobleman's daughter did not belong. She seemed to take delight in doing exactly what she was not supposed to do.

She lay awake nights, Lucien was sure, devising ways to annoy and embarrass her brothers, especially.

When she was seven, she dared her brother Samuel to climb onto the roof. He, six years older, informed her that he wasn't a trained monkey and it wasn't his job to entertain her. She called him a fraidy-cat-mud-for-brains. Then she climbed out onto the steepest part of the roof.

Lucien was the only one agile enough to fetch her down.

He became the one, too, who fished her out of fish ponds and tracked her to the gamekeeper's cottage or the blacksmith's when she went missing. None of her siblings ever had the least idea where to find her or what to do with her.

The cricket incident was typical.

She was eight years old. The boys were organizing a cricket game. She stormed up to him.

"I want to play, Lucien. Tell them to let me."

"Girls don't play cricket," he said. "Go back to your dolls and your nursemaids, brat."

She snatched up a bat and swung it at him—or tried to. She swung as hard as she could, and kept on going. Round and round she went, like a whirligig, and down she went, on her arse.

And there she sat, her disorderly golden hair standing on end and her vivid blue eyes wide open and her mouth open, too, so startled she was.

He laughed so hard, he fell down, too.

She was annoying, sometimes infuriating, generally impossible. And she was a bright, bright spot in his life.

One

Lucien Charles Vincent de Grey, the eleventh Duke of Marchmont, stood on the threshold of the morning room of White's Club, surveying the company through half-closed eyes.

Women tended to read deep meaning in those sleepy green eyes, when in fact there wasn't any deeper thought in his mind than *I wonder what you look like naked*.

Women often got the wrong idea about him. The way his pale gold hair shimmered in certain lights lent his features an ethereal quality. The tendency of one wayward lock to fall over his forehead was deemed poetic.

Those who knew him knew better.

The twenty-nine-year-old Duke of Marchmont was neither ethereal nor poetic.

He avoided deep thoughts and allowed no strong feelings to churn inside him. He took nothing seriously. This included dress, women, politics, his friends, and even—or perhaps most especially—himself.

At present, no woman stood in danger of being deluded, because none were in the vicinity. This was White's, after all, the exclusive preserve of five hundred privileged men.

Several of them had gathered at the famous bow window where Beau Brummell had once presided. Even at present, when the Beau languished in France, hiding from his creditors, seats in that holy place were reserved for a select few.

At the moment the occupants included Brummell's great friend the second Baron Alvanley, as well as the Duke of Beaufort's heir, the Marquis of Worcester. Arguing with them were Lord Yarmouth, Lord Adderwood, and Grantley Berkeley. Of the group, only Adderwood—thin, dark, and perhaps the most levelheaded of the lot—had not been one of Brummell's boon companions. He was Marchmont's. They'd been friends since their schooldays.

Though he broke half a dozen of the Beau's rules daily and, worse, believed it didn't signify, the Duke of Marchmont was one of the Chosen.

He didn't know or care why they'd chosen him. Truth to tell, he considered Brummell an annoying great bitch, and preferred sitting in the bow window when the rest of that lot weren't about, practicing their wit—such as it was—upon passersby in St. James's Street.

Who the devil cared whether this carriage's panels

were too dark, or that fellow's coat was an inch too short or that lady's bonnet went out of fashion last week?

Not the Duke of Marchmont.

He cared about very little in this world.

His sleepy green gaze slid from the collection of wits and dandies at the bow window to a quiet area across the room, where a fellow dozed in a well-padded armchair. As though he felt the ducal regard, the gentleman opened his eyes. Marchmont made the smallest movement of his hand, a gesture universally recognized as *Go away*. The gentleman quickly got up and left the room.

His Grace had scarcely folded his six-foot frame into the chair when he became aware of a buzz of excitement emanating from the bow window contingent. Their attention, he noticed, was not directed at passersby in St. James's Street but at the leather-bound betting book.

After a moment, Lord Adderwood let his keen, dark gaze travel the room until it lit upon his erstwhile schoolmate. "There you are, Marchmont," he said.

"What a noticing fellow you are, Adderwood," said Marchmont. "Nothing escapes you."

"I was about to search the club for you," Adderwood said. "We could not possibly close the betting book without you. What do you say? I say she is."

"Then I say she isn't."

"How much, then?"

"Put me down for a thousand pounds," said the duke. "Then pray tell me firstly, Who is she? And secondly, Is she or isn't she what?"

Every head came up, and every set of eyes swiveled in his direction.

"Good God, Marchmont, where have you been?" said Alvanley. "Patagonia?"

"Busy night," said His Grace. "Don't remember where I've been. Where's Patagonia? Anywhere near Lisson Grove?"

"He doesn't read the papers until bedtime," Adderwood explained to the others.

"I find them an unfailing aid to a deep and dreamless sleep," said His Grace.

"But you don't need to read anything," said Worcester. "They've plastered pictures in all the print shop windows."

"I came the other way," said Marchmont. "Didn't see any pictures. What's happened? Another one of the royal dukes wooing a German princess? No surprise there. I have long waited for one of the royal family to do something truly shocking, like marry an Englishwoman."

Last November, following a long and agonizing labor, the country's beloved Princess Charlotte had produced a stillborn son and died. This sad end to England's hopes—she'd been the Prince Regent's only child and heir—had led her uncles, the royal dukes, to abandon their mistresses and numerous illegitimate offspring in order to commence marriage negotiations with various Germanic cousins.

"Nothing to do with them," said Adderwood. "It's to do with Lexham. We are evenly divided between those who say his lordship has finally taken leave of his senses and those who say he was right all along."

Marchmont's eyes opened a little wider then, and

his indolent mind came to something like attention.

"Zoe Octavia," he said. If they were making bets about Lexham, it must have to do with his long-lost daughter.

A dozen years ago, Lexham had taken his wife and youngest child on a tour of the eastern Mediterranean. This had not struck Marchmont as the wisest enterprise during wartime.

True, the French had surrendered Egypt to the British in 1801, and Lord Nelson's great victory at Trafalgar had demonstrated England's naval supremacy. But the seas remained far from safe. Furthermore, European power struggles meant nothing to the various pashas and beys and whatnot ruling their bits of the Ottoman Empire. Greece, Egypt, and the Holy Land were part of that empire, and rulers and ruled alike all carried on as they'd always done. The slave trade was lucrative, and white slaves were always wanted for the harems—as the pirates lurking in the Mediterranean well knew.

The region was not, in short, the safest place to take any twelve-year-old, fair-haired, blue-eyed English girl, let alone Zoe. They'd scarcely reached Egypt when the fool girl had bolted, naturally, the way she'd so often done at home.

But this time Marchmont wasn't there to track her down, and those who'd searched could find no trace of her. It was believed she'd been kidnapped. Lexham waited for a ransom note. It never came.

He never gave up trying to find her. Though eventually he'd had to return to England, he'd hired agents to carry on the work. They had traveled up and down the Nile, and they'd made their way from Algiers to

Constantinople and back again. They'd heard she was here and they'd heard she was there. They'd gathered rumors and nothing else.

Marchmont had given up hope a decade ago, and locked away Zoe in the mental cupboard with the others he'd lost and the feelings he no longer let himself have.

"What number is this?" he said. "Has anyone kept track of how many females have appeared on Lexham's doorstep, claiming to be his long-lost daughter?"

"I made it to be twoscore," said Alvanley. "The greater number in the early years. It's dwindled considerably of late. I'd nearly forgotten about her."

Though everyone believed him mad to continue searching for her, Lexham had proved sufficiently compos mentis to reject every last one of the would-be Zoes.

"Then I reckon we can put the total at twoscore and one," said Marchmont.

Alvanley shook his head.

"This time he took her in," said Adderwood.

The Duke of Marchmont left his chair and stalked to the bow window.

Berkeley picked up one of the newspapers from the table there and gave it to him.

"Lord Lexham Welcomes Harem Girl," the headline proclaimed.

Marchmont's usually unexcitable—some said nonexistent—heart began to pound in a very strange manner. Not that anyone could tell. His drowsy expression never wavered while he scanned the lengthy article in the *Morning Post*.

"'Mysterious young woman,'" he read aloud. "'Arrived in London on Monday night with Lord Winterton. . . . Family forewarned, gathered at Lexham House, prepared to confront and oust yet another imposter . . .' and so on and so forth." He shook his head as he skimmed the columns. "'The reader will imagine the tears shed upon the joyful discovery—'" He looked up. "I believe I shall be sick. Who writes this drivel?"

He read on dramatically, "'But indeed it was she, restored at last to the bosom of her family, after twelve long years as a captive in the palace of Yusri Pasha.'" He skipped a few more paragraphs. "'Shocking crime . . . Lexham . . . ancient barony . . . youngest daughter kidnapped and sold in the slave market of Cairo . . .'"

With a laugh, he dropped the newspaper onto the table. "Vastly amusing. You didn't happen to notice the date, perchance?"

"I didn't need to notice," said Adderwood. "On the way here, any number of urchins told me my hand-kerchief was hanging out of my pocket. Does there exist an April Fool jest older than that one? I vow, boys must have tried it on Socrates. April Fool was the first thing I thought when I saw the paper. But what, exactly, is the joke?"

"Everyone's forgotten about her," said Alvanley. "Why make her a joke? Why not choose a more timely topic?"

"You saw who brought her home," said Berkeley.

"Winterton." England's second most cynical cynic. The Duke of Marchmont came first. "Even had I failed to observe the date, that name would have aroused my suspicions." Cold-blooded and single-minded, Winterton was not the sort of man who rescued damsels in distress.

"Still, the fact remains, a girl has turned up at Lexham's, claiming to be Lexham's youngest," said Worcester. "That part isn't an April Fool joke."

"Have you seen her?" said Marchmont. He took up the paper again. It made no sense—unless Winterton had suffered a concussion in the course of his travels in the East.

"No one's seen her, except those she claims are her nearest kin," said Alvanley. "And they're keeping mum. Last I heard, they'd cloistered themselves at Lexham House and were not at home to visitors."

In spite of his determined efforts to suffocate it, the Duke of Marchmont's interest was well and truly piqued. His expression remained sleepily amused.

"I begin to understand why Adderwood was about to stir himself to hunt me down," he said.

"You're family to the Lexhams," Adderwood said.

That was no joke. Marchmont knew his former guardian better than Lexham's own children did. The man was no fool.

Yet this young woman had bamboozled him—as well as Winterton, apparently.

It made no sense.

The Duke of Marchmont, however, was never at a loss. If he felt uneasy or doubtful or confused or—as was the case at present—utterly confounded, he ignored it. He certainly didn't show it.

"As a member of the family, I declare that this girl, whoever she is, cannot be Lexham's youngest,"

Marchmont said. "Zoe in a harem for twelve years? If they chained her to a very thick wall, perhaps."

"She was a hoyden, as I recall," said Adderwood. More than once he'd joined Marchmont during those long-ago summer holidays with the Lexhams.

"A bolter," said Marchmont.

He saw her too clearly in his mind's eye.

I want to play, Lucien. Tell them to let me.

Girls don't play cricket. Go back to your dolls and nursemaids, brat.

He shoved the memory back into the mental cupboard it had escaped from and slammed the door shut.

"I hope for Lexham's sake the woman isn't his daughter," Alvanley said. "'Bolter' would be the kindest of epithets Society will bestow upon her."

"Twelve years in a harem," said Berkeley. "Might as well say twelve years in a brothel."

"It isn't the same thing," said Adderwood. "Quite the opposite, actually."

"No one cares whether it is or it isn't," said Marchmont. "No one's going to let facts get in the way of a good scandal."

And this situation was the sort scandalmongers dreamed of, as alchemists dreamt of the philosopher's stone. The tale—of an English girl, a peer's daughter, lost for twelve years in the exotic East among heathens and polygamists—was a feast for the dirty-minded.

"Wait until you see the prints," said Worcester. "Wait until you see the mob outside Lexham House."

"They'd already gathered when I was going home at dawn today," said Berkeley. "Place looked like Bartholomew Fair."

"Clerks, milkmaids, shopgirls, peddlers, pickpockets, and drunkards, all wanting a look at the Harem Girl," said Worcester.

"I heard they summoned troops to disperse the crowd," said Yarwood.

Marchmont would have laughed at this latest example of human absurdity if Lexham hadn't been at the center of it.

It was Lexham whose good name the scandal and notoriety would besmirch. It was Lexham, one of the House of Lords' most dedicated and hardworking members, whose judgment would be questioned. It was Lexham who'd be ridiculed.

The Duke of Marchmont cared about little in this world, and the little began and ended with Lord Lexham. What the duke owed his former guardian could hardly be put into words and certainly could never be repaid.

This nonsense had to be stopped. Immediately. And, as had used to be the case in a Zoe-related crisis, Marchmont was the one who had to do it.

"Put me down for a thousand pounds, Adderwood," he said. "I don't know who she is, but she isn't Zoe Lexham. And I'll prove it before the day's over."

An hour and more after he'd made his bet, the Duke of Marchmont regarded the sea of people in once-peaceful Berkeley Square. Above their heads thick grey clouds mounted, bringing an early darkness to the day.

No one cared about the weather. An earthquake wouldn't drive off this lot, he knew. Waiting for a glimpse of the principals in the latest high-society drama was quite as good entertainment as a public hanging.

Only someone who'd lived in a hermit cave for the past year would find the uproar surprising.

The nation had spent the winter grieving for its beloved Princess of Wales. To ordinary folk, the Princess Charlotte had been one bright, happy image in the depressing lot that constituted the present royal family. The tale of the Harem Girl couldn't have appealed more to their mood and taste if it had been made up special: Spunky English girl (like the late princess) overcomes impossible odds and outsmarts a lot of heathen villains. Better yet, Zoe Lexham's tale was not only heroic but titillating. Visions of Salome danced in their heads.

By this time His Grace was more fully armed with information, as well as better lubricated with alcohol. Over a bottle or two or three, his friends had repeated all the tales they'd heard. Before coming here, he'd stopped at Humphrey's Print Shop in St. James's Street. He'd had to push through the mob gawking at the pictures in the windows.

One caricature showed a well-endowed Zoe Lexham, arrayed in nothing but a large snake, performing a salacious contortion meant to represent oriental dancing. In another, she gyrated lewdly in transparent veils while a turbaned fellow with the prime minister's face offered her the Prince Regent's head on a platter.

Though His Grace lingered over these, he didn't neglect the less obscene pictures wherein, for instance, Lexham featured as a deluded old fool and

Winterton was shown smuggling the girl out of Egypt
in a rug, like Shakespeare's Cleopatra. Several other
prints made reference to an incident last year, when a
woman led some trusting souls in Gloucestershire to
believe she was the Princess Caraboo of Javasu. She
turned out to be a nobody named Mary Wilcocks of
Witheridge, Devonshire.

Marchmont had no idea who the young woman
in Lexham's house might be, and didn't particularly
care. All he knew was that he had not looked forward
recently to anything so much as he looked forward to
unmasking her.

He began to make his way through the crowd,
"accidentally" knocking out of his way those who
failed to move quickly enough. He didn't have to do
this often. The Duke of Marchmont's sleepily ethereal countenance had been caricatured on numerous
occasions. It had adorned print shop windows and
print sellers' umbrellas. The world knew—or thought
it did—all about him. When they saw him coming,
sensible people got out of the way.

Meanwhile, in the small drawing room of Lexham
House, the object of all the excitement sat at a small
table near one of the windows, studying the fashion
plates in the latest edition of *La Belle Assemblée*.

As she had learned to do in the harem, Zoe made
herself the calm in the eye of the storm.

All seven of her siblings had descended upon
Lexham House this morning.

All seven had been closeted with her and her parents in the small drawing room since then. All seven

had spent the time ranting and raving. The numbers, if not the noise, had dwindled in the last few minutes, however.

Her eldest brother, Roderick, had been the last of the brothers to stomp out. A moment ago, he'd followed Samuel and Henry downstairs to the billiard room. There, beyond a doubt, they were all sulking, because Papa had told them they were behaving like hysterical women.

Zoe knew they'd rather remain at Lexham House sulking than go home and face their wives. If all of her siblings were angry with her for disrupting their lives, what could she expect from their women?

It was obvious, too, that her brothers were counting on her four older sisters to wear Papa down.

Augusta, Gertrude, Dorothea, and Priscilla remained at the large central table. There they consumed great quantities of tea and cakes, to keep their energy up for the endless complaints, reproaches, and recriminations they deemed necessary on the occasion. The younger pair, Dorothea and Priscilla, having reached advanced states of pregnancy, tended more to tears, sudden changes of sentiment, and occasional swoons than the elder two.

The storm, which had briefly abated with the brothers' departure, broke out again. Zoe let it rage about her, gathering her wits and saving her energy for the crucial moment.

"She cannot remain in London, Papa."

"You've seen the newspapers."

"If you could see the prints—"

"Lewd, disgusting things."

"Snake charmers and such."

"We are a joke, a circus entertainment for the mob."

"I was obliged to skulk through Town like a common criminal, and sneak here through the garden."

"We had to cover the crests on the carriage."

"Not that there's any point to leaving the house, when one's ashamed to show one's face in public."

"One certainly cannot visit friends. One hasn't any."

"Three hostesses have rescinded their invitations."

"Seven have declined mine."

"We may be sure that's only the beginning."

"One cannot blame them. Who wants the London mob on the doorstep?"

"All of the neighbors in Berkeley Square hate us, except Gunter's. They're doing a brisk trade in pastries and ices, I don't doubt. But the Devonshires will cut us, you may be sure. The Lansdownes, too. And the Jerseys."

"You know what will happen next."

"Riots, I don't doubt."

"*Lady Jersey*—one of Almack's patronesses—only think what that means. We'll be taken off the list!"

A stunned silence, then:

"Good grief! What's to become of my Amy's birthday ball?"

"Call it off. No one will come."

"Parker says we must remove to the country. Can you credit it? Now! At the height of the Season!"

By this time, Mama, easily blown by every emotional wind, had given up trying to decide whose side she was on. She'd taken to the chaise longue, where she lay with her eyes closed. Every so often she let out a moan.

Different language, Zoe thought. *Different clothing. Different furnishings. Yet so like the harem.*

Papa stood at the fire, his back to them all. "Indeed, I can think of no greater catastrophe than to be denied entrance to Almack's," he said to the fire. "Two nights ago you sobbed because the little sister you believed dead had turned out to be alive. Two nights ago you marveled at her courage. Now you can't wait to be rid of her."

Zoe wasn't sure whether her sisters had wept with happiness or shock or outrage.

She'd entered the house and found them all— parents, siblings, and siblings' spouses—in the entrance hall, like an army braced to repel an invader.

What if they don't know me? she'd thought. *What if they don't believe it's me?*

But all she'd had to do was look up and meet her father's cold, suspicious gaze while she let the hood of her cloak slide from her hair. Papa had stared at her for a moment. Then he'd closed his eyes and opened them again. She'd watched them fill with tears. Then he'd opened his arms and she'd run into them.

"My dear girl." Emotion had clogged his voice, but she'd understood every precious word. "Oh, my dear, dear girl. I knew you'd come back." He'd wept, and Zoe had sobbed, too. She was home at last.

Though she'd come back a woman, not a girl, though she'd been gone for so long, he'd known her. They'd all known her, like it or not. Like all of her sisters, she had her mother's dark gold curling hair. But she was the only one who'd inherited Grandmama Lexham's profile and her deep blue eyes.

They couldn't deny she was their own Zoe Octavia.

Then, within twenty-four hours, the trouble started, at which point they all remembered that their own Zoe Octavia was the problem child.

"I don't want to be rid of her," Priscilla cried. "I'm sure I don't, Papa. But we haven't any choice."

"You most certainly do," said Papa. "You can act with courage. You can hold up your head and ignore this foolishness. If we do not feed the rumor mills by hiding and denying, the world will soon find something else to make a fuss about."

"Papa, I wish I could believe that—"

"If it were an ordinary sort of scandal, naturally, that would be the case—"

"But this is like nothing that's happened before."

"It isn't like a political scandal—"

"Or even a crim con case or a divorce."

"A Harem Girl, Papa! When was the last time London had a Harem Girl?"

"They might as well call her Jezebel."

"Some of the newspapers have called her that—and other names a lady must not utter."

"If she goes into any public place—a shop or park or theater—everyone will stare and whisper."

"She won't have a moment's peace, nor will anybody near her."

"Those dreadful journalist persons will follow wherever she goes."

"She cannot live a normal life, nor can we, while she is by."

"Not in London, certainly."

"But if she were to go away, to a quiet place in the country—"

"Dear Cousin Horatio's, for instance—"

"May he rest in peace, poor man."

"And if she lived there under a different name—"

"Ooooh," Mama said faintly. She covered her face with her handkerchief.

"Go away?" said her father. "Change her name? But she's hardly come back!" Papa turned to face them, and Zoe was shocked to see the grief in his face. "My little girl. Twelve years I've spent trying to get her back. Twelve years I've prayed and worried and kicked myself a thousand times for my folly. Twelve years I've raged at myself for not taking better care of her." He met her gaze then. "I shall never forgive myself, child, for what you've suffered. I shall never forgive myself for all the time we've lost and can never recover."

"I'm truly sorry for all the trouble I've caused you, Papa," she said. "I'm sorry for causing everyone so much trouble this time." She closed the book of fashion plates and folded her hands on top of it. "If there's no other way to make it right than for me to go away, then I shall go away."

Her sisters' eyes began to dry. Mama took the handkerchief off her face and sat up a little straighter.

"Well, I'm glad you've decided to be reasonable," said Augusta.

"I shall go to Paris," Zoe said.

Her sisters screamed.

"Or Venice," Zoe said. "I've lived shut away from the world for twelve years. I cannot bear to do that again. But these are cities. They have shops and theaters and parks and such. I shall feel alive again."

"She can't live in *Paris*!"

"What will people say?"

"She has no notion what she's proposing."

"No morals, you see. No notion of what is fitting."

"No notion of what is practical, I should say. What will she live on?"

"Where will she live? Who'll look after her?"

"I'm sure these thoughts never cross her mind."

"She always was the most heedless creature."

Papa said nothing, but he was studying her face. He'd always understood her far better than any of her siblings had. He waited, leaving it to her.

She took courage from his trust in her. "I shall take my jewels and take a different name, as has been suggested," she said.

"Jewels?"

"What jewels?"

"She never mentioned jewels."

"She means some trumpery gewgaws from the bazaar."

"I mean rubies and diamonds and pearls and emeralds and sapphires," Zoe said.

The sisters stilled. Priscilla froze with a piece of cake halfway to her mouth. Gertrude set down her cup.

"Gold and silver bracelets and necklaces," Zoe went on. "*Jewels* is the correct word, is it not? Karim was fond of me, and he was most generous. I thought I must sell all of my treasures to pay for my return home, but it was not nearly as costly as I had supposed. I was glad of that, because I had hoped to share my possessions with the women of my family. But if it is troublesome for me to remain here, the jewelry will allow me to live in another place. I was told that Paris and Venice were not as expensive as London."

Her sisters were looking at one another.

When it came to jewelry, women the world over were the same. If her future and everything for which she'd risked her life had not been at stake, she'd have laughed, because her sisters behaved exactly like the harem women they scorned.

She kept her expression serene. "I would rather stay here," she said.

The silence continued while the sisters mulled this over.

Sometimes the wisest course was simply to offer others a strong motive to solve the problem.

"I don't see how it could be arranged," said Augusta after a moment.

"Even if one were to reeducate her—"

"It won't matter what she does or how she behaves. All everyone will see is the Harem Girl."

"How could one persuade a hostess to have her?"

"No one will have *us* while she's about."

"I doubt the Prince Regent himself could make her welcome in the Beau Monde."

"Unless he married her."

Bitter laughter at this.

"But he's already married, whether he likes it or not."

"One of the royal dukes, then?"

"You're dreaming, Priscilla. They must marry princesses."

"The daughter of a duke is the very lowest they might consider."

"But for Zoe . . . Suppose the gentleman was of exceedingly high rank—"

"If he ranked high enough, the hostesses would not risk offending him. They must accept his wife."

"To offend certain gentlemen is to commit social suicide. Someone like Mr. Brummell is required: a truly fashionable gentleman whose appearance—even if it is only for ten minutes—determines the success of a gathering."

Silence again while the sisters pondered.

A moment later:

"Still, he must stand *very* high. Lady Holland is not invited anywhere because she's a divorcée."

"Lord Holland is a baron. Not nearly high enough."

"How high must the rank be?" said Zoe.

"It's out of the question," Augusta said impatiently. "We waste our time cudgeling our brains. Of the few noblemen of sufficiently high rank, nearly all are married."

"How many are not?" Zoe said.

Dorothea counted on her plump, be-ringed fingers. "Three dukes. No, four."

"One marquess," said Priscilla. "That is not counting the courtesy titles. Ought we to count those?"

"It is an exercise in futility to even contemplate such a thing," said Augusta.

"In the first place, how would one of these gentlemen meet her, when no one will invite her to a gathering?" said Gertrude.

Augusta and Gertrude had always been the killjoys.

"Oh, dear," said Priscilla.

"Even if they could be made to meet her, it's out of the question."

"You're quite right, Augusta. She, a woman of four and twenty—who's lived in a *harem*, who may or may not have been married to a Mohammedan person, who cannot speak proper English, and has no notion of what is and is not a fit topic of conversation?"

Zoe had found out that one was not allowed to mention a great many subjects: certain body parts, pleasuring oneself, pleasuring another, desire, impotence, concubines, eunuchs . . .

The list went on to infinity. She was competent and intelligent, but in this environment she was still too much at sea. She'd recovered her English during the journey home. In coming home, though, she'd entered a world as alien as the harem had been at first. Precious little of what she'd been taught up to the age of twelve had stuck in her brain as well as her native language had done.

"She can learn," Papa said. "Zoe always was a clever girl."

"She hasn't time to learn," said Gertrude. "Papa, if you would only put your parental affection aside—"

"I hope I should never do so."

"That is a worthy hope, I am sure, Papa," said Augusta. "But the difficulty is, it prevents your viewing the matter objectively. What nobleman, I ask you, would want Zoe when he might have a fresh, young, *innocent* bride of eighteen or nineteen?"

The door to the small drawing room opened.

"His Grace the Duke of Marchmont," the butler announced.

Two

As he usually did upon entering a room, Marchmont paused to size up the situation. Even now, after the bottle or two or three, his gaze was not as sleepy as it appeared to be.

He saw:

1. Lexham standing in front of the fire, looking ready to tear his hair out.

2. Lady Lexham fluttering upon the chaise longue, in her best dying moth imitation.

3. At the large central table, the four married Lexham daughters, all in black, a color particularly depressing in women of their complexion. As usual, the two eldest appeared to suffer from an ob-

struction of the bowels. As usual, the
two younger ones suffered the consequences of a lively conjugal life. They
looked ready to drop brats any minute
now—twins or ponies, judging by their
circumference.

4. and at the window . . .

. . . a girl with a book in her lap.

A girl with golden hair and startled blue eyes, the
bluest eyes in all the world, set in a heart-shaped face,
all creamy white and pink . . .

That was as far as Marchmont got. He was aware
of his own eyes widening and a curious galloping
sensation in his chest and a feeling of being set on
fire, then thrown into a deep pool of water. He was
equally aware of the way the pink in her cheeks deepened and the way her shoulders went back while he
stared and the way the movement drew his attention
downward to a figure with the elegant curves of a
statue of Venus he'd seen somewhere or other.

All of this happened so quickly that it disrupted the
already uncertain connection between his tongue and
his brain. Even at the best of times, he might speak
first and think later. At present, thanks to the bottle
or two or three, his mind was in a thickish haze.

He said, "Ye gods, it's true. That dreadful girl is
back."

"Marchmont."

The masculine voice uttering his name in a familiar,

patient tone made him blink. He climbed out of the very deep pool and into the present. He tore his gaze from the girl and aimed it at his former guardian.

Lexham's expression had changed to one all too recognizable: a mixture of exasperation and affection and something else the Duke of Marchmont chose not to put a name to.

"Thank you, sir, I should indeed like a glass—or ten—of something," Marchmont said, though he knew perfectly well that Lexham was not offering a drink. The duke recognized all of his former guardian's tones of voice. When he said "Marchmont" in that way, it meant, *Recollect your manners, sir.*

Nonetheless, His Grace persisted, as he often did, in willfully misunderstanding. "Something strong, I think," he went on. "I find myself in need of a bracer."

Zoe. Here. Alive. It wasn't possible. Yet it must be, because there she was.

He looked at her again.

She looked right back at him, up and down, down and up.

The back of his neck prickled. He was used to women eyeing him. This sort of survey usually occurred, however, in gatherings of the demimonde or in a private corner of an ostensibly respectable social event. It did not happen in the open in an unquestionably respectable domestic setting.

He was not disconcerted. Nothing disconcerted him. Disoriented was more like it. Perhaps he should have had a little less to drink before coming here. Or perhaps he hadn't had enough.

"But of course you want something to steady your

nerves, dear," said Lady Lexham. "I fainted dead away when I saw our Zoe."

This didn't surprise him. The calamity of twelve years ago had sent Lady Lexham into a dangerous decline. While she did recover physically, she did not recover the steadiness and strength of mind she'd once possessed, though he was not sure she'd ever possessed great stores of either quality. These days her ladyship spent much of her time agitated, swooning, or trembling—sometimes all three at once.

At the moment, he himself felt oddly light-headed. "Zoe, indeed," he said. "So it is."

He made himself meet the assessing blue gaze again. The girl smiled.

It was and it wasn't Zoe's smile, and for some reason the image of a crocodile came into his mind.

"And now I've lost a thousand pounds," he went on, "for I made sure I'd find another Princess Caraboo in your drawing room."

"Good grief!" cried one of the sisters.

"Is that what they're saying?" said another.

"What would you expect?"

"I daresay it isn't the worst of the rumors."

Marchmont's gaze swung toward the Four Harridans of the Apocalypse.

"You ought to see the satirical prints," he said. "Most . . . inventive."

"You needn't rub it in."

"You find it all hilarious, I don't doubt."

"If you'd been harried from pillar to post, as we have been—"

"Don't waste your breath. He—"

"You are a duke," came a feminine voice that didn't belong to any of them. It was like theirs but different.

Marchmont turned away from the Matrons of Doom and toward the girl at the window: the girl who was and wasn't the Zoe he'd known so long ago.

She had risen from the chair. Her deep red cashmere shawl set off handsomely the pale green frock and was draped in a way that perfectly framed her figure. The high-necked frock's narrow bodice outlined an agreeably rounded bosom. The fall of the skirt told him her waist was smallish and her hips full. She seemed taller than her sisters, though it was hard to be sure, given that two of them had expanded so much horizontally, and all four of them were seated.

In any event, she was not a pocket Venus by any means but a full-sized model.

Her potently blue eyes held a speculative glint. Or was he imagining that? His vision was in good order. He had no trouble focusing. His brain, on the other hand, was unusually sluggish.

"You speak English," he said. "More or less."

"It was much less at first," she said. "Lord Winterton hired a companion and a maid for me. They couldn't speak Arabic. No one else but he could, and he would not. For all the journey home, I had to speak English. And it came back." She tipped her head to one side, studying his face as though it, too, were a forgotten language. "I remember you."

In the voice that was like and unlike her sisters' he detected no trace of anything one might call a foreign accent. Yet she spoke with a lilt that made the sound exotic. It was a voice with shadows and soft edges.

"I should hope so," he said. "You tried to kill me with a cricket bat once."

She nodded. "I went round and round, then I fell on my bottom. You laughed so hard you fell down."

"Did I?" He remembered all too clearly. The mental cupboard would not stay closed.

"I remembered that while I was away," she continued. "I often pictured you falling down laughing, and the recollection cheered me." She paused. "But you are . . . different."

"So are you."

"And you are a duke."

"Have been for some time," he said. "Since before you went away." Forever. She'd gone away forever. But she was back. He knew her, yet she was a stranger. The world was not altogether in balance.

She nodded, her smile fading. "I recall. Your brother. It was very sad."

Sad. Was that the word?

It was in the way she said it. He heard a world of sorrow in that word. He remembered how she'd wept and how shocked he'd been, because Zoe Octavia never wept. And that had somehow made his own grief all the more unbearable.

"It was a long time ago," he said.

"Not to me," she said. "I crossed seas, and it was like crossing years. To everyone it must seem as though I have come back from the dead. If only I had done so in truth, I might have brought your brother with me."

One devastating moment of shock, a sting within as of a wound opening—but then:

"Good heavens, Zoe!" a sister cried.

"Pay her no heed, Marchmont," said another. "She

has acquired the oddest notions in that heathenish place."

"What does he care? Blasphemy is nothing to him."

"That doesn't mean one ought to encourage her."

"One oughtn't to encourage *him*, either."

"But I must speak to him," the girl said. "He is a duke. It is a very high rank. You spoke of dukes and marquesses. Will he not do?"

A collective gasp from the harridans.

"Do for what?" he said. The wound, if wound it had been, vanished from his awareness. He glanced from sister to sister. They all looked as though someone had shouted, "Fire!"

The intensely blue gaze came back to him. "Are you wed, Lord Marchmont?"

" 'Your Grace,' " Dorothea hastily corrected. "One addresses him as 'Duke,' or 'Your Grace.' "

"Oh, yes, I remember. Your Grace—"

"Zoe, I must speak to you privately," said Priscilla.

Marchmont frowned at Priscilla before reverting to the youngest sister. "*Marchmont* will do," he told the girl who was and wasn't Zoe.

Part of his brain said this was the same girl who once tried to injure him with a cricket bat, who climbed trees and rooftops like a monkey and fell into fish ponds and wanted to learn gamekeeping and blacksmithing and was so often found playing in the dirt with the village children.

But she wasn't the same. She'd grown up, that was all, he told himself. And she'd done a first-rate job of it, as far as he could see.

Since the others so obviously wished to stifle her, he decided to encourage her. "You were saying?"

"Have you any wives, Marchmont?" she said.

"Oh, my goodness," said one harridan.

"I can't believe it," said another.

"Zoe, I beg you," said another.

Marchmont looked about him. The sisters were undergoing spasms of some kind. Lexham had turned away to study the fire, as he usually did when considering a problem.

Marchmont shook his head. "Not a one."

The others started talking at Zoe all at once. A lot of *shush*ing and "Don't" and "Please don't" and "I hope you are not thinking" this or that.

Even had he been thoroughly sober, the Duke of Marchmont could not have guessed what they were about. This was nothing new. It would not be the first time he'd interrupted one of their incomprehensible family squabbles. It certainly wouldn't be the first time they promptly recommenced while he was there. After all, they did regard him as a member of the family, which meant they felt as free to abuse him as they did one another.

He crossed to the table, where a decanter sat untouched, surrounded by wineglasses. He might as well have a drink while he watched the entertainment.

He had lifted decanter and glass and was about to pour when her voice, with its exotic lilt, rose above the rest.

"Marchmont, will you please marry me?" she said.

Mama let out a little scream.

Gertrude leapt up from her chair and tried to drag Zoe out of the room. Zoe broke away from her and moved closer to her father.

"A duke, you said," she told her sisters. "Or a marquess. *He* is a duke. He has no wives. Wife," she quickly amended. In England, it was only one wife to a man, she reminded herself.

"You don't simply offer yourself to the first nobleman who walks through the door," said Dorothea.

"But you said the dukes and marquesses would not come to us," said Zoe.

"I'm afraid to imagine what will be said about this," said Priscilla.

"You said I could not hope to meet such men," said Zoe. "But here is one." And she wasn't about to let him get away if she could help it.

"Ooooh," said Mama. She fell back upon the pillows.

"Look what you've done to Mama!"

"The girl is hopeless."

"Of course he'll tell all his friends."

"Papa, do something!" Gertrude cried as she flung herself into her chair.

Papa only looked briefly over his shoulder, his glance going from Zoe to the tall, fair-haired, shockingly handsome man with the decanter and glass in his long-fingered hands. The Duke of Marchmont's beautifully shaped mouth had fallen open. His eyes had widened slightly.

As she watched, he closed his mouth and shuttered his eyes again.

She'd seen those stunningly green eyes wide open, for one dizzying heartbeat in time, when they'd first lit on her. The impact had nearly toppled her from her chair. She'd felt for a moment like the little girl spinning helplessly until landing on her bottom on a muddy patch of grass.

"I cannot wait," she said. "Marchmont, you are the highest of rank here. Tell them to be silent and let me speak."

"We shall never live this down," Augusta said. "What a tale he'll have for his friends at White's."

Marchmont slowly filled his glass. When that was done, he said, "I must have heard aright, else your sisters would not be shrieking at quite that pitch. You have asked me to marry you. Is that correct, Miss Lexham?"

The last time her heart had pounded so hard was on the day she'd fled the palace of Yusri Pasha and found the gates of the European quarter closed to her. Then she'd been terrified of what would happen to her if she was caught.

Yet she'd been exhilarated, too, to risk everything in one desperate bid for freedom.

This appeared to be her only chance to live the life for which she'd taken that desperate risk.

However grand his rank or handsome his face or splendid his physique, this was still a man, she told herself. Though he hid his eyes, she knew he was mentally taking off her clothes and liked what he saw. She felt, rather than saw, the slight tension in his posture: the alertness of the predator when it marks its prey.

A harem slave would be tearing off her garments about now.

Zoe knew she could not entice him in that way. Not here, at any rate. Not now. She must appeal to him from mind to mind. It must be business. The way men did it.

Or at least it must seem so.

She adjusted her shawl and her own posture, making herself as alluring as she could without being too obvious about it, while she filled her mind with the ritual formulae employed on similar occasions.

In a logical and orderly fashion, she summarized for the duke her sisters' and absent brothers' assessment of the situation and their reasons for wanting to send her away.

"They say the only other solution is for me to marry a man of the highest rank," she went on. "They say others must defer to him. They say that a man so highly placed will want an innocent girl of eighteen. I am not truly innocent, and I am not eighteen, but I am a virgin."

"Ooooh," said Mama.

Zoe went on determinedly, "Yusri Pasha gave me as a second wife to Karim, who was his eldest son by his first wife. But Karim could not make his . . . his . . ."—though Marchmont kept his eyes half closed, she knew the duke regarded her intently—"his instrument of delight. The limb a man uses for pleasure and to make children. What is it called?"

Shrieks from the sisters.

Zoe ignored them. "No one will tell me what it is in English," she said. "If I ever learned the word, I have forgotten it."

He made an odd sound in his throat. Then he said, "*Membrum virile* will do."

The two older sisters put their heads in their hands.

"He could not make his *membrum virile* hard," Zoe said. "He was sickly, you see. He was unable to be a true husband, though he was so fond of me, and

I did everything they taught me to awaken a man's desire. *Everything*. I even—"

"Zoe," her father said in a strangled voice, "it is unnecessary to explain in detail."

"One wishes it were not necessary for her to speak at all," a sister muttered.

"One wishes the floor would open up and swallow one."

"We shall never, *never* live this down."

"Never mind them, Miss Lexham," said Marchmont. "Please continue. I'm all ears." He drank some more.

"I shall be an excellent wife to you," she said, hoping she didn't sound as desperate as she felt. She told herself that if this didn't work, she'd go to Paris or Venice as she'd threatened, though those had never been her first choices. She wanted to live in her native land and have the life she'd dreamt of for twelve long years. It looked as though the Duke of Marchmont was her one chance to have that life. He was handsome and young and healthy and not excessively intelligent, and he desired her. He was *perfect*.

Fate had thrown him in her way. A gift. All she had to do was hold onto him.

Don't panic, she counseled herself. *You know exactly what to do. You spent twelve years learning it.*

"I know all the arts of pleasing a man," she went on. "I can sing and dance and compose poetry. I learn quickly and will learn how to behave correctly in . . . in good society . . . if you will help me, or find me teachers."

She was not calm enough. Her English was faltering as a consequence, but she plunged on. "I know

widows are worthless, but I was never a wife of the
body. I remain a virgin, and a virgin is valuable. Too,
I have jewels, enough to make as great a dowry as a
maiden would have. I shall be a loving mother to your
children. All the children of the harem were fond of
me. In truth, it made me sad to leave them, and I shall
be happy to have children of my own." She paused
and glanced at her sisters. "But not too many."

"Not too many," he repeated. He drank some more.

"I know how to arrange a household," she said.
"I know how to manage servants, even eunuchs—
and they can be impossible. Their moods are more
changeable than a woman's."

"Eunuchs. I see."

"I know how to manage them," she said. "I was the
only one in all the household who could."

The other two sisters put their heads in their hands.
Mama covered her face with her handkerchief.

Marchmont emptied his glass and set it down. His
slitted green gaze came back to Zoe. She couldn't
truly see it, so secret he was in the way he used his
eyes, but she certainly felt it. His slow, assessing look
traveled from the top of her head to her toes, which
curled in reaction. All of her body seemed to curl
under that gaze, as though she were a serpent stirring, lured out of the darkness into the warmth of
the sun. She felt the stirring and curling inside, too,
low in her belly.

"That is a *most* tempting offer," he said.

The room fell oppressively silent, and it seemed to
Marchmont that his voice echoed in it. "To be able to
manage eunuchs is a rare accomplishment, indeed."

The four harridans made no sound. Their youngest sister had succeeded in doing the impossible: She'd rendered them speechless.

"Well?" she said into the lengthening silence.

He poured himself more wine. The effort not to laugh was sure to do him a permanent injury.

He was sure he'd never, in all his life, heard anything so hilarious as Zoe-not Zoe's marriage proposal or her sisters' reaction to it.

That alone was worth the thousand pounds he'd lost in the wager. Hell, it was probably worth the price of marriage. He'd be laughing about it for years to come, he didn't doubt.

But years to come was a very long time, and marrying now would be inconvenient. For appearances' sake he would be obliged to give up his mistress for a time, and Lady Tarling hadn't yet begun to bore him.

"It devastates me to decline," he said, "but it would be grossly unfair to take advantage of you in that way."

"Does that mean no?" said Zoe. Her soft mouth turned down.

Marchmont eyed her grown-up, delectably curving body. "It is no," he said, "with the *greatest* regret. Were I to consent, I should be marrying you under false pretenses. I can accomplish what you require without your having to shackle yourself to me permanently."

He knew that without him she had virtually no hope of a welcome in Society. He was the one man in London who could do what she needed done for her—and he owed it to Lexham to do it. Marchmont had not the smallest doubt in his mind about this. No amount of wine could wash that great debt away.

Her frown eased and her expression sharpened. "You can?"

"Nothing could be simpler," he said.

She let out a little whoosh of air.

Relief?

He was, for an instant, taken aback.

He was, he knew, a matrimonial prize. Unwed women would sell their souls for the chance to become the Duchess of Marchmont. Some of the wed ones, given the least encouragement, would happily do away with their husbands.

But the Duke of Marchmont had never taken himself seriously, and even his vanity was of the detached variety, far from tender. If her tiny sigh of relief wounded his feelings, the blow was merely a glancing one.

She had every reason to be relieved, he told himself. She would not have gone to the extreme of proposing to him if her appalling sisters had not, in their usual way, exaggerated the difficulties of her situation.

"Nothing simpler?" one of them cried. "How drunk are you, Marchmont?"

He ignored her and kept his attention on Zoe-not Zoe. "For reasons which elude me, I am fashionable," he said. "For reasons which elude nobody, I am highly eligible. The combination makes me welcome everywhere."

Zoe glanced at her sisters for confirmation.

"I grieve to say it is true," said Gertrude.

"It is very tiresome, and I find the responsibility onerous, but it can't be helped," he said. "My presence determines the success of a gathering."

"Like Mr. Brummell," said Zoe. "That is what they said. The man must be like Mr. Brummell."

"Not altogether like him, I hope," he said. "If you ever hear of my bathing in milk or discarding a neckcloth because every fold and dent is not precisely where it ought to be, I hope you will be so good as to shoot me."

She smiled then, a slow upward curve of her lips.

Visions of this exotic, grown-up version of Zoe dancing in veils crept into his mind, along with the first part of her qualifications: *I know all the arts of pleasing a man.*

Perhaps, after all, he should have said yes.

No, absolutely not. Though he wasn't altogether sober, he was well aware that the little brain between his legs was trying to take charge of the situation. He told himself not to be an idiot. He shoved the visions into the mental cupboard.

"In short," he said, "you need me, but contrary to your sisters' hysterical assumptions, you don't need to marry me. You don't need to marry anybody until you're quite ready."

Another little whoosh of air. "Oh," she said. "Thank you. You are very handsome and desirable, and I was so glad of that—but I was married from the time I was twelve years old, and it seemed a very long time, and I would rather not be married again straightaway."

"You may leave everything to me," he said.

"That is one of the most horrifying sentences I have ever heard," said Augusta.

"Everything?" said Zoe. She gazed at him expectantly, her eyes like two dark seas, deep enough to drown a man.

He set down his glass. If his mind was sliding into metaphor, he'd had quite enough to drink. "Everything," he said firmly. "Come with me."

"Go with him?" cried a sister.

"Go where?"

"What can he be thinking?"

"Thinking? When does he ever think?"

While the harridans recommenced playing the Greek tragic chorus, Marchmont took Zoe's arm and led her out of the room.

The long-fingered hand wrapped about Zoe's arm was very warm. The heat spread out from there and raced up and down, from one side of her body to the other.

Zoe looked down at his hand and wondered how he did it.

But as soon as they were out of the drawing room, he let go of her. He folded his hands behind his back and walked on. His legs were long, but he did not hurry. She had no trouble keeping up with him.

Aware of servants watching while they pretended not to, she would not let herself stare at him. This wasn't easy. For one thing, the provoking boy she'd known so long ago had turned into someone else: a tall, strong, hauntingly beautiful stranger. That took some getting used to.

For another, this stranger had effortlessly awakened in her feelings she'd heard talked of endlessly but had never experienced. She was still reeling from that discovery.

Still, he was a stranger, and she was relieved not to have to marry him. He seemed to be very conceited. He was nothing like the boy she'd known so long ago.

All the same, she couldn't help wondering what he looked like naked.

She couldn't help wondering what it would feel like if he put those big, warm hands on her womanly parts.

She shivered.

"It is unseasonably cold," he said. "We're in for a filthy night, I don't doubt. The sky was overcast as I left White's and continues to darken. Do you know what White's is?"

She towed her mind back to the moment. "I heard my sisters say you had friends there," she said.

"It is a gentleman's club in St. James's Street," he said. He told her the names of various members, describing his friends in detail, quoting Beau Brummell, and explaining the latest set of wagers in the betting book.

It was interesting, and he spoke in an amusing way. Yet Zoe was aware that he was . . . not drunk exactly, but in a haze.

She was familiar with the haze of intoxicants. In the harem, opium helped bored and frustrated women pass the time. She could not understand why so sought-after and powerful a man, who was free to go where he pleased and do as he pleased, chose to pass his day in a haze.

It was not her concern, she told herself. Yet she couldn't help wondering whether the hazy state dulled his carnal urges or made his *membrum virile* soft.

She doubted it.

He paused at the door to the library.

She glanced behind her. The small drawing room was not very far away. Still, the library was private, at least for the moment. If he wished to touch her she would let him, she decided. Purely for educational purposes. She knew a great deal about men and what they liked and what to do for and to them, but she had not learned what she liked. Karim's touch had never stirred her, nor hers him.

This man would be different. That much was obvious.

"After you, madam," he said.

She walked into the library, her heart picking up speed.

He followed her in, then walked straight to the central window. He flung open the curtains.

A roar went up from the crowd.

Zoe stood stock-still, staring at the back of his head, at the familiar pale blond hair. Yes, he'd always been the boldest of them all, though everyone used to say it was Gerard who was the reckless one. But bold and reckless were not the same thing.

She was aware of footsteps in the corridor behind her, and her sisters' voices becoming more audible. In another moment her brothers would hear the noise outside, and they'd emerge from their lair and . . .

And it would make no difference at all. They would do the same as they'd always done. In childhood none of the others had ever been able to stand up to him. Now he'd been a duke for almost half his life, accustomed to do as he pleased, accustomed to being deferred to.

The library had tall windows, like doors, giving out onto a narrow balcony. Marchmont threw open a pair of windows.

Her sisters let out a collective gasp.

"Good grief!" one cried.

"He's mad!"

"Drunk, is more like it."

"Where is Papa?"

"Why does he do nothing?"

Zoe glanced back. They huddled in the doorway, complaining and objecting, but they came no farther and made no attempt to stop Marchmont.

No, that hadn't changed, in any event. For all their noise, for all the complaining and criticizing, they kept their distance.

He walked out onto the little balcony.

He held up his hand.

The crowd quieted.

"Yes, yes, I know," he said. "Everyone wants to see Miss Lexham."

He did not shout. He scarcely raised his deep voice. But he made it stronger in some way, and it seemed to her that people on the other side of the square must hear him clearly.

"Very well," he said. He turned to her and made a small gesture, signaling her to join him. She looked down at the long fingers, slightly curled, bidding her come. She looked up at his handsome face. A shock of pale hair, the color of early morning sunlight, fell over one eyebrow. He wore a faint smile. She could not tell what sort of smile it was, and this made her uneasy.

She reminded herself that she'd known nothing

about Karim or the world in which he lived, yet she'd soon learned to navigate its treacherous pathways. She'd learned how to amuse and please him. As a result, she'd won his affection and a great fortune in jewels.

This would be easier, she told herself. All she needed to do was find a way into the world to which she properly belonged.

She had come home quietly, Lord Winterton so determined to avert the uproar, which, in the end, could not be averted. They'd kept her hidden in her father's house for two days, behind closed windows and curtains. She'd felt as though she'd never left the harem.

She stepped through the window and onto the balcony.

The crowd fell silent.

So did her sisters.

Hundreds of faces turned upward. Every pair of eyes focused on her.

She went cold, then hot. She felt dizzy. But it was a wonderful dizziness, the joy of release.

Now at last she stood in the open.

Here I am, she thought. *Home at last, at last. Yes, look at me. Look your fill. I'm not invisible anymore.*

She felt his big, warm hand clasp hers. The warmth rushed into her heart and made it hurry. She was aware of her pulse jumping against her throat and against her wrist, so close to his. The heat spread into her belly and down, to melt her knees.

I'm going to faint, she thought. But she couldn't let herself swoon merely because a man had touched her. Not now, at any rate. Not here. She made herself look up at him.

He wore the faintest smile—of mockery or amusement she couldn't tell. Behind his shuttered eyes she sensed rather than saw a shadow.

She remembered the brief glimpse she'd had, of pain, when she'd mentioned his brother. It had vanished in an instant, but she'd seen it in his first, surprised reaction: the darkness there, bleak and empty and unforgettable.

She gazed longer than she should have into his eyes, those sleepy green eyes that watched her so intently yet shut her out. And at last he let out a short laugh, and raised her hand to his mouth and brushed his lips against her knuckles.

Had they been in the harem, she would have sunk onto the pillows and thrown her head back, inviting him.

But they were not in the harem and he'd declined to make her his wife.

And she was not a man, to let her lust rule her brain.

This man was not a good candidate for a spouse.

There had been a bond between them once. Not a friendship, really. In childhood, the few years between them had been a chasm, as the difference in their genders had been. Still, he'd been fond of her once, she thought, in his own fashion.

But that was before.

Now he was everything every woman could want, and he knew it.

She desired him the way every other woman desired him.

It didn't really mean anything. It certainly wouldn't mean anything to him.

Still, at least she felt desire, finally, she told herself. If she could feel it with him, she'd feel it with someone else, someone who wanted her, who'd give his heart to her.

For now, she was grateful to be free. She was grateful to stand on this balcony and look out upon the hundreds of people below.

She squeezed his hand in thanks and let her mouth form a slow, genuine smile, of gratitude and happiness, though she couldn't help glancing once up at him from under her lashes, to seek his reaction.

She glimpsed the heat flickering in the guarded green gaze.

Ah, he felt it, too: the powerful physical awareness crackling between them.

He released her hand. "We've entertained the mob for long enough," he said. "Go inside."

She turned away. The crowd began to stir and people were talking again, but more quietly. They'd become a murmuring sea rather than a roaring one.

"You've seen her," he said, and his deep voice easily carried over the sea. "You shall see her again from time to time. Now go away."

After a moment, they began to turn away, and by degrees they drifted out of the square.

Three

Marchmont had done nothing more than brush his lips over her knuckles.

It was more than enough.

He'd caught the scent of her skin and felt its softness, and the sensations lingered long after he let go and turned away.

Perhaps, after all, he should have said yes. Visions of Zoe dancing in veils swarmed into his brain again.

He pushed them away. He was not about to disrupt his life to marry a complete stranger, even for Lexham's sake.

He turned his attention to the square. It was emptying, as he'd known it would. The mob's excitement abated once they saw that the Harem Girl looked like any other attractive English lady. This was only the first and easiest part of the task he'd undertaken.

Part Two was the newspapers. Unlike the mob,

they wouldn't let go of a sensational story so easily. The stragglers in the square were mainly newspaper men. They wanted a story, and they'd make one up if necessary.

He reentered the library, where Zoe waited, her blue eyes brimming with an admiration and gratitude that even he, who couldn't be bothered to read expressions, could comprehend. He didn't know whether or not he believed what he saw in her face. A dozen years ago, he would have known what to believe. But a dozen years ago, Zoe would never have worn such a melting expression.

This wasn't the Zoe he'd known all those years ago, he reminded himself. In any event, he didn't need to know what was in her heart, any more than she needed to know what was in his. He'd promised to bring her into fashion, and that was all he needed to do.

He turned his attention elsewhere.

Her sisters hovered in the doorway, one black figure standing at each side of the frame and two with enormous bellies pacing in the corridor beyond.

A quartet of crows.

"Who died?" he said.

"Cousin Horatio," said Augusta.

"Ah, the recluse on the Isle of Skye," said Marchmont.

Lexham had taken him there after Gerard died. Some thought it a strange place to take a grieving fifteen-year-old, but Lexham, as always, knew what to do. In hindsight, Marchmont saw how wise his guardian had been not to send the new Duke of

Marchmont back to school. There he'd have to hide his grief. There, among his friends, he'd have no Gerard to boast of, no letters from Gerard to look forward to. Skye and the eccentric Cousin Horatio held no associations with Gerard or their dead parents. It was far away from the world in which they'd grown up, and it was beautiful. He and Lexham walked. They fished. They read books and talked. Sometimes even Cousin Horatio joined the conversation.

The brooding atmosphere of the place and the solitude had quieted Marchmont's mind and brought him a measure of peace.

"He died a fortnight ago," Dorothea said.

"He left his property to Papa."

"The least one might do is wear mourning for him."

Were they thinking of sending their youngest sister to Cousin Horatio's? Zoe on a desolate, windswept island of Scotland's Inner Hebrides? She'd think she was in Siberia. For one who'd spent twelve years in a land where the sun always shone and where even on winter nights the temperature rarely fell below sixty degrees, it would be exactly the same thing: bone-chilling and spirit-killing.

His gaze drifted to Zoe, in her wine-colored shawl and pale green frock. She was the antithesis of mourning, acutely alive and unmistakably carnal.

It wasn't that her garments were seductive. It was the way she wore them and the languorous way she carried herself. Even standing still, she vibrated physicality.

"I did not have enough clothes, and the black dress my sisters found for me was too small," she said, evidently misreading his prolonged survey as criticism. "To alter it was too much work. The maid must take a piece from here." She pointed to the bottom of her skirt, drawing attention to her elegantly slender feet. "Then she must add it to this part, to cover my breasts." She drew her hand over her bodice. "They must put in a piece here as well." She slid her hands along her hips.

"Zoe," Dorothea said warningly.

"What?"

"We don't touch ourselves in that way."

"Most certainly not in front of others who are *not* our husband," Priscilla said.

"I forgot." She looked at Marchmont. "We don't touch. We don't say what we feel in our hearts. We don't lie on the rug. We keep our feet on the floor except in bed or on the chaise longue."

"Where were you keeping your feet?" he said.

She gestured at the furniture. "No chairs in Cairo. When I sit in one, my legs want to curl up under me."

"This isn't Cairo," Augusta said. "You would do well to remember that. But of course you won't." She turned to Marchmont, who was with difficulty maintaining his composure. "Marchmont, you may find this all very amusing, but it would be a kindness to Zoe to face facts: It will take years to civilize her."

She'd got him aroused in an instant, the little witch, and made him laugh at the same time. Zoe Octavia had never been fully civilized. She'd never been like anybody else. Now she was less so.

He let his gaze slide up from the hips and bosom to which she'd called his attention. Up the white throat and delicate point of her stubborn chin and up, to meet her gaze.

It was the gaze of a grown woman, not the girl he'd known. That Zoe was gone forever, just as the boy he'd once been was gone forever. Which was as it should be, he told himself. That was life, perfectly normal and not at all mysterious. It was, in fact, as he preferred it.

"If by 'civilized' you mean she must turn into an English lady, it isn't necessary," he said. "The Countess Lieven isn't English, yet she's one of Almack's patronesses."

"What is Almack's?" said Zoe. "They keep screaming about it, and I cannot decide whether it is the Garden of Paradise or a place of punishment."

"Both," he said. "It's *the* most exclusive club in London, impossibly hard to get into and amazingly easy to get thrown out of. Birth and breeding aren't sufficient. One must also dress and dance beautifully. Or, failing that, one must possess sufficient wit or arrogance to impress the patronesses. They keep a list of those who meet their standards. Some three-quarters of the nobility are not on the list. If you're not on the list, you can't buy an admission voucher and can't get into the Wednesday night assemblies."

"Are you on the list?" Zoe asked.

"Of course," he said.

"Men's moral failings tend to be overlooked," Augusta said.

Marchmont ignored her. "You'll be on it, too," he told Zoe.

"That," said Gertrude, "will take a miracle, and I

have not noticed that you and Providence are on the best of terms."

"I don't believe in miracles," he said. "Not that Almack's signifies at present."

"Doesn't signify?" Augusta cried.

Why would they not go away? Why had Lexham not strangled them all at birth?

"I've disposed of the mob," he said. "Next is the newspapers."

He walked to the door, and the tragic chorus gave way.

He summoned a footman.

"You will find a disreputable-looking being named John Beardsley loitering in the square," Marchmont told the servant. "Tell him I shall see him in the anteroom on the ground floor."

As one would expect, this set off the chorus.

"Beardsley?"

"That horrid little person from the *Delphian*?"

"What is the *Delphian*?" came the lilting voice from behind him.

"A newspaper," said a sister.

"Ghastly, gossipy newspaper."

"He's a vile little man who writes stories for it."

"Sometimes in iambic pentameter. He fancies himself a *writer*."

"You can't mean to have him in the house, Marchmont."

"What will Papa say?"

"Since I am not a mind reader, I haven't the least idea what your father will say," said Marchmont. "Perhaps he will say, 'That was an excellent idea the ancient Greeks had, of abandoning female infants on a mountainside. Why was that practice given up, I wonder?' "

Having rendered them momentarily mute with outrage, he turned to Zoe. "Miss Lexham, would you be so good as to walk downstairs with me?"

Before she stepped out into the corridor, she smoothed her skirts. In another woman, the gesture would have seemed nervous. With her it was provocative. She did it in the way she'd trailed her hands across her bosom and along her hips.

I know all the arts of pleasing a man, she'd said.

He had not the smallest doubt she did. He was aware of heat racing along his skin and under it, speeding to his groin. He could almost feel his brain softening into warm wax, the wax a woman could do as she liked with.

Nothing wrong with that, he told himself. Men paid good money for women who possessed such arts. He'd be paying good money, too, come to that. He forgot about her annoying sisters and laughed— at himself, at the circumstances.

She looked up questioningly at him, and he almost believed she had no idea how provocative she was. Almost believed it.

I'm not innocent, she'd said. That he could believe.

"I was only thinking of the thousand pounds you've cost me," he said.

"You refer to the wager with your friends," she said. "You didn't believe it was me. But why should you? I was worried at first that my own parents wouldn't know me."

"Well, none of us do, do we?" he said. "But it is you, beyond a doubt. And I am far too glad of that to begrudge the money."

"You're glad?" she said, her face lighting up. "You're glad I'm back?"

"Of course," he said. "Did you think I wanted to find that your father had been taken in by an imposter? Did you think I wanted to see him made a fool of?"

She looked away then, and he couldn't see the hurt and disappointment in her eyes—not that he would have noticed. Eyes were reputed to be windows to the soul. The Duke of Marchmont didn't care to look that deep.

That evening

Wearing a wry smile, Lady Tarling opened the oval red velvet box. Within lay a diamond and golden topaz necklace, with matching bracelet and earrings.

"How beautiful," she said. She looked up at the man who'd given them to her. "I'm partial to golden topaz."

Marchmont hadn't known this, but he wasn't surprised. Lady Tarling's taste was exquisite. She was a slender brunette, with large, light brown eyes. She knew exactly what became her, and golden topaz, set off with diamonds, suited her perfectly.

His secretary, Osgood, who was in charge of selecting suitable gifts for His Grace's amours, would know this. Osgood always kept several fine pieces of jewelry on hand, particularly the kind to be used as generous parting gifts, for His Grace was easily bored. This was not a parting gift. It was intended, in fact, to prevent that—until His Grace decided it was time to part.

"I've taken on an amusing task that may keep me away for a short time," Marchmont said.

"Ah," she said, her smile faltering a little.

"An obligation to an old friend," he said. "I've agreed to bring his daughter into fashion—and perhaps find her a husband before the Season's end."

"An old friend. I see."

"You'll read something about it in all the papers tomorrow," he said. "Rumors will be traveling through Almack's tonight."

"But you knew I wouldn't be there to hear them," she said.

Lord Tarling's handsome young widow was not on the patronesses' list. Lady Jersey had taken her in dislike.

"I preferred you not learn about it from one of the cats who will be there," he said, "or from the newspapers. They were likely to give you the wrong impression altogether."

"It must be a curious impression, indeed, to result in such a gift." She gave a little laugh. Her silvery laugh was famous. It was gentler and prettier, many thought, than Lady Jersey's tinkling laughter. This was but one reason Lady Jersey loathed her.

"I've taken Lord Lexham's daughter under my wing," he said.

She closed the box. "But all of his daughters are launched and wed—" She broke off, the truth dawning. She was, after all, both intelligent and well informed. "You refer to the . . ."

He didn't wait for her to hunt for a more tactful term. "The Harem Girl, yes," he said.

"My goodness." She moved away from him to the nearest chair and sat down hard—but tightly clutching the box, he noted.

"There's going to be a ridiculous uproar tomorrow," he said. "Completely ridiculous, as the world will soon discover. For the time being, discretion would be in order. Miss Lexham has some prejudice to overcome: Her recent past is not regarded as respectable."

"And I am not well loved by some who decide who is acceptable and who is not. Your . . . er . . . protégée will want the blessing of Almack's lady patronesses, as well as the Queen."

Queen Charlotte didn't like Lady Tarling, either.

"It will not take long," he said. "By the time she's presented at court, no one will turn a hair."

"You are very confident," she said.

"Oh, Zoe's intelligent and beautiful," he said. "I've no doubt she'll take. It's merely a question of quieting the uproar and retraining her a bit."

"Intelligent and beautiful," Lady Tarling murmured. She opened the box again and studied the jewels therein. "I see."

He didn't know what she saw, and it didn't occur to him to be curious. He was not accustomed to explaining himself and had gone as far as this only because their liaison had scarcely begun, and he wasn't quite finished with her.

It never dawned on him—and why should it?—that she was intelligent enough to perceive this.

Still, he was the Duke of Marchmont, and Lady Tarling was no fool when it came to men. She accepted the gift and pretended it was perfectly normal for him to depart soon thereafter with no other display of affection. She knew as well as anybody that he'd very little of that article to display.

Later that evening

Zoe stood at the window and looked down into the garden. "I could climb down from here," she said.

"Oh, no, miss, I hope not," said Jarvis. "And not in your shift—which maybe we could change for your nightdress?" The maid held up the garment.

"I climbed out of the pasha's palace many times," Zoe said. "They always caught me and punished me. But I did not stop doing it. Do you know why?"

"I'm sure I don't, miss."

"I did it because I knew that one day they would not catch me, and so I must keep in practice for that day."

The day had come, as she'd known it would, and it had come without warning. During the evening meal, Karim had simply fallen off the divan, clutching his throat, and died. His grief-stricken father, at whose side he'd been sitting, had taken to his bed. Within hours, he, too, was dead.

Zoe hadn't waited to find out whether or not these were natural deaths. She'd seen pandemonium, and she'd taken advantage of it. While everybody was running about, the women tearing their hair and shrieking and weeping and the men shouting and arguing and threatening one another, she collected her jewels, stole a cloak, climbed out of a window, and fled through the garden.

Jarvis's voice called her back to the present. "Miss, I do hope you're not thinking of running away now. Her ladyship gave me strict orders—"

"No, no, I'm not running away." Zoe came away from the window. "But I never could abide being confined—to the nursery, to the schoolroom. So I always looked for the way out."

"I suppose, was the house to take fire, it might be useful to know another way out," Jarvis said.

"But it isn't what ladies do, I know," Zoe said. "I've always been the contrary and obstinate daughter. When people say to me, 'No, you can't,' I always think, 'Yes, I will.' In Egypt it was, 'No, you'll never get out of the harem.' Then I got out, and I was arguing with myself, with the fear, the bad genie in the head: No, you'll never get safely home. Yes, I will. No, they won't let you in the house. You'll never get in. Yes, I will. No, they won't believe it's you. Yes, I will. Then today, it was No, you can't have the life you should have had." She laughed. "And then Marchmont came and I thought, 'Oh, yes I will.' And he said, 'Nothing could be simpler.'"

"Yes, miss, it sounds like the sort of thing His Grace would say, and I'm sure he knows better than anybody whether it is or it isn't. Won't you put on your nightdress? You'll be warmer. Lady Lexham said we must remember you aren't used to the climate."

Zoe stalked to the fire and glared at it. "When I

asked him if he was glad to have me back, he said he was. Do you know why he was glad?"

"No, miss, though I couldn't guess why he wouldn't be, like everyone else."

"He said, 'Did you think I wanted to find that your father had been taken in by an imposter? Did you think I wanted to see him made a fool of?' What do you think of that?"

"I'm not allowed to think, miss," Jarvis said.

"He's changed so much," Zoe said. "I hardly knew him. He used to be sweet. He used to have a heart. I used to be able to talk to him and laugh with him. He said he remembered me, but he doesn't, really. And the man I saw today . . ." She shook her head. "He's conceited. I used to think he was the cleverest of all the boys, but now his head is empty. Maybe his brain has shrunk. He's beautiful and desirable and powerful— but I know he will test my patience. I am so tired of being patient with men, Jarvis, so tired of holding my tongue when they're stupid and obnoxious. So tired of catering to them."

"Miss, you don't want to take a chill, I'm sure, and worry Lady Lexham."

Zoe looked round at the maid. She was holding up the nightdress, her brow furrowed.

Until tonight, Zoe had shared her mother's lady's maid. But after Marchmont and the others left, Mama had decided that Zoe must have her own lady's maid to look after her. The housekeeper had sent up three of the girls she deemed qualified. Zoe had chosen Jarvis—formerly Jane the upper housemaid—because, she said, all she saw in her eyes was truth.

Jarvis wasn't yet confident of her abilities as a

lady's maid, and Lady Lexham had given enough instructions and warnings to fill the maid's heart with terror.

Clearly one could not hope to carry on an intelligent conversation with Jarvis while she fussed about the nightdress and her mistress's taking cold. With a smile intended to be reassuring, Zoe signaled the maid to help her out of her shift and into the nightdress.

When the ceremony was completed and Jarvis had relaxed a degree, Zoe startled her by stroking her arm.

"Where I've come from," Zoe said gently, "we say what's in our hearts and we touch, as you do not," she said. "My husband, Karim, gave me a slave, Minhat. With her I could share what was in my heart, as I couldn't do with the other wives or concubines or slaves. You're not a slave, but you are my Minhat. If we can't speak freely together, then there's no one with whom I can do so. My sisters are all crazy. They all think I'm crazy. None of them can be my Minhat. Wherever I go, you'll go with me. When I marry, you'll come with me to my husband's house. You must speak your heart, always."

The maid looked wildly about the room.

"Always," Zoe said firmly. One of the many things she'd learned in the harem was the voice of command. "I have opened my heart to you, Jarvis. It's your turn. Speak to me as my Minhat."

Jarvis shut her eyes, then opened them. She took a deep breath and said, "Very well, miss. Here's what I say. The Duke of Marchmont is top of the trees. Everyone wants him. All the unmarried ladies want to marry him. They say there's plenty of married ladies who'd disgrace themselves if he crooked his finger. Every hostess in Town wants him at her party. All the royal family think well of him. It don't matter how conceited he is or if he's drunk half the time or doesn't have a heart. There's only two things you really need to know about His Grace the Duke of Marchmont: One, he *always* keeps his word. Ask anybody. Two, everybody knows he don't care about much, but what he said to you means he cares about your father. Why else do you think he came to the house today? If I was you, and he was promising to bring me into fashion, I'd muster up all the patience of all the saints and martyrs, because I know he'll do it, no matter what, or die trying."

Then she squeezed her eyes shut, as though she expected a blow.

"Yes, this is correct and wise," Zoe said.

The maid's eyes opened, one at a time. "It is?"

"My pride is hurt and my feelings are hurt only because he doesn't remember that we were friends—of a sort—once."

She had missed him and thought of him. He'd forgotten her. To him, she was only another female. "But that was a long time ago. He's changed and I've changed. We aren't children anymore."

"Yes, miss, that's correct and wise," said Jarvis.

Zoe smiled at her. She'd definitely chosen the right maid. "I must be an adult," she said. "I must be logical and look at the important points, in the way you did. I must have the Duke of Marchmont's help to banish the shame I've brought on my family. I must have his help to be welcomed in Society and live the life I should have had, the life for which I risked everything. If he accomplishes these things, I can find a good husband, and then my father can stop worrying about me. Can you think of anything else?"

"No, miss. I think that covers it well. And if I was you, I'd go to bed now."

To Zoe's amusement, Jarvis started gently shooing her toward the bed, as one does a small child. "You've had a very long and trying day, I know," the maid said. "Too much feeling this and feeling that, I daresay. Too much excitement. After a good night's sleep, you'll be able to look at everything more calm-like."

Zoe let herself be guided to the bed. She climbed into it dutifully and lay down. Jarvis drew up the bedclothes.

"If I do not feel calmer tomorrow," Zoe said as her head sank into the pillow, "there's always Venice or Paris."

"Miss, you haven't even seen London yet, or you wouldn't say such things."

Zoe yawned. "No, I feel no great desire to go to those places—but it was amusing to hear my sisters scream when I suggested it. And there must be an escape route. I must have somewhere to go to, if Marchmont fails me."

"Miss, I'm sure lots of women think of running away when men disappoint us. But if all of us was to actually do that, there wouldn't be a woman left in London."

Zoe laughed. "I like you, Jarvis."

"Thank you, miss. I like you, too. Please go to sleep."

Almack's, later that evening

What Marchmont found especially entertaining was the way everyone in the club tried to be subtle. They were all wild to learn the truth of what had happened at Lexham House, but none dared to ask him outright. Instead they all probed, oh so delicately.

All, that is, except his mad aunt Sophronia.

In a logical universe, she would be firmly excluded from Almack's. But mental imbalance was not necessarily a disqualification. In Lady Sophronia de Grey's case, it was quite the opposite. The patronesses couldn't have kept her out if they tried, and they were too terrified of her to even think of trying.

Tonight, as always, she wore black: an evening dress trimmed with all the magnificent excess of fashionable grief. As always, too, she was swimming in diamonds. He didn't know which of her swains had given them to her or when or why. Aunt Sophronia's past was a mystery he wasn't sure he wanted to solve.

He'd danced with one after another lady dying of curiosity about his visit to Lexham House, and he'd amused himself by deflecting the unsubtle interrogations with his customary wit. The assembly was approaching its final stage when Lady Sophronia at last noticed him and/or remembered who he was. She raised a black-gloved, diamond-studded hand and beckoned.

He excused himself from the group of ladies trying in vain to get a decisive answer from him and moved to where his aunt presided, black plumes bobbing atop her faded blonde hair. About her stood an assortment of ladies of various ages, diplomats, poets, cabinet ministers, and rakes. All wore the bewildered expression usually observed in those who found themselves in Lady Sophronia de Grey's orbit.

When he neared, she waved them away, employing the same gesture he'd used to eject the fellow from his favorite chair at White's.

"You, sir," she said.

He bowed. "Yes, Auntie," he said. "It is I. Your nephew Marchmont."

"I know who you are, absurd boy. What's this I hear about your marrying a snake charmer?"

"I think not," said he.

He could hear whispers from those straining to hear the conversation: *I think not* would be making its way swiftly to the other end of the ballroom.

"No Duke of Marchmont ever married a snake charmer," she said. "And I never thought of you as revolutionary. We may have been French once, but it was a very long time ago, and would we still have our heads, is the question? Quite unnecessary. Only consider the Americans. They shot and stabbed and hanged us like proper gentlemen. Have you met the American ambassador? A pleasant man, but confused."

Most people became that way when attempting discourse with Lady Sophronia.

"She is not from America, is she?" his aunt went on. "They are agreeable enough girls." She looked about her. "I saw one of them a minute ago. Quite pretty. But I can't help thinking they're not English. And then I wonder, 'Who put it into their heads not to be English?' Well, then, who is it, young Lucien? If it isn't a snake charmer, it must be somebody else."

"Your logic, as always, is irrefutable," he said. "It is not only somebody else but something else entirely."

He didn't know where or how the rumor of his marrying Zoe had started, but it didn't surprise him. Members of the ton received much of their gossip via servants. The version that reached aristocratic ears tended to bear small resemblance to the original.

Some of Lexham's servants must have heard Zoe's marriage proposal or had heard there was a proposal. This being exciting news, they'd wasted no time in passing it on.

He saw no harm in letting the rumor drift for a time through the Beau Monde. Society would find itself viewing Zoe not as the Harem Girl but as, possibly, the future Duchess of Marchmont. Once they pictured her in that way, it would be difficult to wrench their minds back to Harem Girl. They would have to start thinking of her as normal.

She wasn't, but that was not his concern.

"Do you remember little Zoe Octavia Lexham?" he said.

His aunt cast her pale blue gaze in the direction of the great chandelier, as though that was where she kept her memory. "Zoe Octavia," she said.

He heard the whispers start up again: *Zoe Octavia.*

His aunt's vague blue gaze widened and sharpened as it returned to him. "The bolter?"

"Yes."

"What nonsense. Lexham misplaced her—in the Holy Land or Constantinople or some such."

"She turned up recently."

"She usually did turn up, eventually," said Lady Sophronia. "But it's been an excessive *eventual*, by my calculations. Is she or is she not a snake charmer?"

"To be absolutely truthful, I am very nearly certain she is not a snake charmer."

"I suppose 'very nearly certain' is the best we can expect in an uncertain world. Is she an American?"

"Decidedly not."

"Very sensible of her. Well, then. It's out of my hands. I leave it to the Queen." She waved her hand. "I say no more. It's up to you. I have a great deal on my mind. You can't expect me to explain everything to you."

He could have stayed longer at Almack's, but he reckoned that (1) his work here was done and (2) his aunt had treated him to as much entertainment as any reasonable man could hope for. He took his leave about the time the words *Zoe Octavia* were making their way into the refreshment room.

Four

The Duke of Marchmont did not even look up when Lord Adderwood burst into the breakfast room. His Grace had been expecting the interruption. Last night, in fact, he'd sent word to the porter to watch for Lord Adderwood in the morning and send him in as soon as he arrived.

Adderwood waved a newspaper under his nose. "Have you seen this?"

Marchmont glanced at it. "It appears to be a newspaper."

"It's the *Delphian*. Have you read it?"

"Certainly not. I never read the papers before bedtime, as you well know."

"I should have bet anything you'd read this one."

"I hope you bet nothing. It pains me to see you lose money, unless it is to me."

"But it's all about the Harem Girl!"

"Is it, indeed?"

"What an aggravating fellow you are, to be sure," said Adderwood. "You must know all about it. You were at Lexham House yesterday. I heard you stood on the balcony with a young woman. This"—he tapped the newspaper—"appears to be the young woman."

"Certainly not," said Marchmont. "That is a newspaper. We settled that a moment ago. Do you not recollect?"

Adderwood threw him an exasperated look, sat down, and opened the paper. "I came straightaway, as soon as I got it. I've only had time to glance—" He broke off, his eyes widening. "Why, this is shocking! Did you know of this, Marchmont?"

"Oh, Adderwood, your lamentable memory. How could I know what is there when I haven't read it?"

Adderwood glared at him over the paper, then cast his gaze down again and began to read aloud:

Miss Lexham's Oriental Ordeal
by John Beardsley

The following DRAMATIC NARRATIVE Comprises a Full and TRUE Account of Events Having Lately Befallen a LADY OF THE ARISTOCRACY, as Narrated by Her to this Correspondent.

Adderwood looked up from the paper. "A dramatic narrative?" he said. "Strange way to go about it."

"Everyone knows that Beardsley fancies himself a

writer," said Marchmont. "As I recall, he once wrote an account of a fire in the form of a Greek epic, in dactylic hexameter."

Adderwood returned to the paper, and in suitably dramatic tone, continued to read:

Cairo, Egypt
Christmas Eve 1817

She couldn't decide whether getting her head cut off was the worst that could happen.

It was a definite possibility, though.

The sun had already set and the nearly full moon continued to climb in the sky. At nightfall, the gates to the quarter of el-Esbekiya, where Europeans resided, were locked, as were all the other gates of the city's districts.

In Cairo only the police, criminals, demons, and ghosts traveled the streets after dark. Respectable people did not go out, and respectable households did not open their doors.

She knew all this. She continued her mad race to the gate all the same. Turning back was out of the question.

She came to a halt and stared at the closed gate, her mind busily sorting out alternatives.

There weren't any.

In minutes the police or the district watchmen would come, and she'd be taken up. Whatever happened after that would not be good. Return to the household she'd escaped was only one possible doom. She might be given to soldiers for their amusement or flogged or stoned or perhaps all three. Or, if they had more important things to do, they'd simply cut off her head.

She beat on the gate.

A face appeared at the grated opening. "Go away," the gatekeeper told her.

"Have mercy," she said. "I carry an important message for the English effendi." She raised one hand a little, to let him see the ruby necklace dripping from her fingers. "May God reward your kindness for aiding me."

And in case God doesn't get around to it straightaway, here's some valuable jewelry.

Her heart pounded so hard she thought it would break out of her chest. She needed all her willpower to keep her hand from trembling as she dangled the rubies before him. They glimmered in the moonlight, easy to identify. In this part of the world no clouds obscured the moon and stars, whose glow was like an eerie form of daylight.

She couldn't remember when last she'd stood in the open, under the moon and stars.

The eyes behind the grate went from the rubies to her veiled countenance. Her cloak's quality would tell him she was not a common prostitute or a beggar. It would not tell him much else. The rubies must do the talking for her. If they weren't persuasive enough, she had other jewels. She'd come from a wealthy household, where even slaves were richly adorned. She'd taken all her portable treasures. She'd earned them.

"Who is it you wish to see, daughter?" The gatekeeper's voice gentled, his mood softened, no doubt, by the sparkling gems in her hand.

Baksheesh oiled all transactions in the Ottoman Empire. If that hadn't been the case, she could never have got this far.

"The Englishman," she said.

"Which one?"

She wished she could say "Mr. Salt," because he was the British consul-general. Unfortunately, she knew—as did everyone else in Egypt—that he was traveling up the Nile with an English nobleman's party.

How many parties of Englishmen had she heard about during her captivity? She wasn't sure who they were. The local women who supplied the harem's gossip had difficulty with European names. All such foreigners were Franks to them, the unpronounceable names unimportant. One must question diligently to ascertain which visitors were English.

She wanted to scream, Help me! This is my one chance. But she had learned to contain herself, to preserve calm while whirlwinds of emotion swirled about her. It was an important survival skill in this world.

She said calmly, "Those Frankish names are impossible to pronounce. It is the man in the great house—not the house of the English consul but the other one. I beg you to permit me to enter. My message is most important. By tomorrow it will be too late, and others will suffer the consequences."

I surely will. I'll be dead, or wishing I were.

The gate opened, only a very little: barely enough for her to squeeze through. It shut quickly behind her, catching the hem of her cloak. She pulled, and the cloth ripped.

Her heart beat so hard she could scarcely breathe. She was afraid that all the care she'd taken would be for nothing. She'd be caught once again, and this time the punishment would be drowning, strangulation, poisoning, or beheading.

Yet hope beat within her, too. It had sustained her for all these years and it had propelled her thus far.

She held out the rubies to the gatekeeper. He lifted his lamp and peered into her veiled face. Since the veil covered all but her eyes, he must see the desperation in them. She could only hope he interpreted it as an underling's fear of failing a master. Those doing the bidding of their masters—and a woman always had masters—had reason to be afraid.

The lowliest harem slave quickly became adept at reading facial expressions; survival depended on the skill. But his told her nothing. Still, it was a wonder she could see straight, so wrought up she was. She had no idea whether he hesitated out of pity or suspicion. Perhaps it was simply a case of his greed warring with his fear of getting into trouble with his masters.

"Take them," she said. "Only show me the way."

He shrugged and took them. He pointed.

She hurried away in the direction he indicated. The house was not hard to find. She pounded on the door.

This time, not an Egyptian porter's but an English servant's face appeared at the small grate.

"Please," she said. Her English was stiff from lack of use. She'd struggled not to forget, but the language was dim in her mind, like the memories

*of family and home. Now the pounding weight in
her chest seemed to press upon her brain as well,
and the words, the precious words, eluded her.*

*"Please. I . . . am . . . Zoe. Zoe . . . Lez. Ahm.
Zoe Lex . . . ham. Lexham. Please help me."*

*Her strength failed her then, as did the cour-
age she'd mustered—not simply to flee the great
palace across the Nile but to endure life in that
prison for twelve years while she tried to preserve the spirit of the girl she'd been. She had
wanted all her courage to survive and to make
her way here.*

Now it gave out, and she slumped to the ground.

Lord Adderwood swallowed hard and furtively
dashed a tear from his eye before he looked up from
the newspaper.

Marchmont, who'd heard the account of Zoe's
escape firsthand, had his feelings well under command.

Adderwood cleared his throat. "Do you know, I
always thought Beardsley a hack of the lowest order,"
he said. "Miss Lexham, it appears, inspired him to
something like competence."

Marchmont noted with satisfaction the use of the
term *Miss Lexham* rather than *Harem Girl* and the
respectful tone employed. "She's the sort of girl who
inspires a fellow," he said.

"It is she, then."

"Beyond a doubt. You'll recognize her the instant
you see her."

"Not at all sure of that," Adderwood said. "You
knew her a good deal better. To me she was always a
blur disappearing into the distance."

"She's not at all blurry at present," said Marchmont. "You'll have your thousand pounds before the end of the day."

In fact, the money would have been delivered to Adderwood's house already. Yesterday, before going upstairs to dress for the evening, Marchmont had notified his secretary. Osgood would have written the bank draft first thing this morning. He knew, as did everyone else, that whatever else the Duke of Marchmont chose to neglect or forget, he never broke his word, and he never overlooked debts of honor.

Everyone knew he'd lost all respect for Brummell when the man had sneaked away in the dead of night, leaving his friends responsible for thousands of pounds in loans and annuities.

Adderwood scanned the remaining columns of newsprint. Half the paper had been given over to Zoe Lexham. The story of her captivity and escape would appear in pamphlet form within hours, no doubt. With illustrations.

"I can hardly take it in," Adderwood said. "Is this all true? You were present when Beardsley spoke to her."

"He took it from her almost verbatim," said Marchmont. "He's even managed to capture her— er—distinctive manner of expressing herself."

While listening to the lilting voice, with its shadows and soft edges, the Duke of Marchmont had been more deeply moved than he would ever admit.

He hadn't, until then, heard the true story of her disappearance. Only then had he learned that she hadn't run away from the servants in charge of her.

Well into her captivity, after Zoe had become fluent

in Arabic, she'd learned that one of her parents' servants had sold her for a vast sum, and the matter had been arranged and carefully planned well before the fateful day in the Cairo bazaar.

Readers would learn, as Marchmont had, that the maid who'd sold her had not lived long. Within a week of Zoe's disappearance, the servant was dead, of a "stomach ailment." But of course she'd been poisoned, Zoe had told her two listeners so matter-of-factly. "She was merely another female, and she'd served her purpose. They wouldn't want to take the chance of her repenting, and telling the truth."

Zoe had spoken in the same quietly devastating way about her capture. She hadn't really understood what was happening, she'd said. They'd made her drink something that must have contained opiates, to quiet her. Perhaps the drug had dulled her senses.

All the same, Marchmont could imagine what it must have been like when the drug wore off: twelve years old, among strangers who spoke a language she couldn't understand . . . twelve years old, torn away from her family . . .

His imagination started again, but he firmly thrust the images into the special mental cupboard.

"I must wonder where a gently bred English girl would have found the fortitude to endure that long captivity," Adderwood said, shaking his head.

"I don't know," said Marchmont. "She didn't dwell on life in the harem. The little she did say dispelled any illusions one might have about a Turkish harem being a sort of earthly paradise. For the man who ruled it, perhaps."

"Where did she find the courage to escape?"

"Zoe never lacked for courage. All she wanted was an opportunity. You'll see when you read on."

One opportunity in twelve years. It had come without warning: The master of the household and his favorite son, both dead within hours of each other . . . the house in turmoil . . . She'd had perhaps an hour at most to seize the chance and act. She'd taken the chance. If they'd caught her that time, they would have killed her, and probably not quickly. The men's deaths, so close together, looked suspicious. "They would have said I poisoned them both," she'd said. Marchmont had learned enough of "justice" in that part of the world to understand what this meant: She would have been tortured until she "confessed."

Marchmont banished those images, too.

He fixed on the images he'd wanted Beardsley to plant in the public's mind, with all the emphasis on her pluck and daring in the face of impossible odds, and her Englishness.

In the course of the interview, the duke had casually mentioned a print of Princess Charlotte—was it only two years ago when the poor girl was alive and well?—titled "Is She Not a Spunky One." In it the princess ascended a ship sailor style, in the process of running away because her father was trying to force her to marry the Prince of Orange. The image, as Marchmont had intended, stuck in Beardsley's mind and influenced his tone.

Marchmont wasn't sure, though, that the resulting sympathetic story was entirely the result of his own manipulations. He'd noticed the way Zoe moved and the way she looked at or away from Beardsley at crucial moments while she spoke.

She was cleverer, too, than anyone could have supposed. Without actually lying, she'd contrived to create the impression that she'd been given as a slave to Karim's first wife. That had reduced the salaciousness factor considerably.

I know the arts of pleasing a man, she'd told Marchmont. She'd pleased a hardened journalist out of his natural cynicism, certainly.

"Almack's must have been atwitter last night," said Adderwood. "Everyone would know you'd gone to Lexham House."

"They not only knew it, but had me racing to Doctors' Commons for a special license," said Marchmont.

Doctors' Commons, which lay in the neighborhood of St. Paul's, was the lair of ecclesiastical lawyers. Therein was the office of the Archbishop of Canterbury, to whom a gentleman applied for a special license. Such a license allowed him to dispense with banns and marry when and where he chose.

A short, intense silence ensued.

Then, "You wouldn't," Adderwood said. "I know you're a careless fellow. I know you regard yourself as under a great obligation to Lexham. All the same . . ." He trailed off, clearly unsure whether he was approaching dangerous waters.

"I'm under the greatest possible obligation," said Marchmont. He could not imagine a greater one.

He'd gone a little mad after Gerard died. He'd wanted to shoot every horse in the stables and shut himself away with his grief.

But Lexham wouldn't let him.

"You're the Duke of Marchmont now," Lexham had said. "You must carry on, for your father's sake. And for Gerard's sake."

Lexham had taken him away on a rambling tour of the English countryside, then up into Scotland, into the Highlands and thence to the Inner Hebrides, whose bleak beauty and isolation had worked their magic. It had taken a long time for Marchmont to calm and begin to heal. Lexham had given up months with his own family and the parliamentary work he loved. He'd given up precious time he'd never get back. He'd done it for another man's son.

There was a debt of honor if ever there was one.

"Still, marriage would be . . . extreme," the duke went on with his normal sleepy amusement. "I've only promised to launch Miss Lexham into Society. It shouldn't be difficult."

Adderwood's eyebrows went up. "Not difficult? It's one thing to captivate one of those inky newspaper fellows. Winning over the ladies of the ton is another proposition entirely."

"Who cares about them?" said Marchmont. "I mean to win over the Queen."

"You're joking."

"It will be amusing, but I'm not joking."

"You think you can arrange for Miss Lexham to be presented at court?"

"Nothing could be simpler."

"You're mad."

"It runs in the family."

"Marchmont, you know the Queen is a stickler for propriety," Adderwood said. "Miss Lexham has spent the last twelve years in what Her Majesty will regard as a dubious situation. One touching story in a grubby newspaper is not going to earn the lady an invitation to court."

"A thousand pounds says I can obtain that invitation," Marchmont said. "It says, furthermore, that Miss Lexham will make her curtsey to the Queen before the month is out."

"Done," said Adderwood.

Lexham House
Wednesday, 8 April

Zoe gave one last, dissatisfied glance at her reflection in the dressing glass and turned to her maid. "Well, Jarvis?"

The maid ran her gaze over the carriage dress Dorothea had donated. It was pale yellow, trimmed in green.

"Very becoming, miss."

"It's last year's style," Zoe said. "Everyone will know. No fashionable woman wears green this year."

And Marchmont was a leader of fashion. Not that he was likely to see what she was wearing.

Not that she wanted him about.

Still, she'd thought he'd be a little more involved in helping her into Society.

Everyone said they must wait until she was presented at court. This, they said, would settle everything.

He'd stopped by briefly on Thursday to tell Mama that he would arrange for the court presentation, but so far the invitation had not arrived. Meanwhile, her sisters were determined to civilize her, a process Zoe found extremely trying.

She had not been allowed out of Lexham House since the night she'd arrived. She'd practiced her English, learned dance steps, read books, and studied household management. She'd memorized fashion plates, as well as the names and activities of all the aristocrats to be found in the scandal sheets. Except for the dancing—which she loved—it had grown very boring—and if she had to spend another ten minutes with her sisters, somebody would die.

They would be here within the next hour, all four of them.

"I could sew on fresh trim, miss, and if I was to—"

"Never mind," Zoe said, waving her hand. "It will do. Now you must go out and find a hackney."

Jarvis's eyes widened in horror. "A *hackney*, miss?"

"Yes, we are going out."

"We can't, miss. Lady Lexham said His Grace would call for you and you might go out with him."

"He hasn't called," said Zoe. "He hasn't been here since Thursday, and then he spoke only to my mother." She'd been with her sisters, learning the correct way to serve tea.

"You can't go out alone, miss," Jarvis said.

"I'm not going alone. You're coming with me."

"You'd do much better to wait for His Grace," Jarvis said. "If he's with you, no one will dare to stare or behave disrespectfully toward you, her ladyship said. She said if anyone else was to go about with you, they would have to call out the guards again and read the Riot Act and if you was killed by the mob, even by accident because of too much enthusiasm, what would she and his lordship do? she said."

"The mob is gone," Zoe said. "Even the newspaper men have left the square. Last night the Princess Elizabeth married the Prince of Hesse-Homburg at the Queen's House. She is the news. I am not the news."

"But, miss, her ladyship said—"

"If we travel in a hackney, no one will know it's me," Zoe said. "No one in my family travels in a hired vehicle."

"That's true, miss, which is why I never fetched one before. And if anyone ever did want one, it's rightfully a task for one of the under footmen or—"

"There is a stand, I believe, not very far away," said the implacable Zoe.

"Yes, miss, on Bond Street, but—"

"Then go to Bond Street."

It was the voice of command. Jarvis went.

A short time later

The maid had been obliged to run up and down Bond Street, waving her umbrella, to procure the hackney, with dubious results. Judging by the creakiness, crumbling interior, and smell, the carriage had probably done service in the time of the first King George, if not the eighth Henry. Still, it moved, which was all Zoe required.

Once they were safely enclosed in the ancient coach, embarked on their journey, Jarvis showed a more adventurous spirit and began naming the sights along the way.

They traveled along Bond Street to Piccadilly, with the maid pointing out dressmakers' shops and furriers, goldsmiths and jewelers, bookshops and print sellers, and houses of the great. They made their way through Haymarket and continued southeastward to the Strand, then headed westward again by another route that took them to Covent Garden.

Zoe gazed out of the coach window, entranced. For a time, the sights of London took her mind off the capricious Marchmont, but only for a time. She did not see how she was to become fashionable with only her sisters to guide her. He seemed not to take this matter seriously. He did not care, certainly, that she'd been cooped inside Lexham House *forever*.

Perhaps he'd forgotten?

It would be easy for a man to forget about a woman when she wasn't right in front of him. Life offered men a great many more distractions than it did women. Then, too, men were so easily distracted.

"Where to next, miss?" said Jarvis. "Would you like to see the Tower? Or would you like to go back?"

"I'm not ready to go back," said Zoe.

"Whitehall, then?"

After a moment's thought, Zoe said, "I want to see White's Club." She knew Marchmont spent a large portion of his day there, not thinking about her or the tortures she'd be undergoing at her sisters' hands.

The driver, amply paid to indulge the lady's whim to wander through London, took them back to the West End. They passed Charing Cross and the King's Mews and the Opera House. At another street, the maid pointed out Marchmont House, nearby in

St. James's Square. They did not enter the square, though, but continued along Pall Mall to St. James's Street.

All the coaches, carts, riders, and pedestrians in London seemed to have crammed themselves into it this day. As they neared the top of the hill, the hackney slowed to a crawl. At White's, close to the corner of Piccadilly, it came to a dead stop. This gave Zoe ample time to study the building. It was handsome but did not look very exciting. What on earth did he find there to amuse him, day after day? Or was it merely a comfortable place in which to get drunk with other idle men?

"There's the bow window," said Jarvis. "The gentlemen gather there and watch the passersby. But only certain gentlemen are allowed."

Several were gathered in the window at present. Zoe couldn't make out their faces, though, through the dirty glass of the hackney's window.

"Curse it," she said. "I can't see a thing." She wrestled the window open and leant out for a clearer view. At the same moment, one very fair head turned to look out of White's bow window, straight at her.

She regarded the gentleman for a moment, then sat back. "Close the window," she told Jarvis.

The traffic gave way and the hackney lurched forward.

Meanwhile in White's

The Duke of Marchmont was half-listening to his friends' unstimulating conversation and gazing out of the bow window in hopes of a diversion when an ancient hackney paused in the street outside and its window went down and a young woman's face appeared.

He blinked.

The face disappeared, the window went up, a space opened in the crush on St. James's Street, and the hackney pushed into it.

He stared for a moment at the place where the vehicle had been and told himself he'd imagined the whole thing. Lexham would never allow a daughter of his to drive about London in a hired vehicle, especially a broken-down one like that.

"That was a deuced pretty girl," said Adderwood.

"Which girl?" said Worcester.

"Hanging out of the window of the hackney. The oldest one in London, I vow. The vehicle, I mean. Not the girl."

"Didn't see her," said Worcester.

"Pity," said Adderwood. "She was a peach. Put me in mind of somebody but I can't think who it is. Did you see her, Marchmont?"

"Yes," His Grace said tightly. "That reminds me. I have an appointment."

While his friends began betting about how old the oldest hackney was, he made his exit.

He did not hurry out of the room. He told himself that Zoe Octavia was her father's responsibility. If she was wandering about London in a ramshackle hackney—and thus couldn't possibly have a family member with her, because they'd all rather set themselves on fire than be seen in a hired vehicle—this was not Marchmont's problem but Lexham's.

The duke told himself that if Lexham chose to let her loose, to get into who knew what kind of trouble, this was Lexham's decision, though one would think the man would know better.

On the other hand, this was Zoe Octavia, who had a pernicious habit of running away. . . .

His Grace took care not to run out of the club and race to the hackney stand in St. James's Street.

He walked at his usual unhurried pace. He selected the least disgusting vehicle he could find. He described the one he'd seen.

The driver knew it. It was famous, apparently, for it was, as Adderwood had asserted, the oldest London hackney in operation.

"I shall pay you fifty pounds to find it," said His Grace.

"I'll wager anything he didn't see me," Zoe muttered. "That would be like him, not to notice. I should have given him more time. Or perhaps not. Perhaps he was too drunk to focus clearly."

"Miss?" said Jarvis.

"Never mind."

She should have waited longer before moving away from the window, Zoe chided herself. She'd watched ladies of the harem do it countless times when they traveled outside the house. If they saw a handsome stranger, they'd let their veils fall "accidentally." Then they took their time about covering their faces again. Even at home they found ways to show themselves to attractive men passing in the street below. They'd peep through curtains or window shutters and be slow to close them or to move away from the window.

She might not have been slow enough.

Marchmont might have been looking at another vehicle or a rider or a pedestrian. She'd shown herself for only a moment. Even if he'd spotted her, he might not have recognized her. He might be in a haze. He had been in a haze when he agreed to introduce her to his world. Perhaps he had only a vague recollection of what she looked like.

She should have allowed for the haze and his not being overly intelligent.

Ah, well, too late to mend it. Either he'd recollected her existence or he hadn't.

A short while later, as the hackney was proceeding westward along Piccadilly, she became aware of shouts nearby.

She looked out of the window. She saw only passing vehicles, horses, people, and, farther to the left, a stretch of hilly meadow dotted with a few clumps of trees.

"That's the Green Park, miss," said Jarvis. "And there's Hyde Park Corner ahead, and on the right-hand side is Hyde Park, where—"

Louder and nearer shouts made Jarvis break off midsentence.

It was their driver who was shouting.

Zoe moved to the opposite window.

A driver in a nearby hackney was gesturing and shouting. Her driver seemed to be arguing with him.

"They want us to stop, miss," said Jarvis. "Oh, my. That's His Grace."

The other hackney was slowing, and the duke was leaning out of the window. Through her vehicle's closed window, Zoe couldn't make out what he was saying, but she recognized the strong, deep voice that could carry effortlessly across a square.

Her hackney came to a stop.

"Oh, miss, he's getting out of the hackney."

Zoe didn't wait for this news. She was already sliding across the seat and grabbing the door handle. She wrenched the door open. It was a good distance to the ground, but Zoe leapt. Jarvis shrieked.

Zoe ran—not toward the other carriage and the man who'd recalled her existence at last—but into a footpath leading into the area Jarvis had called the Green Park.

Five

It was early afternoon, well before the fashionable hour for promenading in Hyde Park. As a result, the Duke of Marchmont's acquaintances were denied the entertaining sight of His Grace leaping out of a hackney near Hyde Park Corner, dashing across Piccadilly, and running—yes, actually running—into the Green Park.

He did not have to run far.

His legs were a good deal longer than his prey's, and he was not encumbered with skirt, petticoat, and corset.

He caught up with her a short distance from the lodge. Most of the park was bare of trees. In the grounds near the lodge and the adjoining area near the smaller basin, though, they provided a degree of shade, as well as a shield of sorts from the observation of passersby in Piccadilly. Those on the footpaths, however, would get an eyeful.

Not that the duke cared who was watching.

He was far too irritated to care.

Though he'd caught up with her, she kept on running, obliging him to trot alongside—or throw himself on her and bring her down.

He was seriously considering the latter course of action when she slowed to a walk, one hand to her side.

She'd given herself a cramp, the little fool.

"You are an idiot," he said, further annoyed to find himself breathing hard.

Though mentally lazy, he was a physically active man, and he'd run only a short distance. If it occurred to him that emotion was making him breathless, the idea did not get far before being thrust into the special mental cupboard with other unwelcome thoughts. "How far did you think you'd get, running uphill, wearing a corset?"

"If I were speaking to you, I would tell you that the corset does not fit properly." She stuck her pretty nose in the air and walked on. "But I am not speaking to you."

Whatever else he was prepared for, it was not this. For one of the few times in his life, he was taken aback. "Not speaking to me? Not speaking to *me*?"

"You promised you would give me a place in your world," she said. "You said nothing could be simpler. A week ago you said this, yet you have done nothing."

This was monstrous unfair. He'd attended the Princess Elizabeth's wedding last night, where everybody behaved with the utmost decorum and where no one could expect any hint of fun. There never was any fun when the Queen was about. He could have been with his friends or with Lady Tarling, but no. He'd gone to the boring wedding, all for the prime opportunity it offered to enlist the Prince Regent in his campaign.

The campaign for Zoe.

But the Duke of Marchmont never allowed anyone but her father to question his actions. Even then, all he did was pretend to listen. He rarely paid attention and certainly didn't explain or defend himself.

"I was busy," he said.

"Perhaps the task isn't as simple as you pretended," she said. "Perhaps it's a joke to you."

It was no joke. Far from it. When a gentleman agreed to do something, he did it. He had been doing it. He'd been so busy on her behalf that he hadn't had time to visit his mistress.

But the Duke of Marchmont never complained and never explained. He remained silent, seething.

She glanced at him, then away. She took a deep breath, apparently to calm herself. "I suppose I ought to remember that you are not very intelligent," she said.

He watched her bosom rise and fall.

His anger seeped away.

She wore a pale yellow carriage dress trimmed with green. Under the bonnet's brim, dark gold curls danced by her ears. Adderwood had called her a peach, and that was more than apt. The warm glow pinkening her cheeks made them seem like sun-kissed peaches, and her soft lips glistened.

If she hadn't been the daughter of the only man in the world for whom he'd lay down his life, the Duke of Marchmont might have tried to find out exactly how innocent she was.

But she was Lexham's daughter, and in a snit about something, and all in all, perhaps it would be wisest simply to humor her.

"I'm shocked, deeply shocked, that no one's told you," he said. "I am not intelligent. You had better explain carefully. And try not to use any big words."

She shot him one of her sidelong glances, a flash of blue suspicion.

"Ask your father," he said. "I'm surprised he didn't warn you what a thickhead I am. I'm sure he's mentioned it to me many times."

"He did tell me so," she said. "He told me not to expect too much."

"Ouch," he said. " 'A hit, a very palpable hit.' "

She rolled her eyes. "I see how it is," she said. "No matter. Some things even you can understand. I need clothes."

"You do? Has my thick brain somehow overlooked the fact that you're naked?"

"Not *these* clothes," she said, drawing her hand down the front of the dress in the most provocative manner. "This is *last* year's dress!"

"How appalling. You must take it off immediately."

"Is that a dare?" she said.

He had replied without thinking. Now images from the past crowded into his mind: Zoe challenging and taunting her brothers, Zoe taking every "you mustn't" and "you oughtn't" and "you can't" and "you wouldn't" as a challenge or taunt.

What he'd jestingly suggested was a dare of the first order. For a lady to take off her dress in public was not merely unthinkably improper; it was practically impossible. Undoing the numerous and complicated fastenings—which were located for the convenience of the maid, not the mistress—would require the agility of an acrobat and a contortionist combined. No lady would get far unaided.

On the other hand, this was Zoe. She'd find a way to do it or die trying. And the process of her finding a way to do it was bound to be entertaining.

The temptation to dare her was almost overpowering.

But he collected his wits and said, "No, it was a joke."

"This dress is no joke to me," she said. "I shall get no respect in Society if I dress like a dowd. My attire must be in the latest mode. I should not have to explain this to you. You told me about Beau Brummell. Even my sisters admit you are fashionable, though it kills them to say so. And I can see it for myself: your dress tells me that you understand these matters."

He said, "Actually, I leave it to my valet Hoare to understand."

"And does Hoare go to the tailor to choose your garments as well?"

"No, I go to the tailor, but I leave the decisions to him," he said. "He knows I don't care. Still, any tailor would know that if he dresses me badly, his reputation will suffer and he'll lose custom."

This seemed to give her pause.

He watched her ponder, and something in her expression made him imagine her mind working, absorbing the few sentences he'd uttered, and filing the knowledge away for future reference. He pictured her mind as a miniature of London's General Post Office, filled with lines of workers at the long benches, neatly filing letters into their proper slots.

"Do you mean to have your valet order *my* clothes?" she said.

"No."

"Did you mean to leave the ordering of my wardrobe to my sisters?"

"Gad, no."

She folded her arms and waited.

He waited, too, drawing out the moment, because sunlight kissed her nose and glanced off the curly tendrils escaping from under her bonnet, and because what might be a smile hovered at the corners of her mouth.

He stood, he was aware, some inches too close for propriety. A passing breeze carried her scent to him.

"I collect it must be me, then," he said.

"Who else?" she said. "You're the leader of fashion. I am to be your . . . protégée—that is the correct word, isn't it?"

It sounded most incorrect and very naughty the way she said it, but he nodded.

"Then you must supervise my dressing," she said.

He could see himself in her dressing room, saying, *Take off your clothes*. He could see himself helping her take them off, starting with . . .

He shook off the image.

Why must she make harmless words sound like the lewdest innuendoes?

"I believe you mean I must supervise your wardrobe selection," he said.

She shrugged, and the motion seemed to travel the length of her body. She moved like a cat, he thought.

She walked on, and he became far too aware of the way she moved: the slow, beckoning sway of her elegantly curved figure. He walked alongside her, and he knew he was too close, because he could hear the brush of muslin against his pantaloons and he could smell the womanly scent, clean and warm.

It seemed to him that the grey spring day had turned into sultry summer.

"You oughtn't to walk that way," he said.

"What way?"

"*That* way," he said. "An Englishman would get the wrong idea."

"To desire me? But that's the idea I want the men to get. I must be popular and receive many marriage proposals."

He hadn't thought of that—or had he? Other men, watching the way she moved her body. Other men desiring her. Other men, tempted.

"You'll get other kinds of proposals," he said.

"Like what?" she said.

"Like this," he said.

He closed the small space between them and brought his arm round her waist. He only meant—or so he lied to himself—to teach her a lesson.

To his shock, she put up no resistance whatsoever. Not even a show of it. She simply melted into him.

She was warm and soft, and the scent of her was like a summer garden with a woman in it. He drew her against him, and the warmth and softness and scent enveloped him.

He slid his hand up her back and along her neck and drew his fingers along her jaw. He tipped her head back and she looked up at him. There was the deep blue sea of her eyes, and there was he, wanting to drown.

He bent his head and brought his mouth to hers.

It was only a touch of their lips, not even a proper kiss, but he felt it ricochet inside him: a stunning jolt of feeling. He didn't know what it was and didn't try to find out. He drew back. It was then, before he could shake off the surprise, that he heard a bird sing out lustily.

The sound penetrated the warm fog of his brain and called him back to his surroundings. The Green Park was far from deserted, and a public embrace was unforgivably, perhaps catastrophically, stupid. It would undo all the work he'd done thus far to make Society accept her.

He drew back. He took his hands away. Then he took himself a pace away, to leave a proper space between them.

He was furious with himself.

"Don't do that," he said.

"Why not?" she said.

He stared at her. "Why not? *Why not?*"

She brought her index finger to her lips and touched the place where he'd kissed her. "A little caress, a little teasing." She studied his face. Then she laughed.

"It isn't funny," he said.

"That's what you say because you can't see the expression on your face."

Expression? He didn't wear expressions. "Zoe."

"Did you not like it?" she said. "I did. I never kissed or touched any man but Karim, and that was like caressing furniture—*soft* furniture," she said with a laugh.

"Zoe, you can't talk like that."

"Oh, I know," she said. "My sisters tell me. You cannot say this, Zoe. You cannot say that. But you aren't my sisters. You're a man of the world."

"I'm a *man*," he said, "and I am not at all accustomed to resisting temptation. If you wish to have a proper launch into Society and be sought after and marry well, you had better not tempt me." A thought struck him. "Ye gods, Zoe, do you even know how to say no?"

She shook her head. "Not in the way you mean. Not to caresses and kissing. All I ever learned in that way was *yes*."

"Oh, my God." If he had been any other man, the kind given to emotional displays, he would have flung his hat on the ground and commenced tearing his hair out.

It was at this moment, finally, that the Duke of Marchmont fully grasped the enormity of the task he'd undertaken.

He could pave her way into Society, but she'd be undermining him at every turn, all innocently. Or perhaps mischievously. This was Zoe, after all.

But Zoe was the daughter of the man who'd stood in place of a father to him. In any event, Marchmont had said he would do it, and he *never* broke his word.

"Very well," he said. "I can deal with this."

Nothing could be simpler.

The words hung in his mind, mocking him.

He looked about him. Nobody who mattered seemed to be about. Perhaps they hadn't been observed. The intimacy had lasted not a minute, after all.

He said, calmly, oh so calmly, "I attended the Princess Elizabeth's wedding last night. The Prince Regent wasn't there—he was ill. But the Duke of York—that is his brother—"

"I know," she said. "I had to memorize all of them."

"Good," he said. "The Duke of York promised to speak to the Regent and see that you received an invitation. He said the royal family were deeply affected by the story in the *Delphian*. The Duke of York thinks it likely that you'll be invited to the Drawing Room being held to celebrate the Prince Regent's birthday."

"On the twenty-third of this month," she said. "This is not his birthday. But his birthday is in August, my sisters told me, and the Season ends in June and everybody goes to the country. No one would be in London to celebrate it then."

Her sisters were the most irksome of women. Still, they'd saved him a good deal of tiresome explanation.

"Exactly," he said. "It isn't like ordinary presentations. You won't be stuck among all the schoolroom misses."

She nodded. "Then it won't be so obvious how old I am."

"Yes, there'll be many other antiques attending."

She smiled. "Good, because I have no idea how to appear young and naïve. It's only a little more than a fortnight from today, and I have more than enough to learn as it is without having to learn how to act innocent."

"Can you contrive not to do anything outrageous or scandalous before then?" he said without much hope.

"If I do not become too bored," she said. "I'm becoming a little bored now." She turned and started back.

He wondered if his hearing was failing. Bored? With him? No one was bored with him. Women never walked away from him. On the contrary, they did everything possible to prolong conversations.

He told himself she was merely being provoking. Bored, indeed. He should have kissed her until she fainted. That would teach her.

Oh, yes. And so much for his promise to make her respectable.

He went after her. "You can't continue wandering about London on your own."

"I am not on my own. My maid is with me."

"A maid is insufficient, and she should not have let you bolt in the first place," he said, though he doubted whether a cavalry could have stopped Zoe.

"I made her do it," she said. "My sisters were coming to the house. They come every day and tell me how to talk and how to walk and how to sit and pour tea and what to say and what not to say."

He felt a twinge of something that could have been the conscience with which he was only distantly acquainted. On the other hand, it could have been fear—far more reasonable in the circumstances.

Zoe let loose in London. Zoe, on her own. Zoe, who didn't know how to say no.

He said quite, quite calmly, "You complained about being cooped up in the house. You've been cooped up in that filthy hackney. What you need is a drive in my new curricle." He leant toward her and sniffed. She still smelled too deliciously like a sunny garden.

He made himself draw away, before scent and sight and sound could lead him to another gross error of judgment.

"You badly need an airing," he said. "I think you've contracted mildew."

She walked on a few steps, then paused and looked everywhere but at him. "I know what a curricle is. An open carriage. Two horses, Papa said. It is dashing. And it goes fast."

Marchmont discerned the gleam in her eye. She was not as indifferent as she pretended.

"I shall take you for a drive in my curricle," he said. "We'll air you out, then we'll drive to the best dressmaker in London, and you may order as many frocks as you like."

He certainly didn't care how much they cost. He couldn't have them billed to him, because word would get out and everyone would assume that Miss Lexham was his mistress. Still, he'd settle finances with her father. Whatever Zoe's wardrobe cost, the price would never approach repaying what Marchmont owed his former guardian.

She continued down the hill. "I have sat in a carriage for long enough. The seats are hard and my bottom hurts."

"You said you were bored," he said. "You complained about your frock being unfashionable."

"Did I?" She gave a dismissive wave, a precise replica of Aunt Sophronia's. "I don't remember."

"Zoe Octavia," he said.

She looked up at him, rolled her eyes, and looked away.

"You are as annoying as you ever were," he said.

"So are you," she said.

"I may be annoying, but I'm the one with the dashing curricle."

After a moment she said, "Does it go *very* fast?"

"There's only one way you'll find out," he said.

"Oh, very well, if you're going to be a pest about it." She let out a sigh. She tucked her arm in his.

The touch sent a wave of pleasure coursing through him.

Gad, she was dangerous, he thought.

Still, he was a man of the world and a man of his word. He could deal with it. At the moment only one thing mattered: He was in charge of her, and while he was in charge, he could keep her out of trouble.

Marchmont House
A short time later

The porter, eyes wide, saw the pair crossing St. James's Square, a female servant trailing after them. He summoned a footman and whispered in his ear. The footman hurried from the entrance hall and fairly flew through the green baize door and down the stairs into the servants' hall, where he found Harrison, the house steward, reviewing accounts with the housekeeper, Mrs. Dunstan.

In appearance, Harrison was everything a duke's chief of staff ought to be. He was tall enough to look down upon all the other servants and most of the house's visitors. His long nose enhanced the effect. His black eyes resembled a raven's: a little too sharp and too bright. The grey streaking his dark hair lent further dignity and probity to his appearance.

"Olney says His Grace is coming," the footman said.

Harrison did not look up from the bill of provisions in his hand. He frowned, though, and the footman trembled at that frown.

As well he should. There was nothing out of the way in the Duke of Marchmont's approaching his own home, even on foot. It was certainly not a matter requiring the attention of the man in charge of running the duke's vast household.

The footman added hastily, "A female with him."

Still Harrison's gaze did not leave the column of notes and very large figures. "What sort of female?" he said.

"Lady," the footman said. "Got a maid with her. Not one of His Grace's aunts or cousins. Olney thinks she's the one from the newspapers. Looks like the etching he saw."

At this Harrison did look up. He exchanged glances with Mrs. Dunstan, whose lips pursed. "The Harem Girl," he said.

Being servants, they were all aware of recent events. They knew their master had taken the Harem Girl under his wing. They knew about the thousand-pound wager with Adderwood. They knew about all of their master's wagers. They knew all of his business.

The Harem Girl business was appalling. However, the nobility did have its whims, and working for the Duke of Marchmont was more lucrative than working for any other peer in all of Great Britain.

Nonetheless, Harrison could not be happy about

the master's bringing to the house a social anomaly.

A harem girl, as any servant would know, stood on a social par with ballet dancers, actresses, and courtesans: marginally higher in rank than a prostitute. On the other hand, Miss Lexham's father's barony was one of the most ancient in England. It was older, by a century or two, than His Grace's dukedom, which was the kingdom's third oldest.

Not that Harrison was ready to believe that the person who claimed to be Lord Lexham's daughter truly was that lady. Others might be taken in by sentimental pieces in the newspapers, but he continued to take a dim view of the entire affair.

A proper lady would not visit a bachelor establishment without a suitable chaperon. A great many people would not deem a lady's maid sufficient chaperonage in the circumstances. Having her mama by, or even one of her sisters or aunts, would have satisfied propriety. But no, the inconsiderate female strutted round St. James's Square on the master's arm, with only a nobody maid following!

Still, Harrison prided himself on never being at a loss in any situation. He couldn't afford to be. The staff would interpret any sign of doubt or hesitation as weakness. In Harrison's view of the world, servants were like dogs or wolves: They could smell fear and weakness. Then their fangs came out.

"I shall deal with the matter," he said.

Marchmont's entrance hall was a great, echoing cavern of a place.

The tall servant, Zoe noticed, did not echo as he crossed the checkered floor. He wafted in like an aroma—like the faint scent of beeswax emanating from one of the rooms nearby.

Her family's London house was an elegant one and efficiently looked after. It was much smaller than Marchmont House, however, which sprawled over a sizable stretch of St. James's Square. Lexham House, too, was more obviously the home of a large family. As diligent as its servants were, they could not always keep up with the endless comings and goings of Lord Lexham's numerous offspring and their spouses and offspring. One might spy a shawl here, a book tossed there, a table or chair not precisely in the correct position.

Such was not the case at Marchmont House so far as she could see, though mainly what she saw was the entrance hall, a handsome public place, intended to awe visitors.

It was scrupulously—no, *scrupulous* was nowhere near the mark. It was *fanatically* maintained.

The mahogany doors glistened. The marble floor's sheen gave it the appearance of pearl and polished onyx. The dark marble chimneypiece gleamed. The chandelier's sparkle dazzled the eyes. Not a single speck of dust, she was quite sure, had ever been allowed to alight upon any surface in this room—or anywhere else in this great house.

The tall man presented to her as Harrison, the house steward, would be responsible for this state of affairs. Thanks to her sisters' lectures on household management, Zoe knew that in the hierarchy of a great—or greatly rich—noble household, the house steward stood at the top of the ladder. He answered only to the master and his land agent. The house steward might be paid two or three times the salary of the next in status: the cook. Slightly below the cook and equal to the master's valet stood the butler.

The structure was quite simple, actually, and Zoe had no trouble making a diagram in her head of all the positions, down to the very lowest ranks, of both indoor and outdoor servants, in Town or in the country.

It was simple, at any rate, compared to the intricate spider's web and ever-changing alliances and hierarchies of Yusri Pasha's household.

Harrison, clearly, did no actual work. The instant the duke removed his hat and gloves, a lower servant appeared, smoothly relieved the master of the articles, and vanished. Other servants hovered in the vicinity.

None of them showed curiosity or any other emotion. All seemed to be at their usual posts. All were correctly dressed and neatly groomed.

And all stood in a state of high tension.

Zoe could feel it. Marchmont seemed oblivious. No surprise there.

"We've only come for the curricle," the duke told his house steward. "I'm taking Miss Lexham for a drive. Have the carriage sent round, and let Hoare know. He'll want to give me a change of something: hat and gloves, I daresay. Meanwhile, we must remember our manners and offer the lady refreshment."

He turned to Zoe. The afternoon light, which made rainbows dance in the chandelier, glittered in his pale gold hair. The one unruly lock had fallen over his forehead, making him look like a careless boy, and she had to fist her gloved hand to keep from brushing it back.

She remembered the touch of his lips. She had not yet quieted the urges the uncompleted kiss had stirred. She had enjoyed that teasing moment very much. She would have liked to enjoy it longer.

"I wish I could say I shall be but a minute, but Hoare cries when I hurry him," he said. "And if I dash out with the wrong gloves or hat, he'll slit his throat. Why do I keep him, I wonder? Any idea, Harrison?"

"I would not venture to say, Your Grace. One might observe, however, that replacing Hoare with a valet of equally high qualifications would consume a great deal of Your Grace's valuable time."

"Harrison always knows the answers," the duke told Zoe. "There it is in a nutshell: It would be even more bother to replace Hoare than it is to put up with him. I shall leave you in Harrison's capable hands."

With that, he sauntered across the hall and through the open door and started up a magnificent stairway.

Harrison flicked a glance at one of the hovering footmen, who hurried toward them. "Escort Miss Lexham to the library—no, no, never mind. That won't do. No entertainment but books. The lady will find it dull."

It was sly, very sly: disrespect couched in a seeming show of concern for her comfort. But no properly respectful servant would presume to know what a lady would find dull or say anything that might be construed as slighting her intelligence. Jarvis, behind her, understood what he'd done, for she gave a barely audible gasp, which she immediately turned into a cough.

The footman comprehended, too. Though he kept his face blank, Zoe saw the smirk in his eyes.

Well, this was interesting.

She beamed at the house steward. "How kind of you," she said. "I never would have guessed that the duke's library was a dull, musty old place. I supposed his collection must be one of the finest in all of England, and his library most elegant and comfortable. But you would know. Yes, I should like to wait in a room that is more pleasant."

The footman's smirk vanished, and he turned pale.

Jarvis made a smothered sound.

Harrison's expression did not change, though his posture became a degree stiffer.

"The morning room," he told the footman. "See that refreshments arrive promptly." He bowed to her and wafted out of the room.

Neither woman spoke until they were comfortably seated in the morning room and the footman had run away.

"Oh, miss, I never," Jarvis whispered. "What he said and what you said. *His* library musty."

"It is not his library but the duke's," said Zoe. "He will do well to remember that. He should remember his place, always, and treat all of his master's guests with the greatest respect. This much I know."

"Yes, miss. He needed a setdown and you gave him one. But . . . well."

"Do not be afraid of him," Zoe said. "He is simply a bully. There is usually at least one in a household, though that one is not always at the top. You must never let such persons cow you, whether they are men or women. You do not answer to anyone but me. Remember this."

"Yes, miss," Jarvis said, looking about her doubtfully.

"There is no need to be frightened," Zoe said. "I do not believe he will try to poison us."

Jarvis's eyes widened. "Good gracious, miss!"

"It is most unlikely," Zoe assured her. "In the harem, they were always plotting to murder Yusri Pasha's third wife, so disagreeable she was. But they were too busy quarreling with one another to organize a proper plot."

"Oh, my goodness, miss!"

Zoe brushed off the maid's alarm with a wave of her hand. "When my sisters were teaching me about running a great household, it seemed like the most tiresome of a number of boring duties. In a house like this, though, it could be most interesting."

The Duke of Marchmont did not notice anything out of the way among his staff. He scarcely noticed his staff except when, as at the present moment, they were annoying him.

A full quarter hour after he'd left Zoe in Harrison's care, the duke stood in his dressing room in his pantaloons and shirtsleeves, watching his valet take up and reject yet another coat and waistcoat.

"Hoare, we shall *not* drive in Hyde Park at the fashionable hour," said His Grace. "No one will be taking any notice of me but the lady—and that will not last long. The fashion plates and fabric swatches will soon absorb all her attention."

"Yes, Your Grace, but the lady—what is she wearing?"

"Ye gods, you don't mean for us to *match*?"

"Certainly not, sir. But it is necessary to achieve the correct tone."

Marchmont silently cursed Beau Brummell. Valets used to be sensible fellows before the Beau came along and turned dress into a religion. "Carriage dress," he said impatiently. "Pale yellow with green trim. A year out of date, she informed me."

The valet regarded him with a panic-stricken expression.

Marchmont did not know or care what had thrown the man into a panic. He only wished he had not hired the most high-strung valet in London.

They would be at this all afternoon and into the evening if the master didn't take matters in hand.

"That coat," he snapped, pointing. "That and the green waistcoat."

The valet's eyes widened. "The *green*, sir?"

"The green," Marchmont said firmly. "It will amuse Miss Lexham."

"Oh, dear. Yes, Your Grace."

"When the lady is bored, appalling things happen. We must strive for a little inconsistency, perhaps a hint of originality. We do not wish to be thought dull, do we?"

"Good heavens, Your Grace. Certainly not."

And at last, Hoare began to bustle.

Six

The duke made Jarvis ride with Filby the groom in the seat behind the carriage.

Neither servant was happy with the arrangement. This was perfectly plain to Zoe.

But she knew it was not Marchmont's business to make servants happy. It was their job to make him happy, and judging by the set of his jaw, they were making a hash of it.

The groom, plainly, was mortified to be seen sharing his seat with a female. Jarvis, equally plainly, was terrified of the curricle and her high perch thereupon. But there was no room for her inside the carriage. It was built to hold the driver and a companion.

Zoe was not sure what the proper procedure was for a maid in such cases. She only understood that Jarvis must accompany her to the dressmaker's, and this was the simplest way to do it.

In any event, it was Marchmont's curricle, he was the master, and everyone else must like it or lump it.

If he did not want to keep his restive horses waiting, then everyone had better move quickly—or be moved quickly, as Zoe discovered.

His way of helping her into the high vehicle was to wrap his gloved hands round her waist, lift her straight up off the pavement, and toss her onto the seat.

She was still tingling from the contact when his big body settled next to hers. He muttered something about "damned finical servants." Then, more clearly, he addressed the horses: "Walk on, my lads."

Though they seemed as eager to be gone as he was, the beautifully matched horses set out slowly from St. James's Square and proceeded calmly through the narrower and more crowded streets.

This sedate pace did not last for long, though.

The driver, Zoe was aware, was as restive as the horses. She had been taught to be keenly sensitive to a man's moods. She was acutely aware of tension. The impatience or restlessness or whatever it was throbbed along the side of her body nearest his.

At last they reached a broader thoroughfare. The horses began to move, faster and faster. Zoe heard Jarvis shriek each time their pace increased. Yet they moved so steadily, stepping beautifully in time. They were big, powerful, high-couraged animals, yet Marchmont controlled them absolutely, without seeming to do anything. The lightest flick of the whip—and that not touching them—the slightest motion of his hands on the reins, were the only outward signs.

The wind ruffled the fair hair under his sleek

hat. Other than that, he seemed almost still on the outside, all the power fiercely contained within him—something the animals, surely, sensed and responded to.

The buildings and lampposts sped by, giving way to greenery, then buildings again. She held onto the side of the carriage as they passed riders, coaches, wagons, and carts and while the world went by in a blur, as though it were a dream.

It was like flying.

It was wonderful.

She laughed. She was a bird, flying, free. He glanced at her, and when he turned away he was smiling a little.

Then, by degrees, they began to turn into narrower streets again, and the pace slowed. After a time she recognized Bond Street, where Jarvis had found the ancient hackney.

Zoe had expected him to return to St. James's Street, where Mrs. Bell's Magazin des Modes stood. Mrs. Bell was very fashionable. She featured prominently in *La Belle Assemblée*.

But he turned into an unfamiliar street.

"Grafton Street," he said, though she had only glanced inquiringly at him and he had not appeared to be looking anywhere but at the way ahead. "We start at Madame Vérelet's."

She was about to ask him who Madame Vérelet was when another vehicle barreled round a curve ahead, straight at them.

Marchmont saw it coming: an antiquated coach and four, overburdened with baggage and traveling far

too fast for this busy street. It had shaved the corner
of Hay Hill to half an inch, but then the vehicle went
wide.

The duke easily stopped his pair in time, but the
bloody fool on the coach box drove straight on at
them. At the last instant, he pulled the horses hard
to the left. He missed the curricle, but the weight
on top of the coach shifted, overbalancing it. The
coachman fell off his box. One of the wheelers
shrieked at the same time the duke heard the crack
of splintering wood. After that, it was difficult to
sort anything out, amid the din and confusion.
Horses plunged and screamed, people ran into and
out of shops, shouting and shrieking and getting in
the way.

Marchmont leapt down from the curricle, leaving his team to Filby, who was on the pavement as
quickly as he.

The duke started toward the overturned coach. It
had fallen on top of some of the luggage and lay pre-
cariously on a great trunk.

The leaders had broken loose, but some men farther
along the street caught them. The wheelers, meanwhile, were wild, one bleeding and clearly maddened
by pain and fear, the other in a panic.

Marchmont shouted orders. A boy ran up and
nearly had his head kicked off, but he caught hold
of the injured animal. The duke caught the other one
and was calming the frantic beast when he heard a
familiar voice cry, "Someone fetch a doctor!"

He looked back and saw Zoe, half under the coach
and pulling at the door of the insecurely balanced
vehicle.

"Get away from there!" he shouted. "It's going to collapse!"

She ignored him and tugged at someone inside. The trunk bulged and the coach sagged downward.

"Zoe, damn you, get away from there!"

To his horror, she crawled under the coach.

"Someone hold this curst animal!" he shouted.

All that held up the old coach was the trunk. One wrong move and it would fall . . . and crush her.

Someone came and took over the animal. At the same instant, before he could get the wretched girl away from the coach, she gave another pull.

The trunk gave way.

The coach seemed to fall so slowly, while he was still lunging for her, before it landed with a great crash and a choking cloud of dust.

"Zoe!" he roared, and plunged into the wreckage.

She'd seen the boy hanging out of the door. Zoe feared he was badly injured, but she hadn't time to check. She pulled him out and dragged him out of the way. An instant later, the coach hit the ground and flew apart.

"You idiot." Marchmont's voice easily penetrated the clamor about her.

He took the boy from her and carried him into the nearest shop. He demanded a doctor, and one soon arrived. Then he went out and supervised those tending to the horses and damaged coach.

When a constable arrived, Marchmont ordered the coachman taken into custody and charged with drunkenness, disturbing the King's peace, and endangering public safety. The coachman was taken away.

All this happened in a remarkably short time. Zoe watched the street's concluding events through the shop window while behind her the physician attended to the boy.

Marchmont, she saw, could be remarkably efficient when he chose—or when he had to be. Or perhaps he was not so much efficient as impatient and intimidating.

He came back inside the shop at last. He didn't look at her but folded his arms and leaned against the door, stone-faced, until the boy came to his senses and proved able to remember his name, the date, and the present sovereign. Zoe caught only the last part of this, because the boy said it loudly: "King George the Third. *Everybody* knows that."

He had a lump forming on the back of his head and a number of bruises and scrapes, but the doctor pronounced him fit to return home.

"My groom will take him home in my carriage," Marchmont said. These were the first words he'd uttered since reentering the shop.

He watched them drive away until they were out of sight. Then he turned his attention to Zoe, who'd followed him out of the shop. He eyed her up and down.

She was dirty and bedraggled, she knew, but she didn't care. She was still exhilarated, because she'd saved the boy from serious injury, perhaps death. The big, cumbersome coach could have crushed him when it fell. He could have been impaled on a jagged piece of wood or metal.

She'd saved him. She'd been free to act, free to help, and she'd done something worthwhile.

Marchmont did not look either exhilarated or be-draggled. He still had his hat on. His neckcloth seemed crisply in order. The coat that so closely followed the contours of his big shoulders and upper body showed spots of dirt here and there but no tears. The green waistcoat hugging his lean torso hadn't ripped any-where or lost buttons. The pantaloons clinging to his long, muscular legs were very dirty, though. Her gaze trailed slowly down, to his boots. They were scuffed and coated with dust.

She became aware of a soft, slapping sound. He had taken off his gloves. He slapped them against his left hand.

Slowly she brought her gaze up.

His face was as hard as the marble in his house's entrance hall. His eyes were angry green slits.

"That way," he said, jerking his head toward a shop.

She looked in the direction he indicated. The shop bore a black sign with the word VÉRELET in gold let-ters. That was all. On either side of the door, bay windows held a splendid array of colorful fabrics and delicious bonnets.

"Clothes?" she said. "Now?"

"My curricle is on its way to Portland Place with that wretched boy. What do you suggest instead? Per-haps a leap off Westminster Bridge?"

She had trained herself ages ago to keep her temper in check, because survival in the harem often de-pended upon keeping a cool head. She told herself she could do it at present.

She reminded herself of her conversation with Jarvis. Zoe needed this man's help in order to live the life she'd risked everything for. She needed his help to banish the shame she'd brought on her family. She needed this help if she wanted a chance to find a good husband. Once she was wed and settled, her father could stop worrying about her.

She told herself all this, several times. Then she lifted her chin and entered the shop.

Marchmont's heart still pounded.

It was as though his brain had overturned, like the coach, and boxes had fallen out and broken, spilling their contents.

He heard himself shout, "No! Don't!" and heard Gerard laugh in the instant before he went over the fence. Again and again the scene played in his mind: Gerard, galloping ahead of the rest of the boys, heedless as always.

Marchmont would never know why he'd shouted the warning, whether he'd seen or sensed something amiss with the fence ahead or the ground or his brother's horse. He'd never know what it was that had made him slow his own mount and cry, "Look out!"

But Gerard wouldn't listen. He never did.

"No! Don't!"

Gerard only laughed, and on he galloped, toward the fence, and over it.

And then he was dead. Like that. In the blink of an eye.

Again and again the scene played in Marchmont's mind.

He followed Zoe into the shop, staring hard at her back, at the stains and dirt and ripped ruffles of the carriage dress. He concentrated on these and thrust the unwanted images back into the dark place they'd escaped from.

Madame Vérelet's was a large shop. As he finally took note of his surroundings, he felt as though he'd entered an enormous birdcage. What seemed like hundreds of females fluttered about the place, bobbing and clucking, picking up buttons and ribbons, pretending to be busy sewing or putting trimmings into drawers and taking them out again. They opened books and flipped through pages, then shut them. They bent their heads together and whispered. They darted furtive looks from him to Zoe and back again, again and again.

Madame Vérelet bustled out from a back room quite as though she'd been deeply engaged in important business there for this last hour. A man less cynical than Marchmont might be taken in. Another man might believe that Madame was too elegant and dignified to take any notice of public disturbances on her doorstep. Madame, after all, was a great artist, not one of the rabble who gathered at accident scenes.

Marchmont, though, hadn't any doubt that she'd been gawking out of the shop window along with all her employees, and had hurried into the back room only when she saw him coming.

She made him an elegant curtsey. "Your Grace," she said.

He gave the little wave of his hand. "Everyone out."

"Out?" said Zoe.

"Everyone but *you*," he said. The women darted for the door leading into the back of the shop, where the workrooms were. They all tried to squeeze through at the same time, with a good deal of pushing and elbow thrusts. Madame did not fly, but she did not linger, either. She shoved aside one girl who didn't get out of her way quickly enough.

"Miss?" said Jarvis.

"You, too," said Marchmont.

"She is required to stay with me," said Zoe.

"Out," he told Jarvis. She hurried after the seamstresses and shopgirls.

Zoe folded her arms. Her face took on a mulish expression.

He knew this expression. He'd seen it scores of times. She'd worn it a moment before she'd picked up the cricket bat. He was aware of this, in the churning stew that was his mind; but since it was a stew, he wasn't capable of calm and logical thinking. The pose and the expression only made him angrier.

He didn't wait to hear what she'd say.

"Are you utterly mad?" he said, his voice low and taut. "Are you deaf? Are you completely without brains? Did I not tell you to get away from that coach?"

"You had the horses to deal with," she said with a calm he found maddening. "I could not leave the boy there. He was hanging out of the door. I knew he was hurt. He might have been bleeding. What if he bled to death while you dealt with the horses? What if the coach fell on him?"

What if it fell on you?

"He wasn't bleeding," he said.

"You didn't know that."

"I didn't need to know!" he snapped. "It was a thoroughly decrepit coach and four, and if it had fallen on you, it would have smashed you to pieces! And that's if you were lucky. If you'd got a piece of it stuck in your gut, you'd die by inches." Such accidents happened all too frequently, the victims lingering in agony for days, sometimes weeks.

"The same could have happened to him," she said. "What would you have me do?" Her voice rose. "Nothing?"

"Yes!"

"That is completely unreasonable!"

"I don't care. When I give an order—"

"An order?" Her eyes were a stormy sky flashing lightning. Hot pink color flooded her cheeks. "You do not order me!"

"Yes, I do. You're my responsibility. I'm in charge of you."

"In charge?" she said. "Of me?" Her voice went up another notch. "I did not agree to this. I did not agree to be stifled!"

"Oh, very good. Give the shopgirls an earful."

"You were the one who chose this place. You are the one who chose to make a scene. You did not care who was listening. I do not care, either. You cannot shout at me."

"I most certainly can."

"Then shout, but I will not listen to you. I will not be ordered. I will not be stifled. For twelve years I was stifled. If this is how you mean for us to go on, then our agreement is cancelled."

"Agreement?" Whatever else he'd expected, it wasn't this. He blinked and told himself he couldn't have heard correctly. "Cancelled?"

"That is what I said."

"You can't be— You think you can do this without me?"

"I shall not do it with you, that much is certain." She folded her arms and stuck her nose in the air. "I release you from your promise to help me."

His heart was beating far too fast.

"Good," he said. "That's a relief."

"A greater relief to me," she said. "Go away. I hate you. You are impossible."

"Good-bye," he said. "And good riddance."

He turned his back and started for the door.

Something struck his hat and knocked it off. He did not turn around.

He left the hat and stomped out.

Though Marchmont had made Zoe so furious that she could hardly see straight, she'd been aware of Jarvis slinking out of the back room and into the shop when the shouting commenced.

Remaining conscious of her surroundings had become second nature. She had learned early in her time in the pasha's palace to watch from the corner of her eye the comings and goings of wives, concubines, servants, slaves, and eunuchs.

After glancing at the design book she'd thrown at Marchmont, then at his hat lying by the door, Zoe turned to the maid, who had a death grip on the handle of her umbrella.

Jarvis crept closer. "I'm sorry, miss. I know he said I was to go away, but they told me when they made me your lady's maid that I was in charge of you and was not to let you out of my sight and if anything happened to you it would be my fault."

An image arose in Zoe's mind of the terrified maid beating a murderous Marchmont off with an umbrella.

Though her heart still pounded and outrage lingered—along with a painful awareness of having thoroughly destroyed her future—the image helped her recover her composure, if not her equilibrium.

"Summon the dressmaker," she said. "As long as I am here, I shall buy clothes."

Jarvis hurried to the door through which the shopgirls and seamstresses had escaped. Evidently the maid moved too quickly, because when she opened the door, the dressmaker stumbled into the room, and her helpers after her.

They had been piled up against the door, eavesdropping, obviously. Not that they needed to. People three streets away must have heard the row.

Now the women tumbled out, tripping on their hems and one another's feet. Caps got knocked askew and smocks came undone. One girl fell backward over a footstool, and another cracked her head against one of the overhead drawers that had been left open when they'd fled. An occasional "Ow!" and "Get off my foot!" punctuated their arrival, along with some expressions in French that Zoe didn't understand.

Madame quickly straightened her magnificent lace cap, gathered her dignity, and approached.

"I need clothes," Zoe said.

Madame examined Zoe's dirty, torn carriage dress with a pained expression and nodded. Zoe wasn't sure whether the woman was pained because her dress was torn and dirty or because it was a year out of date. She suspected the latter.

"I need everything," Zoe said.

"*Oui, mademoiselle.*" The dressmaker glanced at Marchmont's hat on the floor near the shop door.

Jarvis edged closer to Zoe and whispered, "Miss, I think she's wondering who's going to pay."

"I am well able to pay my own way," said Zoe. "I don't belong to him. He does not pay for me."

She told herself she didn't belong to him or need him. She would go to Paris or Venice. It would be more agreeable than London. There would not be so many rules, for one thing. Gertrude had told her that the Parisians and the Venetians were quite wicked and immoral and tolerated all sorts of impropriety.

In one of those wicked places she would easily find a man who could awaken in her the feelings that Marchmont did. She'd find other men who could make her feel like a serpent slithering out of the cold darkness into the hot sun.

Other men who weren't unreasonable and despotic.

A prince, perhaps. That would show him.

She beat down the memory of his mouth touching hers and the longing that still had not subsided.

"Everything," she repeated. "And everything in the latest mode."

"*Oui, ma—*"

The bell over the shop door tinkled.

Marchmont strode in.

He picked up his hat but did not put it on. He did not look at her or anybody else. He crossed the room, set his hat down upon a table, dropped in the most provokingly calm manner into the chair beside it, picked up a book of fashion plates from the table, and began turning the pages.

He was impossible, infuriating. Yet the world brightened at that moment. She hadn't realized how heavy lay the weight upon her heart until now, when it lifted, and the regret and guilt trapped there evaporated.

She regarded the pale gold head, the one unruly lock falling over his forehead, the large but graceful hands holding the book, the long legs. . . .

She remembered the warmth of his gloved hand against her back and the touch of his fingers on her jaw and the jittery shock that had raced through her at these mere nothings of caresses. She remembered the light touch of his lips and the ache it had made in her belly.

She turned her back on him and began explaining to Madame what she meant by "everything."

"Everything," Zoe said, "down to my undergarments. My sisters' stays are so tight against my breasts that I can hardly breathe—and this includes the ones they wear when they are pregnant. But you see, they are smaller in the back even when their breasts are enormous from breeding. My mother's corsets are very handsome and comfortable, but they are too big. She is older and more plump. All the women of my family are shorter than I, and we are not shaped the same. My bottom—"

A strangled sound came from the chair by the table.

Zoe ignored it. "My bot—"

"This," came the deep masculine voice from behind her.

Madame looked that way. "Ah!" she said.

Zoe turned.

He was holding up the fashion plate book. It was

open to a picture of a magnificent gown. "This will be perfect for the Prince Regent's Birthday Drawing Room."

Zoe crossed the room and stared hard at the design, not him.

It was splendid, daring and dashing. It was *red*.

"It's very French," she said. The difference from English style was unmistakable. Had she not memorized *La Belle Assemblée*, which included not only illustrations but detailed descriptions of the latest fashions in Paris?

"You're an exotic," he said. "Your apparel ought to be something out of the ordinary. All the world will be studying you. Give them something they can see and easily put a name to, and their tiny brains won't be forced to imagine."

Though she knew it was in her best interests to do so, Zoe was not ready to forgive him. He had been unreasonable and tyrannical. He had hurt her feelings.

The coming weeks were going to be extremely trying.

Still, the gown was magnificent. It was so very, very *French*.

She looked at him.

He lifted his gaze from the book he was holding and met hers. "Why don't we buy the clothes now and argue later?" he said. "I have an engagement at eight o'clock. Hoare must have at least two hours to dress me for it or he'll cry. That leaves us time either to quarrel or to order your wardrobe, but not both."

"You are abominable," said Zoe, and she flounced away.

* * *

Zoe expressed her disgust with him in the time-honored fashion of women everywhere, by shopping exhaustively.

The sums she spent would have daunted most men, certainly, for she was determined to have everything of the best and most fashionable, from head to toe. Among other things, she bought dozens of corsets. Unlike other modistes, Madame employed her own corset maker, in order to assure a perfect fit for her gowns.

As she'd made clear earlier, Zoe had strong opinions on this topic.

Before she went into the fitting room, she not only explained to Madame precisely how her breasts ought to be most comfortably and attractively arranged but demonstrated, by holding them in the desired position.

"Not in front of the shop window, Miss Lexham, I beg," the duke said. *And not in front of me.*

"I forgot," she said. "I must not take hold of my breasts before others who are not my husband." She turned to Madame. "I lived in another place, and the rules there are different for what is said and done and what is not."

"*Oui, mademoiselle,*" said Madame. "Let us go into the fitting room, if you please." She kept her face neutral. From elsewhere in the shop, Marchmont heard giggles.

"I don't want the short kind," Zoe said as Madame led her to the curtained alcove. "They press the ribs under my breasts, and they do not enhance the shape in the way I wish. I want the kind that comes to here." She indicated the place on her hips. "And it must have the shape that makes the pretty curve from the waist and makes the bottom— But no. Augusta said I should not mention my bottom. It is vulgar, she said. Jarvis, what is the word they use? For the same thing?"

"That's *derrière*, miss," said a scarlet-faced Jarvis.

"A French word, yes. Now I recall. My French is execrable. What little I learned as a girl, I forgot. Thank you, Jarvis. What I wish, Madame Vérelet, is for the corset to shape exactly to my *derrière*. When I wear a dress of fine muslin or silk, I want the shape behind to make a curve, very round." She curved her hands over her buttocks to demonstrate.

"Miss!" said Jarvis.

"Oh, yes." Zoe released her *derrière*. "I forgot."

She disappeared into the fitting room. Madame closed the curtain, but it was only a curtain. Marchmont could hear Zoe talking about her breasts and hips and *derrière*. He heard the rustle as Madame took out her tape and measured. He heard her murmur the measurements to the assistant, who wrote them down.

His mind instantly produced supporting illustrations.

He remembered the softness and warmth of her body melting against his.

His body reacted as one would expect, his temperature climbing upward, along with his cock.

And that was a bloody damned waste of energy, when the gods only knew when he'd have time for amours, at the rate things were going. He told himself it was only for a fortnight—if he didn't kill her before that.

He looked round the shop at the hordes of females. "Someone get me a drink," he said.

When he returned her to Lexham House, Marchmont promised to call the following day.

"I don't care," said Zoe, nose in the air.

They stood in the vestibule while a parade of footmen unloaded parcels from his curricle. Most of Zoe's frocks would not be ready for several days. However, when the Duke of Marchmont entered Madame Vérelet's shop, all of her other customers dropped in priority to forty-second place. She had ordered her seamstresses to alter a few garments intended for other ladies who were not the Duke of Marchmont's protégée.

Zoe was wearing one of these dresses. The duke had ordered her damaged gown burned.

He and she had spent an hour in a shoe shop as well, where she made sure he saw her prettily turned ankles, the evil little tease.

They had bought stockings, too, heaps of them.

He banished from his mind the provocative glimpses he'd had of her legs. Like it or not, he needed to think. With Zoe, a man needed his wits about him.

"It hardly matters whether you care or not," he said. "I shall come to collect you at two o'clock. If you choose to spend the day in this house instead, you're welcome to do so. I certainly have sufficient to occupy me. I shall not die of grief because I cannot escort a sulky young woman about London."

"If you find me so disagreeable, I wonder why you came back into the dressmaker's shop," she said.

"What sort of paltry fellow do you take me for,

to be put off by a temper fit?" said he. "Especially one of yours. It was hardly the first I've seen, and I am certain it won't be the last. You ever were a pain in the a— Ah, Lord Lexham, I see you have escaped Westminster's clutches."

"Temporarily." Zoe's father, who'd quietly entered the vestibule between servants, stood watching the parade of parcels. "Zoe's been shopping, I see," he said.

"Oh, this hardly signifies," said Marchmont. "These are merely some fripperies and trinkets we bought in the futile attempt to sweeten her ghastly temper."

Zoe stormed out of the vestibule, hips swaying, skirts swishing.

"Never mind, sir," Marchmont said, pitching his voice so that she'd hear him. "I promised I would see this thing through, and I shall, no matter what."

Seven

Zoe might have become calmer and more rational if her sister Augusta hadn't condescended to join the family after dinner that evening.

She had nowhere else to go, she said. She still did not dare show her face to her acquaintance. She wondered if she ever would dare, or whether she ought to remove to the country permanently.

"After Zoe's carryings-on this day, I do not see how even the Duke of Marchmont can restore the family honor," she said.

As Marchmont had predicted, news of their contretemps, in Grafton Street and in the dressmaker's shop, was already making the rounds of the Beau Monde. Augusta enlightened their parents.

"Oh, Zoe," Mama said. "How could you?"

Even when Zoe gave her version of events, her father, to her dismay, did not take her side.

"Marchmont was right to shout at you," said

Papa. "In his place I should have done the same. That was damned reckless of you, to pull a child from an overturned carriage. You should have left it to Marchmont. He's perfectly capable of dealing with such matters."

"You made him look ridiculous," said Augusta.

"I?" Zoe said. "I have not noticed you or any of my other sisters showing him any respect. All of you criticize him and say he is useless and lazy—"

"We don't say it in *public*. But you act like a ten-year-old child—and an ill-bred ten-year-old at that. Throwing a vase at him. Does that not strike you as childish?"

"It was a book!"

"Oh, Zoe," said Mama.

"You are very lucky he came back, after the vulgar display you treated him to," said Augusta. "But he at least thinks of Papa and his obligation to him. You think of nobody but yourself."

"Obligation?" Zoe said.

"He's under no obligation to me, I'm sure," said Papa.

"You know he has always regarded you as a father," Augusta said.

Did you think I wanted to find that your father had been taken in by an imposter? Did you think I wanted to see him made a fool of?

The words hung in Zoe's mind. She remembered Jarvis's interpretation of his words: *Everybody knows he don't care about much, but what he said to you means he cares about your father.*

Now the memories flooded in, of the summers

when Lucien and Gerard joined the Lexhams in the country. The two families had often spent weeks together, but she didn't remember the early times, when the boys' parents were alive. She didn't remember what the duke and duchess looked like or sounded like. She remembered vividly, though, the dreadful time after Gerard was killed, when Lucien shrank into himself and avoided everybody. Papa took him away, only the two of them, for what had seemed to her a very long time: months and months. When they returned, Lucien was himself again, or nearly.

Marchmont had returned to the dressmaker's shop because of Papa. Zoe looked at her father.

"Obligation has nothing to do with it," Papa said. "Everyone knows that Marchmont would never run away from a fight. Everyone knows that he regards his word as sacred."

I promised I would see this thing through, and I shall, no matter what, he'd said.

"It's all pride, and nothing to do with me," Papa said. "Really, Augusta, you have a knack for twisting things about."

She did have that knack. Augusta was a killjoy of the first order.

Pride or obligation, it hardly mattered, Zoe told herself. For her, Marchmont was simply a means to an end. She needed to remember this. She needed to remember this was all he was to her.

Perhaps Papa's reproof subdued Augusta temporarily. Or perhaps she couldn't at the moment devise another way to abuse her sister. Whatever the reason, she reverted to the subject of Almack's.

Mama and Papa, who did not find this subject nearly as stimulating as Augusta did, moved away, Mama to her needlework and Papa to the chair beside her and a book.

Would she one day find a man with whom she'd sit in that way? Zoe wondered. Would she and this unknown husband ever be quietly content in each other's company? While such a prospect might not be fashionable, Zoe decided it might not be as boring as some might think.

"Marchmont will be there," Augusta said, drawing Zoe from a domestic reverie in which a man who too closely resembled the duke sat by the fire with her.

"Where?" Zoe said.

"Almack's, of course," said Augusta. "Were you not listening? The patronesses will be devastated if he doesn't appear. He's as important to them as Brummell used to be."

"I think they'll be devastated tonight," Zoe said. "He said he had an engagement at eight o'clock."

"That leaves plenty of time for Almack's," said Augusta. "The doors don't close until eleven. His engagement is no doubt with Lady Tarling," she added, lowering her voice so that their parents couldn't hear—not that they offered any signs of listening to what was said on the other side of the room.

"Lady Tarling?" Zoe quickly ran through the names she'd memorized from the newspapers and scandal sheets. This one was unfamiliar.

"His mistress," Augusta whispered.

Zoe felt a sharp stab within, which she told herself was foolish. He was a handsome, rich, and powerful man. All the virgins would want him for a husband.

All the not-virgins would want him for a lover. "He must have many concubines," she said.

"I am sure I know nothing of such things," Augusta said. "However, he and her ladyship are exceedingly discreet, which is all propriety requires. She is a widow, after all, and widows and married women are allowed more freedom, as I am sure I have explained to you."

"All widows have freedom but me," said Zoe.

"Nobody knows what you are," Augusta said. "How can you be a widow when by rights you could not have been properly married because the man already had a wife?"

Zoe doubted she'd been properly married in any sense, even by the standards of the world she'd escaped. She was a widow who couldn't really be a widow because she hadn't really been a wife because she remained a virgin. There was a social conundrum if ever she'd seen one.

"I can promise you that Lady Tarling will not accompany Marchmont to Almack's," Augusta went on. "Lady Jersey hates her and refuses to put her on the list. Lady Tarling pretends it doesn't signify. She makes a point of going to bed before midnight on Wednesday, in order to rise at dawn to ride in Hyde Park. She's a fearsome horsewoman. Everyone says that's what attracted Marchmont to her in the first place."

Zoe doubted it was the lady's horsemanship that attracted Marchmont, but she filed away the information. She pondered it later that night when she woke from a bad dream about the harem.

The next morning, she, too, was up at dawn.

Marchmont House
Early Thursday morning

Jarvis stood in the anteroom, clutching her umbrella.

Under Dove the butler's disapproving glare, she spoke rapidly to a barely awake Duke of Marchmont.

"I am so sorry to trouble you at this hour, Your Grace, but Lord Lexham has already gone out and Lady Lexham is in bed with a headache and not to be disturbed and none of Miss Lexham's sisters or brothers has called yet this morning and I did not know what to do." She took a deep breath and hurried on, "Your Grace, so far as I know, Miss Lexham has not been on a horse in twelve years, and she doesn't know London. She took a groom with her, but I fear he doesn't realize how long it's been since she rode or how little she knows of London and I'm sure he doesn't understand my mistress at all and it is very easy for her to—er—confuse the servants, especially the men."

In other words, Marchmont thought, Zoe had gone out against her father's orders and lied to the stablemen to get her way . . . exactly as she used to do.

He was not amused.

He had not slept well.

On Tuesday night the Duke of York had assured him that the Prince Regent would invite Zoe to the Birthday Drawing Room.

On Tuesday night, Marchmont had felt confident the matter was settled. He was not so confident at present.

Last night at Almack's, the Duke of Marchmont was once more the topic of conversation. A highly exaggerated and distorted version of events in the Green Park, on Grafton Street, and in the dressmaker's shop circulated through Almack's ballroom.

He'd made light of it, as he always did. When Adderwood asked whether it was true that Miss Lexham had thrown a footstool at him, the duke replied, "I heard it was a book of fashion designs. In any event, it would hardly be the first time a lady has hurled a missile at my head and is unlikely to be the last. Harriette Wilson once threw a snuffbox at me, as I recall."

He knew that wouldn't be the end of the matter. White's betting book would be full of Zoe today.

This didn't worry him. Nothing the ton was talking about was scandalous, merely entertaining. The abortive embrace was nowhere mentioned.

What worried him was the Queen. She was a stickler of the first order, and if she owned a sense of humor, she hid it well. She was polite and gracious and suffocatingly correct. He was not sure what she'd make of the stories. He supposed it was too much to hope they wouldn't reach her.

For all he knew, the invitation had not yet been sent. Even if it had been, it could be rescinded. If it wasn't rescinded, Zoe could still be snubbed. At a Drawing Room, this would be catastrophic.

Such thoughts were not conducive to tranquility.

Now, roused from a not-so-sound sleep and hastily dressed by a fretful Hoare, His Grace was not in the best of humors. His narrowed gaze moved from the maid to his butler.

"I do apologize for troubling Your Grace," said Dove. "I explained to this person that she ought to have brought her problem to Lord Lexham's butler. We at Marchmont House have no control over the doings of Lord Lexham's stablemen. Despite my earnest entreaties, she was most insistent upon speaking to you."

She must have threatened Dove with the umbrella, Marchmont thought.

"Mr. Harrison is out buying provisions, Your Grace, else I should have consulted him," Dove added.

"What the devil has Harrison to do with it?" Marchmont said. "Do you need him to tell you the matter is urgent? Was the maid's anxiety for her mistress not plain enough? Send to the stables. I want a horse. *Now*."

The Hyde Park Zoe discovered in the early morning was amazingly quiet and stunningly beautiful. A faint mist hung over the place, making the leaves of the trees shimmer. There was green, green, green as far as the eye could see, and the sheen of water in what her groom had told her was the Serpentine, a man-made river created in the time of King George II on the orders of his consort, Queen Caroline.

The view Zoe took in was easily worth the guilty conscience. She'd lied to the grooms. Wearing her mother's habit, she sat upon her mother's saddle on her mother's horse. None of these articles, including the horse, fit her. She could only hope that she didn't end up as a tangled heap of broken bones.

Ahead of her at present stretched the King's Private Road. This was the road known as Rotten Row, the groom explained. It was strictly for riding, he said. Only the reigning sovereign was permitted to drive along this particular road.

At this hour, Zoe knew she'd little chance of encountering any sovereigns driving to or from Kensington Palace. At the moment, she didn't even see another rider.

But as she was taking in the acres and acres of glistening greenery, a slim, elegant rider on a superb gelding approached. The horse's dark coat matched the lady's hair. Her wine-colored habit was of the highest quality and latest fashion. Her groom's livery was splendid.

This had to be Marchmont's concubine.

Zoe felt the twinge again, but sharper, augmented by envy. The lady was breathtakingly elegant and utterly sure of herself. *She* didn't need lessons in how to stand or sit or pour tea.

As she neared, Zoe touched her crop to her hat. She couldn't remember whether it was proper to acknowledge a rider to whom one hadn't been introduced. On the other hand, failing to do it might be construed as a snub.

Zoe didn't want to snub this woman.

She wanted to kill her.

It was wrong and stupid to feel this way, of course, but she couldn't help it. She was uncivilized.

To her surprise, the lady returned the salute. She didn't pause to speak, though, but rode on.

Zoe let her pass, then followed, slowly at first. But as Lady Tarling's horse picked up speed, Zoe encouraged hers to do the same. Before long, Zoe was riding alongside the lady on the broad path.

Lady Tarling glanced her way, smiled, and raised her eyebrows in inquiry. Zoe returned the smile and nodded. And so the race began.

By the time Marchmont found them it was too late to do anything. They were galloping headlong down the hill from a stand of trees. He dared not get in their way, lest he distract them and cause an accident.

In his mind an image flashed of Zoe, in the summer before she vanished, galloping ahead of him on a narrow bridle path. She'd bolted and taken a fractious mare for a mount—daring herself and everyone else, as she too often did—and he'd gone after her, his heart in his mouth.

When he caught her and scolded her, she told him he was stuffy. She complained of her French lessons and mimicked her French tutor's efforts . . . until Marchmont was clutching his stomach, laughing helplessly.

In less than a twelvemonth she was gone, and all the brightness went out of his world.

Now he watched, heart pounding, until at last the two riders slowed and turned onto the road that would take them across the Serpentine. When they returned to Rotten Row they seemed to exchange words, but briefly. He made his way back to the Row and waited.

Lady Tarling rode ahead. When she reached him, he resisted the urge to shout at her for endangering Zoe. His mind knew—if his gut didn't—that Zoe endangered herself.

He schooled his features and his voice and greeted

the lady politely. She was flushed with the exercise, and her dark eyes were dancing.

"Ah, Duke, you have your hands full, I've heard—and now seen," she said. She looked as though she would say more, but she only shook her head and laughed. Then she rode away.

Zoe dawdled, pretending to be enraptured by the view. She was probably catching her breath. Not on a horse in twelve years! She must be numb as well as exhausted.

He waited.

At last she trotted sedately to him. He would not be surprised if she pretended not to see him and trotted right past him, but she slowed and stopped.

"How beautiful it is," she said. "Everywhere I look, there's greenery. I cannot remember when last I saw so much green. In Egypt, you know—"

"Are you insane?" he broke in impatiently. "You haven't ridden in twelve years. That gelding is too wide for you, and the saddle is too short. Yet you raced with a complete stranger on terrain you don't know. I saw you gallop headlong down a hill. You could have been killed."

She looked at him in the way most people looked at his aunt Sophronia when she made one of her dafter pronouncements.

"But of course I've ridden in recent years," she said. "Many times. Sometimes we traveled up the Nile on holiday or to abuse the peasants. Then the men would let me ride in the desert. Sometimes a camel, sometimes a donkey, and sometimes a horse. They knew I couldn't run away then. I tried, but it was no use. All the desert looks the same, and in no time I'd be lost. They had no trouble catching me, and it amused them. It was a game to them."

She spoke of the Egyptian experience with less emotion than she'd employ to describe a pair of gloves or slippers. But he could see the scene too clearly and Zoe in it. The vision upset him, adding to the stew of fear and anger inside.

While he struggled to beat down emotion, she looked calmly about her.

"I like this place," she said. "I did not realize it was so large." Her gaze came back to him. "I must like her, too, though I find I'm very jealous."

"I don't care whether . . ." He paused, trying to think past the fear and rage he couldn't quite command. "Jealous?"

"She's so elegant," Zoe said. "She knew who I was, I believe, but she did not snub me. That was generous. If I were your concubine, I would be very suspicious of protégées."

"She is not my con—"

"Her seat is excellent. Better than mine."

He would like to get his hands on the person who'd turned her mind to Lady Tarling. He ordered himself to be *calm*.

"Her saddle fits her," he said. "Her mount fits her. She did not steal her mother's—"

"No." She held up her hand. "You will *not* scold me. This was fun. I want fun. I want a *life*. In Egypt I was a toy, a game. I was a pet in a cage. I vowed never to endure such an existence again."

He stared at her in outraged disbelief.

He told himself her English sounded well enough

but her grasp of meaning was less than perfect. He told himself a great many sensible things, but his gut reacted to the accusation, the patently unfair accusation. She was equating him with the swine who'd caged her and treated her like a pet and a game.

"I drove you all about London yesterday," he said. "I took you to buy dresses and underthings and shoes and stockings. And I told you I would take you for a drive today."

"I needed to ride."

"You might have said so."

"I didn't know it then. And even if I had known it, you would not give me a chance to say what I wanted. We'll do this, you say. We'll do that. I will collect you at two o'clock, Zoe. I will make you respectable, Zoe, whether I like it or not, for your father's sake, and because I said I would, and I always keep my word."

"I know the words are English," he said, "but the thinking must be Arabic, because I cannot make heads or tails of it."

She signaled her horse to walk on.

"Oh, no," he said. "You will not utter cryptic remarks and dismiss me. I will not be dismissed."

She ignored him.

He dismounted and stalked to her. He brought her horse to a halt.

"Get down," he said.

"No," she said.

"Coward," he said.

Her blue eyes flashed.

"Go ahead, then," he taunted. "Run away."

Her eyes were blue murder but she let him help her

dismount. Her bottom must be sore, and her legs would soon be aching painfully.

"You need to walk," he said.

"No, I don't!" She stamped her foot and winced. "I'm only a little stiff. I do not wish to walk with you."

"I don't care."

"You care about nothing," she said. "What about the horses? You cannot leave the horses in the middle of the bridle path."

"Your groom will deal with the horses."

"I am not going to walk with you," she said. She tried to mount her horse.

He could have amused himself watching her try to climb into the sidesaddle unaided, but he wasn't in the mood to be amused. He grasped her hand and dragged her away from the horse and started toward the Serpentine. "I think I'll drown you," he said.

She kicked him in the shins and ran.

The attack being the last thing Marchmont expected—though it should have been the first, he later realized—he was slow to react. Stiff-legged and tired though Zoe must be, she made surprising progress during that moment's delay, and disappeared into a stand of trees.

It was sheer stubbornness propelling her, he told himself, and that wouldn't take her far. She'd had almost no exercise in recent weeks, her muscles were tired—though she might not realize it yet—and she was dragging a train of heavy cloth.

The trouble was, she didn't need to go far to get lost—or to trip over that accursed train and stumble

and crack her skull against a tree trunk or fall into
the Serpentine and drown.

"I shall drown her, I vow," he muttered, and ran
after her.

He watched for a flash of blue and soon found her.
She was near the Serpentine but not on the footpath.
He easily closed the distance between them, but she
kept at her shambling run.

When he came within a pace of her, he reached out
to grab her arm. He stepped on her train and his boot
tangled in the hem, jerking her off balance. Down
she went, and so did he, on top of her.

As they struck the ground, his hat fell off. Out of
the corner of his eye he saw hers roll away. Nearer
to hand, her bosom rose and fell with her labored
breathing. He raised his head and chest to take his
weight off her, but he didn't roll off her completely.

Damp curls clung to her temples and near her ears.
Her skin was pink with exertion. She was scowling
up at him, blue eyes glittering.

"What the devil is wrong with you?" he said.

Her hands came up. Instinctively he drew back. But
she didn't scratch his eyes out or punch him as he expected. She slid her fingers into his hair and grasped
his head. She pulled, bringing his face to hers, and
kissed him full on the lips.

At the first touch, he felt the skittering shock he'd
experienced the day before, but deeper and stronger
this time, as though he'd touched an electrifying ma-
chine. This time, though, he didn't draw away. Her
mouth was soft and warm and her scent and taste
spilled into him, sweet and fresh and warm, like a
summer garden.

Inside him a riot seemed to be going on, of feelings. He didn't know what they were and didn't care. About them was springtime, cool and damp, but she tasted like summer and he craved the heat. Her hands slid down to his jaw and her mouth was searching for more from him. She was by turns insistent and coaxing, and he was all too willing to be led.

His brain slowed and he forgot everything else but the warmth and scent and taste of her. She brushed her tongue over his lips, and the shock he felt this time was a familiar one: the rush of pleasure at an invitation.

All of his senses responded to her, all shouting *yes*. In the warmth and rightness of their deepening kiss, all the turmoil—the anger and fear and frustration and confusion—melted into simple, inescapable need.

He sank onto her and wrapped his arms about her. He rolled onto his back and she went with him. No hesitation, no thought. Only *yes*.

The world went away. Nothing remained and nothing mattered but the teasing and tantalizing discovery of a kiss, slowly deepening. Nothing remained and nothing mattered but the ripely curved body melting against his.

He dragged his hands down her back and up again to trace the line of her spine and the angle of her shoulder blades and the slope of her shoulders and the curve of her neck.

Her hands moved over him, too, in the same unhesitating way her mouth had claimed his. He felt that touch in every cell of his body. The barrier of his clothing was nothing. He was acutely aware of his own skin, its nerve endings quivering.

His heart pumped harder and his breath came faster and heat raced downward. He slid his hand up over her waist and belly and higher still, to cup her breast. She made a sound against his mouth like a purr and a moan mingled. Her mouth and her hands roamed as boldly and possessively as his—over his shoulders and back and under his coat, then settling on his buttocks to press him against her, to rub herself against his hardened cock.

He broke the kiss only long enough to roll her onto her back again. She laughed deep in her throat, and his answering laugh was thick. He was drunk with the heat of tasting and touching her, and he drunkenly wanted all and he wanted it *now*.

He reached down to drag up her skirts.

He was aware of something else, something far away, but it vanished from his consciousness when her hand slid down below his waist to where his erection pushed against the flap of his breeches. That touch emptied what was left of his mind. He grasped a handful of her thick skirt and pulled it up. He slid his hand under the cloth and along her stockinged leg.

He heard noise, somewhere, but it was not important. What was important was his hand moving up over her stocking. What was important was the warmth of her skin underneath and the beautiful curve of her leg.

"Good grief, are you completely lost to reason?"

A part of his consciousness took in the words, but they meant nothing. It was noise to him, a crow cawing. His hand slid further upward.

"Stop it!"

Thwack.

"Stop it! Heaven help me, it is like trying to separate dogs!"

Thwack. "Get off!"

Something was hitting his back.

Thwack. "Now! Do you hear me?" *Thwack*. "Get off her this instant!" *Thwack*. "Get off!"

Bloody hell. Not the idiot maid. Not now. Where in blazes had she come from?

He closed his eyes, took a long breath, and summoned his mind back into his skull.

He would kill the maid and throw her corpse into the Serpentine.

He rolled off Zoe, opened his eyes, and looked up.

The maid was there, yes, but well out of reach. She wasn't the one who'd attacked him. Jarvis stood, shoulders hunched and fists pressed to her mouth, a few feet behind and to the right of Priscilla, mountainous belly heaving as she brandished the tightly furled umbrella.

"Have you taken leave of your senses?" Priscilla cried. "Good God, Marchmont, what is wrong with you? Rutting with my sister in Hyde Park! Like dogs! What will people say?"

Eight

Marchmont didn't answer. He stayed where he was, regarding Priscilla through half-closed eyes while he waited for his erection to subside and his breathing to return to normal.

Zoe raised herself up on her elbows and glared at her sister. "I am going to kill you," she said. "Are you a crazy woman, to interrupt at such a time? I do not care how pregnant you are. There is no excuse—"

"Excuse?" Priscilla cried. "You cannot—cannot—" She waved the umbrella. "You cannot do what you were doing. You cannot do that—here—*in Hyde Park!*"

Marchmont took his time sitting up. After another moment, he swung up onto his feet. He held out his hand, and Zoe took it. She rose awkwardly. Passion having cooled—and far too abruptly—she must be paying the price for her gallop.

"The exceedingly round lady is right," Marchmont said. "We ought not to do this in Hyde Park."

"But what is she doing in Hyde Park, I want to know," Zoe said. "She should not even be awake at this hour."

"It's a good thing I was," Priscilla said. "And why should I not be here at this hour? It's not as though I have entertainments to keep me up late. Augusta said we must not show our faces at Almack's until you've made your curtsey to the Queen—whenever that is, *if* it ever is, which, given today's escapade, I think highly unlikely."

If the Queen refused to meet Zoe, it would be his fault. He'd promised to make her respectable.

"You know no one does anything else of any importance on Wednesday nights," Priscilla raged on. "It is the most vexing thing, to be trapped in the house with a husband who is determined to be contrary in *everything*. I could not abide Parker's sarcasm and went to bed early. Then, when I went to visit Mama this morning, I saw Jarvis returning to the house—*without you*—and knew instantly something was wrong."

"Did Jarvis not tell you that I was dealing with the matter?" Marchmont said.

"Indeed, you are dealing with it splendidly, I see," said Priscilla.

"Of course Jarvis told her," Zoe said. "But my sisters will not leave me in peace." She reverted to Priscilla. "None of you will let me out of the house. Marchmont is too busy with his concubines to take me out."

"I don't have any concu—"

"I cannot meet the Queen for a fortnight. Today, all I want is to enjoy his body—but no, you must interfere, even though nobody is here to see what we do."

"You're not allowed to enjoy his body!"

"It was only kissing and fondling," Zoe said.

Only, he thought.

"Only?" said Priscilla. "He's a man. Did you imagine he'd be content with preliminaries?"

"I know what to do to content him," Zoe said.

"Heaven help us," said Priscilla.

Amen, he thought. He looked at Zoe. He could still taste her, and her scent seemed to have entered his skin. Remembering the press of her hand on his swollen cock, he stifled a groan.

She didn't know how to say no. Neither did he—even when his honor depended on it.

Priscilla's fit continued. "You are most fortunate I did come," she said. "The world is more than ready to view Zoe as damaged goods. If anybody else had witnessed this, she would be *ruined*, and you're the last man on earth who'd be able to restore her reputation then." She turned toward the maid. "If you utter one syllable of this, you will be turned off without a character."

"Leave Jarvis alone," Zoe said. "She is not your maid and she would never do anything to make trouble for me. Give her back her umbrella, in case somebody tries to kill me and she must beat them off."

"You're as ridiculous as he is," said Priscilla. But she returned the umbrella to the maid, who said, "I'll be on the footpath, miss, if you need me," and moved out of hearing range.

Priscilla wasn't done with them yet. "If anyone gets an inkling of what happened here today—"

"Enough," said Marchmont. "I'll marry her."

Zoe stared at him.

"You weren't taught how to say no," he said. "I've never had to."

She remembered the taste of his mouth and the wicked game his tongue had played with hers and the fire his hands had made on her body. She remembered the possessive way he'd squeezed her breast. She remembered her hand upon the front of his breeches and the heat and size of his arousal.

That was wonderful.

But she remembered, too, the way he'd ordered her about and showed no regard for her feelings. She remembered Lady Tarling.

He would never be a faithful husband, not even a loving one. He would never give his heart fully. He would engage his wife's heart, then he'd grow bored and abandon her. That wasn't the kind of marriage Zoe wanted. She wasn't that desperate. If she had to, she'd run away to Venice or Paris. If she did wed, she must have a marriage like her parents'. After twelve years in the harem, she would settle for nothing less.

Her problem was simple enough: She had no perspective. She needed to meet other men.

"I can say no to this," she said. "You're not thinking clearly, and no wonder. You've been aroused and all the blood has gone out of your brain to fill your *membrum virile*. Even I am confused, and I'm a woman and women are not so much ruled by our lust. The trouble is only that Priscilla is making us feel ashamed."

"You *ought* to feel ashamed," said Priscilla.

"I don't," said Zoe. She shrugged. "He is very beautiful and desirable, and his *membrum virile* grows hard so easily. I scarcely have to touch him. And what other men do I see?"

"Thank you," he said. "I think."

"Marchmont, you said you would see this through," Zoe said. "You said it wasn't necessary for us to wed. I believe you. I *trust* you."

"That is one of the most frightening sentences I've ever heard," said Priscilla.

Zoe lifted her chin. "All of my sisters said no invitation would ever come, but you have arranged it."

That got Priscilla's attention. "Invitation?" she said. "What invitation? You can't mean . . ." She trailed off, looking from Zoe to Marchmont.

"The Duke of York has promised to see that Zoe is invited to the Prince Regent's Birthday Drawing Room on the twenty-third," he said.

"The Birthday Drawing Room?"

"It is preferable, in the circumstances, to a Drawing Room reserved for presentations," said Marchmont. "Zoe won't be mixed in with a lot of girls barely out of leading strings."

"The Birthday Drawing Room," said Priscilla. "Good grief, Zoe, why didn't you say so?"

"I forgot," Zoe said. "He told me yesterday, but I was so angry with him that it went out of my brain."

"Oh, my goodness! The twenty-third. That's only

a fortnight away!" Priscilla grabbed Zoe's arm and started to drag her away.

"What are you doing?" Zoe said. "I cannot go with you. Mama's horse is on the bridle path."

"Let him deal with it," Priscilla said. "You're coming in my carriage. The sooner you get away from Marchmont the better. Come along, you absurd creature. Forget? How could you forget such a thing? Stop dawdling. We've not a minute to lose."

Lexham House
Friday afternoon

Zoe stood in the corridor outside the open door of the large drawing room, preparing to enter. The two younger of her sisters were in the corridor with her, to provide guidance. The two older ones were inside. Augusta was playing the queen. Gertrude was playing Mama.

For one who'd navigated the deadly shoals of Yusri Pasha's court, the rules governing court presentations were laughably simple.

Not so simple were the hoop petticoats. Her mother, grandmothers, and great-grandmothers had worn these interesting undergarments beneath the elaborate gowns Zoe had seen in family portraits. In olden times, though, a dress's waistline had been at a woman's natural waist or lower, and this made for some balance between top and bottom. Nowadays, the waists came up under one's breasts, and the gown spread out from there, forming a dome, somewhat flattened fore and aft.

"You could not wear this in the desert," Zoe told her sisters. "If a sandstorm came, it would lift you up and carry you to Constantinople."

"What nonsense," said Augusta. "There are no sandstorms in London."

"You needn't worry about winds," said Dorothea. "You need only step down from the carriage. Then it's merely a few steps into the palace."

"The train is heavy enough to act as an anchor," said Priscilla with a giggle. "Oh, Zoe, how droll you look."

Zoe wore one of Priscilla's gowns. A pearl grey silk confection adorned with ruffles and lace, it was the size of a tent sufficient to house a family of Bedouins. The dress was a few inches too short, but there was plenty of train to make up for the hemline.

Moving forward in a relatively empty space like the corridor of Lexham House had felt strange, but it had not proved very difficult. That, however, was only the beginning, her sisters assured her.

"The palace doorways are wide enough to pass through, but you must be prepared to contend with a tremendous crush of people on the stairs and in the corridor," Dorothea said. "You must practice and practice if you wish to move gracefully, particularly when you're presented to the Queen."

"You must make your way up a crowded staircase," said Gertrude. "You must gracefully maneuver your hoops and train among not only other ladies in hoops but men wearing swords. You must make a very deep curtsey to Her Majesty, and be careful not to get the plumes in her face."

"Take care they don't fall off, either," Dorothea said.

"You must contrive to rise again without stumbling or dropping your fan and gloves," said Gertrude. "Then you will back out of the royal presence, curtseying as you go."

"Without getting tangled in your train," said Dorothea.

"Yes, yes," Zoe said impatiently. "But one thing at a time. Let me get through the door first."

Augusta walked away to the far end of the drawing room and took her place upon her "throne." This was a chair the servants had raised up on bricks, to bring her to approximately the level at which the Queen would sit.

Gertrude positioned herself nearby.

Dorothea and Priscilla remained in the corridor, to offer instruction as needed. "Are you ready, Augusta?" Dorothea called.

"Of course I'm ready," said Augusta. "The question is whether Zoe is."

They had closed one side of the double doors leading into the large drawing room so that Zoe could practice maneuvering through a more confined space.

She brought her elbows down to compress the hoops, as Priscilla had shown her. Then she concentrated on the route she meant to take to Augusta, took a deep breath, and sailed over the threshold at the same instant Dorothea cried, "Zoe, wait! The train!"

Too late.

Zoe's foot tangled in the forgotten train, and down she went. She let go of the hoops and put her hands out to break her fall. The hoops sprang out as she went down face foremost onto the carpet, and the gown billowed up around her.

She heard the snort behind her, but she was preoccupied with determining the simplest and quickest method of getting upright unaided. The corset required her to bend from the hips. After a quick mental survey of the options, she pressed her hands into the carpet and pushed herself up onto all fours. Then, hands still braced on the carpet, she lifted her bottom into the air while she straightened her legs. She carefully walked her hands back as close to her feet as she could, then angled her spine upright.

Another, louder snort came from behind her, then a bark of laughter. Deep, masculine laughter.

She turned toward the doorway, where Marchmont stood, one hand braced against the door frame while he laughed.

And laughed.

And laughed.

Tears streamed down his face.

He shook his head and composed himself. He took out a handkerchief and wiped his face. Having erased all signs of mirth from his face, he walked into the room and sat in a chair. Her two younger sisters broke into giggles. He made a strangled sound, then exploded into laughter. Then they were all laughing, even Augusta.

"Do you know," Zoe said to the room at large, "that is much more difficult than it looks?"

"Falling on your face?" said Marchmont. "But you make it look s-so easy." And off he went into whoops.

* * *

During this one unguarded moment, Zoe could watch him, and she did, utterly bemused. Something had happened, and she wasn't sure what. The world had changed somehow. Or perhaps something in her mind had changed or a key had turned in a keyhole, unlocking something hidden away and forgotten.

Then, as his laughter began to subside, she saw what it was.

This is he, she thought. *This is the boy I used to know. This is Lucien.*

The moment passed and the green eyes shuttered, but she could still discern the amusement glinting there.

"The Birthday Drawing Room will prove more entertaining, I suspect, than some might wish," he said.

"I shall not embarrass you," Zoe said.

"Oh, nothing embarrasses him," said Gertrude. "Never fear for that. It's the rest of us who'll be mortified. It's Mama who'll be there, humiliated."

"She will not be humiliated," Zoe said. "I won't fall. I'll learn everything. If I can learn to dance in veils without killing myself, I can learn to get through a door wearing hoops."

She became acutely conscious of his slitted green gaze. She knew he was either picturing what was under the hooped petticoat or imagining her dancing in veils. She glanced down at his hands and remembered yesterday. Her skin had memorized every place where those hands had touched her. Every one of those places tingled. In the airy space under the hooped petticoat, her Palace of Delight tingled, too.

"I'd always thought the Dance of the Seven Veils was a myth," he said.

"It isn't," Zoe said. "It's very beautiful and arousing to men—well, not to Karim, but then, *nothing* aroused him."

Not like you, she thought. The trouble was, she'd thought of him in that way far too much. She really needed to meet other men.

"That is an unsuitable topic of conversation," said Augusta, who'd quickly regained her normal pomposity.

"You had better go away, Marchmont," said Gertrude. "You do not take this seriously, and you are a bad influence."

"Zoe can practice her gymnastics later," said Marchmont. "I must mount her."

Augusta turned purple. Even Zoe looked taken aback.

"Out!" Augusta snapped. "Out!"

"Certainly not," Marchmont said. "I am in charge of launching Zoe into Society, and she can't make a respectable show if she isn't properly mounted. We can't have her riding in Hyde Park looking like a quiz, on a borrowed horse on a borrowed saddle and wearing a borrowed habit."

At the moment, in her borrowed finery, she made anything but a respectable show. It was the first time he'd ever seen her not wearing day dress, with her bosom covered. At present, it was on full display. Overfull display. They had stuffed some lace into the bodice for decency's sake, but it was obviously too small, and the lace was being asked to do more than the laws of physics allowed.

Zoe laughed. "Oh, it's a word play. *Mount* means two things. Very funny, Marchmont. I'll be happy to let you mount me."

The two younger of her sisters covered their mouths. Augusta and Gertrude glowered.

"I'm sorry to interrupt your presentation lessons," he said. "But the matter can't wait. We're due at Tattersall's in an hour."

"What is Tattersall's?" Zoe said.

"The grand mart for horses," Priscilla explained. "It's quite close to Hyde Park Corner. They've room for more than a hundred horses, as well as carriages and harnesses and hounds."

"The auction is not until *Monday*," Augusta said. "And Tattersall's is for men only."

"Like a gentleman's club," Priscilla told Zoe.

"Women do *not* enter," said Gertrude. "Unlike a gentleman's club, they let in persons of high and low degree, including some of unsavory character."

"For a lady to go is unthinkable," said Augusta.

"True," said Marchmont. "But the rules do not apply to me. I thought it unwise and dangerous to choose a horse for Zoe without her participation. I've made arrangements. What's the good of having a duke in charge of these matters if he doesn't use his . . . er . . . duke-ness?"

"Baksheesh," Zoe said. "It works magic, I know."

He knew what baksheesh was. He'd learned about it when she'd told her story to Beardsley. London was not altogether different from Cairo in that way. Bribes worked wonders.

"That, too," he said. He didn't know or care what

the special arrangement had cost. He left financial wrangling to Osgood. "But we have a limited time. Can you get out of that contraption quickly?"

"Oh, yes." She lifted up her gown, reached under, and started wriggling about as she hunted for the petticoat ties.

"Zoe!" Gertrude cried.

"Someone help me get out of this," Zoe said.

"Not here!" Augusta shrieked.

Zoe paused, the front of the dress pulled up to expose her knees and more. Her garters were plainly visible. They were red.

She did not appear to be wearing drawers.

She let the garment fall, dragged up the train, and ran out of the room. "Jarvis?" she called. "Where is Jarvis?"

He muttered something about making sure she didn't tumble down the stairs and followed her out.

It was the feeblest excuse. The truth was, he couldn't take his eyes off her. It wasn't simply the expanse of smooth flesh on display, either. It was the way she moved in the hooped skirts, the way they exaggerated the sway of her hips, and the way the skirts billowed about her. She was like a ship under full sail, gliding along the passage as though she glided on water.

He was dimly aware of her sisters saying something. He shut the door behind him, to shut them out.

She had the train over her arm, but the way she held it hiked up the skirt on one side. He remembered what he'd seen, what he knew: under those hooped petticoats was only air and skin.

His mouth went dry.

She rounded a corner. He could have—and should have—stopped then if he'd known how, but he didn't.

Temptation glided ahead of him, and he couldn't turn away.

Though the corridor was carpeted, she must have heard him, because she turned her head to look at him over her shoulder. She gave a little laugh and broke into a run.

Then he became aware of the staircase looming ahead and a chair against the opposite wall and a table beyond that, with a great china dragon standing on it—and scores of obstacles elsewhere. If she tripped and fell against the table, the dragon would fall on her head.

"Zoe, stop!" he called.

She stopped abruptly, dropping the train. She started to turn, lost her balance, and tottered toward the stairs.

He lunged toward her and pulled her upright and dragged her away from the stairs.

He pushed her against the nearest wall, solid and safe, and tried to calm himself.

Impossible. His heart was racing, churning with panic and anger and desire everlastingly put off.

Red garters and stockinged legs and the memory of her hands on him and the taste of her mouth and the scent of her skin. In his mind he saw her as she was long ago, galloping away, never to return. He saw her as she was yesterday, in his arms, yielding and eager and curving and soft and turning the cool spring day into summer.

"Don't, don't, don't," he said. He didn't know

what he was saying. Nothing made sense. But she was here, and he could feel her breath on his face. He could hear her inhale-exhale, fast and shallow, like his. He was aware of the rustle of silk and the gown billowing about him, a silken, feminine cloud.

"Damned hoops," he said. Then his mouth was on hers and she gave way instantly, her lips parting to his, her hands reaching up into his hair. To hold him.

As though there was any danger of his running away.

He'd never run away. It was always she.

He had her now, though, and all the balked lust of yesterday exploded into life at the first taste and touch. Their kiss was deep and wild, nothing civilized about it at all, but he was worlds away from civilization at this moment.

He broke away from her mouth to press his face into her neck and drink in the scent of her while his hands slid over the silk and lace encasing her. He was heatedly aware of her hands moving over him. She wasn't afraid to touch. She wasn't afraid to explore his body. Far from it. Her hands stole under his coat and waistcoat, and dragged over the front of his shirt. Then those restless hands moved behind and lower, to grasp his buttocks and press him closer. She rubbed herself against him.

He slid his hands over the silk and ruffles and the frustrating layers between them. He wanted skin, but the dress entranced him. The silk draped over the hoops was the most sensuous and seductive of traps, yielding to the pressure of his hands and billowing up again when he released them.

He grasped a fistful of silk and ruffles and lifted

up the front of the dress. The silk and lace whispered against his coat sleeve while he reached under and his fingers slid over her stocking and upward, to pause on a garter.

Red.

No drawers.

His hand stole upward, to skin.

She moved against his hand. He trailed his finger upward, to the junction of her thigh.

"Oh," she said.

She was so soft in that softest of places.

"Oh." She squirmed against his hand.

Then, "Oh!" she said, and pushed him away. Hard.

So hard that he dropped the front of her dress and stumbled backward.

Then he heard the approaching footsteps.

It was then that he came to his senses—or as close as he could get. He looked down in despair at the incriminating evidence: his cock standing at attention, a great bulge straining at the flap of his breeches.

He bent down and made a show of helping her gather up her train. He was explaining the most efficient way of carrying it when her father rounded the corner and stalked toward them.

"Marchmont," he said. "I want a word with you."

She'd heard the door shut shortly after she left the drawing room. She'd known it was Marchmont behind her. She knew his step, and she'd trained herself to hear far stealthier footfalls than his.

All the same, she was amazed she'd heard her father coming. All the world had narrowed to Marchmont and what he did to her. She could not remember when anyone or anything had absorbed her as fully as he did when he kissed and caressed her.

She really needed to meet other men.

"You'd better go to your maid," Marchmont told her.

"Not yet," said Lexham. "This involves Zoe, too."

Marchmont's countenance, which had been almost human a moment ago when he'd got her all stirred up, reverted to its usual tell-nothing expression.

It was a face she couldn't marry, couldn't think of marrying: a beautiful house with all the doors closed and the windows drawn. The women in his life would always be shut out.

And she, unlike most of them, would know what he used to be and could envision what he might have become. She'd heard his laughter and watched his face before, in the drawing room. She'd seen and felt him come alive when he pushed her against the wall and when she thought he'd ravish her and it hadn't occurred to her to do anything but let him.

Then she'd been caught up in the excitement and danger. It was so deliciously wicked, in the corridor, with her hoop petticoats going up and down like ocean waves. It was thrilling, too, knowing that any minute she and Marchmont might be caught.

The trouble was, any minute they might be caught and he'd think he had to marry her. So would everyone else.

Her body liked the idea, too much. Her heart and mind and pride knew better. When she wed, she wanted an eager and happy and, yes, loving bridegroom. She did not want a man doing his duty—no matter how beautiful and exciting he was and how wild he made her when he touched her.

"Perhaps we ought to adjourn to a less public environment," said Marchmont.

Papa stared at him. "What's brought on this attack of stuffiness? The trials of managing Zoe into respectability? But if it were easy, Marchmont, then anyone could do it, and you'd be bored." He held up a thick envelope. "Know what this is, Zoe?"

"It looks official. Like the Sultan's firman."

Papa laughed. "You're close, child. Only observe the seal. This is your invitation. Arrived a moment ago, direct from Carlton House." He clapped Marchmont on the shoulder. "Lady Lexham will be in alt. I know you said it would come. I know my girls are all in a frenzy about it. But my lady didn't want to get her hopes up."

The frozen expression on Marchmont's face melted slightly.

"But that's weeks away, I understand," Lexham went on. "And my lady and I agree with Zoe that she needs to practice her social skills before that. With strangers. Men, in particular. She's had all the experience she needs in dealing with women, and she is a woman herself."

Marchmont's gaze slanted briefly at Zoe before returning to her father. "Men," he said. "You want her to meet men."

"*Other* men," Zoe said.

"She suggested it last night," Papa said.

Marchmont looked at her. He gave very little away,

but she was trained to notice. His eyes held some emotion, and it didn't seem to be relief.

She told herself it was stupid to try to read his mind. They had been interrupted in a moment of passion. His mind would be muddled with balked lust.

"Mama said we could have a small dinner party," she said.

"With men," said Marchmont.

"No more than twenty guests," said Lexham.

"With a lot of men she doesn't know," said Marchmont.

"That's the point," Zoe said. "I need to practice how to behave with men I don't know."

"But I'll want your help with the list, Marchmont," said Papa. "I'm liable to fill the places with a lot of fusty politicians."

"They must be the kind of men who'll wish to talk to me and dance with me and flirt with me," said Zoe. "The kind of men who might wish to marry me."

"He understands," said Papa. "Eligible men, of course. He'll know who's most suitable, in the circumstances."

"Eligible men," said Marchmont.

"We shall give Zoe an opportunity to dip her toes into the social waters in a small way, among those disposed to accept her, before she tackles the mob at the Queen's House."

"Dip her toes, yes," Marchmont said. "I beg your pardon if I seem preoccupied. I quite agree, and I should be happy to help you with the guest list, but the present time is inconvenient. Zoe and I have an appointment to see a man about a horse. Then we must have her measured for a saddle and riding habits."

"Ah, yes," said Papa, "I meant to attend to that. We had a bit of a to-do yesterday, I understand. Threw Priscilla into a panic. But Zoe always did that, I reminded her. You remember, don't you, Marchmont?"

"Yes."

"You needn't worry about the horse, Papa," Zoe said. "Marchmont will take care of that. But he's right. We cannot stop now. I must change out of these contraptions."

"In any event, I should want some time to decide exactly who merits the honor of meeting Zoe before the Queen does," said Marchmont. "I'll send a list tomorrow."

"Splendid," said Papa. He clapped Marchmont on the shoulder. "Well, then, run along, Zoe. Mustn't keep the horses waiting."

"I beg you, *don't run,*" said Marchmont. "But do make haste."

There was only one man in all the world whose opinion and respect meant anything to Marchmont.

To debauch that man's daughter—under his roof!— was the act of the most swinish of scoundrels.

He and Zoe had had a narrow escape. The error must not be repeated. Marchmont must be on his guard against her at all times, because she was not going to guard herself.

Besides, she wanted to meet other men.

Marchmont stuffed the hooped petticoats and the frothy silk gown into the special mental cupboard.

He stuffed the low-cut bodice there, too. He shut the door and turned his mind firmly to Zoe's horse and saddle and habit.

She wanted to meet other men, and rightly so.

Her only trouble was an inability to say no.

She simply needed close chaperonage.

She must have realized this, because when she came downstairs a miraculously short time later, she had her maid with her, armed with the ever-present umbrella.

He and Zoe behaved with unfailing correctness all the way to Tattersall's and during the time they spent there. They did not relax propriety for an instant, all the time at the saddlery and thereafter, during the purchase of a dozen riding dresses, the first of which was promised for Monday.

The errands completed, Marchmont took an immaculately polite leave of her and she of him.

Then he went home and drove himself mad selecting and discarding the names of eligible gentlemen. After which he dressed and went out and got very drunk.

The following morning, while nursing a headache, he tore up the list and wrote another one. He tore that up and wrote another. Two dozen tries later, he summoned a footboy to deliver the list of recommended invitees to Lord Lexham.

Marchmont did not return to Lexham House. She didn't need him, he told himself. Her sisters would ready her for the presentation.

Perhaps he'd see her at the dinner party. If he decided to go. If he had nothing better to do. He wouldn't be needed there. Her parents could watch her well enough. She'd get no opportunities to not say no.

She wanted to meet other men. She was quite right. It was perfectly reasonable. He should have thought of it himself, in fact.

He did not ask himself why he hadn't.

Nine

The Duke of Marchmont didn't know where Zoe had found the dress. It looked like Vérelet's work, but he was positive he'd had nothing to do with ordering it.

He would never have ordered the *corsage* to be made so tight or cut so low. If there was an inch of lilac-colored satin covering her bust, it was the narrowest inch he'd ever seen.

And there were Adderwood and Winterton, on either side of her—the golden-haired half-naked angel between two leering dark devils. Not that they were obvious about it. But he knew that they—along with Alvanley, who sat opposite her—were staring at her breasts while pretending not to. He knew how to do that, too.

He emptied his glass.

The dessert course was in the process of being set out, and he was well on his way to being drunk.

Other men.

Lexham had decided to err on the side of caution. Ten guests only. Of the men Marchmont had suggested, Lexham had selected only Alvanley and Adderwood, the two youngest. Marchmont had put Adderwood on the list only because he couldn't *not* add him. The stout Alvanley was less of a problem. No one could ever accuse him of being handsome.

But Lexham had discarded the Earl of Mount Edgcumbe, along with several other steady, older gentlemen. He'd invited Winterton instead.

In addition, he'd invited Adderwood's sister Amelia, Lady Lexham's sister Lady Brexton, Marchmont's spinster cousin Emma—one of the indigent relations he supported—and the American ambassador, Mr. Rush, and his wife.

With only a dozen at table, the conversation was general, ranging freely up and down and across the board.

The meal had reached its last stages, and Adderwood was running the show, thanks to the opening the American ambassador had given him. Rush had marveled at the British press and its propensity to tell everybody everything about everybody and everything. From newspapers, Adderwood easily turned the conversation to books.

He was at his most charming this evening, the lecherous swine.

"Walter Scott seems to be highly popular here," Rush was saying. "I heard of a dinner at which the hostess asked each of her guests to write down on a piece of paper the Scott novel he liked best. She received nine slips of paper, each one with the name of a different novel."

"I heard of that," said Adderwood. "The guests she asked were all men. If one were to ask women to name their favorite books, I suspect the slips of paper would bear the titles of horrid novels." He turned to Zoe, using the opportunity, Marchmont had no doubt, to ogle her assets. "What do you say, Miss Lexham? Scott or a horrid novel?"

"What is a horrid novel?" said Zoe.

"A book in which a lot of bizarre and terrifying events are told in a desperately romantic fashion," said Winterton.

Before he could continue, Marchmont said, "Typically, an innocent maiden finds herself in a decaying castle where she is hunted by depraved men, haunted by ghosts, locked into dungeons, attacked by vampires or werewolves or both. There's usually a madman in the picture."

"It sounds like Cairo," she said. "*Afreets* everywhere."

"*Afreets?*" said Adderwood.

"Demons," said Winterton, the know-it-all, before Marchmont could answer.

"Everyone there believes in ghosts and demons and giants and *jinn* and the Evil Eye," said Zoe.

"Good heavens!" said Cousin Emma. The only excitement in her life was the periodic summons from Aunt Sophronia to accompany her somewhere—excitement that even Emma, whose life was numbingly dull, would rather do without.

"They think all sicknesses can be healed with magic spells and charms," said Zoe. "I don't need to read a horrid novel. I've lived in one."

"No, no, Miss Lexham, you want something more improbable than that," Marchmont said. "Pieces of gigantic suits of armor appearing in the garden. Corpses resurrected via dismemberment, neat stitchery, and electricity. You are too real."

She frowned. "Too real?"

"Not at all," said Adderwood. "Miss Lexham is precisely real enough."

"I meant that the rigors of your ordeal might be too painful for some of the ladies," said Marchmont. He couldn't believe she was going to talk about the harem after all his work trying to put it out of people's minds.

"I wasn't referring to an ordeal," said Zoe. "I thought we were speaking of the absurd things in these stories. Ghosts and such. It's the same elsewhere. *The Thousand and One Nights* is famous in Egypt. I saw that my father has this book in his library, but in French."

"Oh, yes," said Amelia Adderwood. "I've read those stories."

"I've read them, too," said Cousin Emma. "Magic lamps and flying carpets."

"To us, all those impossible things are make-believe, fantasy," Zoe said. "To those among whom I lived, the stories are true."

"Very well, then, Scheherazade," said Marchmont. "Tell your tales. I'm sure everyone here is longing to hear the secrets of the harem." He emptied another glass and glanced at the nearest footman, who quickly refilled it.

"That isn't what I meant," she said.

"Sometimes you speak English and think in Arabic," he said. "It's charming but confusing to some of the company."

"I think we all understand Zoe well enough," said Lexham.

Marchmont heard the reproof in his voice, but the doting smile Adderwood bestowed upon Zoe—or her breasts—put it straight out of his mind.

"Then I shan't recommend *Frankenstein* to you," Adderwood told her. "You may find *Pride and Prejudice* more to your liking. The heroine is an independent-minded young lady of wit and charm. You are sure to find more in common with her."

I'm going to be sick, Marchmont thought. Who'd ever have guessed that Adderwood could be so treacly? The breasts under his nose must have turned his brain to syrup. Marchmont said, "That one I found more harrowing than *Frankenstein*."

"You're joking," said Miss Adderwood.

"He usually is," said Alvanley.

"Not at all," said Marchmont. "*Frankenstein* was too improbable to alarm me. *Pride and Prejudice*, however, was all too probable. It had me on tenterhooks: Would this one marry that one? And so many marriages to fret about. So many choices. Would the ladies choose well or ill? Would Fate intervene, and destroy this one's chance of happiness? Would the aunt get her way? Would the sister— But I don't want to spoil it for you, Miss Lexham."

"We may be sure, given your observations, that Miss Lexham has not the smallest inkling what the book is about," said Adderwood. "Meanwhile I'm all agog to learn that you've read a book."

"You do me a shocking injustice," said Marchmont. "I most certainly did not read it. I allowed my valet to tell me the story, while I was dressing for dinner at Carlton House. A lengthy and tearful process, I regret to say—tearful on his part, that is."

"Marchmont's valet is famous," said Adderwood. "He's been known to faint at the sight of an over-starched neckcloth."

"He cries when Marchmont puts anything into his pockets," said Alvanley.

"He wept while he related the tale," Marchmont said. "Whether it was the story or my buttons that made him sob, I cannot say."

"What a remarkable servant he must be, to entertain you while he dresses you," said Mr. Rush.

"I should never let him make a habit of it," said Marchmont. "On this occasion, I invited him to tell me. Miss Austen's books were favorites of the Prince of Wales, Miss Lexham, and one wishes to appear *au courant* when one attends His Highness." Again he emptied his glass. Again it was refilled.

"Everyone knows what the Regent's favorites are," said Adderwood. His gaze reverted to Zoe's breasts. "But Miss Lexham is *terra incognita*."

And if you think you're going to explore that territory, Marchmont thought, *think again*. He said, "By *terra incognita*, Adderwood means—"

"I know what he means," Zoe said. "Do you not remember, Marchmont? How dreadful I was at

French, and how Papa said I might study Greek and Latin, as the boys did?"

"Ah, I recollect," he said. "I recall your French tutor saying that when you spoke his beautiful language, he had only one desire, and that was to have his ears cut off. I used to picture him holding his ears and screaming in pain whenever you attempted to *parler*."

"Marchmont will have us believe he knows everything there is to know about you, Miss Lexham," said Adderwood. "As though he wasn't conceited enough before. It gives him an unfair advantage."

"Adding insult to injury," said Alvanley, "he's kept you to himself for all this time."

"An eternity," said Marchmont. "A whole fortnight."

And I'm the one who kissed her first. I'm the one . . .

The thought fell away as he realized the occasion on which he would not be the first.

Other men. She wanted to meet other men. He'd offered to marry her and she'd said no. She wanted to meet other men.

And that was when she said, "But Marchmont is one of the family. He's like a brother to me."

He froze.

She beamed at him.

"I should call that a decided *disadvantage*," said Winterton.

Before Marchmont could lunge across the table and strangle Zoe, her mother rose. The other ladies instantly heeded the signal and followed her out of the room, leaving the men to their port . . . and mayhem and murder if they so chose.

One hour later

"'Remembered an appointment,'" said Adderwood as he followed Marchmont into the drawing room. "You sly devil. She's the peach."

Adderwood was still alive. Marchmont wasn't sure why.

Oh, yes. Because she wanted to meet other men, and how could she meet them if Marchmont killed them? However, she'd met Adderwood this evening. Technically, it would be all right to kill him.

Later, though. Mustn't get blood all over the drawing room.

"Appointment," he repeated blankly. "The peach."

"The girl in the antiquated hackney," said Adderwood. "The girl you chased into the Green Park. The girl who pulled the boy out of the smashed carriage. The girl who threw the book at you. All those stories we heard and couldn't believe. The ones you never actually confirmed or denied."

"Oh, that peach," said Marchmont.

"It's all clear now. Of course you knew her the instant you clapped eyes on her. She hasn't really changed, has she? That is to say, she's grown up and grown beautiful. It's a good thing you're so constantly besieged by beauties that you're immune."

"A good thing, yes."

"I am not, however. Had I undertaken the task of launching her into Society, I couldn't possibly have remained aloof. I should have offered for her instantly, to make sure no one else got a chance."

Marchmont looked back longingly at the door

leading out of the drawing room. "Why did we leave the dining room so quickly?" he said. "I wasn't done drinking."

"You're bored, I know," said Adderwood. "Bored with us. We're all so proper, trying to make a good impression on Miss Lexham."

"A good impression—on *Zoe*?"

"I know. Everyone supposed it was to be the other way about: Could the exotic creature meet the standards of English Society? There are bets on at White's. But that's no surprise to you."

"Everyone is so predictable," said Marchmont.

"Indeed we are. And now she's turned the tables, and we're all falling all over ourselves trying to meet her standards."

That would be me, Marchmont thought. *I'm the standard*. Because she hadn't met other men.

He had the unpleasant suspicion that he'd set the standard too low.

"It's a great bore for you, I know," said Adderwood. "As silly as watching everyone chase after Harriette Wilson a few years ago. No, sillier, because this time it's a lady and we must be on our good behavior. Poor Marchmont, what a martyr you are. I don't blame you for wanting another bottle— or another dozen. But I know you well, and I can see you're rapidly approaching the point where you start quoting Shakespeare and falling into the fire. Either you must begin drinking tea or we must make our excuses."

"Tea?" Marchmont said. "I'd rather hang. I do *not* spout Shakespeare when I'm in my cups."

"Always," said Adderwood. "Henry IV, usually."

"Oh, that. 'I know you all, and will awhile uphold the unyoked humor—' "

"Uphold yourself for a bit, there's a good fellow," said Adderwood. "It'll be over soon. She'll be off your hands in no time, and wed before the Season ends."

Marchmont's gaze went across the room, to where Zoe sat with Amelia Adderwood and the indigent cousin, the three of them giggling.

"If she takes—as it appears she'll do—I wager she'll have her pick of suitors," Adderwood said.

"Suitors, undoubtedly," said Marchmont. "Whether any succeed is another matter entirely."

She wouldn't. Not so soon.

I was married from the time I was twelve years old, and it seemed a very long time, and I would rather not be married again straightaway.

"She's a woman," said Adderwood. "They all want to rule their own households."

"I shouldn't count on that in her case, if I were you," Marchmont said. "Certainly I shouldn't be so foolish as to wager on it."

Adderwood's eyebrows went up. "Marchmont advising a fellow against a wager. Now I've heard everything."

"I tell you because you're my friend and I deem it unfair to let you throw money away in that cause," Marchmont said. "Miss Lexham has told me she doesn't want to be married straightaway. This shouldn't surprise you. Having read her story, you must understand her wishing to enjoy her freedom for a time."

"Women change their minds," said Adderwood. "They're famous for it."

"Do you fancy you can change hers?"

"Perhaps. If I can't, somebody will. Once she's going about in Society, once she begins meeting Englishmen and finds herself endlessly wooed and pursued, I think she'll change her mind. How do you know what 'straightaway' means to her? It could mean tomorrow. Next week."

"You don't know Zoe."

"And you don't know everything," said Adderwood.

No one knows her better than I do, Marchmont thought.

"A thousand pounds," he said. "A thousand says she finishes the Season as Miss Lexham."

"Done," said Adderwood.

Zoe, as always, was aware of everything going on about her. She was most palpably aware of Marchmont prowling the room like one of Yusri Pasha's caged tigers.

She was aware, too, that her plan wasn't working.

Papa had shaken his head over Marchmont's list and muttered something about "old men" and scratched off most of the names. Even so, even though he'd kept the two youngest ones and added Lord Winterton, and even though these younger men had seemed disposed to admire her—well, at least Adderwood and Alvanley seemed to do so; Winterton seemed merely to find her amusing—even so, she found herself as unmoved in their company as she had been with Karim.

Alvanley was not handsome but very witty. She felt nothing.

Adderwood was not only handsome but charming and witty. She felt no heat, no thrill.

Winterton was as handsome as Marchmont, and others might view him as more romantic, with his dark hair and eyes, but she felt no excitement of any kind in his company, either. He was the man who'd rescued her, and she would always be grateful. But she couldn't feel more than gratitude.

None of them had succeeded in blotting Marchmont from her mind.

Still, that was only three eligible men, she told herself. When she was finally moving freely in Society, she'd meet many, many more. The odds were in her favor.

In the meantime, she must do something about Marchmont. He'd had a great deal to drink. He must have an unusually strong head for liquor. Any other man, she thought, would have been carried out to his carriage by now.

She knew he was uneasy about this dinner. She knew he thought it a bad idea. Otherwise he wouldn't have put a lot of elderly bachelors and widowers on his list of "eligibles." He was worried she'd misbehave and spoil everything.

Too, he was jealous.

It was very difficult to enjoy the company and concentrate on other people when he was prowling about, cross and bored and wanting to fight somebody.

Men, she knew, would fight over women merely to prove who was the bigger and stronger male. It didn't matter whether they really wanted the woman or not.

She drifted from one group of guests to the next until she saw him talking to Alvanley, near the windows. Then she approached. "I should like a word with His Grace," she said.

Alvanley gracefully made himself scarce, as she'd known he would. He was not as competitive with Marchmont as Lord Adderwood was.

"What word is that?" Marchmont said when his friend had moved out of earshot.

"I lied," she said, lowering her voice. "I have bushels of words. But first—I'm sorry you're so bored. I know this isn't the group you chose. But for some reason Papa seemed to think your list was a joke."

"The Earl of Mount Edgcumbe," he said. "That's what did it, probably. An agreeable fellow—but his eldest daughter is three years older than you. I know what you're thinking."

She was thinking he was a man, and possessive. About her. She knew this signified nothing. It was merely competition with other men. But her body, which noticed no other men, was aroused by this one, a snake drawn to the heat.

"You were trying to protect me," she said. "You thought I'd be safer with more mature gentlemen."

"Is that what you're thinking?"

"I'm thinking, too, of how grateful I am," she said. "Your friends Lord Adderwood and Lord Alvanley are amusing. And your cousin Miss Sinclair is very clever."

Miss Emma Sinclair had proved to be not only clever but informative. She thought the world of her cousin Marchmont and didn't hesitate to say so. Tonight Zoe had learned that the duke supported this lady, along with numerous other relatives. Though a woman of high rank, Miss Sinclair, like too many other spinsters, had no income; and, like them, she had no respectable means of earning a living or even any idea or training in how to go about earning one.

Marchmont, who made such a show of caring about nothing and nobody, obviously cared about Miss Sinclair. He supported her. Generously. And that was only part of the story. Miss Sinclair had told Zoe that he not only supported his mad aunt Sophronia but let her live in grand style in a magnificent old house he owned, a few miles from London. These, Zoe had learned, were by no means the only relatives to whom he was generous.

She knew it was a gentleman's obligation to look after his dependents. She knew a duke had a great many dependents. All the same, the discovery had made her heart ache. In so many ways he'd changed, and not for the better. But in other ways he was Lucien still, impossibly annoying at times—as he'd always been—yet kind, deep down, in the heart he kept so well hidden.

"I'm glad they amuse and entertain you," he said. "You needn't worry about my being bored. I am not so dangerous as you are when that happens."

He was a great deal more dangerous than she. His mood hung over the drawing room like a storm cloud. She wasn't sure others felt it—or recognized what it was if they did feel it—but she did, and it was wearing on her nerves.

She smiled up at him. "But I'm not dangerous tonight. I can be proper when it's absolutely necessary."

"You've done well," he said. "Everyone's in love with you."

But not she with them.

"Maybe I shouldn't have mentioned the harem," she said. "You seemed displeased."

He waved this away, the slightest gesture of his hand. "It didn't signify."

"And you shouldn't worry when men stare at my breasts," she said.

She caught the flicker of surprise before he hid his eyes again. "There they were—are," he said, and she felt, rather than saw, his green gaze drift downward. "Unavoidable."

"But that's the purpose of evening dress," she said. "To display."

"You have undoubtedly achieved the purpose," he said.

"You're very protective," she said.

"Yes, like a *brother*."

Oh, she was trying to be patient and understanding. She reminded herself of how much he'd had to drink. She reminded herself that men could be the most irrational of creatures. She told herself a great many sensible things, yet she felt her temper slipping.

"I'm sorry if I hurt your manly pride," she said, "but it would be best for everyone to think of us in that way. One must change the way people view us—I had in mind our public quarrels. It's the same as letting Mr. Beardsley believe I was the slave of Karim's first wife. In people's minds I stopped being a concubine and turned into a Jarvis."

"There's nothing to explain," he said. "No need to. I was . . . amused."

She very much doubted he'd been amused, but before she could respond, Lord Adderwood approached.

And in the nick of time, too, because she was strongly tempted to pick up the nearest heavy object and apply it to the duke's skull.

"Monopolizing the lady again, I see," said Adderwood.

"Not at all," Marchmont said. "I was about to take my leave. I thank you for a most entertaining evening, Miss Lexham." He bowed and walked away.

Zoe did not pick up a porcelain figurine from the pier table nearby and throw it at him. He continued walking away, unmolested, and not long thereafter, he was gone.

Later, at White's

The Duke of Marchmont waved his wineglass as he declaimed:

> *I know you all, and will a while uphold*
> *The unyoked humor of your idleness:*
> *Yet herein will I imitate the sun,*
> *Who doth permit the base contagious clouds*
> *To smother up his beauty from the world,*
> *That when he please again to be himself—*

"I knew it," Adderwood said. "I knew we should have Prince Hal tonight. Someone call a servant—better yet, a brace of them. Let's get him home before he falls into the fire."

Ten

Afternoon of Thursday, 23 April

The Duke of Marchmont had arranged with Lexham to collect the ladies and take them to the Queen's House in his state coach. The vehicle was one he employed on ceremonial occasions, and it was large enough to accommodate comfortably a pair of ladies in hooped petticoats and two gentlemen encumbered with dress swords. Only three would travel in the carriage today, though, because Lexham was otherwise engaged.

Marchmont arrived a little before his time, more uneasy than he'd ever admit to being. He'd attended too many levees and Drawing Rooms to view them as anything more than social events.

This occasion, though, could determine Zoe's future. It could decide whether she would move freely in the ton, as all her sisters did, or be pushed to its fringes, permanently on the outside looking in.

While he waited at the bottom of the main staircase, however, his mind wasn't on the challenge ahead but on the dinner party of the previous week. In the cold light of the following day, and in the dark misery of the world's vilest headache, he had not been happy with his behavior.

He hadn't seen her since then. He'd told himself he didn't need to. He'd done all he could. He'd helped her order her wardrobe for the Season—or at least the start of her wardrobe. He'd accomplished the impossible by finding a horse lively enough to suit her while not the sort of fire-breather liable to kill her. He'd had her measured for a saddle and fitted for riding attire. He'd obtained the crucial invitation to the Drawing Room.

The rest was up to her, and if she—

The sound of rustling fabric made him look up.

She appeared at the landing.

She paused there and smiled, then flipped open her fan and held it in front of her face, concealing all but her eyes—while meanwhile, below, the low, square neckline of her gown concealed almost nothing.

The deep blue eyes glinted as they regarded him.

"How splendid you are," she said.

He wore a satin frock coat with an extravagantly embroidered silk waistcoat and the obligatory knee breeches. Under his arm he carried the required chapeau bras. His court sword hung at his side.

"Not a fraction as splendid as you," he said.

She was beyond splendid. She was . . . delicious.

Younger women viewed court gowns as ridiculous and old-fashioned. They were, certainly, when one tried to combine today's fashion for high waists with the great skirts of olden times. But he'd told Madame Vérelet to drop the waistline of Zoe's court gown. The bodice and petticoat were a deep rose sarsnet. The combination of vibrant color and lowered waist created a more balanced effect. The layers of silver net and the delicate lace trimming the drapery and train made her seem to be rising out of a cloud upon which sunlight sparkled, thanks to the diamonds her mother and sisters must have lent her. The gems adorned the gown, her neck and ears, her plumed headdress, her gloved arms, and her fan.

It helped, too, that Zoe didn't seem to regard hoops as an encumbrance. Judging by the way she descended the stairs, she seemed to have adopted them as an instrument of seduction.

She closed the fan and made her way down slowly, every sway of the skirts suggestive.

His mouth went dry.

"Ah, well done, well done," came Lexham's voice beside him.

Belatedly, Marchmont discovered his erstwhile guardian, who must have come out into the hall while Marchmont was gawking at Zoe and getting exactly the sorts of ideas he strongly suspected she wanted him to have, the little devil.

When she reached the bottom of the stairs, her father walked to her and kissed her cheek. His eyes glistened with unshed tears. "How glad I am to see this day arrived at last," he said.

If all went well, this day would give Zoe the life she would have had if she had grown up in the way her sisters had done.

If all went well.

Lady Lexham followed Zoe down the stairs a moment later. "Isn't she lovely?" said she. "How clever you were about the dress, Marchmont. There will be nothing like it at court today—and next week, everyone will want the same thing."

"That's why he's a leader of fashion," said Zoe.

"And all this time I thought it was my wit and charm."

"Try to be dull on the way to the Queen's House," Zoe said. "I have a thousand things to remember: what to say and what not to say. Mainly it's what not to say. If I were wearing the usual kind of dress, I could simply tell Mama to kick me if I said the wrong thing—but with all this great tent under me, it would take forever to find something to kick, and by then I should have disgraced myself."

"Never fear," said Marchmont. "If I detect the smallest sign of your going astray, I'll create a diversion. I'll accidentally trip over my sword."

"There, you see, is the mark of a true nobleman, Zoe," said her father. "He'll fall on his sword for you."

"I said I'd get her through this and I shall," said Marchmont. "I shall do whatever is necessary." His gaze reverted to Zoe, floating in her cloud of rose and silver. "Ready, brat?"

She smiled a slow, beatific smile, and a summer sun broke out upon the world.

"Ready," she said.

* * *

It was the most amazing sight. As they neared the Queen's House, Zoe watched long lines of carriages advancing through the Green Park from Hyde Park. Others—from the Horse Guards and St. James's, Marchmont said—came by way of the Mall. Along both routes people crowded, watching the parade of vehicles. She heard the blare of trumpets and the crack of guns.

As they neared the courtyard, where they were to alight, she saw another line of carriages going the other way, heading toward what Mama said was Birdcage Walk.

"I wish I could open the window," she said.

"Don't be silly, Zoe," said her mother.

"You want to hang out of it, I don't doubt," said Marchmont. "Your plumes will fall off into the dirt, and the dust will coat your gown. You may open the window when we depart. Nobody will care what you look like then."

"It's beyond anything," she said. "Everyone said there would be a great crowd, but I had no idea."

The carriage stopped and she took her nose away from the glass to which it had been pressed. She smoothed her skirts, not because they needed it but because she relished the feel of the silver net, like gossamer. "I feel like a princess," she said.

"The princesses are agreeable enough ladies, but I fear you'll outshine them," said Marchmont. "Perhaps I should have let you hang out of the window after all."

She smiled at him. She couldn't help it. He'd tried her patience the week before, but she had missed him, and seeing him at the bottom of the stairs today had made her heart lift. Descending the stairs, she'd felt as light as a cloud.

He had called her "brat," as he used to do so long ago.

And though he'd stood in all his grandeur of court dress, looking every inch the duke he was, descended from a very long line of them—for all that pomp, he was Lucien, too.

The coach door opened.

It was time.

They all knew who she was, and Marchmont wasn't in the least surprised.

Only the London mob—ordinary people—had been present when she'd appeared on the balcony of Lexham House. Few if any members of the aristocracy would have been in that crowd, mingling with the unwashed. He doubted that anyone in the entrance hall of the Queen's House had seen any more of Zoe than the caricatures and the single etching that had accompanied Beardsley's story. Pamphlets having sold like Holland bulbs during the tulip craze, a book version had come out this week, the more expensive editions containing colored illustrations of her adventures.

That was all anyone in Society but the handful who'd attended the dinner had seen of Miss Lexham.

The world knew who she was all the same. Even the Beau Monde was capable, in desperate circumstances, of putting two and two together. Its members observed him and observed her mother and drew the logical conclusion.

They also drew away, insofar as the crowded quarters and court dress would allow. The hall was the customary seething sea of people, the ladies with their gloved hands down, keeping their hoops compressed— and out of range of the gentlemen's swords.

He was aware of some of the ladies compressing a little more tightly and edging away from Zoe, as though in fear of contamination. He fumed, but there was nothing he could do except remember the names of each and every lady who did this and resolve that each and every one of them would live to regret it very much, indeed.

He felt a hand on his arm and looked down. It was Zoe's hand, encased in its long white glove, with diamond bracelets hanging from the wrist. She'd had to draw near to touch him, her elbows being occupied with keeping the hoops out of danger. Her scent wafted up to him, rising, he was all too aware, from the warm flesh abundantly displayed mere inches from his nose and framed in lace and rose-colored satin. The bottommost and largest diamond of her necklace nestled in the inviting valley between her breasts.

"You look very dangerous," she said in an undertone. "You can't murder them only because they're . . . shy." She smiled up at him.

"I was not looking danger— 'Shy'?"

"Let's pretend that's what it is."

He preferred to imagine himself knocking their plumed headdresses off their heads.

"Never mind them," she said. "They don't trouble me. When first I went into the harem, almost everyone tried to make me feel unwanted, and they were much less inhibited about it than English ladies."

"I'd always imagined women in the harem as subtle," he said, trying to match her carefree smile. He was used to wearing masks, but this was beyond him. She put up a brave front, but he knew that the stupid women about them had hurt her feelings—and they didn't even know her!

"'Go away you filthy thing,' they would say," she said. "'Why did you come here? No one wants you.' They called me names. They locked me in cupboards. They played silly tricks. They were like spiteful children. But those women were never allowed to grow up, really. This is nothing." She shook her head and the plumes bobbed.

"It may be nothing to you," he said. "It's something to me."

"No one here can hinder or help me now," she said. "You got me here. The rest is up to me." Her blue gaze shifted toward the staircase. A partition divided it as far as the first landing, where the stairway separated into two branches. One part of the mob was aimed upward on one side while another was aimed downward. Nobody seemed to be actually moving, but that was normal.

"They'll have a difficult time keeping away when we climb the stairs," Zoe said. "That should be amusing."

He didn't think so.

It took three-quarters of an hour to get from the bottom of the stairs to the top. The parade was making its way slowly through four rooms, and as they reached the corridor, she could see them all through the open doorways: the plumes bobbing, some colored, most of them white, the lacy lappets dangling over the ladies' shoulders, the jewels blinking in the light, and the billowing gowns in every color of the rainbow.

It was very beautiful, and the sight alone would • have made her happy. She was home, among her people—even if some of them didn't want her.

Marchmont was here, her knight, ready to slay dragons for his protégée. He looked very dangerous, indeed, glowering at the company through those slitted eyes—and with a sword at his side, no less.

But he could not slay any dragons for her now. He could not present her to the Queen. Mama must do that, and Zoe must make herself presentable.

They entered the saloon, and Zoe saw her, finally: an old and clearly unwell lady under a red velvet and gold canopy. She sat on a red velvet and gold chair. The chair was not raised very high, merely two steps above the floor. The princesses and ladies-in-waiting stood nearby.

People walked up to the Queen and bowed and curtseyed. Ahead of Zoe, one girl, who seemed dreadfully young, was being presented. She wore a modest, ivory-colored gown.

But Zoe was not a young girl. She was different, and it would have been silly to pretend she wasn't.

Today wasn't a presentation day, though, and Zoe would not stand out so much from all the young virgins in their maidenly gowns. Most of the ladies and gentlemen who paused before the elderly figure on the velvet chair were well known to her. She said a few words to the girl, Zoe noticed, but merely nodded to most of those who made their bows and curtseys.

Zoe watched it all, fascinated.

Then there was no one left ahead of them. Mama moved up to the canopied place and there was Zoe, right behind her. Mama said something, but Zoe couldn't hear it because her ears were ringing.

Don't faint, she commanded herself. *You've come this far, all those miles from the palace of Yusri Pasha, all those miles from captivity.*

She glanced away from the Queen and her gaze fell upon Marchmont, who stood among the diplomats. Though his beautiful face was as unreadable as always, she discerned the conspiratorial glint in his green eyes. She remembered how he'd called her "brat."

The dizziness passed, and she was sinking into her curtsey—deep, deep, deeper than anyone else could do, because she'd lived in a world where one prostrated oneself before superiors, and everyone was a woman's superior. There a woman was merely a possession to be bought and used and discarded upon a whim.

Here at least a woman could be *somebody*.

She sank nearly to the floor, and it was like sinking into a dream, so unreal: the elderly woman under the red velvet and gold canopy and the mirrors on either side reflecting the splendor all around: the room's rich furnishings and the colorful dress of the company and the plumes and glittering diamonds and the sparkling chandeliers.

As she rose, she became aware of the Queen's puzzled expression and a pause, a stilling of the atmosphere. A silence fell, as though all the world held its breath.

Then the old lady on the red and gold velvet chair said, "We are glad of your return, Miss Lexham."

Confounded, utterly confounded, utterly lost, Zoe yet managed to say, "Thank you, Your Majesty," because it had been drummed into her as a safe thing to say. She couldn't have said any more than that in any case, she was so thunderstruck by the Queen's words.

Glad of your return.

Queen Charlotte said, "You favor our good friend, your grandmother. We shall look forward to seeing you again."

Zoe understood this was a signal to withdraw. She murmured thanks and started backing away.

One did not turn one's back on the Queen.

One of the princesses—Zoe wasn't sure which one—stepped forward before she could commence curtseying herself out of the room.

The princess said, "We greatly admire your courage, Miss Lexham."

Only that. One quick sentence and one quick smile before she returned to her sisters.

Zoe had to be content with that, though she had a hundred questions to ask. But in such a crowd, the royals hadn't time to talk to everybody. Most of the time, they let people pass with no conversation at all.

She was halfway to the door when a very fat gentleman, most elaborately dressed, stopped her. "We are very glad of your return, Miss Lexham," he said.

She dared to look up into the pale blue eyes. She saw tears there.

She became aware of Marchmont: She felt his presence before she actually saw him.

"Your Highness," came his deep voice from some-where above her right shoulder. "I thank you for your kindness."

"A brave young woman," said the Prince Regent—for that was who the fat gentleman was. "Stay a moment with us, Marchmont."

Zoe breathed thanks and curtseyed and curtseyed and curtseyed until she was safely out of the room.

She found her mother and met her gaze but only squeezed her hand, because she couldn't trust herself to speak.

She was afraid to say anything. She didn't want to spoil it. She was afraid she'd wake up and find it was all a dream and the Queen had not given her the golden gift of approval, with a princess and the Regent himself echoing it.

She couldn't stand stock-still, gaping, though, so she blindly followed her mother into the sea of people, the voices rising and falling around her.

What seemed like hours later—and might have been, progress through the rooms was so slow—she felt a hand at her elbow. Even without looking she knew it was Marchmont's hand. But she did look up at him, into his beautiful face, and saw the smile hovering at the corner of his mouth.

"Well done," he said.

A thousand feelings welled up in her heart. She looked away, because she knew her eyes would tell everything, and *everything* was far more than she wanted him to see.

He guided her through one room after another and on to the staircase and a descent as slow as the ascent.

Again a crowd milled about them, but if the ladies were holding their skirts over-tightly and edging away, she didn't notice.

She'd done it. She'd made her curtsey to the Queen. She existed, in the world into which she'd been born.

They spent an eternity getting down the accursed staircase, and Marchmont was dangerously near exploding with impatience by the time they reached the entrance hall.

"It will be a while before we can get through this crush to the courtyard," he said. "There's a painting I want you to see in the next room."

"But my mother will be looking for me," she said.

"Everybody's mother will be looking for her," he said. "And there's my mad aunt Sophronia, whom I should prefer to avoid for the moment." He'd glimpsed the figure in black from time to time as they'd made their progress through the rooms. With any luck, she would be gone by the time they went out for their carriage. "Come along."

He took Zoe's hand, gave a quick glance about, and slipped into a quiet corridor. He was an old hand at finding his way through royal quarters. He knew all the nooks and crannies. The Duke of Marchmont had his role to play at court, and he'd danced attendance on royals in one way or another for nearly half his life.

"Well done," he said as soon as they were out of view. "Oh, well done, Zoe Octavia." Then he laughed and tossed his chapeau bras onto a nearby chair. He grasped her waist and lifted her up as he'd done on occasion when she was very young.

She gave a surprised laugh, and round he went once, twice, thrice.

Don't stop, Lucien, she used to say. *Make me dizzy.*

"Oh," she said. "Oh." And he felt her lips touch the top of his head. "Thank you."

He let her down then because he knew he must. He let her down slowly but not as slowly as he wanted to. He wanted to bury his face in the silk and lace of her skirts and then in the warmth of her bosom.

But he let her down as though she were a child still, and he kept his head well back—resisting temptation, though she would think he was avoiding the feathers of her headdress.

"That was all," he said. "I had to do it."

"I'm glad you did," she said. "That was how I felt. It was very difficult to keep in my feelings."

"Well, then, now we've got it out of our systems, we can carry on with proper dignity."

Marchmont found slipping back into the sea of aristocrats more difficult than slipping out of it. The entrance hall was even more crowded at present than it had been when they arrived. Eventually, though, he and Zoe reached the courtyard.

Being a head taller than much of the company, Marchmont had no trouble scanning the crowd. He soon spotted Lady Lexham. She looked very worried.

The worried look, he surmised, was not on account of Zoe, for her ladyship would trust him to look after her daughter. It was on account of the tallish woman with the great black plumes waving from her head.

"It appears that my mad aunt has got your mother

in her clutches," said Marchmont. "Aunt Sophronia can be entertaining in the right time and place. This is not the time or place. There's no help for it, though. We must attempt to rescue your mother— Oh, drat the woman! She's taken Emma hostage, too."

"I have faced the Queen," Zoe said. "I can face anything today."

"You say that because you've never dealt with my lunatic aunt," he said.

He'd dealt with her, though, time and again. He led Zoe to the cluster of women. They stood before his carriage.

"Oh, there you are, dear," said Lady Lexham. "I was trying to explain to Lady Sophronia. She seems to believe this is her carriage."

"Never mind him," said his auntie. "Marchmont has his own carriage."

"That *is* my carriage, Auntie," he said. "There is the ducal crest, plain as day."

"This is no time for your jokes, Marchmont," said his aunt. "Get in, get in," she told Lady Lexham, waving her diamond-encrusted, black-gloved hands. "The company is waiting. You, too, Emma."

"But Cousin Sophronia," Emma said, "as I recall, your carriage is the one with the blue—"

"Is that the bolter?" said Aunt Sophronia. Her gaze had fallen upon Zoe.

"Yes, Auntie, and I brought her and her mama here in that—"

"Get in, get in, Emma," said his aunt. "What are you waiting for? Do you not see the carriages lined up behind us?"

Emma threw Marchmont a panicked look. He gestured her to get into the carriage. With a look of resignation, she obeyed.

"Zoe Octavia," said Lady Sophronia. "Is that you?"

"Yes, Lady Sophronia." Zoe managed to negotiate a curtsey while being jostled by the milling crowd.

"*That* was a curtsey," said his aunt. "How everyone stared. Most exciting. They should write it down and put it in a book. But we've no time at present for snakes. Marchmont will bring you to dine with me. Lady Lexham, if you please. Without swords, we shall fit three comfortably."

"Please go ahead," Marchmont told Lady Lexham. "She never admits she's wrong, and we should be hours redirecting her. Zoe and I will take my aunt's— that is to say, the *other* carriage."

He saw the other two ladies safely into the carriage and told his coachman to take them all to Lexham House.

He watched them drive away.

"Will you know which one is your aunt's carriage?" Zoe said.

"Certainly. It's my carriage. They're all my carriages. If I let her have her own, I'd never be able to keep track of her. This way, I have at least a modicum of control over her doings. Some wonder why I have not put her in an asylum. But I've always maintained that every great, ancient family must have at least one mad relation living in a haunted house."

Zoe smiled. "I didn't know you owned a haunted house."

"Baldwick House *looks* as though it's haunted,"

he said. "And appearances are everything. Ah, here comes her carriage."

Very much as she'd done on the way here, Zoe watched the passing scene through the window. They left the palace along with a long parade of other vehicles. Crowds lined the way here, as well, and progress was slow, an endless series of stops and starts, but she didn't seem to mind the snail's pace.

"So much green," she said. "In Egypt there's only a narrow strip of green along the sides of the river. And it isn't the same green at all. We had gardens, too, but nothing like this—so many trees and acres and acres of grass. And there's the canal. I see it sparkling between the trees. I'm so glad to be home."

Every word made the duke's heart ache, but the last words most of all. Though he'd seen her smile and heard her laugh, he'd never seen her so happy as she was now, the lighthearted Zoe he'd known so long ago.

She turned from the window and smiled at him.

"I'm glad to see you so happy," he said.

"It's all your doing," she said.

"Not very much needed doing," he said.

"Ah, yes. 'Nothing could be simpler,' you said."

He had the royal ear—several of them, in fact, and a scribbler like Beardsley wasn't the only one who knew how to tell a story.

Still, it wasn't all his doing.

All the royals had to do was look at her to be disposed in her favor.

Zoe had told him she wasn't innocent, but she was,

in ways that some might not understand. This innocence shone in her eyes and warmed her smile. It had
made the Prince Regent teary-eyed. He'd said he wept
because she reminded him of his daughter.

She didn't resemble Princess Charlotte physically.
What she reminded everyone of was the life and hope
the princess had represented. And this was partly because Zoe wasn't practiced in hiding her feelings. She
had glowed, visibly, when the Queen made her welcome. Her joy had vibrated through the saloon. The
Regent had felt the joy. He'd seen the glow.

What had she said, shocking everyone so, on the
first day—was it only three weeks ago?—Marchmont
had seen her?

*I crossed seas, and it was like crossing years. To
everyone it must seem as though I have come back
from the dead.*

That's what they'd seen, those royals who'd seen
and borne shame and disappointment and madness and the early deaths of loved ones: They'd seen
life and courage and hope.

Zoe had glowed like the summer sun, and it was
impossible to look at her and not feel the warmth and
the optimism of her spirit.

That's what the Regent had seen. That, combined
with youth and good nature and beauty, had touched
his sentimental heart.

Marchmont realized he'd been woolgathering and
staring at her for rather a long time. He discovered
that she hadn't turned back to the window and the
fascinating greenery outside. She was watching him.

"Are we done being proper?" she said.

"Oh, no," he said. "That part's only begun."

"But isn't this improper?" One gloved, braceleted hand took in the vehicle's interior with a little sweep. "To be alone in a closed carriage? I wondered whether the court presentation changed the rules."

"It doesn't," he said. "But others' rules don't apply to Aunt Sophronia. She makes her own." He forced his mind away from the dangerous fact of being alone with Zoe in a closed carriage. He wrenched his attention from the warm bosom so generously displayed an arm's length away, and changed the subject. "You swept all before you, too. That curtsey my aunt remarked upon was the most spectacular I've ever seen."

Also the most arousing, but he wouldn't let his mind dwell on that, either.

"Once I learned the way of it, I had no trouble," she said. "I've prostrated myself wearing very complicated clothing. Everyone imagines we were always naked in the harem—or wearing a few veils—but that was not the case."

He'd seen her naked a thousand and one nights, in his dreams.

"We were naked in our thoughts and feelings, though," she went on. "That has been one of the hardest things about coming home: *not* saying what's in my heart."

What was in her heart was not his concern. What was in his was not her concern. "You don't need to say anything," he said. "You show it."

"That, too, is a difficulty here."

"You're happy," he said. "That shows. This was

what you wanted—the life you would have had if those swine hadn't torn you from it. Today that life begins, with royal blessing."

She folded her gloved hands in her lap and looked down at them. "My heart is too full for words. You think I'm ungrateful and capricious, but that isn't so."

"I never thought you ungrateful," he said. He remembered the light kiss on the top of his head and the whispered *thank you* and the sweetness of that moment.

"But capricious?" she said. "Because I flirt with your friends?"

"Oh, that." He waved his hand. "Perhaps I was overprotective."

"Oh, Marchmont, is that what you call it?"

Jealous and possessive and selfish was what he'd called it the day after.

Then he'd told himself, *Out of sight, out of mind.*

"What do you want me to call it?" he said lightly.

"What it is," she said. "Not what's convenient or witty or agreeable to your pride. But you'll never do that, will you?"

To his consternation, she began to cry.

Zoe *never* cried.

She brushed away the tears. "Never mind. I'm too excited. I need some air. I'll walk."

"You can't walk. *No one* walks in court dress, from court."

She flashed her *Is that a dare?* look and reached for the carriage handle.

The carriage, which had stopped for the hundredth time, lurched into motion as she was leaving her seat and leaning toward the door. She lost her balance and fell on the floor in a heap of hoops and waves of satin and lace and net, her plumes tumbling forward.

She reached up for the door handle. He grabbed her hand.

"Let go of me!" she said. "Let me go."

"Don't be an idiot."

She tried to pull free.

"Stop it," he said. "If you open the door you'll fall out onto your head."

"I don't care!"

"Zoe."

She was trying to pull away, still.

He kept his grip on her hand and got his other arm under her shoulder and hauled her up.

She struggled all the way, squirming, feathers flying and diamonds flashing.

"Stop it, drat you!"

"No, no, no."

He pulled her up and onto his lap, and held her there, his arms wrapped about her. Her tiara had slipped forward. The plumes tickled his cheek, and she wouldn't stop squirming.

His manly parts couldn't distinguish between a struggling sort of squirm and an invitational sort of squirm. They came to attention and his brain thickened.

He was lost in the cloud of satin and lace and net and the scent of Zoe and the warmth of her.

"If you don't stop," he said, "I'll drop you on the floor and hold you down with my feet."

She reached up and grasped a fistful of his hair. She brought her face close to his. "Possessive," she said. "The word you want is *possessive*."

He didn't know what she was saying. Her mouth was a breath away from his and her scent was everywhere, in the cloud of satin and lace and net and femininity. The cloud billowed about him.

His hand slid up to the back of her neck, to cup the back of her head, and he kissed her.

Eleven

Zoe knew what he wanted. She'd known from the moment she'd stood on the landing and caught Marchmont's first, startled expression before he hid it.

Liar, liar, liar, she thought.

He lied with words and he hid his eyes, but his kiss didn't lie. It was hot and fierce.

His body didn't lie. She felt his heat and his arousal against her thigh, even while she struggled in his lap. She still struggled, though she knew she'd never be free of him. She squirmed under the big, gloved hands clasping her waist because she needed to. She did it for the pleasure of it, for the heat and the wild sensations racing through her blood. The thrill of it. The excitement.

She'd been trained to yield, but she wouldn't yield to him. He would have to admit what he wanted and fight for it.

She turned her head away, breaking the kiss,

and his hands tightened on her waist. She twisted this way and that, but he wouldn't let go.

He kissed her neck and her shoulder and pushed aside the top of the sleeve with his mouth and kissed the place he'd bared. He lifted his head, and she thought he'd give up then, that his conscience or honor or some other horrible thing would get the better of him, but he breathed in deeply and she knew he was drinking her in, the way she did him.

The more she struggled, the warmer it became, there in the closed coach. From the corner of her eye, while she refused to give way and tried to turn away, she saw his golden head sink down, and then she sucked in her breath as his mouth touched the top of her breast. The hoops had folded up, crushed between them, and one big, gloved hand slid down to her knee.

His mouth was on her breast, his tongue dipping under the lace edging the bodice's neckline. His hair brushed her chin, and the smell of him was all around her, inescapable: the clean, starched scent of his neckcloth and the fragrance of his shaving soap and above all the scent of his skin, and the combination of all these things, a scent like no one else's in all the world.

The combination was fatal to her, as inevitable as kismet.

She turned a little toward him and beat on his shoulders, and then his hand came up and closed over her breast, and she gasped. The shock and pleasure of it raced through her and vibrated in the place between her legs.

He pulled her round to face him, and she couldn't make her hands beat on his shoulders anymore. Her arms went round his neck, and when his mouth found hers, she gave up the kiss she'd held back.

This was the kiss she'd longed for. This was the caress she'd longed for. This was the heat and excitement only he could make inside her.

He'd stolen away with her for a moment, and lifted her up and spun her in the air, and all of her being had soared with happiness and triumph.

Oh, and love.

He'd set her on her feet again, slowly, reluctantly, and she'd acquiesced, because what choice had she?

She hadn't wanted him to set her on her feet.

She'd wanted him to push her against a wall and have her then and there.

Now, behind his back, she was pushing down her gloves and pulling them off, heedless of the bracelets. One fell off and another remained on her wrist, bare now. She slid her naked hands into his hair and held him so while the kiss deepened from longing to passion and while thinking dissolved into feeling.

She felt him move then, too, tearing off his gloves without breaking the kiss, and this time when she squirmed, it was toward him. But the hoops were in the way. She pulled up one side of the gown, but he pushed her hand away, and then his naked hand was on her knee, and moving up under the petticoat, sliding over her stocking and over the garter and up, onto her skin, and it was beautiful, a rush of pleasure so deep that she seemed to fall to the bottom of the world.

His hand slid higher.

"No drawers," he said, and it wasn't words but a groan. "Oh, Zoe."

"To be proper above and wicked below," she murmured.

"Oh, Zoe."

The carriage lurched again and she nearly fell off his lap, but his arm braced her. But the other hand was still under her skirts, still on her skin, sliding upward with a slowness that was torture. She buried her face in his neckcloth.

He cupped her Palace of Delight, and she let out a cry and then another as he stroked her.

Now, now, she wanted to scream.

She was ready as she'd never imagined she could be ready. She reached down and laid her hand over his breeches front, where his *membrum virile* pushed against the cloth. She found the buttons and undid them, quickly, impatiently. Then she found his manly place, and she closed her hand over his instrument of delight. It was *nothing* like Karim's.

"Zoe."

She stroked up and down its length.

It was very large and hot and hard.

It couldn't possibly fit inside her.

She didn't care. They'd make it fit somehow.

She'd learned a hundred positions, and she simply turned a little and bent her knee and got her bent leg up against his hip, her foot on the carriage seat.

His hand came away from her pleasuring place and slid over her hand and pushed it away from his rod of joy. She rocked against him, as close as she could get, skin to skin.

There were a thousand roads to pleasure. This was only one.

"You," he said thickly.

She lifted heavy-lidded eyes to meet the smoldering green of his gaze.

She leaned toward him and ran her tongue over his lips.

She licked his chin.

He made a sound, a laugh and a groan combined.

"We have to stop," he said.

She kept on rocking, pressing her soft treasure against his hard one. She was lost in pleasure, in the dark world of the passions. She was lost in the scent of him and the low sound of his voice, so rough. The carriage rocked under them and the satin gown rustled against his breeches.

It was wicked and beautiful, and she hung in the hot darkness of desire, rocking against him, skin to skin, pleasuring herself.

"*Zoe.*"

She brought her hands up and pushed down the top of her dress and grasped her breasts. Eyes closed, she rocked.

He made sounds. Words, growls—she didn't know. She was deranged with passion and pleasure and heat, beautiful animal love.

He grasped her waist. "You have to—"

And then he growled deep in his throat. His hand came between them, to her pleasure place, hot and damp. And then she felt it, the great hot thing that couldn't fit and she didn't care.

He pushed, and her eyes flew open.

"Oh," she said. "Oh."

He pushed again, and her head sank onto his neck. She bit her lip. It hurt.

He pushed again, and she swallowed a cry of frustration. It was very uncomfortable.

Then she felt his hand again, so caressing, in her soft place, and inside her something gave way and she could feel him inside, filling her, and she whispered, wonderingly, "Oh, this is—oh, this is *very good*."

He made the sound again, half laughter, half groan.

Then he moved, and she moved with him, rocking as she'd done before, but this time he was inside her. And this time the pleasure strengthened and seemed to rise inside her like a rocket. Higher and higher it went. And then it struck the top of the heavens and burst, and its remnants cascaded down, through her and around her, sparks of happiness trickling down in the darkness.

Mad, mad, mad.

He held her tightly while he came back to himself and she came back to herself.

He held her tightly while reason returned and said, *Mad, mad, mad.*

"Oh, Zoe," he said, when he could find his voice.

"Oh," she said softly. "That was *splendid*. Now I understand why the women carried on so. It's most agreeable—except for the painful part in the middle. But that was because of my virgin barrier. Before that part and afterward, it was *very good*."

He drew back a little to look at her.

She gazed at him dreamily and rocked a little, back and forth.

It was the shameless rocking. He might have come to his senses if not for that.

Or probably not.

There she was, smiling her wanton smile, her breasts hanging out of her dress.

"You have no inhibitions, have you?" he said.

"My English came back so quickly and easily," she said. "Inhibitions seem to need a great deal more time than three weeks. I didn't have much time for them—I was so busy practicing curtseying out of a room backward without tripping over my train or the hem of my gown or dropping my fan." She stroked his cheek.

He turned his head and kissed her hand. The scent of their lovemaking was there, and his mind started to thicken again.

Think of her father, he told himself.

And that was like a pail of ice water dumped on his privates.

Lexham, the one man in the world for whom he'd lay down his life.

. . . whose youngest and dearest daughter Marchmont had just dishonored.

He took her hand and kissed the back of it. As he did so, his gaze strayed to the window. "Curse it," he said.

"What?" she said. "What?"

"We'll be there in a moment," he said. "We need to put our clothes in order very quickly. We need to pray that the sun's glare on the coach window prevented anyone's seeing what we were doing."

This was another coach meant for formal occa-

sions. A heavy vehicle, older and larger than the one
that had brought them here, it was built like a man-
of-war, and richly fitted out. It would not jounce
about a great deal when people were not sitting quietly in their respective seats. Onlookers wouldn't be
able to make out what transpired inside the carriage.
The windows were small, the interior dark. Still, the
two footmen standing on the footboard at the back
might have heard the sounds and known what they
signified.

Never mind.

It didn't matter whether anyone had seen or heard
or guessed what the Duke of Marchmont had done.
He'd done it, and he knew what he had to do next.

He shifted her back onto her seat and helped her
clean herself and put her clothes in order. Then he
attended to himself. In the process, he found some
spots of blood on the inside of his breeches' flap and
some on her petticoats.

It was only a very little, and that discovery eased
one weight from his mind. He hadn't hurt her so
badly as he'd imagined.

He shouldn't have hurt her at all.

He should have been content with keeping his cock
out of a place where it didn't belong.

But no. He couldn't be content with touching her
and pleasuring her with his hands and letting her pleasure him with her hand, her wicked, wicked hand.

Never mind. It was done, and at least there was no
obvious evidence on the outside.

The matter could be dealt with quietly.

Quietly, that is, if she would cooperate.

He knew Zoe too well to count on that.

He had better be careful how he approached this. He took a moment to determine the best way to put it to her. Then, "Zoe," he said.

She was giving a few final adjustments to the lace at her neckline. "You'd better fix my headdress," she said. "I can't see whether it's straight or not."

He adjusted her tiara. He brushed from her hair and his coat bits of feathers that had got loose during the orgy.

"Zoe," he said.

She looked up at him and smiled the beatific smile.

"Zoe, would you mind very much becoming the Duchess of Marchmont?"

The smile faltered a little. She gazed at him for a long, long time.

He made himself wait.

"It's because of this," she said, her hand sliding to her belly. "Because I'm not a virgin anymore."

"I know I should have controlled myself," he said. "I know you wanted to meet other men—but even if we hadn't done what we did . . . Zoe, I'm sure I wouldn't like it at all if you did that with someone else."

Those were not the smoothest remarks he'd ever uttered, but he felt anything but cool and composed at the moment. He was too painfully aware of having destroyed her chances of choosing a husband for herself. He was too painfully aware of having betrayed her father's trust. At the same time, he didn't regret what had happened, and it was quite true that he didn't want her to choose another husband.

"Possessive," she said.

"Yes," he said.

Her expression brightened again. "Only a crazy woman wouldn't wish to be the Duchess of Marchmont," she said.

It wasn't quite the answer he'd expected—but what should he expect? "Does that mean yes?"

She nodded, plumes bobbing.

He started to lean forward, to kiss her.

The carriage stopped.

He glanced out of the window and sat back hastily. "Drat. We've arrived at your house already— and speaking of crazy people, there's a trail of black feathers to the door."

Zoe knew there were girls in books who declined financially advantageous offers on noble principles. She knew there were fictional girls who threw everything away for love. She certainly knew that only a short time ago she'd decided that Marchmont would not make a good husband.

She still believed that.

He was the kind of man who was quickly bored. He'd soon grow bored with his wife. He'd stray, and no matter how discreet he was, she'd know, and it would hurt her.

All the same, she knew what she had done and she knew that sort of thing led to babies and she knew that having relinquished her virginity, the correct thing to do was to marry the man she'd relinquished it to. If she didn't, she'd not only shame her parents and—if a baby did result—be ostracized from the world she'd worked so hard to get into, but she'd be throwing away the chance to be one of the premier ladies of the realm.

She'd brought this on herself. She would have an unfaithful husband, as other women did, and she would simply have to live with it, as other women did. .

It wasn't as though there weren't any compensations. Marchmont was extremely handsome and extremely rich, and she had greatly enjoyed losing her virginity to him—except for the moment when it actually went.

Only a crazy woman would decline his offer. Zoe was uncivilized, and she hadn't got her inhibitions back yet, but she was not insane.

She could leave madness to Lady Sophronia, while basking in the knowledge that she'd soon be a duchess and she and Marchmont could do more of what they'd done in the carriage. And no one could object then, at all.

Zoe and Marchmont found everyone gathered in the large drawing room. Everyone included, along with Lady Sophronia and Lady Emma, Zoe's parents, sisters, brothers, and the assorted spouses.

Mama must have told them of Zoe's success, because there was a chorus of "Well done" and "I knew you could" and such when she and Marchmont entered.

Lady Sophronia soon reclaimed the audience's attention and launched into a detailed description of what the attendees had worn to the Birthday Drawing Room. It was the usual family hubbub until her ladyship's gaze lit upon Marchmont.

"You, sir," she said. She had the same kind of commanding voice Marchmont had. The noise in the room abated.

He looked up from his conversation with Samuel. "Me, Auntie?"

She beckoned with one diamond-covered hand. Marchmont left Samuel and approached the corner where she presided, with Emma Sinclair nearby, looking worn out.

"You," said Lady Sophronia.

"Yes, it is I," he said. "Your nephew Marchmont."

"I know who you are," she said. "You're the one who played tricks on me."

"Did I, Auntie?"

"Don't play the innocent with me. You deliberately encouraged me to get into the wrong carriage. I never was so surprised in all my life as when I found myself at Lexham House instead of on my way to Kensington."

"How shocking," he said.

"You tricked me," she said.

He made a show of thinking hard. "Hmmm," he said. "Ah, yes, it comes back to me. I had something I wanted to say to Zoe Octavia. In private."

He glanced at Zoe, and the devil glinted in his green eyes. That look put straight into her mind vivid images of what they'd done in the carriage. Her skin became very hot.

"I cannot believe it," said Augusta. "That was most improper. Indeed, Zoe, you ought to blush. To drive unchaperoned with a gentleman immediately after Mama presented you to the Queen. I vow, it is as though you deliberately—"

"Her Majesty took particular note of Zoe Octavia," Lady Sophronia said in her commanding voice. "Everyone there remarked it. The Princess Sophia— or was it the Princess Elizabeth? Never mind. One of them drew her aside for a word. The Regent spoke to her. I recall nothing of the kind occurring at *your* presentation, Augusta Jane."

Augusta subsided in confusion.

"We shall not ask what you had to say to Zoe Octavia, Lucien," Lady Sophronia continued. "These are private matters best understood by the young people involved. I myself was young until Friday of last week." She turned away from Marchmont to address Mama. "We were not so prim in the old days, were we, my dear? A dull king and a court that drove us witless with boredom. But *we* were not dull. I always say there is nothing like a man in knee breeches. A man, that is, possessed of a good leg. Lucien, you see, has his father's legs, my late brother. My legs, too, have been remarked upon in their time. My ankles, as you know, have inspired odes."

It was going to be interesting, indeed, being the Duchess of Marchmont, Zoe thought. Among other things, she was going to acquire some colorful relatives.

While his aunt held her audience spellbound—or dumbstruck or vertiginous, as the case might be— Marchmont casually strolled to Lord Lexham's side and said in a low voice, "I should like a word with you, sir."

Lexham's eyebrows went up.

Marchmont's conscience became very shrill, painting lewd pictures of what he had done with this gentleman's youngest daughter. "About Zoe," he said.

Lexham glanced toward Zoe. She was watching his aunt, and wearing, instead of the customary look of embarrassment and/or confusion and/or horror, a small smile.

He wanted to kiss the corners of her mouth where it turned up that very little bit.

"My study," Lexham said, and led the way there.

Marchmont closed the door behind him when he entered. "I want to marry Zoe," he said.

"Do you, indeed?" said Lexham. He stepped behind his desk, which was heaped with papers, as usual. "What's done it? The hoops? The plumes?" He picked up a piece of paper, frowned at it, and set it down again.

"I'm not joking," said Marchmont.

"I didn't think you were. But you know, she did make you a most handsome offer some weeks ago, as I recall, and you turned it down."

"As I recollect, I said at the time that I was tempted but accepting would be taking unfair advantage," said Marchmont. "She believed then that she had no alternative."

She didn't have one now, either.

"I thought she wanted to meet other men," Lexham said. "I thought that would mean more than two fellows she hadn't clapped eyes on before."

"I find that I prefer she meet other men *after* we're married," said Marchmont. "I'm possessive, you see."

"Are you, indeed?"

"Zoe explained it to me," Marchmont said.

"In the carriage," said Lexham. "When you were quite private."

Guilt ate at Marchmont like acid.

"Where I proposed," he said. "Contrary to my aunt's assertions—"

Lexham put up his hand. "My lady told me what happened. Lady Sophronia has her own distinctive view of the world. The rest of us must bear our doubts and uncertainties, but she is always certain. We all know how difficult it is to persuade the lady out of a misapprehension. You could hardly make the rest of the company wait while you embarked upon that Herculean labor. You'd make quicker work of cleaning the Augean Stables."

"I owe her thanks for this particular hallucination," Marchmont said. "When I found myself alone with Zoe . . . Well, I believe it's enough to say that I realized I didn't want her to marry anybody but me. She said she'd have me. All we want is your consent."

There was a long pause. Lexham left the place behind his desk and walked to the fire. He stood there, looking into the grate, as he so often did when cogitating.

After a time he looked at Marchmont. "I notice that you don't say you're over head and ears in love with Zoe."

Marchmont found himself at a loss how to answer, a rare experience for him, though not surprising in the circumstances. When he'd set out this day, the last thing he'd expected was to be standing here, asking Lexham for his daughter's hand—and all the other delicious parts of her.

He was over head and ears in lust, beyond a doubt.

He had no idea what anyone meant by love in these cases. He'd always assumed it was a euphemism for a strong attraction.

"You don't say, either, that without her your life would be a desert," Lexham added after a moment. "But that isn't the sort of thing you'd say." He shrugged. "And it isn't the sort of thing I could easily stomach. No, I suppose I don't expect it, though I'm not altogether surprised at this turn of events. You've always had the knack of dealing with her, and I'll feel less anxious trusting her to you than to anyone else I can think of."

Ah, yes, I'm to be trusted. Give me half an hour alone in a carriage with your daughter and her virtue's done for.

Lexham nodded to himself. "Then, too, she'll be a duchess, and I'm no different than any other father in wishing to see my child well set up in life. Yes, it will do, it will do."

Marchmont let out the breath he hadn't realized he'd been holding.

Lexham gave him a quizzical look. "Did you think I'd say no?"

"She's been back for only a few weeks," Marchmont said. "I thought you might tell me I was too hasty—or you weren't quite ready to give her up."

"I shan't see her any less than I do at present," said Lexham. "She lives under my roof, but I'm hardly ever at home. And when I am at home, my daughters usually turn up, I find. They're the very devil to get rid of." He laughed then. "Come, Marchmont, give me your hand."

His former ward did so and thanked him.

"A most satisfactory day this has turned out to be," Lexham said. "The royal family has smiled on my daughter, and she's netted herself London's most sought-after bachelor. A duke, no less." He laughed. "I always said Zoe was a clever girl. Well, then, you have my blessing, Marchmont. Now let me speak to her."

Late that night

Zoe stood at the window, looking down into the garden. This time she'd obediently donned her nightgown, as well as the heavy wrapper Jarvis had insisted she wear.

"Miss, I hope you're not thinking of running away this time," said Jarvis as she turned down the bedclothes.

"If I did, it would only be to get away to think," Zoe said. "I can hardly believe all that's happened in one day. My head is a jumble."

Marchmont at the bottom of the stairs . . . the presentation . . . Marchmont lifting her up and spinning her about . . . the wondrous end of her virginity . . . and then he'd asked her, and *yes* she'd said, because no other answer was possible.

She smiled. He must have had a very anxious few minutes while she was alone in the study with her father.

The duke needn't have worried.

Yes, she was uninhibited, as Marchmont said. She

was not a fool, however. She knew better than to tell Papa what had happened during the return from the Queen's House.

She had only assured her father that Marchmont had had no trouble persuading her to become his duchess. "I've never felt about any man as I do about him," she'd said, and that was simple truth.

"The Duchess of Marchmont," Jarvis said in awe-filled tones. "I can hardly take it in myself."

"I still haven't taken it in," Zoe said. "What chance had I to think, with all of them about?"

The hubbub attendant on her arrival from court was nothing to the uproar ensuing this evening at the family dinner celebrating her debut. When the dessert course arrived, her father said he had an additional treat for them all. That was all the warning he gave before announcing her engagement to Marchmont.

"It was funny," she said. "Everyone was so surprised. Well, not so much Priscilla. She wasn't quite as much aghast as the rest of them. But it did stop some of my sisters fussing about my traveling alone with him in a closed carriage. They all assumed he took the opportunity to propose because he was blinded by my finery. They couldn't imagine why any man in his senses would marry me—and they could see he wasn't drunk when we arrived at Lexham House." She laughed. "They thought it was the dress—and perhaps it was." He seemed to find her hoops as exciting as she did.

"Miss, if His Grace hadn't asked, there's a hundred who would," Jarvis said loyally.

"That's a hundred who don't know me," Zoe said.

"I know he won't be an easy husband, but I won't be an easy wife. Still, we understand each other well enough . . ." She let out a sigh. "And I'm afraid I do love him."

"Nothing to be afraid of, miss. I've no doubt he loves you, too. Leastways, he will, once he comes to know you better. Come to bed, please. You'll be needing your rest after such a day. And we'll be very busy in the next few days, packing your things and getting you ready to move to Marchmont House." She shook her head. "Oh my, oh my, I can hardly believe it. Back into that house—that Mr. Harrison—and this time you'll be his mistress. I do wonder what's going through his head."

Zoe approached the bed. "Oh, yes. Harrison. I'd forgotten about him."

"I haven't," said Jarvis. "I'm glad at least I shan't be going there as a housemaid. As you said, I answer only to you—and I shan't have much to do with him in any event, except at mealtimes. Not that I complain, miss. It's an enviable place to have. Lady's maid to the Duchess of Marchmont. Who could have thought it!" She shook her head in wonder.

"I only thought of Marchmont," Zoe said. "I never thought about the house, that great, immaculate house and all the servants. My goodness. I'll be mistress there. What fun!"

"Miss, you said I could say my opinion, and my opinion is, Mr. Harrison isn't going to be much fun."

Zoe looked at her. "You're not afraid of that man?"

"Yes, miss, I'm afraid I am."

"Pish. Nothing to be afraid of. Yusri Pasha's chief

eunuch—now *that* was a man to fear. It took me years to understand him. But this one, who has all his manly parts?" Zoe paused. "The servants do keep all their manly parts in England?"

"Miss, I don't think it's allowed to make eunuchs here," Jarvis said.

Zoe waved her hand dismissively. "Then there's nothing to be uneasy about. I do know how to manage a household, and I'll manage that one."

Twelve

By Thursday night, the rumors were racing through the Beau Monde.

The servants, as usual, heard the rumors long before their betters did.

At Marchmont House, however, rumor swiftly turned into certainty, and members of the duke's upper level staff knew well before nightfall that calamity had struck: Their master was marrying the Harem Girl.

They knew it because he told them so.

After the Birthday Drawing Room, when the Duke of Marchmont returned to change from court dress into evening dress, he summoned Harrison into his study. Osgood was there, too, as he always was, to write down whatever needed writing down. He did a great deal of writing down wagers lost and won.

He knew, therefore, that he could expect a draft for a thousand pounds from Lord Adderwood, who'd bet that Miss Lexham would not make her curtsey to the Queen before the end of the month.

He did not know until this moment that His Grace had lost the wager regarding Miss Lexham's being wed before the end of the London Season.

"I'm getting married," His Grace informed his two employees. "To Miss Lexham. Next week, perhaps."

Both men maintained their usual wooden expressions. Both offered the correct form of congratulations.

Both felt queasy, albeit for different reasons. Osgood feared that a lady in the house would upset his neat order and disturb his papers.

Harrison, who had no intention of letting any female interfere in any way with his arrangements, was mortified at the prospect of having to abase himself to a person who had made a spectacle of herself in the newspapers—one who had, furthermore, administered to him a setdown that a certain footman had repeated to another. Harrison had dismissed both servants without a character.

His Grace knew nothing about this. His Grace didn't know one footman from another.

"I shall make a note for a special license," said Osgood. "And the purchase of a ring."

"I planned to go to Doctors' Commons for the license tomorrow," said the duke.

"Yes, Your Grace," said Osgood. "Have you any particular requirements regarding the ring?"

"Indeed, I do," said His Grace. "I shall see about that, too, tomorrow. While I'm in the neighborhood, I'll stop at Rundell and Bridge."

Rundell and Bridge were royal goldsmiths and favorites of the Prince Regent. The shop at Number
Thirty-two Ludgate Hill included among its regular
customers not only English royals and nobility but
those European crowned heads who'd managed to
keep theirs attached to their necks.

If Harrison had ever worn an expression, it would
have grown grimmer. But all his thoughts were written on the inside.

His master, to his knowledge, had never personally
selected and purchased a piece of jewelry for anybody
since coming into the title. It was Osgood's responsibility to buy the gifts His Grace gave to his amours.
The duke's wishing to visit Rundell and Bridge himself
and choose the engagement ring himself boded ill. The
Harem Girl, clearly, had her hooks in him very deeply,
indeed.

"I must pay a brief call tonight," Marchmont said casually to his secretary. "I shall wish to bring a gift."

"Yes, Your Grace."

No more was said. No more needed to be said. The
duke was getting married. A gift to the party he was
not marrying was in order, and Osgood would be
expected to have a suitable parting gift on hand.

The duke gave no further instructions. It wouldn't
occur to him to do so. Osgood, who operated inde-
pendently of the household staff, knew exactly what
was required of him. Harrison, as usual, would ascertain what needed to be done next in his sphere and
would communicate these requirements to those in
the lower ranks.

When the duke went up to dress, he let Hoare know
of the impending nuptials in the same offhand way.

Hoare wept, but then he wept over buttons and over-starched neckcloths. The only reason Marchmont hadn't sacked him was that he was used to him and it was too much bother to get used to somebody new. Everybody knew this, including Hoare.

After the master went out again, Harrison summoned the valet, cook, butler, and housekeeper to his luxurious parlor. He gave them sherry and assured them that Marchmont House would continue to run as it had always run. There would be a slight augmentation of the staff in order to properly attend to the increased responsibilities. Otherwise, all would go on as usual. While there was bound to be a short period of adjustment at first, he did not expect significant interference or disruption in the day-to-day operation of the duke's establishment.

To Mrs. Dunstan he later confided, "I foresee no difficulties whatsoever—fewer, in fact, than might attend had His Grace chosen differently. The Mohammedans do not believe in educating women. Everyone knows there's little in ladies' heads but fashion and scandal. This lady will know even less of household matters than the average English gentle-woman, and she will be less inclined to tend to them. We must not look upon this as a catastrophe but as an opportunity to enlarge the establishment."

Had Mrs. Dunstan harbored any lingering anxieties or doubts, Harrison's confidence banished them. The following day, all the upper servants were cheerfully bustling about and bullying their inferiors, to prepare the house to receive its new mistress.

As to the unpleasant episode during her brief visit

to Marchmont House—Harrison refused to let it trouble him. Once the lady lived under his roof, he told himself, she, like everyone else, would live by his rules.

Later that night, the duke paid a call to Lady Tarling.

Wearing the same wry smile she'd adopted on a previous occasion, she opened yet another velvet box. This one was green. This one contained a set of three gold floral bouquet brooches, set with colored diamonds.

They had been made to be worn separately or attached to form a tiara.

"How beautiful," she said.

"I'm getting married," he said.

She nodded and looked up. She was not surprised, except at how little the news surprised her. "I see."

"I preferred that you not read about it in the papers first," he said.

"Thank you," she said. Whatever others might say, she had never deemed him entirely heartless. Or if he was, his good breeding masked it well.

She had heard rumors already. One always heard rumors, half of them nonsensical, but this one she'd found believable. Perhaps she'd seen this day coming weeks ago, on the night he'd brought her the other generous gift. It might have been then, or maybe on that morning in Hyde Park. She wasn't sure when it was, but at some point it had become clear to her that this man had given his heart elsewhere, a long time ago, whether he knew it or not.

Being prepared as well as intelligent, she accepted

the news good-naturedly and congratulated him as a friend would do—and really, he'd been no more than that in recent weeks.

For what small regret she might feel, the magnificent brooches were more than adequate consolation.

By Friday afternoon, Marchmont had obtained the special license and ordered the ring. He went next to White's, where he settled various wagers about whether he was or was not engaged to Miss Lexham and placed a bet against himself that he'd be married before the end of the month.

Thus, by the time Society descended upon Hyde Park at the fashionable hour, everybody knew and everybody was talking about it.

At six o'clock, the Duke of Marchmont appeared in Rotten Row. He rode alongside Miss Lexham, who wore a rich blue riding dress of the latest mode. Those able to get close enough said the color matched her eyes exactly. A dashing plumed hat perched on her dark gold tresses. She rode a spirited gelding, which she managed with ease.

The lively beast did want managing, for their progress was slow. Even bitterly disappointed mamas and their equally dismayed unwed daughters hid their feelings. They, like everyone else, wanted to be known to the next Duchess of Marchmont. Everybody was made known to her except the ladies who'd shied away from her at the Birthday Drawing Room. These Marchmont somehow failed to see.

On Friday evening he dined *en famille* with the Lexhams.

The family gathered in the library after dinner, as they always did on informal occasions.

It was then Lexham said, "I heard about that ridiculous wager of yours, Marchmont."

"So many fit that category," said Marchmont. "To which one do you refer?"

"The one about whether you would or would not be wed by the end of the month. May I point out, firstly, that there's only one of you—and some might take this as a sign of your turning into Lady Sophronia—and secondly, you've less than a week until the end of the month. Would it not be logical to settle it with Zoe?"

Zoe had been exceedingly proper all through dinner. Her dress was exceedingly improper. Once again her breasts were insecurely tucked into the world's tiniest bodice. At present she stood at the window, looking down into Berkeley Square, where, at this hour, she was unlikely to see anything.

From where he sat, Marchmont had a profile view of her. The candlelight glimmering in her hair and throwing part of her face into shadow made her seem remote, even mysterious. He felt uneasy and found himself wondering whether he did know her, after all. Then he told himself he was ridiculous: It was only a trick of the light.

Thrusting aside doubt, he said, "I find I'm not in favor of long engagements. Zoe, would you mind being married next week?"

"Next week?" said Lady Lexham. "But I thought that was one of your jokes. A short engagement, indeed."

He remembered then that Zoe was the last of their

children. They'd probably want to send her off in style, with a great party. It was, after all, no small thing to have one's daughter marry a duke. The trouble was, this duke had been one of the family for so long that it was easy, here, to forget his adult position in the world. Here, in some ways, he still felt like Lucien de Grey. Even when he was a boy, the Lexham family rarely used his title. Only in company was he "Lord Lucien." Zoe had called him that only when she was poking fun at him—or furious with him.

"How thoughtless of me," he said. "You'll want a great breakfast or dinner or ball or some such. Those things take time, I'm told. Well, then, sometime in May, perhaps."

Zoe turned away from the window and gazed at him in the way she sometimes did, as though she thought she could read him. Nobody could read him, he knew.

"A wedding feast?" she said. "Is it necessary?"

"I think your parents would like it."

"You may find this impossible to believe," said Lexham, "but my lady and I were young once, too. Life is short and unpredictable. Your parents hadn't long to enjoy their happiness. Make the most of time, I say. But there, what does Zoe say? You're subdued this evening, my dear. Have you become awestruck, suddenly, at the idea of becoming a duchess?"

"Not yet, Papa," she said. "I was only debating which dress to wear to my wedding." She gave Marchmont an absent smile. "I don't like long engagements, either. I think it would be fun to marry on the last day of the month." She laughed, and it was Zoe's laughter, easy and light, and the sound brightened the room. "I want to see you pay yourself for the wager."

On Saturday morning the Duke of Marchmont arrived at Lexham House in a state of uncertainty. It was a feeling he rarely experienced and one he didn't like. This time, though, he couldn't shake it off or thrust it into the special mental cupboard. It clung to him like a great, prickly cocklebur.

He wasn't expected, but it never occurred to him to send notice ahead, since he'd never done it before.

He found Zoe in the breakfast room, surrounded by her sisters, all of them cawing and squawking as usual.

"There you are," one cried as he entered. "It simply can't be done."

"Out of the question," said another.

"She has no trousseau."

"After all our hard work to make the world accept her," said Augusta, "and then for her to be married in such haste, and in this appalling hole-in-corner way? Unthinkable. We must have at least a month."

"June would be better," said Priscilla. "Dorothea and I expect our confinements in May."

Zoe looked at him, rolled her eyes, and recommenced buttering her toast.

"The Duchess of Marchmont," he said, "may wed when and where she pleases. Nothing the Duchess of Marchmont does is ever hole-in-corner. If the Duchess of Marchmont wishes to make haste, then the world must make haste with her. Your-Grace-that-is-to-be, when you've finished your breakfast, I should like to speak to you in a place where your sisters are not. I shall await you in the library."

He went to the library.

It was blessedly quiet.

He wasn't.

He walked to the fireplace and stared into the grate. He walked to the window and took in the view of Berkeley Square. One carriage. Two riders. Two people walking in the direction of Lansdowne House. A small group emerged from Gunter's and walked toward the little park. He remembered what the square had looked like a few weeks ago, on April Fool's Day, the day he'd come here intending to unmask an imposter and found instead the girl he'd lost twelve years ago.

Now they were engaged to marry.

Thirty days, from the time he'd walked into the small drawing room of Lexham House and spied her sitting in the chair to the day he'd set for their wedding: this coming Thursday, precisely at the end of the month.

Thirty days, start to finish.

Thirty days, and he'd be finished as a bachelor.

That didn't worry him. It was bound to happen sooner or later. It was his duty to wed and beget heirs, a duty drummed into him practically since birth: Though Gerard had been the heir, carrying on the ancient line was too important a matter to be left to only one male of the family.

Wedlock didn't worry Marchmont. He foresaw no great changes in his life. What worried him rested nearer to hand.

He left the window and paced.

Hours, days, months, and years seemed to pass before something made him turn toward the door.

He must have heard her footfall without fully realizing. She paused in the doorway.

Her posture was correct. Her morning dress was correct, covering her arms and her bosom completely. But no other Englishwoman stood in quite that way. No other Englishwoman could linger for a moment in a doorway and create images in a man's head of her falling back onto pillows, her clothing disordered, her gaze sleepy with desire.

"Thank you for silencing them," she said as she entered. "You'll wonder why I let them carry on so and don't argue with them. The trouble is, if I do argue, it takes forever to finish my breakfast, and everything gets cold. In the harem, we had outbursts all the time, much worse than this. Women screaming, threatening, complaining, hysterical. I tell myself I'm used to it. I tell myself to let it wash over me, to pretend it's a storm raging outside. But it's *very* aggravating, and I'll be so glad to move into your house, and make rules about how many sisters may be allowed at a time and what times they are allowed."

It had never occurred to him that she might make rules in his house; but the realization came and went, quickly supplanted by the momentous thing that was about to happen, and about which he was experiencing doubt such as he hadn't known since boyhood.

"Whatever you like," he said distractedly. "I have something for you."

Her entire being seemed to still. "A gift?"

"I'm not sure one calls it a gift." He patted his coat.

Which pocket had he put it in? Which one had he finally settled on? He'd taken it out and put it back a hundred times. "One moment. I know it's here somewhere. Hoare became hysterical, because it spoiled the line of my—Ah yes, there it is." He drew out the small velvet case from the pocket concealed in the lining of his tailcoat's skirt.

She stiffened and folded her hands over her stomach.

"What's wrong?" he said.

"Nothing," she said. "I think I know what's in the little box."

"In general terms, I daresay you do." He opened the container, his hands a degree less steady than they ought to be. He told himself this was absurd. How many times, to how many women, had he given jewelry?

He took out the ring and stared at it. Somehow, this morning in the shop, it hadn't seemed quite so . . . quite so . . .

"My goodness." She raised her tightly folded hands to her bosom. "It's big."

It was enormous, and perhaps, after all, too large for her hand: a great, brilliant-cut center diamond surrounded by smaller ones. He should have given the goldsmiths more time. They'd had to hurry. They'd misunderstood. They'd got it wrong. But no, Rundell and Bridge never got it wrong.

"Rundell was shocked," he said. He was uncomfortably hot, and not in the good way, the lustful way. "He showed me scores of elegant, tasteful diamond rings. But I told him I wanted a great, vulgar stone, one that people could see flashing from a mile away."

"Oh, Marchmont," she said.

"Perhaps you could unclench your hands," he said.

"Oh, yes," she said.

"Give me your hand, please," he said.

She drew nearer. She put out her hand.

His heart beating unevenly, he slipped the ring onto her slim finger. It fit, as it ought to do. He'd been there, hadn't he, when she was measured for gloves—for everything.

His heart continued its erratic nonsense all the same.

She held her hand up and watched the diamonds flash in the daylight streaming through the windows. There wasn't a great deal of sunlight in this room at this time of day, but it flashed.

"It's *wonderful*," she said softly.

"It is?"

She nodded, gazing down at it. She took in and let out a long breath. He watched her bosom rise and fall.

"It's *perfect*," she said. "Elegant, tasteful rings are for lesser women. The Duchess of Marchmont must wear a diamond that could serve as—as a lighthouse beacon in an emergency. Oh, Marchmont."

She laughed then, and flung her arms about his neck. Her soft body went along.

He wrapped his arms about her and pulled her close. He buried his face in her hair and drank in the summer scent of her. She tipped her head back, inviting him, and he bent his head to accept the invitation. His mouth touched hers, soft and warm and fraught with memories: the Green Park and Hyde Park and the wild heat in the corridor of this house and in their mad coupling in his aunt's carriage. His hold of her tightened.

A loud "ahem" came from behind him.

He and Zoe hastily sprang apart.

"The thirtieth, I see, will be not a minute too soon," said Lord Lexham. "Marchmont, we had better find a way to keep you occupied. Come along to my study. Let us reach an agreement about the marriage settlements before we summon the lawyers and they begin wrangling."

On Sunday, Priscilla arrived at the crack of dawn. She was obviously overflowing with news, because she pushed past Jarvis and burst into Zoe's bedroom mere moments after Zoe stepped out of her bath.

It was harder to bathe in England than it had been in Cairo, but daily bathing was one Mohammedan custom Zoe refused to abandon. Here she had only a portable tub, not a great pool, and no coterie of slaves to wash and massage her and remove the hair from her body and oil and perfume her. But the English were not troubled by hair, and she didn't need the other attentions. The tub served the main purpose.

"He chose it *himself*," Priscilla said.

"Chose what?" Zoe said as Jarvis wrapped the dressing gown about her.

"The ring."

"What ring?"

"That monstrous great stone of yours. The engagement ring."

"Oh," said Zoe. "That was obvious."

More obvious than she could have supposed.

He'd hidden it well, but she had been trained to see

and hear what men hid. She was coming to understand him better. She was learning to read him better.

He'd thought about her.

He'd cared about whether she liked the ring or not. Cared deeply.

She felt a sob welling in her chest.

She told herself not to be a sentimental idiot. She told herself his caring was only his pride. She told herself not to imagine he cared deeply about her. Even if that was true for the moment, it wouldn't last. He was a handsome, wealthy, powerful man. Every woman wanted him, and he knew it. To expect him to give his heart to one woman only was ludicrous.

She told herself she understood this about him and she could live with it, must live with it. But she cared and would never stop caring—he had lived in her heart all the time she'd been away—and she wanted him to feel the same.

She kept the tears back while she moved to the fire, where her morning chocolate awaited on a tray, alongside the newspaper.

She must have done too good a job of hiding her feelings, because Priscilla, apparently thinking her insufficiently impressed, said, "You don't understand, do you? Marchmont *never* does that. His secretary always buys gifts. For everyone. Royals and relatives and mistresses alike."

"If one of his concubines has a diamond from him like that," Zoe said, "I shall have to accidentally break her finger. And his head will accidentally collide with a chamber pot."

"*No one* has a diamond like that," said Priscilla. "Oh, Zoe, may I see it again?"

Jarvis was told to fetch the ring. She brought it in its little box to Priscilla, who only opened the box and looked at the ring but didn't touch it. "Put it on," she said.

Zoe did so. The morning light caught in the facets and flashed rainbows.

"Osgood has excellent taste," Priscilla said. "And he can indulge his taste because Marchmont never cares what anything costs and refuses to be bothered with choosing gifts. He refuses to be bothered with anything that looks like a decision or a responsibility. All the world is agog that he chose your ring himself."

Zoe had simply assumed he'd chosen it. She hadn't realized how significant this was. Oh, this made it worse. He was making her feel special. She'd never be able to steel her heart against him, and he'd break it.

"There's no making him out, to be sure," said Priscilla, "but I'm very glad for you, indeed."

She left minutes later.

When the door had closed and her sister's footsteps had faded away, Zoe looked down at the diamond on her finger, the immense center stone surrounded by smaller ones, like a queen surrounded by her attendants.

She told herself not to be an idiot. She told herself not to be a sentimental fool. But how could she help it? He'd taken care about her ring, and he'd truly wanted her to like it—and that was too sweet of him, more sweetness than she could bear.

Her chest heaved and a sob escaped her. Then another. And another.

She put her face in her hands and wept.

* * *

The night before the wedding, Zoe held a little party in her bedroom.

The guests were her sisters.

"A party in your bedroom?" had been the first reaction. "Whoever heard of such a thing?"

She had waved her great diamond ring in their faces, and the fussing subsided.

They had all married well. They all owned heaps of fine jewelry. Zoe's engagement ring, however, had a magical effect upon all of her sisters, not only Priscilla, the least insane of them all.

Zoe had ordered little sandwiches and delicate pastries and tea and lemonade and champagne.

When they'd supped and drunk and gossiped and offered the usual marital advice, she had Jarvis bring out the treasures Karim had showered upon his second so-called wife and favorite toy.

Rubies and garnets, sapphires and emeralds, diamonds and pearls and topaz of every color. Necklaces and bracelets and rings.

She gave them all away to her sisters, all but a few pieces she'd reserved for Jarvis.

They were shocked into silence.

Then, finally, Priscilla spoke up. "You said you'd share, I remember, Zoe, but all of it? Are you quite, quite sure?"

"That was my old life," Zoe said. "I won't take it with me into my new life."

In the end, in spite of what Zoe's sisters had claimed about hole-in-corner affairs, the wedding turned out to be large and complicated.

Once they'd invited all of Zoe's siblings and their
spouses, they'd had to invite Marchmont's aunts and
uncles and cousins. And then, since Adderwood must
stand at his side, the other fellows must be asked,
too. There were royals, too, who must come. Even
leaving out the respective nieces and nephews, the
large drawing room of Lexham House became suffocatingly crowded.

Or so it seemed to Marchmont.

At last the clergyman appeared, and Zoe entered
the room soon thereafter, wearing a shimmering silvery confection that made Adderwood say in an undertone, "Oh, this is deuced unfair. Some fellows get
all the luck. She looks like an angel."

Zoe Octavia was not an angel, not by a long
stretch, but at this moment she looked purely innocent. At this moment it seemed to Marchmont that
she was the most beautiful creature he'd ever seen. As
she joined him before the clergyman, he felt a surge
of pride, which was not at all surprising, and a quick,
deep stab to the heart, which was.

The ceremony began. No one speaking up when
the time came to declare "any just cause, why they
may not be lawfully joined together," and neither
of them announcing any impediments, it continued
to the end, through each promise and "I will," and
through her father's giving her to be married, his eyes
sparkling with unshed tears, while his wife sobbed
openly. On it went through Marchmont's placing the
wedding ring on Zoe's finger and wedding her and
worshipping her with his body—the easiest of promises to make—and on through psalms and the prayer

for fruitfulness and more prayers and advice from St. Paul.

It seemed to him that he'd spent a lifetime marrying Zoe, but at last the Solemnization of Matrimony came to an end.

At last she was the Duchess of Marchmont—*his* Duchess of Marchmont. His wife.

He had a wife.

He was responsible for her. He'd sworn it before heaven and before witnesses.

. . . to love her, comfort her, honor and keep her in sickness and in health; and, forsaking all other . . .

Forsaking all other.

It dawned on him, then, what he'd done.

He'd given his word.

There was no turning back, no undoing.

His life was going to change, like it or not.

Thirteen

Some hours later

Zoe remembered the wedding ceremony vividly. Events thereafter were not so clear. A great many guests. Speeches and introductions. Food and more talk. A sea of people to wade through.

She hadn't slept soundly the night before, and by the time it was all over, and she and he left Lexham House, weariness overcame her. She fell asleep in the carriage during the short drive to Marchmont House and didn't wake up until the vehicle stopped. She'd started out on the seat opposite Marchmont, but when she woke she was sharing his side of the carriage. He had his arm around her.

When she looked up at him, he laughed. "Am I that boring?"

"Getting married is hard work," she said.

"Your labors aren't quite done," he said. "Now

you've got to meet the servants. Brace yourself. The good news is, it will soon be over."

He was right. It didn't take long.

They found all the staff awaiting them in the gleaming entrance hall. Harrison made a formal welcoming speech. The duke introduced his secretary, Osgood, and Harrison introduced the upper servants. And that was all.

The formalities completed, the duke took Zoe by the hand and whisked her up the carpeted stairs.

"That's the lot," he said. He looked down over the iron railing, where below, the numbers of servants dwindled. They marched out of the entrance hall, a small army in strict order of rank. "I didn't realize there were so many. I don't recall ever seeing them before in that way, all at once and in one place."

There were a great many, yet their numbers didn't daunt Zoe. In Cairo she'd lived among hordes of slaves and servants, and before long she knew each and every one.

This day she studied the faces of Marchmont's staff, because she meant to know all of them, too. She'd noticed that the footman who'd attended her the first time she'd been here was absent.

Not surprising. In Yusri Pasha's palace, if the chief eunuch was reprimanded or embarrassed, he usually executed any witnesses to his discomfiture.

"It was gently hinted to me by certain of the ladies that my new bride might require time to rest and otherwise prepare herself for the wedding night," Marchmont said.

"I shall need time to change my clothes, yes," said Zoe. "I'm glad I chose to be married in this gown.

It's very beautiful. But to get it off will be the most tedious process. A thousand tapes to tie and pins to take out and buttons and hooks, and then all the things underneath."

"Well, I would be happy to help, of course," he said.

She could picture him undoing her, bit by bit, taking off her clothes, layer by layer, and she felt as though she walked next to a moving fire, so heated she became.

She looked up and found him looking down at her. Heat flickered in his green eyes.

"I should look forward to that, in fact," he said. "But perhaps tonight is not the best time for complicated ceremonies."

It most certainly wasn't. With a few words and a look he'd made her unbearably impatient for this night's bedding. She was more impatient than most new brides since she had an excellent idea of what it would be like. Tonight it would be far wiser to let Jarvis get her out of the wedding dress and into something much flimsier. The less time Marchmont spent undressing his new bride, the more time he could spend making love to her.

"Yes, let us have complicated ceremonies another time," she said.

They had reached the first floor. He led her down one side of the gallery landing to a corner where a pair of mahogany doors met.

"This will take you to the duchess's apartments," he said as he opened one of the doors. "You'll find a connecting door between our bedrooms. I thought we might sup quietly together this night, in the great bedroom, rather than dine in state."

She squeezed the hand clasping hers. "Thank you," she said. "I'd like quiet. I've almost forgotten what it's like."

"Not too quiet," he said.

She looked up at him from under her lashes. "Not too quiet," she said. "As you wish. I vaguely recollect promising to obey."

"I supposed it would be the one item about which you'd have only the dimmest recollection." He lifted her hand to his lips and lightly kissed her knuckles. "I shall look forward to seeing you again in a little while, Your Grace."

Your Grace.

The two words hung in the air after the door closed behind her.

That was when it truly sank in: who she was and who she'd be from now on . . . and how far she'd come since the night she'd pounded on an unknown Englishman's door in Cairo.

She'd found the courage to escape her old life.

She'd find the courage for whatever her new life turned out to be.

Later

Zoe's quarters, she discovered, were about twice the size of her mother's apartments.

Given this, she could hardly be surprised at the vastness of Marchmont's bedroom. She was impressed nonetheless.

It was larger than the large drawing room of Lexham House, and it was the antithesis of austere.

His Grace, she saw, liked his comfort. Furthermore, the leader of fashion was no slave to the latest fashions in décor.

His bedroom was a delightful hodgepodge of furnishings of various styles and times.

A great tester bed dominated one wall. Its canopy rose nearly to the ceiling. From it hung curtains of gold and green velvet and silk. Nightstands stood on either side, a set of steps on one side. She took in chairs, tables, a bookcase, and a chest of drawers. In one corner of the room stood a lacquered Chinese screen and nearby, a matching cabinet. On the walls hung several beautiful paintings, including one of his parents. Though she had no memory of them, the style of clothing and the physical resemblance told her who they were.

A thick, richly designed carpet covered most of the floor—and that was considerable acreage—while elaborate plasterwork adorned the ceiling.

This marble chimneypiece was even more impressive than the one in the entrance hall. Before the fireplace stood a table laid for two and a pair of well-padded armchairs.

Zoe stood in the center of the room, hands clasped under her chin while she turned, taking in her surroundings.

Jarvis had dressed her in the nightclothes Zoe had carefully chosen for her wedding night: a simple muslin nightdress under a muslin wrapper embroidered in green, pink, and gold silk thread.

Shortly after she entered, Dove appeared, with a small train of footmen behind him, bearing trays and a silver bucket. Zoe watched them set out the supper—

an array of dainty dishes, small sandwiches like those she'd served her sisters, and cheeses, fruits, and pastries. Champagne cooled in the silver bucket, which was filled with ice. She knew that Marchmont House had its own icehouse, as did other great houses.

Marchmont stood over the servants, giving orders, moving a dish a fraction of an inch this way and another that way. She watched him for a moment and remembered what Priscilla had told her: that Marchmont bothered about nothing and nobody.

But he'd bothered this time. He'd thought about this and planned it and decided what it ought to be.

For her.

She looked down at the great diamond on her hand, the wedding ring nestled alongside, and a lump formed in her throat.

Oh, heaven, he truly could be sweet, like the Lucien she'd known long ago. How was her heart to withstand such sweetness? And if he captured her heart, how would she bear it when he grew bored with her?

Never mind. She'd survive somehow. She always survived.

And that day was sometime in the future.

Now he wasn't bored.

And for now, she knew how to make sure he stayed not bored.

At last everything seemed to be in order. Marchmont knew he couldn't fault Cook, for the man had done exactly what he was told to do. If it all added up to too much or too little, the duke had no one to blame but himself.

He waved the parade of footmen out of the room

and waited until they closed the door behind them. He poured the champagne, took up the glasses, and turned toward the center of the room, where he'd last seen Zoe, slowly going round and round, taking it all in.

He had no idea whether she approved or not. He tried to tell himself he didn't care. She had her own rooms, which she could furnish as she pleased.

Yet he couldn't help wondering whether she found his bedroom old-fashioned and cluttered, with its odd assortment of furniture from various generations. Some of the pieces came from other houses, and had belonged to the earliest holders of the title. Other pieces had been his grandparents' and parents' purchases, and a few, his own.

She wasn't there.

"Zoe?"

No answer.

He set the glasses down on the table. He looked toward the door that led to her bedroom. She couldn't possibly have . . .

Then he heard it, a faint rustling from behind the Chinese screen.

He'd had one of the nightstands containing a chamber pot moved behind the screen. She must have found it while he was busy with the footmen. For his bachelorhood, it had stood in the open, near his bed. But now he was married, and he knew that women tended to be more circumspect about such things than men.

He turned away and began to whistle.

He heard a giggle.

He turned toward the sound.

She stepped out from behind the screen.

She was wearing a smile. And the great diamond ring. And a great deal less clothing than she'd been wearing when she first entered his bedroom.

Then she'd worn a lace-trimmed nightdress under an embroidered, lace-trimmed wrapper of fine muslin.

Now she wore only the wrapper.

He couldn't see through it. While fine, the muslin was not transparent, and she was not standing in front of the fire. Where she stood, firelight and candlelight and shadows danced on the pink and green and gold embroidery, making the garment a shimmering veil.

The shadows and shimmer outlined the curves of her body, not fully revealing but calling attention to every alluring undulation.

He swallowed hard.

She began to sing. Her voice was low, barely above a whisper, and the melody was in a strange minor key. He felt it, like a touch, skimming over his skin. He couldn't have understood the words even if she'd sung louder, but his body understood the message and every fiber of it came fiercely alive.

Then her hands went up, sinuous as snakes, and she began to dance.

She moved with the fluid grace of a ballerina, but it was nothing like any ballet he'd ever seen. Her hands, her hips, the movement of her head and her eyes, glancing toward him and away—every gesture was exotically, unmistakably suggestive.

She moved about the room, but it was like the motion of a wayward breeze, advancing, then retreating. Now and again her hand went to her hair, and he caught the glint of a hairpin dropping. The devil danced in her smile and called to him from her eyes. Around him she danced, her hair tumbling loose, and he turned, mesmerized, following her.

She danced backward toward the bed and her hands glided down over her body, pausing to cup her breasts, then slid lower, her fingers skimming over her waist and belly. Further down they moved, to trace the shape of her hips and buttocks . . . then they moved to the front, under her belly, sliding over the triangle between her legs.

He'd bedded women, experienced and talented women, but they might have been wooden puppets compared to her.

She was all fluid carnality, shameless beyond shameless.

She caught hold of one of the carved posts at the foot of the bed and let her fingers trail over the carvings. Then she let go, to let her hand drift over the bedcover while she moved to the side of the bed.

In one easy motion she glided up and onto the bed. She settled into the middle of it on her knees. She lifted her hands above her head and pressed the palms together, like a prayer, and swayed there, her torso moving in ways the human body couldn't possibly move.

All the while she sang in the low, lilting minor key words he couldn't understand but whose meaning was obvious.

He'd long since forgotten about the supper he'd so carefully planned.

He'd forgotten everything in all the wide world.

He simply moved toward her, unthinkingly, because thinking wasn't necessary even if it had been possible. She could have been Eve, apple in her hand, Eve the temptress.

She brought her hands down as far as her heart, the palms still together, the gesture as fluid as silk. Then she opened her hands and smiled and curled her two index fingers, beckoning him.

He went, moving to one side of the bed, but as soon as he placed his knee on it, she laughed, and slipped out of the bed on the other side as easily as she'd slipped onto it.

He moved away from the bed and started toward her. She darted away, laughing again.

He tried a few more times, but she danced away from him. When she leapt onto the bed again, he leapt onto it, too. She scrambled away before he could get his hands on her.

He climbed off the bed. "Zoe Octavia," he said.

She backed away. "Lucien Charles Vincent," she said, and in the low voice, with its shadows and soft edges, his name became unbearably intimate. She stuck out her tongue, the brat. Oh, but not a brat. She'd become a woman, and this woman was sin incarnate.

She backed toward the table—their supper—and he thought she'd stumble over it, but she only paused and took up a glass of champagne. She drank, and laughed, and the champagne dribbled down her chin and onto her breast. The moisture spread outward and downward, making the thin cloth cling to the swelling curve of her breast. He watched the bud tighten, and his mind shut down.

He strode to the table, took the glass from her hand, and set it down.

She looked up at him, letting her head fall back. Her mouth curved into a slow, wicked smile.

"You devil," he said. Then he lifted her up and carried her to the bed and tossed her onto it.

She didn't bounce up or try to slip away.

She lay there, looking at him while she dragged her hands through her hair, scattering what remained of the pins and letting it fall in shimmering curls about her neck and shoulders. She untied the fastening band of the wrapper and let it fall open. The firelight and candlelight danced on her skin and flashed from the great diamond on her hand.

He threw off clothes. Dressing gown. Slippers.

She stretched out her arms, reaching for him, and he forgot about the rest of his garments. He climbed onto the bed and dragged her up and into his arms and kissed her. It was the first time he'd held her since her father had appeared in the nick of time in the library. Since then he'd thought of other things, yes, but always of her, of this, as well.

He'd meant to give her a proper wedding night, slow and romantic, to make up for their hasty coupling in the carriage, but the seductive dance, her wanton ways, put paid to that fantasy.

He gave her the hot kiss she deserved, deep and thoroughly lascivious. He dragged his hands over the thin muslin, down her back to the curve of her bottom. He broke the kiss and threw her back down onto the bed, and she laughed, her eyes as dark as midnight. He drew his hands down from her shoulders to her breasts, and he filled his hands with her, soft and so warm.

She put her hands over the sweet place between her thighs. "Here," she said. "I want you here."

"I know where it is," he said.

She laughed again and he laughed, too, as he released her breasts. He unbuttoned the flap of his breeches. His cock sprang out, and that made her laugh, too.

"He wants me," she said.

"How can you tell?" he said.

This time her laugh was deep in her throat as she reached for him. Her hand closed over him and traveled the length of his swollen rod. He gasped and pulled her hand away. "Not now," he said. "I don't need any help, thank you."

She found this hilarious. "Oh, Lucien," she said between giggles.

Lucien. Again. And again the sound of his own name, in that lilting, shadowy voice, reached deep, as deep as the secret places of his heart, places he'd hidden even from himself.

He stroked up her leg, and she stretched under his touch like a cat. He had meant to take all night, but her sensuous movement was another death blow to careful plans. Every motion of her body frayed the threads of his self-control.

He knelt between her legs and brought both hands to her knees. She moved, bringing herself closer to him, and planted her feet alongside his hips. He stroked her and she squirmed in pleasure, and he felt the pleasure—the damp heat of her, against his fingers—and then there was no thought of finesse or thought of any kind at all.

He plunged into her and watched her head rise from the bed, and fall back, and "Oh, Lucien," she gasped.

"Duchess," he said hoarsely on a thrust.

"Duke," she answered and pushed against him.

"Your Grace."

"Your Grace."

On and on, silly words murmured amid laughter and cries of pleasure and kisses; and all the while they were joined in the simple, mad way of lovers, moving as desire and heat drove them.

And when they reached the peak and there was nowhere else to go, she flung her arms about him and held him tightly. He gave way then, and release came in a rush of happiness. He let himself sink onto her soft, warm body and into the scent of her, like summer, and the scent of their lovemaking, and it felt like heaven to him.

When at last they lay together, spent, he moved off her and settled onto his side. He drew her up against him and held her there, her back curved against the front of his body.

She was safe. Secure. And above all, she was his as, he now knew beyond any doubt, she'd always been meant to be.

Fourteen

Friday, 1 May

"I should like the table moved nearer to the window," Zoe said, with a longing glance at that bright corner of the room. "The garden is beautiful, and the garden block makes a pretty backdrop. London is so green. I shall never grow tired of looking at the greenery. It's a wonderful scene to watch while one breakfasts."

"I don't care where the table is and I don't care which table it is," said Marchmont as he came away from the sideboard. "All I want is *a* table—any horizontal surface will do—on which to set my plate and a chair on which to plant my carcass."

He set down his plate and sat in his chair. He made a sweeping gesture, encompassing the breakfast room. "Arrange the house as you like. You're mistress here."

"As I like?" she said. "Anything?"

He nodded. "You're welcome to trouble about furniture arrangements if it amuses you. I only ask that you keep me out of it." He sliced into his beefsteak. "If Osgood becomes hysterical because you move his papers from one side of the desk to the other or Harrison drops into an apoplectic fit because you turn the China Room into a sitting room or Hoare faints because you change the curtains of my dressing room, I do *not* wish to hear about it."

The speech surprised her not in the least. "I'll deal with it," she said. "I've dealt with eunuchs."

"So you have."

"They can be exceedingly temperamental."

"I daresay." He regarded her for a time. "Zoe, this is your house. Do as you wish with it. The place has done well enough for me, but I suppose it wants a woman's touch. So my aunts declare—and that includes the not-mad ones. They say it lacks warmth or some such." He resumed eating.

He was doing it again: He was being sweet.

But then he'd reason to be amiable, she reminded herself.

She knew she'd pleased him last night and this morning. He'd made her glad for all her years of training—and that was something she couldn't have imagined only six months ago. Since her skills had been wasted on Karim, she'd expected them to remain unused forever. As his widow, she was unlikely to be able to employ them with other men. Widows were worthless, unwanted. Besides, she was old—past twenty—practically a crone.

Her skills were not wasted on Marchmont. She'd

made him laugh and she'd set him on fire and he'd done the same to her. She told herself not to place too much importance on his sweetness. A man was usually more malleable immediately after a night and morning of passion.

Furthermore, she knew he truly didn't care what she did to his house. He left most of his life to others. He was fortunate to have efficient and conscientious servants. Obnoxious, too, some of them, but efficient.

Harrison, for instance. He might be a bully, but for all she knew that was a result of his having to assume complete control. He had become overbearing, perhaps, because the master made no decisions and bore no responsibility at all.

"I shall want to look at the household records first," said Zoe.

"To move a table? All that wants is a pair of footmen."

"I want to understand how this household is run," Zoe said.

"Harrison runs it," said Marchmont. "He does a fine job. Have you noticed anything wrong or lacking? I mean, apart from the breakfast table being too far from the window."

"A gentleman who lives alone does not have the same requirements as a gentleman with a wife and family," Zoe said.

"Family," Marchmont repeated. He met her gaze, then his drifted downward. Though they had the table between them, she knew his mind had fixed on her belly, and he was wondering if his seed was sprouting there.

"One must make adjustments. One must accommodate the increase of the duke's family," she said.

Marchmont House was splendid, but, except for his bedroom, it was like a beautiful museum. It felt cold and anonymous. As stuffy and strict as the Queen was reputed to be, even Buckingham House had more personality.

"I'm sure Harrison will make all adjustments and accommodations necessary," he said, returning to his meal. "You don't need to trouble yourself about it. I can't imagine why you'd want to spend time looking at numbers in ledgers instead of riding or driving or shopping or visiting friends."

"I expect to be very busy with all of those activities in the coming weeks," Zoe said. "These early days of our marriage, when I'm not so busy, would be the best time to learn the ways of this household."

"I have no idea why you need to learn anything about it," he said. "I can't understand why you'd want to give yourself a headache looking at account books and such."

"The books often explain more clearly than the servants can," she said. "They show the patterns of the house, the ebb and flow."

He shrugged. "As you wish. But you are not to give yourself a brain fever. I was hoping to show off the new Duchess of Marchmont in Hyde Park later today."

"And I shall be honored to be shown off," she said. "Any day you wish. I promise not to rave or froth at the mouth in public."

"Afterwards, what is your preference? The theater? Or shall we spend the night quietly at home?" He glanced across at her, and heat sparked in his sleepy eyes. "But not too quietly."

She slipped off her slipper and stretched her leg out under the table. She brushed her foot against his leg, then higher, and higher still.

He set down his cutlery. His slitted green gaze moved to the footmen posted on either side of the sideboard. "Out," he said.

They went out.

"Come here," said the duke to his wife.

Monday, 4 May, in the duke's study

The interlude after breakfast led to another and another. They were newlyweds, after all. And then, as important newlyweds in London, they had to be seen here and had to be seen there. The Duke of York gave a great party on Saturday night. The Queen was there, and several princesses and royal dukes and certain members of the nobility, the Marchmonts included, naturally. As they were taking tea, the Queen suddenly fell ill. She was taken back to Buckingham House in Lord Castlereagh's carriage, because her own wasn't ready.

Zoe and Marchmont left soon after Her Majesty did. They went home and did what newlyweds usually do.

It wasn't until Monday that Zoe found the time to begin examining the household. She commenced the review shortly after Marchmont had dressed and taken himself off to Tattersall's.

Osgood, she found, was happy to indulge her curiosity. He proudly showed her his domain: the neat piles of correspondence, the diary with its beautifully penned entries, the tidy ledgers listing Marchmont's personal expenditures.

After Osgood came Harrison.

Harrison was a horse of a different color.

A power struggle instantly ensued.

"Your Grace, I should be happy to explain the rules of the household," the house steward said. "We follow the rules written down by His Grace's grandfather, the eighth Duke of Marchmont. Some minor adjustments have been made to accommodate modern requirements."

"It's a great house, and I understand there must be ceremony and strict rules," Zoe said. "The rules here will not be the same as those in other houses. I do not expect to make any but minor changes, and perhaps very few. Still, before I think about what I will and will not do, I must review all of the current records."

"Mr. Dove and Mrs. Dunstan will be happy to answer any questions Your Grace has regarding the household matters."

Zoe knew better than to let him fob her off on the butler and housekeeper. This was about control, and she must have it.

"I shall speak to them, naturally, in due course," she said cheerfully. "But I shall begin by reviewing the books. I want to see all of them for the last six months. The ledgers. The accounts for provisions. The inventories."

"Your Grace, I shall deem it an honor to explain the

provisioning of the household," said Harrison. "You should not find anything lacking. If you do, however, the matter will be attended to with a word, a mere word. Every member of this staff is not content merely to meet the needs of the family, Your Grace. We view it as our duty to anticipate. If there is aught amiss with Your Grace's apartments, Mrs. Dunstan will wish to know of it, that she might correct the oversight *immediately*."

"I expect no less," Zoe said.

"Thank you, Your Grace. We should wish you to have only the highest expectations of the staff of Marchmont House."

It was obviously time for the voice of command.

"I expect my orders to be heeded," Zoe said in the implacable tones that might have startled some people but with which Jarvis was familiar.

The tone clearly startled Harrison, because he became more wooden.

"I expect you to anticipate my desire to review everything to do with the running of the household whose mistress I am," she said, watching the faint color rise in his face. "I do not expect to have to explain myself again. I expect to find in the library by three o'clock this afternoon the household records— all of them—for the last six months, and the most recent inventories." She chose the location on purpose, remembering Harrison's veiled insult on her first visit—the implication that she was too ignorant to appreciate books. "I'll begin reviewing them immediately."

"Yes, Your Grace," Harrison said, his lips barely moving. "Very good, Your Grace."

He went out of the room in his usual stiff way, but this was the stiffness of suppressed fury. It practically came off him in waves. The other servants would have no more trouble than Zoe did in sensing it. Unlike them, though, she wouldn't shrink away from his rage.

She'd had plenty of experience with bullies. She knew that some created an atmosphere of barely suppressed violence. It could be quite frightening to those at the bully's mercy. But she wasn't at anybody's mercy, and she wouldn't be intimidated or manipulated.

Given the condition of the house, she expected Harrison's records to be irreproachable. But that wasn't the point.

The point was, Who was in charge?

Marchmont clearly wasn't.

She would have to be. As a woman and, worse, the notorious Harem Girl, she could never hope to have the respect of the servants and control of the household if she accommodated the house steward instead of seeing that he accommodated her.

It was not the Duchess of Marchmont's business to make servants happy. It was their job to make her happy. If it turned out they were underpaid for the job, she'd correct that. But it would be fatal to her authority to expect of them any less than the absolute obedience Marchmont received.

A few hours later

Servant problems.

Marchmont had never had a servant problem. He

was not supposed to have servant problems. Servant problems were Harrison's problem.

Now Marchmont had a wife. She had not been in the house for four days, and he had a catastrophic servant problem.

He found Zoe in her dressing room, frowning at a carriage dress Jarvis held up for her inspection.

"Out," he said, making the go-away gesture at the maid.

Jarvis darted out of the room, taking the carriage dress with her.

Zoe stared at him.

"Harrison is threatening to resign," he said.

She frowned. "That's strange."

"Do you think so?" he said.

"It's very strange," she said. "He simply came to you and said he wished to resign?"

"He tells me you asked to see all of the household records and—and I hardly know what else."

"Inventories," she said. "It's my responsibility to review these records, to fully understand the management of this household."

"You've impugned his integrity."

"I think not," she said. "I think this is about getting his way. You are the Duke of Marchmont. He's your house steward. Where will he obtain a more prestigious position? If he leaves because of a small thing like this, then something is very wrong in this house."

"Something is clearly wrong," Marchmont said tightly. "We had peace here, and all running smoothly, and look what you've done."

"I've done what is my responsibility," she said.

"You don't need to be responsible," he said. "Harrison has been with this family for twenty years. He started as a footboy. If ever there were a trusted retainer, that is one—and you've implied he isn't trustworthy."

"Have I, really?" Zoe said. "Because I wished to do what every woman of my family does?"

"Every woman of your family is not the Duchess of Marchmont," he said.

"Quite true. My responsibilities are greater than theirs."

"Your responsibility is to bear my children," he said. "And to spend my money. And to entertain yourself in the Beau Monde you were so determined to be part of."

"That's all?" she said. Her voice had grown dangerously quiet, and there was a light in her blue eyes that even he could read, whether he wished to or not. But he was too angry to heed the warning.

"It's bourgeois," he said, "to fuss about records and inventories, like a common shopkeeper."

"Common?" she said. *"Common?"*

She snatched up a hairbrush and threw it at him.

He dodged instinctively, and the missile flew by him and struck the door frame.

He was not allowed to throw anything back.

He was not allowed to throttle her.

He stormed out of the dressing room and, soon, out of the house. He went to his club. He stayed there through the remainder of the afternoon and well into the evening and drank steadily.

That night

The Duke of Marchmont was not carried into the house in the early hours of morning. He didn't even stagger—not so one would notice. He'd drunk a great deal, but it wasn't enough. Sobriety came and went, and when it came, it was too bright and cold, like a day of dead winter.

His bride had placed him in an impossible position.

There was Harrison saying the duchess was dissatisfied with his services and offering to resign if the duke so wished it.

What was Marchmont to say to that? What could he say but "Her Grace cannot be dissatisfied with your services. Clearly there's a misunderstanding. I'll look into it."

Look into it!

Why must he look into it? Why must he be placed in the ridiculous position of negotiating between his house steward and his wife?

Zoe shouldn't have put him in this position.

Why couldn't she leave well enough alone?

The arts of pleasing a man, indeed. Drive his house steward to resign. Drive her husband out of his own house. Oh, yes, how pleasing that was!

As pleasing as his house was at this dreary hour. Dark and quiet as death. All of them abed except the night porter . . . and Hoare waiting and no doubt whimpering upstairs . . . and the husband who'd been driven out of his own abode.

He strode more or less steadily across the entrance

hall, through the main doorway and on to the great staircase. As he grasped the handrail, he glimpsed, out of the corner of his eye, a glimmer of light to his left. He turned away from the stairs and crossed to the door of the anteroom. A fire still burned in the grate and a lone candle burned in the candelabrum standing on one of the tables. More light filled the doorway to the library.

He went to the library door.

She sat at the great table, her back to him. The candlelight shimmered in her hair, which was coming down. Dark blonde tendrils clung to the back of her neck.

The table was heaped with books and stacks of paper. As she dipped her pen into the inkwell, she must have become aware of him, because she turned and looked over her shoulder toward the doorway.

"You're working very late," he said.

"It's most interesting, what I'm finding here," she said. Her voice was cool.

He advanced into the room. She recommenced writing.

"It must be fascinating indeed, to keep you up so late," he said.

"It is," she said.

As he neared, he saw an ink smudge on her cheek and another at her temple. He was still angry with her, but the smudges were adorable, and she looked so weary and cross, like a child forced to do sums against her will.

She'd despised sums, he recalled. Yet she'd insisted on studying ledgers, column upon column of the numbers she'd hated.

"It's too late for such work," he said. "You're all over ink. Come upstairs and let's get you cleaned up and into bed." He thought about washing her . . . everywhere . . . and his cock began to swell.

"I'm not quite done," she said.

"Zoe," he said.

"Marchmont," she said crisply.

He supposed she wanted him to apologize. He was tempted. She really was adorable, all smudged with ink and cross. But she was cross with him, and she had no business to be, after very nearly driving his house steward out of the house.

Then what would become of them? England could manage well enough without a monarch. It had survived a mad king and his not-exactly-mentally-balanced son, even during wartime. Marchmont House could not manage without Harrison.

"The numbers will still be there in the morning," he said. "You need sleep."

And he did not want to get into his great, cold bed alone.

"I'll be along in a little while," she said. "As soon as I finish these calculations."

She gave the slight, go-away wave of her hand.

Was she *dismissing* him?

"As you wish," he said, and stormed out.

The Duke of Marchmont's bedroom faced east. When he woke, the angle of the sun told him it was late morning. No one had to tell him he was alone in the bed.

No one had to tell him he was an idiot, either.

He'd figured that out the second time last night he'd

woken after a bad dream. In it Zoe rode away on a black horse and disappeared, forever.

He winced, recalling what he'd said. *Bourgeois. Common.* What had possessed him?

He wasn't sure. Panic, perhaps, because he'd found himself required, suddenly, to do what he'd never done before. He'd found himself required to pay attention and make a decision.

He'd decided wrong, unsurprisingly.

He heard a light tap at the door connecting his room to Zoe's. His sinking heart cautiously lifted. "Yes," he said. "Yes, come in."

His heart lifted another degree when she spilled through the door in a delicious confection of a morning dress. Made of a cream-colored muslin trimmed in pink, it had long, loose sleeves and an abundance of lace. "You look like a sugar cake," he said.

She looked tired, too. He saw shadows under her beautiful eyes. His conscience said, *Your fault, your fault, you beast.*

She beamed at him, just as though he wasn't a beast.

His heart lightened further.

"Zoe," he began.

But before he could embark on his apology, a train of footmen entered behind her, some bearing trays.

Those unencumbered set about moving a table and chairs in front of the fireplace. Then they set out the dishes. Then they went out via the room's main door, which the last servant discreetly closed after himself.

"When I came up this morning, you were asleep," she said. "I didn't want to disturb you."

"Come here," he said.

"Come eat your breakfast," she said.

As he did every night, Hoare had laid out Marchmont's dressing gown on the back of a chair, near at
hand. She took it and held it up, playing valet.

More coals heaped upon the duke's head.

He climbed out of bed, donned his slippers, and
obediently thrust his arms into the sleeves. He tied
the sash and said, "I must beg your pardon, Zoe. I
behaved badly yesterday."

"Oh, thank you." She flung herself at him and threw
her arms about him in her usual impulsive way.

He wrapped his arms about her and held her tightly.
"I should never, never have taken Harrison's side
against you," he said. "I don't know what I was thinking. Evidently, I wasn't thinking at all. Please forgive
me." He buried his face in her hair and inhaled the
fragrance of her, clean and warm and summery.

He stood for a time, simply holding her.

She'd been lost for far too long. She'd returned. She
was his. He'd made her his. No one had forced him to
do this. Now it was his job to look after her and
honor her, a job no one had forced him to accept. He'd
given his word, of his own free will, in the moment
he'd said, "I will."

After a time, she drew away. "Thank you," she said.
"I wasn't easy about coming to you this morning. But
now that I'm forgiven—"

"Oh, no," he said. "I asked you to forgive *me*. I
haven't decided whether to forgive you." Her eyes
widened, and he laughed. "A joke, Zoe. I couldn't
resist. Gad, what is there to forgive? I told you to do
as you pleased, not as Harrison pleased."

"Come, let's eat breakfast," she said. "I must talk

about sums, and that isn't something you can bear on an empty stomach."

"Sums," he said.

What foreboding he felt was simply due to the prospect of dealing with numbers. She'd been staring at long columns of them. She'd been writing them down. Though she'd scrubbed the smudges off her face, faint ink stains remained on her fingers.

She took his hand, and he let her lead him to the breakfast table. "This is the darkest part of the room," he said. "I thought you preferred to breakfast in the sunlight. My windows overlook the garden."

"I assumed your head would ache this morning," she said.

"I wasn't nearly as drunk as I'd planned to be," he said. "Getting drunk turned out not to be as much fun as it ought to be." He held out a chair for her and she sat. He took his place opposite. It wasn't far away. This was a good deal more intimate than even the breakfast room, one of the most informal rooms in the house.

They ate for a time in comfortable silence. He was used to silence and used to living alone. But he knew she savored the quiet, after so many riotous mealtimes at Lexham House. As for himself, he was content this day simply to have her near and not in a mood to throw things at him.

He seemed to be in a very bad way, stupidly attached to his wife.

When at last he set down his cutlery, she drew out a few sheets of folded foolscap from a pocket hidden in the folds of her dress.

"Those would be the sums, I collect," he said, eyeing the papers with loathing.

"A few notes, only," she said. "Merely some examples to support the main premise. The main premise is that you are being grossly overcharged and overprovisioned, and that, in short, members of this household have been cheating you."

It was, perhaps, the last thing he could have expected to hear her say. He understood the words but couldn't take them in. He looked at the papers in her hand. He looked at her, into her troubled countenance.

"I never expected this in a household so well run," Zoe said. "I didn't suspect anything was amiss until Harrison made such a fuss about letting me see the records. Even then cheating was only one of several possibilities that occurred to me."

"Harrison," he said. "Cheating me." It was beginning to sink in, though he still felt numb.

"The first thing I noticed was the quantity of provisions," she said. "It might have made sense if you entertained on the most lavish scale every single evening. But I know you don't. You dine away from home most of the time, according to Osgood, who keeps track of all the invitations and appointments. I haven't yet sent for your cook—or any of those who might be involved—to hear how they explain the quantities and prices. I didn't want to do this until I'd spoken to you."

"I can't . . ." He remembered her sitting in the library, toiling over the books until long after midnight. She'd still been at it when he left in a sulk.

Yesterday afternoon and night and early this morning she'd studied and calculated.

"Oh, Zoe." He held out his hand, and she put the notes into it. He looked down, and the notes and numbers were a blur.

"I know such things happen," she said. "My sisters warned me. They said I must immediately study the records, and talk to the upper-level staff, to show that I understand how a household is run. They said I must assert myself at the beginning, or I would leave a void and others would move in to fill it. Then I should never have control. I knew this was true, because it's the same in the harem."

He hadn't understood at all. He'd inherited his title. He'd inherited his position in the world. He'd never had to assert himself or prove who he was. The Duke of Marchmont simply *was*.

"Sometimes the cook or another orders more than can be used, and sells the extra," she went on. "Sometimes they make arrangements with, say, the butcher. He charges more than what the correct price should be, and he and the servants split the profit. But it isn't only the food and drink. Your laundry bills are ludicrous, even for a fashionable gentleman. Some of the tailor bills are forgeries, I think. I would not be surprised if we discover that some of the merchants whose names appear on the bills don't exist."

He stared blindly at the notes in his hand.

"I'm sorry," she said. "One expects to discover minor pilfering. That happens everywhere, and it's nearly impossible to prevent. This is beyond anything

I could have expected. It's very, very wicked. A betrayal of trust of the worst kind."

The first blank shock was ebbing, and anger rushed in to fill its place. Harrison, whom he'd trusted, who'd stood before him, so piously correct yesterday.

A part of him still didn't want to accept it.

Yet he knew in his heart it was true.

His trust had been betrayed.

All the same, he saw with painful clarity how easy he'd made it for others to betray him.

He gave the notes back to Zoe, rose from the table, crossed the room, and pulled the rope, to summon a servant.

A footman appeared within minutes.

"Send Harrison to me," said Marchmont. "Now."

"I'm sorry, Your Grace," said the footman. "Mr. Harrison isn't in the house."

Zoe wasn't surprised when they discovered that the house steward had run away, apparently during the night.

When his rooms were searched, his belongings—and a number of things that didn't belong to him—were gone.

Mrs. Dunstan had gone out to the market early this morning and had not come back. Neither of them had warned Dove and Hoare. These two must have assumed that the new duchess would never in a million years make heads or tails of the household records, else they'd have vanished, too.

By the end of the day, after questioning every member of the staff, Marchmont was left in no doubt whatsoever that his upper servants, led by Harrison, had been systematically siphoning off a portion of his income—and this had been going on for as much as a decade.

Hoare, for instance, had cultivated a network of tailors, glove makers, haberdashers, laundresses, and so on, all of whom overcharged His Grace and split the excess with the valet, who paid a percentage to his other partners in crime. The others—cook, butler, housekeeper—did the same in their own spheres.

Some of the lower servants knew what was going on, some suspected, and some knew nothing. Those who knew had been afraid, until now, to inform. They believed that no one would take their word against Harrison's, and they were terrified of what he would do if they tattled.

Situations at Marchmont House were highly paid and of high status. One couldn't hope to do as well elsewhere. Furthermore, one mightn't find any work anywhere else, because Harrison let offending servants go without a character. A servant who hadn't a letter of recommendation was unlikely to find another good position. Too, Harrison could be vindictive, spreading poison about those he'd dismissed. No one within ten miles of London would hire them for even the most menial positions.

"He was a bully, as I knew," Zoe said after the last of the servants, a scullery maid, had left the study.

"I didn't," Marchmont said. "I never noticed anything amiss. I had no idea that most of my servants lived in fear of him. Even if I had noticed, I probably would have thought that was as it ought to be. But fear and respect are not the same thing. Gad, Zoe, what a mess."

He got up and walked to the fire and gazed into the grate, his hands clasped behind him.

It was the way her father so often stood, thinking as he stared into the fire.

"I'm sorry," she said. "You trusted these people and they betrayed your trust."

He shook his head. "Not everyone can resist temptation. If I had taken responsibility, they wouldn't have been tempted. I set a bad example. I was not the master of the house. Someone had to be. And it's too tempting, when one has great power, to abuse it." He turned back to her. "What would happen in the harem, in such a case? Off with their heads?"

She nodded. "No one would care whether they were truly innocent or guilty."

"I know I ought to have the lot of them—Harrison, Cook, Dove, Dunstan, Hoare—taken up and prosecuted. But they'll hang—and then I'll always wonder whether, if I'd behaved differently, none of this would have happened."

"If Harrison and the housekeeper have any sense, they'll be on their way out of the country by this time," Zoe said. "It doesn't seem fair that they should escape and the others hang."

"The others are equally guilty. We can add to that the crime of stupidity for lingering in the house a minute after you'd opened the ledgers." He still studied the burning coals.

"It wouldn't be the first time servants have under-estimated my obstinacy," Zoe said. "When you came to the library last night and told me to come to bed, I wanted to. I wanted us to kiss and make up. I didn't want to keep staring at those columns of numbers. You know I never liked sums."

"I know."

"But I'm like the dog with the bone. As soon as I saw something wasn't right, it became a challenge, to find out exactly what was wrong and how and where. It was the same in the harem. If I weren't so obstinate, I should never have got away. But I was determined to master the place. And because I mastered it, when the time came, I found the way out."

"Oh, Zoe." He turned to look at her, but she didn't need to read his face. She heard it all in his anguished voice. She went to him. It was instinctive. She put her arms around him, the way she'd done this morning, because she loved him—she couldn't help it—and she wanted him to be happy.

His arms went around her, the way they'd done this morning, warm and strong and reassuring. He kissed the top of her head, and the tenderness of that small touch made her heart ache.

"Your mother and father never gave up hope, but I did," he said tightly. "I gave up on you, on everything. You never gave up."

"I'm stubborn," she murmured against his chest.

"Don't give up on me, Zoe Octavia. Don't ever give up on me."

"I won't," she said.

And *No, I won't*, she thought. *I'm afraid I never will.*

Fifteen

Only a few short weeks ago, the Duke of Marchmont couldn't be bothered to decide which waistcoat to wear.

Now he found himself holding the power of life and death over his felonious servants.

He had to make a decision, and he had to do it quickly. Dove, Hoare, and Cook were locked in Harrison's parlor, guarded by an army of footmen and maidservants.

Marchmont wanted to seek Lexham's advice, but that seemed like passing off responsibility.

He wanted to seek Zoe's advice, but that would be cheating, too.

He sent Osgood and Zoe out of the study.

He paced. He stared into the fire the way Lexham always did, hoping to find the answers there, as Lexham so often seemed to do. The coals produced only the usual glow and heat, smoke and ashes. They offered no solutions.

Finally he returned to the writing table, where he'd laid out the various pieces of evidence. He looked at Harrison's records. He looked at Osgood's. He skimmed the diaries. He traced the expenditures. Osgood's accounts included a great many wagers. The totals the duke had lost must easily match, if not surpass, the servants' pilfering, outrageous as it was.

Marchmont didn't care about money. Or he hadn't, until today. Yesterday Zoe had spoken of his "family," and he knew she wasn't referring to the mad aunt and indigent relations he supported, fully or partially.

She referred to the children he and she hoped to have.

Suppose they had eight, as Lexham had done. Or more. King George and Queen Charlotte had produced fifteen children. The fourth Duke of Richmond had fourteen. Worcester's father, the sixth Duke of Beaufort, had ten.

Marchmont's eldest son would inherit everything. But the duke must pay to care for and educate them all. He must find places for the younger males and pay for the girls' come-outs and weddings and the wardrobes that went with these. He must provide dowries as well.

He didn't care about money. A gentleman didn't.

But a gentleman was honor bound to care for his family, and a family needed money. A duke's family needed pots of it. He had pots of money, so much that ten years' steady and zealous thieving had not attracted anybody's attention.

He continued scanning Osgood's neat entries: some thousands to found an Infirmary for Diseases of the Eye. A subscription to a Samaritan fund. A contribution to a society for the deaf and dumb, another for the indigent blind. He gave money for the relief of wounded soldiers and sailors. He contributed to funds for widows and orphans. He gave to churches and hospitals and asylums.

He'd presided over any number of dinners devoted to one charity or another. To him these were social obligations, more or less like appearing at court. Most of his friends attended. Such an event was merely another dinner, where one must endure too many speeches.

At least he hadn't spent all his money stupidly or selfishly. The wretches below, locked in Harrison's room, had not, after all, stolen more than he'd given away or squandered unthinkingly.

Marchmont thought of the money thrown away on great dinners for his friends, where he'd drunk prodigious quantities, and spouted Shakespeare, as he was wont to do when three sheets in the wind.

I can see you're rapidly approaching the point where you start quoting Shakespeare and falling into the fire, Adderwood had said at the dinner where Marchmont had become so stupidly jealous of his friends' interest in Zoe.

Though he wasn't drunk at present, Shakespeare wandered into his mind:

> *The quality of mercy is not strained,*
> *It droppeth as the gentle rain from heaven*
> *Upon the place beneath: it is twice blessed;*
> *It blesseth him that gives and him that takes:*
> *'Tis mightiest in the mightiest; it becomes*
> *The thronèd monarch better than his crown . . .*

He rang, and a footman came.

Which one was this? There were so many of them. Perhaps it was time to start learning who these people were.

"What's your name?" said Marchmont.

"Thomas, Your Grace."

"Thomas, I shall want my cook, butler, and valet brought to this room. But first ask the duchess if she would be so good as to return here."

Thomas went out.

When the trio entered, Marchmont had taken his place behind the handsome French desk a previous Duke of Marchmont had acquired during the time of Louis XV.

Zoe sat by the fire, her hands folded in her lap.

"You must be here," he'd told her. "They all need to understand that you and I are united in this."

"If you cut off their heads, I'll watch, if I must," she said. "But I'll throw up afterwards."

"I'm not going to cut off their heads. This is England, not Egypt. And certainly not France."

He'd made a joke of it because that was what he always did. Whatever else he changed, he refused to become too boringly serious.

He hadn't told her what he did mean to do, and she hadn't asked.

No one had any idea what he meant to do.

During the time locked up in Harrison's room, the larcenous trio must have realized they were headed for the gallows. Dove, who'd previously spent most of his time proclaiming his ignorance of all wrongdoing, looked pale. Cook, who'd been truculently unforthcoming, was looking worried. Hoare's eyes were red with weeping, and he trembled.

"I've decided to let you determine your fate," said Marchmont.

They all looked at one another, then up, though not enough to meet his gaze directly.

"You may continue to assert your innocence," he continued. "In that case, I shall turn you over to the authorities with the evidence we've amassed and let a judge and jury decide the matter. If they find you innocent, you'll go free. If they find you guilty, you'll be transported or hanged." He paused to let this sink in.

The miscreants looked at one another, then at the floor. But not at him.

"The alternative is to admit what you've done and give us the names of all your confederates, both in this house and outside of it," Marchmont went on. "In that case, you'll be spared criminal proceedings. You will not be spared punishment, however."

Another pause.

He was aware of Zoe watching him in that intent way she had, as though she'd peer into his soul. *Good luck*, he thought. He might have one, but he doubted she'd find in it anything worth the trouble of examining.

"You'll perform ten years' penance," he went on. "You will do this in London, where we can keep an eye on you. Each of you will toil for ten years in one of the charitable enterprises I support. You will receive no pay but your room and board and whatever clothing is necessary to perform your duties. Should the enterprise come to an end or the establishment burn down, as often happens, you'll be assigned another situation. You'll do penance for a full ten years. Not a day more or less."

He looked hard at each of them in turn. "That is how long you worked for me and abused my trust. For the allotted time, you'll do, to the best of your abilities, the work required of you. At the end of this time, if your performance merits it, you'll receive a letter of commendation bearing my signature." One last pause. "If you break the terms of our agreement, I shall leave you to the official system of justice."

The three servants decided against testing the mercy of the English judicial system and accepted the duke's brand of justice.

This left Marchmont two extremely tedious tasks: First, he must make arrangements for the trio's dispersal among appropriate charitable establishments. Second, he must fill five crucial positions in the household.

"Here's responsibility with a vengeance," he told Zoe after the three were led out of the room. "We've no one to supervise the lower servants, no one to prepare the next meal, and most important, no one to dress me."

"I shall dress you," said Zoe.

"Do you know a day coat from an evening one?" he said.

"No," she said.

"Do you know whether a waistcoat for day ought to be embroidered or plain?"

"No."

"Have you any idea where to find my stockings?"

"No."

"Come here," he said. She went to him, and he wrapped his arms around her and rested his chin on the top of her head. "You are the silliest duchess there ever was."

"I know where you keep your *membrum virile*," she said against his coat.

"You don't need to know that, so long as I do," he said.

"Then find it," she said, "and let us go to bed and make love and sort these matters out afterwards, when we're happier and calmer."

"Make love?" he said. "You want to make love now, while the house is tumbling down about our ears?"

"The house is not falling down," she said. "We merely need servants. But you've been so brave and clever and wise and frighteningly ducal today that I'm on fire with lust. If you don't wish to go up to bed, then throw those papers and books on the floor and ravish me on the desk."

There was not another woman like her in all the world, he thought.

"Very well, if it pleases Your Grace," he said.

"I think it will."

He pushed everything off the desk.

"Perhaps you should lock the door," she said.

"If anyone interrupts, I'll cut off their heads," he said.

"It excites me when you're masterful," she said.

He picked her up and tossed her onto the desk. He unbuttoned his pantaloons.

Later

Zoe put the undercook in the cook's place and had Jarvis, as the highest-ranking woman servant, supervise the female staff. After talking to the menservants, Marchmont decided not to promote the under-butler—whose greatest skill seemed to be obsequiousness—but to make Thomas, the most experienced of the footmen, his butler and valet.

All of this was for the time being only.

Other households might make do with a combination butler-valet or housekeeper-lady's maid. Other households did not have porters or under-butlers or steward's boys. The Duke and Duchess of Marchmont did not make do. They had everything and more. It was their patriotic duty to be waited upon by scores of servants, whether they needed them or not, and the servants were as well aware of this as they were.

Still, the staff performed admirably in the circumstances, and Zoe and Marchmont were able to go out to the theater as they had planned, and afterward to a ball at Hargate House, where Zoe danced with the Earl of Hargate, three of his five sons, and most of Marchmont's friends.

The duke and duchess knew rumors would start circulating soon, regarding the sudden disappearance of their senior staff, but that was for tomorrow and the days to come. For this night, all people talked about was what a handsome couple the Marchmonts made and how amiable and witty the duke was—wittier and in better spirits than anyone could remember seeing him before.

The happy couple returned home at half past two in the morning.

They did not see the shrouded figure skulking in the shadows of the square.

Wednesday, 6 May

April showers, the wags said, came in May, the result of what some still deemed the misguided change, several generations earlier, from Julian to Gregorian calendar.

A glance out of the window told Marchmont that one April shower was in the offing this morning. Black clouds were massing overhead, and an un-May-like wind blasted through St. James's Square.

It was not the most inviting day to go out, but the Duchess of Marchmont needn't worry about bad weather. He'd ordered a closed carriage for her. Servants would hold an umbrella over her head when she walked the few paces between vehicle and door. Furthermore, as she pointed out to him, she wasn't sweet enough to melt.

She needed to visit her parents, and that errand oughtn't to be put off. They already knew she was happy and well, because they'd seen for themselves—at Lexham House and various social gatherings. But she wanted to seek their advice regarding the servant problem, particularly the matter of finding a house-keeper.

Marchmont couldn't go with her. He'd sent for his solicitor, to work out the details of Cook's, Dove's, and Hoare's philanthropic servitude. It was a tedious process, sifting through all the possible situations, and deciding where the miscreants would do the most good. This matter couldn't be put off, either. He could hardly keep them locked up in Harrison's room indefinitely.

He did leave his solicitor for long enough to see his wife off, though.

"This is exciting," she said as they crossed the entrance hall. "It's my first time out alone as a married woman."

"Not entirely alone," he said.

Jarvis trailed behind her mistress, umbrella in hand as always.

"I told her she needn't come," Zoe said. "I told her there would be two big, strong footmen standing at the back of the coach and a burly coachman driving, and we're only going a short distance."

"We must hope that the housemaids don't run amok while she's away," he said.

"What do housemaids do when they run amok?" Zoe said.

"I don't know," he said. "Excessive dusting?"

She smiled up at him, and he could actually feel his heart melting. Marriage had a deleterious effect on a man's dignity. If he didn't watch out, he'd be giving her idiotish smiles in return.

He pretended the feathers of her bonnet needed straightening. Then he had to adjust the satin puffs at her shoulders. Then he had to step back and regard her critically.

Then she had to laugh at him and step closer and grasp his lapels.

"Zoe, you're *wrinkling* me," he said reproachfully. She tugged.

He bent and kissed her, there, in front of the servants. When he straightened, he noticed with amusement that Jarvis was pointedly looking the other way and the footmen and hall porter were carefully looking at nothing.

Marchmont walked with her to the door and out of it, and down the steps to the waiting carriage. He helped her in and closed the door behind her.

He watched the carriage proceed westward, round the fence enclosing the circular pond in the center of the square. When he saw the vehicle turn into King Street, he started back into the house. He'd scarcely crossed the threshold and the door hadn't yet closed behind him when he heard horses shrieking, people shouting and screaming, and a thunderous crash.

He leapt down the short flight of steps and ran through the square and into King Street.

Everyone about him was screaming and shouting, but it was all background noise. He was aware of people running out of buildings, but they were shadows. He saw bodies on the pavement and in the street. Blood everywhere. People crowded about the overturned carriage. He pushed them out of his way. He saw the crest. His crest.

Zoe was in there.

He saw her in his mind's eye, galloping ahead of him on a narrow bridle path, the sky grey, the tree leaves shining, the ground slick with wet. It was the last time she'd run away. The last time he'd chased her, exasperated, as always, and afraid, as always. It had rained for two days and she was supposed to be safe at home, studying her Greek and Latin. She'd promised to study very hard, because she was going abroad, to visit Greece and Egypt and the Holy Land with her parents.

It was the last time she'd run away, the last time he'd chased her. Not a year later, she was gone. Forever.

Gone forever.

Someone was shouting at him, but the sounds made no sense.

He was climbing up onto the wreckage. He had to fight to wrench open the door.

The first thing he saw was the ostrich plumes. They didn't move.

Nothing moved.

His heart stopped moving, too.

"Zoe."

Then, louder. "*Zoe.*"

A small movement. A feather quivering.

But the wind was whistling through the street on this dreary day—the same wind that had blasted through the square only a moment ago, ruffling the water in the basin.

He reached down, his hand shaking.

The feathers fluttered.

One slim, gloved hand moved, rose, and reached for his.

His heart gave such a lurch that he nearly fell off the vehicle. Then he was clasping her hand tightly, so tightly. "Zoe."

"Lucien."

She shook her head and looked up. The bonnet tilted over one blue eye. "What are you doing up there?"

He remembered little of what happened immediately afterward. He'd fallen into some kind of frenzy, and all the world seemed to have gone mad, too. People had crowded into King Street from everywhere.

He vaguely recalled the footmen helping him get Zoe and her maid out of the carriage. The footmen accounted for two of the bodies he'd seen. They'd been thrown or had jumped from their perch behind the carriage. They were bruised and their livery was torn and filthy, but that was the worst of their sufferings.

Marchmont carried Zoe back to the house in his arms. One of the footmen tried to carry Jarvis, but she wouldn't have any part of it, instead limping after her master and mistress, umbrella tightly clutched in her hand.

Bystanders helped carry the coachman back to the duke's coach house on a litter.

Some of the blood Marchmont had seen was the coachman's, apparently.

But most of it must have been the horses', given what the servants told him later.

It took a while to sort things out.

There were witnesses, as there usually are, but everyone told a different story, and all told it at the same time. In any case, Marchmont refused to wait about to listen.

John Coachman had had the best view of events. He was in no condition to be interrogated, though, even had Marchmont wished to question him. He didn't. He left his servant in the physician's care, waiting only to be sure the man was not fatally injured.

Then he returned to Zoe, whom he'd carried up to his bedroom.

He wouldn't have left her, even to see about the coachman, but she'd assured him she was unhurt—and she wanted to bathe.

By the time he returned, she was clean and dressed in one of her pretty nightdresses, sitting up in his bed, propped up by a brace of pillows. If she hadn't sat there so quietly—too quietly for Zoe—wearing a small furrow between her brows, he might have believed the accident had not disturbed her in the least.

He went to the bed, sat down on the edge, and took her hand.

"It's no use," she said. "I really don't know what happened. It's a great jumble in my head. I know Jarvis was talking about Almack's, but I was looking the other way. Before I turned, I heard noise—shouting and screaming—and then . . ." She frowned. "But I don't know what came next. One moment all was well. Jarvis was speaking. Then there was a dreadful noise." She considered. "Did I think it was a riot? No, it was the horses. It was like Grafton Street. The cry they made because they were frightened and hurt. Then there was a great thump . . . I think. The next thing I knew, I was looking up at the carriage door and there you were, looking down at me. And I thought it was so curious that the carriage door should be up there and you should be looking down at me." She shook her head. "I am useless. You had better ask Jarvis. She saw something."

He looked at the maid, who was fussing over the tea tray she'd carried up herself.

"Jarvis, can you enlighten us?"

She frowned as she placed the tray on Zoe's lap.

She looked from Zoe to Marchmont and back again.

"Tell him," Zoe said. "Whatever you saw, tell him."

"If the coachman was derelict, I want to know," Marchmont said tightly.

"Your Grace, I don't think he was," she said. "I was looking out of the window, and there was Almack's, and I said, 'Your Grace, that's Almack's,' because I wasn't sure my mistress knew where it was. Then I saw a man run out from Cleveland Yard straight into our path. I screamed, because I thought we'd run him down. When the horses started jumping in the air and making such a noise, I thought that's what happened: They'd trampled him or he'd got under the wheels or something. But that's as much as I thought, because the next thing I knew, we were going over—and I don't remember much of that. I know I grabbed for my mistress. All I could think was she would hit her head. I d-didn't want her to hit her h-head."

And then, to everyone's amazement, the stolid Jarvis burst into tears.

Late that afternoon

Marchmont having sent word to Lexham House, Zoe's mother came to look in on her.

The duke returned to his study. During the crisis, his solicitor had carried on without him. Evidently, Marchmont's directions were clear enough, because Cleake had narrowed down the selection to half a dozen charities.

The last thing Marchmont wanted to do at present was to find positions for untrustworthy minions. However, he'd played Solomon, and had to carry through his decision.

"Cook to the orphanage," he said. "Dove to the home for aged and infirm soldiers. And Hoare to the school for the blind."

Leaving Osgood and Cleake to make the arrangements, he proceeded to the coachman's quarters at the coach house.

John Coachman had a broken collarbone and a sprained wrist and many bruises. He was not happy about being immobilized, and furious about the accident, his first since he'd entered the duke's service.

"Your Grace, I never in all my time seen anything like it," he said. "Like a madman he was—running out of the yard into the street and attacking the poor creature."

"Attacking?" Marchmont said. "He went after the horse?"

"He had something in his hand, Your Grace. Didn't know what it was then, but it's clear it had to be a knife. What I knew was, he was making for the horse, and meant trouble. I went for him with the whip, the bastard, and took a strip off him, I'll warrant. He howled at it. I heard him howl. But I wasn't quick enough, sir." With his good hand, the coachman wiped a tear from his eye. "I reckon they had to put down the near side grey, did they, Your Grace? The one he was bent on killing? They took me away before I could look at the poor beast—either of 'em."

"The second coachman and the others will do what's necessary," Marchmont said. If the horse—or both—had to be destroyed, that would have been done promptly. "They are only waiting for me to leave before they speak to you."

"Those fine cattle, sir," the coachman said. He swallowed and went on more gruffly, "The sweetest-natured beasts. For Her Grace. I said she must have the sweetest, prettiest pair in the stables."

"So she must," Marchmont said. "Let's hope they survive. But whether they do or don't, we must get to the bottom of this. You say a man ran out of Cleveland Yard and straight at the horse and attacked it—he attacked the *horse*?"

"Oh, he did, Your Grace. I went for him, but he stuck her. Poor, innocent creature that never did him nor anybody any harm. We was going so slow she never had a chance. That bastard—begging Your Grace's pardon. If I ever get my hands on 'im—"

"Did you see his face?"

The coachman's expression became grim, indeed. "I saw. I won't forget it in a hurry. He tried to cover it up—burnt cork or some such. And he'd got some cloth wrapped about his head, like a turban, but he weren't no more Turk than I am. You ask Joseph and Hubert, Your Grace. They must have seen him, and they'd know him better than I do, seeing him every day."

"Seeing whom?" Marchmont said. He knew the answer already but didn't want to know it, didn't want to believe it.

"Harrison, sir. I'd stake my life that's who it was. And I'll stake him, too, only let me get a chance."

Sixteen

That night

Despite her travails of the day, the Duchess of Marchmont, resplendent in a ball gown of Clarence blue and white, appeared at Almack's Wednesday-night assembly with her husband.

The scene of the crime was the last place Marchmont would have chosen. But this was where Zoe wanted to be.

"If I keep away, the place will become too important in my mind, and I'll always be afraid of it," she'd told him. "Better to go right away, the same day, before it can take hold of my mind. And what's the likelihood of someone trying to do exactly the same crime in the same place twice? Besides, I have a beautiful gown, special for my first time at Almack's. And I want to dance."

"Oh, a special gown," he said. "Well, that settles it, then."

He was a great, besotted idiot, and he gave in, though he wasn't settled at all.

Still, he'd done all he could. He'd gone to Bow Street and spoken to the chief magistrate, Sir Nathaniel Conant. Tomorrow's news sheets and journals would carry descriptions of both Mrs. Dunstan and Harrison. Even now, Bow Street Runners and metropolitan patrollers were looking for them. If the two servants were still in London—which the runners seemed to think unlikely—they'd soon find them. If the pair had done the intelligent thing and fled, they'd be found eventually. Marchmont had offered large rewards for their capture, jointly or separately.

He didn't care about Mrs. Dunstan—unless she'd aided Harrison in this attack—but he wanted to see Harrison hang.

Though it was a short, easy walk to Almack's from Marchmont House, they'd driven in Marchmont's sturdiest carriage, with guards discreetly accompanying them.

He and Zoe arrived at the club without mishap, and when he saw everyone's head turn toward his wife, and the admiration and envy in those gazes, his heart swelled with pride.

Mine, he thought. The finest female in the place, and she was his.

She did look splendid in the gown, though the blue satin bodice, as usual, showed a good deal more of her bosom than he deemed necessary—enough, he suspected, to constitute a threat to public order. But it was the fashion, and he was the most fashionable husband in London, and so he must not break any fellows' noses for looking where she was so flagrantly inviting them to look.

After greeting the hostesses and making the few introductions still necessary—for the Countess Lieven and Mrs. Drummond-Burrell had not yet formally met Zoe—Marchmont said, "I must apologize for the little contretemps this morning, ladies. My wife had been told repeatedly that it was next to impossible to be admitted to Almack's. I never dreamed she'd try to *break* in."

The witticism quickly made its way through the assembly.

The runaway carriage had suffered far greater damage than it caused. It had scraped a bollard and damaged a fence and nicked some brickwork. Had the accident happened later in the day, when the street was busier, the damage and injuries would have been considerable. At present, the worst he and Zoe had to deal with was the talk. It seemed as though the gossips and newspapers had hardly finished with one matter related to Zoe than another came along to tantalize them.

She would be plastered in all the print shop windows by tomorrow, he had no doubt. But the notoriety that would have brought social ostracism to the Harem Girl merely made the Duchess of Marchmont interesting.

"How brave you were to come out this night," Lady Jersey told her. "The excitement would have prostrated me. I should have kept to my bed for a fortnight."

"If I could not leave my bed for two weeks, I would

have to try a variety of positions," said Zoe. "Prostrate is all very well, but Marchmont would find it boring, night after night—or day after day."

He whisked Zoe away, leaving Sally Jersey and her associates to debate whether the Duchess of Marchmont had actually said what they thought she'd said.

"That was droll, what you said about my breaking in," Zoe told him.

"You're going to attract enough of a crowd as it is," he said. "By tomorrow, everyone will know the lurid details, and I shall have the most popular wife in all of London. I thought a little humor this evening would give us some respite. Tomorrow the melodrama begins, I daresay."

By tomorrow, everyone would know that the accident wasn't an accident and an attempt had been made on the Duchess of Marchmont's life. He'd kept the fraud quiet, but that would get out eventually, and so the circus would continue.

Tonight, though, most people knew only that there had been an accident. A few stories circulated about an anonymous madman attacking the duke's horses. A madman had killed Spencer Perceval almost exactly six years ago and another had tried to kill Lord Palmerston, the secretary of war, a month ago. One constantly read of murders attempted and committed by madmen.

Generally speaking, though—and with the notable exception of Lady Sophronia de Grey—the patronesses excluded lunatics from their list.

Tonight, all was well, and Zoe could flash her great lighthouse beacon of a diamond and dance to her heart's content. She was alive, beautifully and fully alive, teasing his friends and astonishing the ladies, and living the life she'd wanted.

Late Wednesday night

Harrison was a London servant, born and bred. He knew every inch of the metropolis: the high, the middling, and the low. He'd made a great many friends among certain types of tradesmen and publicans. He had no trouble finding lodgings within easy walking distance of Marchmont House.

They were only temporary, he'd assured Mary Dunstan. As soon as he'd collected the money he'd secreted in various places, they would go to Ireland and start fresh. They had planned to become innkeepers in London. They would simply change locations, Harrison assured her.

On Wednesday evening, though, when he came back to the lodgings, and Mary Dunstan asked him if he'd got all the money, he said, "We want something better than money, my dear."

Then he told her what he'd done that morning: how he'd lurked in the mews and learned the duke's coach was setting out for Lexham House.

"I knew the route they'd take," he said. "Don't I know the routes they always take, wherever they mean to go? Don't I always know everything? Isn't it my job to know everything, even before it happens? I knew what would happen before it happened this morning. I knew it and I was ready, waiting for her when they turned into King Street."

He'd been waiting, knife in hand—one of several

he'd taken from the kitchen before he ran away. It was a beautiful knife, and Mary didn't blame him for taking it. She'd taken things, too.

But it was to be for their inn, for the cooking.

It wasn't for what he'd used it for.

She couldn't believe her ears when he told her. He was drunk. She tried to make herself believe he was simply drunk and boasting. But what man boasts of such things?

"I couldn't hang about to see the smash-up," he said. "That's the devil of hiring the best. John Coachman saw what I was about, and I got a taste of his whip. The horses panicked and the carriage went amok and overturned, for all his care, but it wasn't as I pictured. No time to wait about to tally the damage. I thought she'd get the worst of it, but no. It was the horses and the coachman, curse her."

He found a bottle and opened it. He filled his glass and drank, and stared at her. He slammed the glass on the table, and she jumped.

"Don't look at me like that!"

"I was only wondering whether you had time to arrange for the post chaise," she said composedly.

Mary Dunstan had had years of practice acting calm no matter how she felt. A housekeeper always had to appear to be in complete control of everything. Other servants must never believe they could rattle her. She must always be as steady as a rock. She must always be sure of herself. Those beneath her must look upon her as omniscient and omnipotent, a version of the house steward, lower in status but equally formidable. Those above her must be able to take her competence completely for granted.

"What post chaise?" he said.

"The one to take us to the boat that will carry us to Ireland," she said.

"Ireland." His lip curled. "Savages. Bog trotters."

"We can't remain in London," she said.

"No, we can't," he said. "Everything's ruined because of her. No London inn for us, thanks to her. No future here. No future anywhere. No *future*."

"If you don't like Ireland, we can go to France," Mary said calmly. "The English appreciate a proper English hostelry there. Good food and drink and clean, dry linens and spotless floors."

He wasn't listening. He drank some more. "Ruined," he said. "Twenty years climbing to the top. And then, all at once, there am I, on the bottom." He snapped his fingers. "Like this she knocked me down. And I'll knock her down. I'll finish her, I will, like this"—another snap—"I'll finish her, because she finished me."

He went on ranting and drinking, and Mary Dunstan pretended to listen calmly. But she was a paragon among housekeepers, and a good housekeeper saw ahead. It didn't take much looking to determine what she must do.

Saturday

It didn't take Marchmont long to replace nearly all of the upper servants. Everyone and their grandmothers, he found, wanted to work at Marchmont House.

And this time, determined to Take Responsibility, he interviewed everyone and their grandmothers. Or so it seemed. Scores of applicants came from an agency. Scores more received word of the vacancies via the servant gossip grapevine, and came on their own initiative. Osgood proposed some candidates, as did Cleake and Zoe's sisters and sisters-in-law.

Sorting them out was tedious. It would have been unbearably so, had Marchmont done it alone. But Zoe was there, taking notes and occasionally asking a question. Mainly she left it to him until they were alone. Then she had a great deal to say, some of it hilarious, and some stunningly perceptive. Their one major dispute was about the butler. In the end, they agreed to keep Thomas in that position.

Since none of the house steward candidates satisfied them, the position remained unfilled for the time being. The household operated relatively smoothly in spite of the vacancy. Not as smoothly as it had under Harrison's despotic reign, but nothing like the chaos Marchmont had dreaded. He'd imagined servants pestering him constantly, asking questions he didn't know the answers to.

Evidently, they pestered Thomas and Osgood instead.

With their world restored to something like order, the duke and duchess were preparing to go out to a rout when Marchmont received a message from Bow Street: Mrs. Dunstan had been caught and was in custody.

Ten minutes later

Being well aware that Marchmont was protective to an extreme, Zoe wasn't at all surprised when he told her she was not going with him.

She had no objection to being protected by a big, strong man when the occasion called for it. A woman in jail, however, could do her no harm. There was no rational reason for him to leave Zoe behind—and she had no intention of encouraging him to be irrational.

"There's no need for you to upset yourself," he said as she followed him into his dressing room.

"I will not interfere," she said. "This is your business. I only want to hear what she has to say."

"I'll tell you what she has to say."

"I want to see her face."

"I'll describe it."

She shooed away Ebdon, his new valet.

"I don't want to be kept in a cocoon," she said when she and Marchmont were alone.

"With any luck, I'll be back in plenty of time to dress for the rout. There's nothing cocoon-like about going to a rout. You'll be surrounded by people. You'll have no protection from their elbows and feet and perfumes or lack of bathing."

"If I'm present, the housekeeper might be more forthcoming," she said. She advanced to help him out of his coat. "She might say more than she would when only men are present."

"I don't deny you might be helpful," he said. "You were immensely helpful in hiring new servants. You were especially helpful in finding me a valet who doesn't cry and faint. He is shockingly calm. I am not sure he breathes."

"Only in the discreetest way," said Zoe.

"He doesn't blink, certainly. But a valet is one thing and a lot of constables and lawbreakers is quite another. The Bow Street magistrate's house is no place for a lady."

"I know," she said. "The place will be filled with drunkards and prostitutes and pimps and thieves and murderers. Just like Yusri Pasha's palace. Sometimes they made us watch when others were punished. I saw them strangle a slave girl, and I've seen slaves whipped many times. I know how they make a eunuch. What do you think I'll see at Bow Street to shock me?"

"That isn't the point," he said. "Merely because you once lived among unspeakable people doing unspeakable things doesn't make it right for you to spend your time among the dregs of London. The point is, you're the Duchess of Marchmont, and she doesn't frequent low places."

Having peeled off the snug coat, she started unbuttoning his waistcoat.

"You're the Duke of Marchmont, and you mean to frequent this place," she said.

"I'm a man."

Oh, I know, she thought. The waistcoat undone, she let her hand stray over the front of his shirt. "A big, powerful man," she said. "With big hard muscles and a godlike instrument of delight."

"Flattery will get you nowhere," he said.

"I'll be safe with you," she said. "Who would dare to trouble me when you're by my side? Even at Almack's, everyone was amiable to me for your sake." She let her hand slide over his muscled chest. She felt the heat begin, low in her belly, the snake of desire stirring.

"No time for that," he said gruffly. As her hand slid downward, he gently lifted it away. "Everyone was amiable for your sake, Zoe, not mine. Because you're pretty and amusing—and because they were worried that if they weren't amiable, you'd hit them with that great diamond of yours and break their skulls."

She smiled up at him. If he was making a joke, he was calming, and he would take her with him.

"I see what will happen," he said. "You'll fondle and flatter and smile me into it. I might as well admit defeat, instead of wasting time fighting you. But you'd better run along—and dress quickly, because I will not wait one extra minute for you."

She reached up and grabbed his neckcloth, and pulled his face toward hers and kissed him hard. He was turning into a far better husband than she'd dared to hope for. He was not the shallow, capricious man she'd believed him to be. He was truly kind and truly caring . . . and she was afraid she was falling quite hopelessly in love with him.

Two hours later

The Bow Street Office stood a short distance from the Covent Garden Opera House, and on the same side of the street.

Zoe and Marchmont were able to bypass the busy courtroom at No. 3—where, Zoe supposed, the thieves and prostitutes and pimps and drunkards were gathered at present. This was because Mrs. Dunstan was being kept in a room in No. 4, the house adjoining. Here, among other things, Bow Street held its prisoners.

The housekeeper had been taken to a room separate from the felons' room, in consideration of Marchmont, who'd asked to interview her privately. Otherwise she would have been shackled in the one room with all the other prisoners, Zoe learned.

A Runner had caught Mrs. Dunstan before she could board a Dover packet, bound for Calais.

She had not been cooperative, the Runner explained before Zoe and Marchmont entered the room. The housekeeper insisted she didn't know where Harrison was. She had not been involved with him in any way, she said. She had left the duke's house in a temper, she claimed, because the new mistress had questioned her methods. She refused to hang about, she said, and be accused of incompetence, and have her authority undermined in front of the rest of the staff.

"That's her story, Your Grace," said the Runner. "Doesn't matter how we ask or what we ask. It's always the same."

When Zoe and Marchmont entered, they found Mrs. Dunstan seated stiffly upright upon a bench against a wall. Though the room was dimly lit, Zoe saw her eyes blaze at their entrance. She didn't need to see it. The woman radiated hostility. But she was impotent, her ankles chained.

"Oh, Your Grace has come, have you?" she said. "You and she, to see me like this, in chains, like a common thief."

"I should say, madam, on the contrary, that you are a most *uncommon* sort of thief," Marchmont drawled. "I should say you are a genius among felons. Your aptitude with figures is a true marvel of sleight of hand."

This small show of bored arrogance instantly lit a very short fuse.

"What did you ever have to complain of us?" she burst out. "We did our work. There's no better-kept house in all of London. Everyone said so."

The officer attempted to intervene, but Marchmont held up his hand. "Let her have her say," he said.

"Oh, I'll say, all right," she spat out. "Not one of all those servants in that great house ever gave you any trouble at all, did they, Your Grace? But you don't know what a trouble it was to us, to keep it that way. Everything always done for you. Like magic, wasn't it? It was the best-run house in London, in all of England—and you had to bring her in and spoil it."

She shot Zoe a murderous look before reverting to Marchmont. "What did we ever do that harmed you? We had a right to our perquisites and more, for all we did and how well we did it. When did you ever need to take any notice of the running of the house, Your Grace? When didn't the windows sparkle and the floors shine? When was the sheets ever dirty or damp or the fires not lit when wanted? When was the dinner not laid exactly to the minute, whether you and your guests sat down on time or half an hour late? When was it ever cold or overcooked? When did you ever have to ask, 'Why wasn't this done?' When did you ever have to ask for anything? Wasn't it always as you wanted, before you even knew you wanted it? What was so wrong that *she* must come in and start looking for a fault? Why did she ever go looking in those books but because she couldn't find any fault anywhere else?"

"Yet such a great fault there turned out to be, in those books," Marchmont said. "And there, you see, is the nub of the matter: theft and fraud, fraud and theft. So unnecessary. You might have asked for an astronomical salary, and I'd have paid, without question—because what did I care? Instead, you made a great deal of unnecessary work for yourselves with your clever conspiracy. I would have paid you as much as you stole and cheated me of, and I'd never have noticed or cared what it cost. But no, you must commit forgery and fraud and theft and make it a hanging matter, you foolish woman."

"I won't hang! I did nothing wrong!"

"You disappeared at the same time Harrison did," Marchmont said. "Why didn't you two simply go abroad? It's easily enough done. If Brummell could sneak away unnoticed, with that famous face and physique, surely you could. But no, you must hang about and plot with Harrison to attack my horses. For what? Spite?"

"I never did that!"

"John Coachman and two of our footmen saw Harrison take a knife to one of my horses," said Marchmont.

"I had nothing to do with that!"

"You and Harrison fled my house at the same time," Marchmont said. "You didn't warn the other servants. They all stayed. One can only conclude that you and Harrison were in communication and still are. One can only conclude that you aided and abetted a violent attack."

"I never did! If I'd known what he was about, I

would never have stayed with him. I'd have run to Dover before today, and your dirty Runners wouldn't have caught me."

"But you did stay in London for a time. With Harrison."

She realized, too late, what she'd revealed. She bowed her head and pressed her fist to her mouth.

"I don't care about you," Marchmont said. "I should be very sorry to see you hang simply because you were silly. But if you'd anything to do with what I'm bound to see as an attempt on my wife's life—"

"It wasn't me!" she cried. "I didn't know until he came back and told me."

"He came back and told you," Marchmont repeated quietly.

"I didn't want to stay in London, but he said we had to. He had to get the money we'd put aside."

"My money," Marchmont said with a thin smile.

"We were going to become innkeepers," she said. "When he went out, I thought it was to do with the money, and making arrangements. But it wasn't, was it?"

"He was watching us," Marchmont said. "Watching where we went and what we did. He was waiting for his chance."

She nodded. "He told me afterward, and it was then I knew he must be out of his senses. He always had a temper, but I never knew him to do violence. He never needed to. No one dared to sauce him or cross him. He'd gone wrong in the head, that was clear. But I had to wait, because I feared he'd try to kill me if I left him, knowing what I knew."

She told them how Harrison had regretted not being able to stay to watch.

Zoe saw Marchmont's hands clench, but he unclenched them immediately. His countenance told nothing, as usual, except to her. He wore his customary, sleepily bored expression. He controlled himself as he always did. He hid his feelings as he always did.

"The way he talked—it wasn't like him," the housekeeper went on. "I didn't see until then how bad it was with him."

The housekeeper went on to describe a degree of vengefulness others might have found shocking. Zoe wasn't shocked. She'd seen worse cases than this, murderous rages and vendettas over trivial matters: a hair comb, a bracelet.

Harrison had devoted twenty years to climbing a ladder of power. Then, when he thought himself securely at the top, she had come along. In a matter of days, he'd fallen off—and this time there could be no climbing back.

Mrs. Dunstan snapped her fingers, drawing Zoe's attention back to her. "That's what he did, again and again," the housekeeper said. "Snapped his fingers. 'Like this she knocked me down,' he said. 'And I'll knock her down. I'll finish her, I will, like this.' He snapped his fingers and 'I'll finish her,' he said, 'because she finished me.' He drank and talked mad like that and finally he drank himself senseless. He fell onto the bed, dead to the world. Then I packed up and ran."

"But he's still here?" Marchmont said. "In London?"

"He knows where to hide," Mrs. Dunstan said. "No one knows London like he does, and no one has the kinds of friends he has. He can hide right under

your nose and you'll never know. He knows everything, doesn't he? Knows what you're going to do
before you do it. A proper servant, he is. And like a
proper one, he'll find a way to do it, whatever it is."

Since Mrs. Dunstan could tell them only where Harrison had stayed last, there was nothing more for
Marchmont to ask her. Zoe had nothing to add. He'd
done a fine job of provoking the woman to reveal
what she knew.

She told him so when they were back in the carriage and on their way home.

"She was right, you know," he said. He looked out
of the carriage window into the lamplit streets, where
the pedestrians were merely anonymous dark figures,
hurrying along the pavement. "It was a wonderfully
well-run house. They did their jobs brilliantly. I took
them completely for granted."

"But that's the way it ought to be with good servants," Zoe said.

"I understand that," he said. "But I know, too, that
had I paid the slightest attention—taken an interest, however cursory—none of this would have happened."

"You can't know that," she said. "Some people
are simply dishonest. Many are corrupted by power.
Harrison was no lord, but in his world, he wielded
great power."

"If he was corrupt, I should have been the one to
discover it," he said tightly. "Because I didn't, I endangered your life."

"That's illogical," she said. They were sharing the
carriage seat. She drew nearer to him and took his
hand. "You're a clever man—much cleverer than you

let on—but your logic isn't good. If he's gone mad, then his mind has become diseased. That's no more your fault than the state of any wretch in Bedlam. If he hasn't gone mad, then he's evil. You didn't make him evil. You didn't corrupt him. That was the path he took. For the upper-level staff he hired the kinds of people he could corrupt. For the lower levels, he chose the kind he could bully." She twined her fingers with his. "I told you I could manage a household. With the troublemaker gone, all will be well."

"Nothing will be well until I see that man hang," he said.

"The Bow Street Runners will find him," she said. "You're the Duke of Marchmont, and you've offered a large reward. They'll ignore every other task in order to hunt him down. These are men who know London, you said. They must know it as well or better than Harrison does. It's their business to know it. Finding people is their livelihood. He won't get away."

"No, he won't." His grip on her hand tightened. "I don't care what it costs. I've doubled the reward. I'll triple it if I have to."

"They'll find him," Zoe said. "Leave it to them. We'll go to Lady Stafford's rout and count how many people step on our feet and how many elbows stick into our ribs. Shall I wear the lilac gown or the blue?"

"We're not going to the rout," he said. "We're going home and you are not leaving the house until that man is in custody."

Seventeen

For a moment, Zoe couldn't form a thought, let alone speak. It was as though she'd plunged into a deep, cold well.

To be trapped in a house for who knew how long, after she'd only begun to taste freedom, and while everyone else about her was free—when she wouldn't have even the companionship, such as it was, and the amusements, such as they were, of the harem . . .

Her heart was racing, and her mind raced, too, pointlessly.

All the past rushed at her in an icy wave of panic—the moment they'd taken her away in the bazaar . . . the voices speaking a language she couldn't understand . . . the darkness . . . the men touching her . . . she, screaming for her father, until they gagged her . . . the drink they'd forced down her throat that brought strange dreams but never complete oblivion . . . the slaves stripping off her clothes—

She shook it off and made herself stare out of the window and breathe, slowly. This was England. She was in London, with her husband. She was safe, and all he wanted was to keep her safe.

He was upset, she reminded herself. When men were upset, their instincts took over, and their instincts were not always rational. Even she was disturbed by what had happened, though the danger was nothing to what she'd lived with day after day and night after night in the harem.

She made herself answer calmly. "I know you wish to protect me, but this isn't reasonable."

"Harrison isn't reasonable," Marchmont said. "We're dealing with a man who's either deranged or evil. You said so yourself. He thought nothing of brutally attacking a dumb animal. He didn't care what a creature maddened with pain would do. He didn't care who else might have been injured when the horses panicked. There's no predicting what he'll do."

"There's no predicting how long it will take to find him," she said. "It could be days or even weeks. What if he comes to his senses and runs away from London, as he should have done? What if he falls into the Thames and drowns? His body might never be found. You'd make me a prisoner in Marchmont House indefinitely?"

"I am not making you a prisoner," he said. "I'm making sure he can't get at you."

"It's prison to me," she said. "You ought to understand this. I thought you did. I was kept caged for twelve years. I lived in a vast house, larger than yours—a great palace with a great, walled garden. A prison is a prison, no matter how big or how beautiful."

"It's not the same."

"It's the same to me," she said. "I can't abide to be confined."

"And I can't abide risking your life," he said. "Until we know he's in custody or dead or abroad, you'll stay home. You said the Runners would find him. You said they had every reason to do so. You were the one reassuring me about this. Reassure yourself."

"You cannot keep me in the house," she said.

"I can and will. Don't be childish, Zoe. This is for your own good."

"Childish?" she said. "*Childish?* I risked my life to be free. You don't know what they would have done to me if they had caught me. I risked my life for this." She waved her hand at the window, where the shadowy figures hurried along the pavement, and riders and carriages passed in the busy street. "I risked everything to be in a world where women can go out of their houses to shop and visit their friends, where they can even talk to and dance with other men. For twelve years I dreamed of this world, and it came to be my idea of heaven: a place where I could move freely among other people, where I could go to the theater and the ballet and the opera. For twelve years I was an amusing pet in a cage. For twelve years they let me out only for the entertainment of watching me try to run away. Now I have my own horse, and I can ride in Hyde Park—"

"Only listen to what you're saying," he said. "Everything you want to do will expose you. Hyde Park is completely out of the question."

"You can't do this," she said. "I won't be locked up. I won't hide from that horrible man. He's a bully, and this is bullying, and you're letting him do it. You're letting him make the rules, because you're afraid of what he'll do."

"He's not making any rules, Zoe! *I'm* making the rules. You're my wife, and on the day we wed, I promised to look after you—and you promised to *obey*."

She started to retort, but paused.

She knew that keeping his word was a strict point of honor to him.

Everyone knows that he regards his word as sacred, Papa had said.

When she had promised to obey, she'd given her word, too. To fail to keep her word to him would be dishonorable, a betrayal of trust.

"I did promise," she said. "And I shall obey."

They traveled in silence the rest of the way home. All the while Marchmont's gut churned.

He heard it over and over: the snap of the housekeeper's fingers, and the words she'd repeated.

I'll finish her, I will, like this.

The words echoed in his mind as they entered Marchmont House and crossed the marble entrance hall.

He heard them as he and Zoe climbed the stairs.

He was aware—oh, very well aware—of his wife walking alongside him with all the light and life gone out of her, and he knew he'd killed her happiness and humor and delicious insouciance.

He told himself she was making too much of it. The trouble was, he knew why she made so much of it.

Her freedom was precious to her, far more precious than it was to other Englishwomen, who simply took it for granted, the way he'd taken his servants and his smoothly running household for granted.

He remembered what she'd said that first day, after she'd proposed to him and he'd declined.

I was married from the time I was twelve years old, and it seemed a very long time, and I would rather not be married again straightaway.

Yet she had married again, straightaway, because he'd lacked the will to resist temptation.

She'd never had a chance to be courted by other men.

She'd never had a chance to decide for herself which of them she truly wanted.

He'd wanted her, and he'd had to have her, and that was that.

Still, he'd hardly condemned her to a life of misery. Being married to him offered more freedom than most other women had, including other aristocratic women. No doors were closed to the Duchess of Marchmont. She would never lack for money to buy whatever she wanted. She could still flirt with other men and dance with them.

And she could go where she pleased, to a point.

Until tonight.

I want fun, she'd told him that day in Hyde Park after she'd raced with Lady Tarling. *I want a life. In Egypt I was a toy, a game. I was a pet in a cage. I vowed never to endure such an existence again.*

He watched her enter her apartments, then he walked on to his.

He told Ebdon he would not be going out this evening, and ordered a bath. The odor of Bow Street seemed to cling to his skin as well as his clothes.

The bath should have calmed him. It didn't.

The new valet had laid out a clean shirt, pantaloons, and stockings. The duke stood and gazed at them for a long time. He felt so weary, suddenly, not in his body but in his mind and heart, as though he'd carried a great burden, inside, for an endless time.

"Give me my dressing gown," he said.

He didn't bother with the clothes readied for him, to be worn under his damask dressing gown: the full costume of "undress." He shrugged his naked body into his dressing gown and slid his bare feet into his slippers. The maroon leather mules had pointed, upturned toes, in imitation of Turkish fashion.

Like a pasha's. Like the men in another world, who kept their women caged.

"Plague take me," he said.

"Your Grace?" Ebdon was obviously baffled. He bore his confusion like a man, however. No weeping or fainting or trembling. Merely a slight crease between his brows.

"I'll be back in a minute," Marchmont said.

He left the dressing room, crossed his bedroom to the connecting door, and walked in.

He found his wife in her bath, her face on her arm, resting on the linens draping the tub. She was weeping.

"Oh, Zoe," he said.

She'd been so lost in misery that she hadn't heard him approach—another bad sign. She was losing her old skills. She didn't care. She was too wretched to care. She loved him, and she wanted to be a good wife. She knew he only wanted to protect her—but she couldn't bear this, to have the walls close in on her again, so soon.

She wiped her eyes and looked up at him. "I'm sorry," she said. "I know it's mad to feel this way, but I can't help it."

He simply reached down and lifted her up, out of the bathtub. He grabbed a towel and wrapped it about her, then he wrapped his arms around her and pulled her close. He buried his face in her damp hair.

"You're all I have left," he said. "You're all I have left."

His voice was hoarse, broken.

"Lucien," she said, her face against his chest.

"You're all I have left, Zoe," he said. "They're all gone—everyone I ever loved. Gone forever. You, too, I thought. But you weren't. You came back from the dead—and if I lose you, I don't know what I'll do."

She held him tightly, as tightly as she could.

His parents. His brother. Gone.

He'd had her family, but it wasn't the same.

Everyone I ever loved.

You, too, I thought.

She was one of them, one of the loved.

Loved. He loved her.

It was as simple as that.

Her heart lifted, the way it always used to do when she caught sight of him, when Lucien came back from school to spend the summer with them. When he came, her world brightened.

"Lucien," she said softly. She had learned Latin and

Greek, and she knew *lux* was the Latin for "light." Her heart lifted, because he was the light of her life and had been from the first day she met him. "Oh, Lucien, we're both a little mad."

"No," he muttered into her hair. "You're the mad one. I'm completely sane." He lifted his head and drew away a little and looked down at her. "Let's get you out of that wet towel."

He got her out of the wet towel and dried her off with another one, in front of the fire.

He played lady's maid, kneeling before her, the towel in his hand. He lifted one slim foot onto his thigh and gently dried it, and she shivered.

He looked up, and there she was, all creamy skin with touches of pink in the special places, and a dusting of gold between her legs. She was all curving womanliness, and she was looking down at him, her blue eyes filled with something he couldn't put a name to. How could he, when he'd never troubled to read a woman's gaze?

In her case, perhaps, he didn't need to. Perhaps, after all, they simply understood each other. Perhaps they always had.

He slid his hands up from her foot, up along her calf to her knee and along her thigh, and up, to the downy place she had so many names for.

"Your Golden Flower," he murmured, lightly drawing his hand over the feathery curls, still damp after her bath. "Your Palace Of Delight."

"My Secret Abode," she said. She slid her fingers into his hair. "My Hidden Treasure and my Throne of Love and my Lion's Head."

"Your Lion's Head?" He caressed her so lightly.

She made names for the caresses, too: the Teasing Feather and the Gentle Glove and the Fire Touch.

"Oh, yes," she said. "This part of me is very dangerous when hungry for lovemaking."

She combed his hair with her fingers. "My lover's hair is like silken candlelight," she said softly. "My lover is the candlelight in the night and the first rays of the sun on the horizon and the last rays, too. My lover is my light."

He looked up, his gaze locking with hers. "I had better be this lover you're talking about," he said.

She laughed and let go of him. She stretched her arms above her head, stretched like a cat, and he watched her beautiful breasts lift. She was completely at ease in her body, in her nakedness.

How could he think of stifling a soul so free?

"My lover leaps upon me, like a tiger," she said.

He caught hold of her buttocks and pressed his mouth to her Hidden Treasure, and he felt her tremble.

He caressed her with his mouth and his tongue and felt her fingers tighten in his hair while her body vibrated with pleasure.

Then, after he'd driven her to the peak and made her cry out, he slid his arm behind her knees and brought her down.

Her eyes were dark and unfocused, her face flushed.

She gave way to passion in that unhesitating, liquid way of hers. She caught his mood—or he caught hers—and simply yielded to feeling.

Tonight the feeling was stormy.

She sat on the rug and opened her legs, and he

crawled between them. She pushed open his dressing gown and raked her hands over his skin, and it was his turn to tremble while she explored him, running her fingers over muscles that bunched under her touch. She explored him as though he was new to her, a lover she'd never seen before . . . and yet as though, too, she knew him as well as she knew herself, and knew he belonged to her.

From the first she'd been this way, unhesitating, as easy with his body as she was with her own.

But there was more between them tonight than simple possession.

You're all I have left.

There it was, the thing buried in the deepest recess of the hidden place in his heart, in the dark cupboard he hadn't been able to keep shut since the day she returned. He'd uttered the words, and they still beat in his heart.

She was all he had left, and she was precious to him.

He raked his hands over her, too, in the same way she touched him. He moved his hands over her skin, over her firm breasts and along the delicate angles of her collarbone. He traced the circle of her waist and the swell of her hips, the fine bones of her wrists and ankles, and she stretched and moved under his touch, the restless tigress tonight.

He caught hold of her hair with one hand and grasped her chin with the other and kissed her hard. She broke away, and made as if to pull away. He pulled her back, and she let her head fall back, and she was laughing, in that way she did, low and beckoning. He pushed her thighs apart, and thrust into her, and she laughed again, and wrapped her legs about his waist.

We're both a little mad, she'd said, and perhaps they were.

They joined this night in a maddened way, in a long, ferocious coupling, as though there was no more time left, as though this was the first time and the last time.

That, at least, was what he thought of it later.

Now, though, while he was inside her, there was nothing in his mind, nothing in the world but her and this moment and the heat and pleasure of the lovers' storm they made.

It raged and quieted and raged again. Then she cried out, again and again, words he didn't understand and one he did: his name. Then he let himself spill into her, and he sank down onto her. He lay there, for a moment, feeling her heart beat against his chest. Then he rolled off her and onto his side. He pulled her up against him and buried his face in her neck.

She lay there, listening to his breathing quiet.

She was dear to him and he was dear to her, and this was what was most important.

Karim had doted upon her and showered her with jewels, but to him she was only a pretty toy. If she had displeased him, he would have given her away—or even had her killed—without a second thought.

"There was no bond," she murmured.

"That was English," he said, "but I couldn't quite make it out." His voice was low, sleepy.

"Never mind," she said. "Sleep."

"How can I sleep at a time like this?" he said.

She turned her head a little, but she couldn't see him. She felt him lift his head, though. He brushed his cheek against hers.

"I thought I understood what had happened to you," he said. "But I understood only a part. When you told your story to John Beardsley, I thought I'd heard all there was to hear. But I think it was all I *wanted* to hear. I didn't want to know any more. When you vanished—"

His voice caught, and he paused. "If I'd been there, Zoe, I'd have found you. I wasn't there. I couldn't bear to think of that. And so I made myself stop. I—I don't know what it was, exactly. But I stopped. Thinking. Caring. It was harder than I let on, to carry on, after Gerard died. When you were gone, perhaps I simply lost heart."

She hadn't realized. All she'd known, when she first saw him after her return, was that he wasn't the same. She hadn't been the only one damaged by her captivity. Her parents had suffered. Her brothers and sisters, too, though perhaps not as deeply, because they were starting families of their own.

"I caused more pain than I knew," she said. "I told my family I was sorry, but I didn't understand what the trouble was. I didn't understand why Mama had grown so nervous and flighty or why my sisters and brothers were so angry with me. They said I made a disruption, and I thought the disruption was my coming back. But the disruption was my disappearing, and the years Papa spent trying to find me, and what happens to a family when they can't know for certain what's become of a loved one."

"But it wasn't your fault," he said. "Everyone knows that now. Everyone knows you didn't run away."

He knew the story itself: the stroll through the Cairo bazaar and the maid who'd sold her—the maid who'd claimed Zoe had run away, and whom everyone had believed, because Zoe was famous for running away.

"As though I were so mad as that," she said, "to run away in a crowded place, where no one spoke my language. But everyone except Papa would believe I would do such a mad thing, because I was the wild daughter, the rebellious one. I'm daring, Lucien, but even at twelve I had some sense."

He kissed the nape of her neck. "Not much, but some," he said.

She smiled.

"I should have got the truth out of that maidservant," he said, "if only I had been there."

"Even if you had got it out of her before they killed her, would that have made a difference?" Zoe said. "Once they had me, do you think they'd give me up? Have you any idea how valuable I was?"

"Yes," he said. "I know how valuable you are."

"I was a rare, rare creature to them," she said. "I learned this later—that I was like one of the magical beings in the *Thousand and One Nights*. The slavers had followed us from Greece. They knew they'd get a lot of money for me: White slaves are valuable—and I wasn't merely a Circassian but an English girl. My coloring was different. Everything about me was different. How many twelve-year-old, blonde, blue-eyed European girls turn up in that part of the world? Especially during that time, when Europe was at war. They knew the pasha would pay a fortune for me, for his sick son. For the magic. The slavers knew Yusri Pasha would believe I would have the power to arouse his favorite son Karim's desires at last, and he would produce sons."

"And none of this would have happened but for an easily corrupted servant," Marchmont said.

"They had all the reason in the world to make it happen, one way or another," Zoe said. "They offered her more money than she could hope to earn in twenty years. If they hadn't got to her, they would have got to someone else in our party. They would have found a way. They were very determined."

"I should have been there," he said.

She turned to him then. "You were seventeen years old. What would you have done that Papa didn't do?"

"I would have found you," he said. "I always found you."

She turned round fully and rested her head in the hollow of his shoulder. His fingers threaded through her hair. "No," she said. "They killed the maid to make sure she'd say nothing. If you had found me, they would have killed you without hesitation. For years, I was terrified that you or my father would burst into the palace and be killed. Even when it became obvious that I was useless—that I couldn't cure Karim and he'd never sire sons—even then they wouldn't have given me back. He was his father's favorite, and I was Karim's favorite toy, and they'd kill anybody who tried to take me away from him. If you'd found me—and they'd killed you, what would I have done, Lucien?"

He said nothing for a time, only kept drawing his fingers through her hair, caressing, soothing.

She lifted her hand and laid it over his heart, and felt its reassuring beat while she lay there, safely snuggled against his big body.

"I worry that you'll be killed in a carriage crash," he said after a long silence. "I worry that you'll fall ill so suddenly, as my parents did, and die. I worry that you'll fall off your horse and break your neck, the way Gerard did. I worry that you'll die in childbed. I try to push these thoughts from my mind—I used to be so good at not thinking. But since the trouble with the servants began, I've become . . ." He paused. "Not Aunt Sophronia—not yet, I hope. But I seem to be not altogether rational."

"All of those things you worry about can happen," she said. "They can happen to me and they can happen to you—except for the childbed part." She grinned up at him. "Unless you die of fright when I grow as gigantic as my sisters."

He moved his head back to look at her. "If you grow as gigantic as they, I shall certainly die of fright."

She pulled away from him to use her hands to draw a big mound over her belly. "The women of my family tend to become as big as houses," she said. "Very round houses."

Though the room was dimly lit, she had no trouble seeing the laughter dance in his eyes.

"You're picturing it," she said.

He nodded. His lips trembled. Then it burst from him: a great whoop of laughter.

He rolled away onto his back and laughed and laughed.

She laughed, too.

This was the boy she'd known so long ago, the boy who'd fallen down laughing when she tried to hit him with a cricket bat.

She remembered how, when he'd finally sobered, he'd stood up and marched to her, and plucked her up off the ground as easily as if she'd been a rag doll. He'd carried her, kicking and hitting and calling him names, back to the house and up to the schoolroom and plunked her into a chair.

"Learn something, you stupid girl," he'd said, and walked out.

And she had learned something: Greek and Latin, because that's what boys learned and she was determined to know what boys knew. She'd learned not only how to do sums but harder kinds of mathematics, like geometry and trigonometry. She did this not because she enjoyed the subjects but because boys learned those things—and she was determined to show *him*. She'd never been the best or most conscientious student. Still she'd learned some things that most girls didn't know: how to hide fear and how to think logically and how to jockey for position and how to be dogged and how to fight when one had to. Such knowledge had helped her survive the harem. It had helped her escape the harem. And it had helped her remove a blight from this great house.

Perhaps, too, what she had learned, in the schoolroom and in the last twelve years, had helped remove a shadow from this man's heart.

When they sobered at last, she sat up and bent over

him and kissed him. "If something bad happens," she said, "we must promise each other to remember all the times like this when we laughed. And until something bad happens, we must enjoy ourselves. We are most fortunate people, Lucien. I am a most fortunate woman, and I mean to enjoy my good fortune as much as I can."

"I should enjoy it better," he said, "had we only the normal concerns of life. A deranged servant out to murder my wife is not a normal concern."

She sat back. "In the harem, there was always somebody wanting to kill somebody," she said. "I heard it was even more dangerous in Constantinople, in the sultan's palace."

"That's why I've become deranged and you haven't," he said. "To me, this is outrageous. To you, it's normal."

"If he were here," she said, "trying to poison my food, or creeping into my room with a knife, I would know what to do."

"You would?" he said.

She nodded.

He thought for a time. Then he climbed out of bed and pulled on his dressing gown.

"Where are you going?" she said.

"To ring for a servant," he said. "All this talk of poisoning reminds me that we haven't dined. I'm famished." He crossed the room and pulled the rope. "And you've given me an idea."

Eighteen

Monday, 11 May

*Everything goes into the newspapers. In other
countries, matters of a public nature may be seen in
them; here, in addition, you see perpetually even the
concerns of individuals. Does a private gentleman
come to town? you hear it in the newspapers; does
he build a house, or buy an estate? they give the information; does he entertain his friends? you have
all their names next day in type; is the drapery of a
lady's drawing-room changed from red damask and
gold to white satin and silver? the fact is publicly
announced.*

The observations the American ambassador,
Mr. Rush, recorded in his diary about the amaz-

ing English press were much the same as those he'd made at dinner on the night he and his wife and a few privileged others had met Lord Lexham's youngest daughter.

And so it was hardly surprising that the amazing English press would report the doings of the Duke and Duchess of Marchmont. Anyone who could read would read in the newspapers that the new duchess had made substantial changes in the household staff and was shortly to embark upon an extensive refurbishment of Marchmont House in St. James's Square.

Anyone who could read would read in the papers that the Duke of Marchmont meant to set out on the following day for Lancashire, on urgent legal business related to one of his properties there.

His Grace's former house steward, Harrison, could read, and did so, while he drank his coffee in the room he'd taken at the Black Horse Inn in Haymarket, immediately after Mary Dunstan's abrupt departure.

" 'Normally, His Grace's agent would act in his place,' " he read aloud as he'd always used to do when he and Mrs. Dunstan breakfasted together. " 'But the matter of these fishing rights has apparently reached a pitch such that his personal attendance is wanted to avert a lawsuit.' Oh, certainly. That's what sends my lord duke out of London at the height of the Season to travel some three hundred miles, to the wilds of Lancashire. Fishing rights, my foot. It's *she*. She's driven him out of his house."

Had Harrison given his temper time to cool, he

could have spared his master the ignominy of running away from his wife. But Harrison had acted rashly and botched the business. Not only had the Harem Girl failed to die in the carriage smash-up, but she'd escaped with scarcely a scratch.

She'd gone out dancing that same night—at Almack's! She—the Harem Girl—at Almack's!

A proper lady would have taken to her bed for a fortnight. She wasn't a lady. Why were only a handful of servants able to see her for what she was?

"We could have told him she was common," he said, as though Mary Dunstan were still with him, listening as she always did. "She's made turmoil in his house. His Grace can't abide that. He likes his peace."

He sighed deeply. "I knew him better than he knew himself, did I not? It was my responsibility to do so. What's he to do without me? Where's he to go for peace and quiet? White's? That's well enough for some, who haven't anything better to do. It won't do for him. To spend all his days and nights there? Out of the question. He'd be bored witless. Where else, then?"

Harrison considered. "Unwise to go back to the dashing widow. The Harem Girl would hunt him down. Vulgar scene bound to ensue. I know her sort. Knew the instant I clapped eyes on her, she was never Lord Lexham's daughter. It was the Princess Caraboo all over again, and she took them all in. Even the Queen. Not that it's so hard to fool a sick old woman."

He returned to the newspaper. The article went on

to share with readers one of the duke's humorous remarks. According to an unnamed source at White's Club, when asked about his impending journey, his grace had said, "If your wife was redecorating the house, would you hang about?"

Harrison repeated the riposte aloud, and laughed. "Have I not always said the master was the cleverest wit in London? 'Would you hang about?' Ha, ha. That is good."

His amusement faded when he remembered that he would not, ever again, be present to hear one of the duke's witticisms. He would not be able to enter the hostelry where the crème de la crème of London's servants gathered, and tell his envious friends what his clever master had said and done lately.

"Where shall I find another like him?" he said. "Where should I find another place like that one? Ireland? France?" He shook his head. "Oh, Mary, Mary. How could we hold our heads up if we sank to that: presiding over one of those hovels they call inns in those savage countries."

But Mary wasn't there to answer. She'd run away, and the Runners had caught her, as he'd warned her would happen.

Naturally the Runners were looking for him. He knew they'd be doing their sharpest looking along the roads leading out of London. He'd explained to her: He had friends in London, so many friends who owed him and who would make sure he wasn't caught. They wouldn't want to risk his telling all he knew about them. For him, there was no safer place to be than London.

"Oh, Mary, Mary." He glanced sadly about the empty room. "I was in liquor that day. It frightened you, I know."

He wasn't the kind to drink to excess. He'd done it because of the horses.

He'd acted too hastily, and he'd paid for it. He'd heard the horse's screams in his head long after he fled King Street. He'd seen the blood even when he closed his eyes. He'd begun drinking and had kept on drinking until he was senseless and couldn't hear or see any of it anymore.

He'd always been so proud of His Grace's cattle: the finest beasts in London. When he'd burst out of Cleveland Yard that day, he'd attacked in a frenzy. When the hot anger dissipated, he'd grieved for them.

She, he would hurt without a second thought or the smallest regret afterward. She'd destroyed him, utterly. She'd killed his future and made a fool of his master and polluted the house.

Now, when it was too late, the duke had discovered his mistake. Why else would he leave his new bride behind and set out on a lengthy journey at the height of the Season?

Harrison set down the newspaper and refilled his coffee cup. He stirred in a few lumps of sugar and added a generous dollop of cream. Though he'd fallen on hard times and was temporarily inconvenienced, he was far from impoverished. The room might be smaller than what he was used to, yet it was comfortably appointed, and his friends kept him properly provisioned.

This wasn't much solace for a man utterly and irrevocably ruined, who had no future worth having.

Still, so long as he remained in London, it was better to be comfortable than not.

He was exceedingly sorry for Mary. She'd hang for sure. She should have known him better, after all these years, than to take fright over a few drunken ravings. In any case, she could do him no harm and their enemies no good. She didn't know who his friends were. He had helped line the pockets of the high, middling, and low. He had friends among the goldsmiths, linen drapers, and furniture makers. He knew tavern keepers and innkeepers, fishmongers and bakers and vegetable sellers, tea and coffee and spirit merchants, the candle makers and coal merchants and more. There wasn't a trade in London in which he didn't have at least one friend.

Mary didn't know who they were. She'd always preferred not to know. Thus she wouldn't know, any more than the Runners and patrollers and constables and magistrates did, where he was.

He put her out of his thoughts and turned his mind to dealing with the cause of all their troubles.

He turned his mind to the first day he'd met the Harem Girl and the way she'd humiliated him in front of a footman. Keeping that incident at the front of his mind would keep off regrets. The next time, he wouldn't need to stupefy himself with drink. Next time, he'd leave everyone else out of it. He'd do what any good servant must do. He'd remove from Marchmont House what should never have been allowed into the house in the first place.

He couldn't expect thanks for it, but he was used to being taken for granted. A proper servant, in fact, took pride in being taken for granted. And as always, the good servant must derive his satisfaction from a job well done.

Tuesday, 12 May

The Duke of Marchmont took leave of his wife with a reluctance obvious to onlookers on the other side of the square. He didn't care how obvious it was.

When she followed him out to the traveling chariot, he gave his neighbors the shock of a lifetime by making his horses wait. Instead of springing into the carriage, he held her hand and repeated all the instructions he'd already given—twice—indoors.

"You will not leave the house," he said. "You will not step into the garden until the footmen have patrolled it first for intruders. And then you must have Jarvis with you at all times. With her umbrella. Promise me."

"I promise, I promise," she said.

"While you're here, the servants can keep you safe. Outside of the house, you're vulnerable."

"I know."

"I'll be back as soon as I can."

"I know you will."

"Perhaps, after all, it would be wiser to take you with me," he said.

"It'll take me hours to pack, and if I go with you, the journey will take twice as long," she said. "Men never make a fraction as many stops as women want. This way, you'll be back in a few weeks—perhaps as little as a fortnight. Then we can enjoy the rest of the Season."

"I can't believe I must leave you alone while I go away to quarrel about fishing rights, of all things, at such a time."

"They wouldn't send for you if it wasn't necessary." She stroked the front of his coat. "Please don't fret. I won't be alone. I'll be safer here than anywhere else. And I shouldn't enjoy going out to any sort of entertainment without you, in any event."

"I worry that you'll be bored, Zoe. When you become bored, terrible things happen."

"I won't be bored at all. I'm excited about refurbishing the house. I'll have plenty to do, looking at fabric swatches and paint charts and deciding how to arrange the rooms. If I begin to feel dull, I'll send for my sisters to argue with me."

He gazed down at her for a long while, into her sparkling blue eyes and sunny countenance. "Perhaps you won't miss me very much after all."

"I shall miss your body very much," she said. "But while you're gone, I can think of new and different ways to make use of it."

He wondered what new and different ways she could devise that she hadn't already done. Still, she did seem to have a boundless imagination.

He laughed and grasped her waist and lifted her off the pavement. "I'll keep that notion in mind, to warm me at night in my cold, lonely bed."

He kissed her, and she wrapped her arms about his neck and gave him a no-holds-barred kiss in return. She didn't care who was watching, either. She never held back. With Zoe it was all or nothing, always.

He set her down again slowly, relishing the feel of her soft body sliding along his. They were scandal-

izing the neighbors, no doubt. Ah, well, he was besotted with his wife. What did he care who saw? Let
them watch and let them talk about it all they liked.

Friday, shortly after midnight

His prey was bound to go out eventually, but Harrison couldn't wait for eventually. He only waited to
make sure the duke didn't suddenly change his mind
and return. He listened for rumors and quietly absorbed the information ordinary servants exchanged
in their various gathering places.

Half the world had observed the vulgar public fare-
well in St. James's Square. The other half heard from
those who'd seen. It was her doing, of course, hanging on His Grace's neck like a harlot.

But her lures didn't bring him back. The duke had
not changed his mind and returned on Tuesday or
Wednesday. Thursday having passed as well, the
duke would be hundreds of miles away.

The moon, approaching its full, would set in about
two hours, but at present its illumination cast shadows in St. James's Square. In the shadows, well away
from the streetlamps' narrow circles of light, Harrison patiently waited.

He stood and watched as the hall porter fastened
the shutters of Marchmont House. From where he
stood, he couldn't hear the man latch the doors, but
he knew he'd do so. Shortly thereafter, the porter
would trim the lamps in the entrance hall and passages.

Harrison bided his time, knowing the routine of

the house. This night, the servants would all be abed. If the master and mistress had gone out, a few must wait up for them. But the master was away and the mistress had not gone out. The hall porter would soon be dozing in his chair. The others would have taken to their beds for the delicious luxury of a few extra hours of rest. They'd be dead asleep. A fire or explosion might rouse them but not much else.

If he were still the house steward, he'd be prowling the corridors, to make sure the male and female staff were in their proper beds. He'd never tolerated any improprieties of that kind. Pregnant maids were dismissed without a character, and the males responsible paid fines.

But he was no longer in charge of them, and the duke hadn't yet replaced him. There was only Thomas, lately jumped up to butler, and only adequate for that position.

Still, Thomas might be on the prowl, jealous of his new rank and wanting to show off to the new mistress how conscientious he was.

Harrison waited a little longer, watching for any telltale flicker of light.

But he saw none. Only darkness.

And when he slipped in through the servants' entrance, he heard only the familiar silence of a sleeping household.

Boy and man, Harrison had lived in Marchmont House for twenty years. He knew every inch of it. As house steward, he'd walked these corridors late at night. He could find his way to any part of the house blindfolded.

Still, the Harem Girl might have had furniture moved about. She'd had the table of the breakfast room moved, hadn't she? She was unlikely to leave anything else alone. Not wanting to risk tripping over an illogically placed chair or table, he carried a small candle, as he always used to do during his nightly inspections.

A good servant goes unobtrusively—preferably invisibly—about his business. To make sure of this, Harrison had always kept the house well maintained. No creaky hinges or squeaky floors announced one's passage from one room to the next.

He made his way noiselessly to the Duchess of Marchmont's rooms. The housemaids slept in the attics. Her Grace's lady's maid, however, had a small room adjoining Her Grace's.

He set the candle down on a nearby table in the corridor and cautiously cracked the door open to listen. He heard no snoring. He didn't hear Jarvis moving about, though. He left the candle on the table in the main corridor, slipped through the door, and waited while his eyes adjusted to the darkness of the passage. Then he moved along and found the door to Jarvis's room. When he opened it, he easily made out her form under the bedclothes.

Swiftly and soundlessly he passed through her room, then through the boudoir, where he removed a small pillow from the chaise longue. He continued his progress, passing through the dressing room. These rooms, having full windows, were not quite as dark as the maid's, and his eyes had adjusted. He had no trouble finding his way to the door of the duchess's bedroom.

Her room would be a degree lighter still. Some

moonlight would penetrate the curtains, and the dying coals would give off a faint glow. It would be all the light he'd need for his simple task.

He pressed his ear to the door and listened.

Silence.

He had a well-sharpened penknife, but only for an emergency. Knives were untidy. Blood was the very devil to get out of damask.

The pillow was best. Suffocation left no evidence. If he wrung her neck, he'd leave bruises. Still, he'd do what he had to, as discreetly as possible, as a good servant always did.

He opened the door.

He trod quietly over the carpet, toward the bed, and parted the curtains.

He took the pillow in both hands and bent over the figure under the bedclothes.

It sprang up suddenly, and something clanged against his skull.

He dropped the pillow and pitched sideways, onto the floor.

Harrison lay too still. Marchmont cursed silently as he climbed out of Zoe's bed.

He'd made himself be careful. He'd wanted the man alive. He'd wanted to watch him hang. This was too easy a death for the villain who'd tried to kill Zoe.

About him, the servants emerged from their hiding places. One hurried to the fire and lit a taper, then began lighting the candles.

As the gloom receded, Harrison made a small movement and moaned. The candlelight showed no pool of blood about his head.

Marchmont breathed a quick sigh of relief and eased his iron grip on the candlestick. His heart was pounding, as though he'd run for miles and miles.

If Zoe had been in the bed . . . if he'd been an instant too slow . . .

But she hadn't been in the bed.

He'd agreed to use her as bait, making a great show in the square of leaving her behind while he went on his long journey, but he had refused to let her actually lie in her bed to await a would-be assassin.

She came out from behind the door, another candlestick in her hand. "Just in case," she'd said.

Tonight, as had been the case since Tuesday night, they'd had servants under the bed and in every possible hiding place, all ready to come to his aid.

She had insisted on being there, too.

The best Marchmont could do was persuade her to stand behind the door, while he hoped there wouldn't be a scuffle and she wouldn't hit him by accident.

"Somebody tie his hands and get him out of this room," he said. "I can't bear the sight of him. Hubert, find the hackney and make haste to Bow Street. Tell them we've got him."

Not knowing where Harrison was or when he was watching, they hadn't kept one of the duke's carriages ready. Harrison would have noticed and become suspicious. Instead, Marchmont had paid a hackney to make a circuit of a few nearby streets, over and over, while waiting to be summoned to the house.

Harrison said nothing while they tied his hands and hauled him up onto his feet. But when they tried to lead him to the door, he refused to move.

"Oh, that is a fine trick, Your Grace, a fine one

indeed," he said. "You took me in completely. I watched you drive away myself, and had word from a friend at Barnet, who'd seen you stop to change horses. But it wasn't you in the carriage, I see."

Marchmont had changed places with Roderick, the tallest of Zoe's brothers. Along the road, people would notice only the ducal crest. How many people outside of London knew exactly what the Duke of Marchmont looked like? They'd see a tall, fair-haired gentleman and the crest on the carriage, and that would be sufficient.

He didn't explain any of this. Harrison deserved no explanations.

"I should have anticipated a trick," Harrison said. "I mistook that show in the square before your departure, too. That I, of all people, should underestimate my master's cleverness is a sorry state of affairs, indeed."

"Come along, Mr. Harrison," Joseph said. "Please don't make a greater spectacle of yourself than you have already."

"Yes, a spectacle, certainly," said Harrison. "Well, well, how we shall laugh about this tomorrow, when we read it in the newspapers. Another one of His Grace's jokes, eh? I told you all, did I not, that there wasn't another master as amusing as His Grace."

The house steward's gaze shifted to the new butler. "So, Thomas, you've been put in charge, I hear. Like the work, I daresay. Fancy yourself His Grace's house steward next, no doubt. Twenty years, you give your best. Do without sleep and without thanks, and it comes to this."

Harrison's shoulders slumped and he began to

weep. "Twenty years. All my work. Ruined, ruined, ruined. 'I'll see those books,' says she. Oh, yes, she must see the books. What's books, to twenty years' devoted service?"

"I should have given you credit for the twenty years' devoted service," said Marchmont, "had you not tried to kill my wife. Twice. I owe you nothing. Our account is balanced." He gave the little wave of his hand. "Take him away. If he gives trouble, do what you must, but keep him alive. I want to see him hang."

After they left, Zoe saw the change in her husband. The exhaustion he'd hidden from the others was plain to her. All these days of waiting, unsure exactly what Harrison would do. And all the while Marchmont couldn't be sure he was doing the right thing and the best thing.

Zoe had told him, "Harrison knows this house better than any of us do. He knows it better than he knows his own body. If I don't go out, he'll come here to get me, and he'll think he's safe, because he knows everything about us and about the house."

She'd been right, and Marchmont's plan had worked.

Harrison had been caught, in the act.

And his master was so unhappy.

Zoe put her arms about her husband, but he gently disengaged himself.

"I beg your pardon," he said. "I need a moment. You're accustomed to being almost murdered. This is a novel experience for me."

He moved away and drew a chair nearer to the fire and sat. He put his head in his hands.

She sat on the rug, cross-legged at his feet. She

waited until she heard his breathing slow and she knew he was calming.

"Twenty years," she said. "A long time. Your parents were alive when he began to work here."

"Yes." He did not look up. "He started as a foot-boy. His father was a footman here but died young."

"He was like a member of the family, then," she said. "No wonder you grieve."

"I'm not grieving," he said. "I want him to hang."

"He was here when your parents were alive, and when Gerard was alive. He was here all the time I was gone. He was a part of your life—"

"And I trusted him. Implicitly. And he betrayed my trust. Yes, yes. I know." He looked up. "He was, in so many ways, the perfect servant. I can't help thinking he would have been altogether the perfect servant had I paid attention."

"Perhaps," she said. "Whatever happens, the Mohammedans say it's the will of God. They would say it was the will of God that your servant became corrupt and stole from you. They would say it was the will of God that, when he was caught, instead of repenting, he turned to violence. And so I wonder if maybe you think *you* are God. You think that because you looked the other way, it's your fault this man turned bad. Well, perhaps that's what happens when one is a duke and everyone defers to him. He thinks he's God."

"I don't think . . ." He trailed off.

She said nothing.

He regarded her for a long time. "You told me you could dance and sing and compose poetry. You told me you knew all the arts of pleasing a man. You told me you could manage a household—even eunuchs. You never mentioned you could argue philosophy, too."

"Being in the harem gives a woman plenty of time to think," she said. "I think about these things. Especially I think about the way men think. And most important to me is the way *my* man thinks."

"Or doesn't."

She smiled and leaned back and rested her head against his leg. "I'm glad I married you, because your heart is kind and generous. You're so angry with this servant, and you hate him, yet you grieve for him and think of the ways you could have prevented what's happened. While you're thinking this, I'm thinking of how cruel fate has been to you, taking your mother and father and your brother. I know you've tried to close your heart. But you didn't close it to me, and you don't even close it to a man who has so cruelly betrayed you. I don't mind anymore that I love you."

She felt his body go still then. She was aware of the atmosphere changing.

She felt his fingers threading through her hair.

He cleared his throat. "Zoe, I think you said you love me."

"I did say it. I do love you. With all my heart."

"I see." There was a long pause, then he said, "For how long has this been going on?"

"I don't know," she said. "Sometimes I think it started a long, long time ago."

"You might have mentioned it."

"I didn't want to encourage it," she said. "I thought it was a bad idea."

He laughed.

She looked up.

"I feel the same way," he said. "*Exactly.*"

She took his hand from her head and brought it to her mouth and kissed each knuckle. She would have done more, but a servant appeared and said, apologetically, that a Bow Street officer was downstairs and wishing to speak to His Grace.

It was a long night and a long fortnight for the Duke of Marchmont.

Harrison was one responsibility one couldn't pass to others. Marchmont went to Bow Street and gave evidence at the preliminary hearing. Harrison was bound over for trial and sent to Newgate Prison. The trial took place swiftly, as was usual, and the jury swiftly found Harrison guilty. The question of his sanity was raised, but his demeanor was what it had always been. Judge and jury observed the speech and behavior of the perfect servant. The judge sentenced him to be hanged alongside Mrs. Dunstan.

It was what Marchmont had said he wanted. It was what the man deserved.

And yet . . .

And yet . . .

And yet there was Shakespeare again.

The duke explained it to his duchess after they supped together in his room that evening. After days spent at the trial and days dealing with the trial's aftermath, he was in no mood for socializing.

The servants had taken away the small table and the remains of their supper. Master and mistress sat together companionably by the fire, their chairs close together.

"So there was Shakespeare in my head again," he said, "and that damnable speech from *The Merchant of Venice*. 'The quality of mercy is not strained' and so forth."

"I don't remember," she said. "Tell it to me."

He recited Portia's speech.

Zoe's eyes filled with tears. "Oh, Lucien." She put out her hand and he took it in his, and he was grateful he'd married a woman who understood.

"What could I do?" he said. "I said I wanted him to hang, but when it came to it, when I saw the judge put on his black cap, I was heartsick. I know you believe that Harrison chose to do what he did—but I'll never know if he would have behaved differently had I chosen to truly be the Duke of Marchmont, instead of acting as though it weren't true."

"If, if, if," she said softly. "Who knows the answer to 'What if?'"

"I don't know," he said. "Since I don't know, I must give Harrison the benefit of the doubt. I called on the Prince Regent and asked for mercy for my servants. The sentence is to be commuted to transportation."

She eased her hand from his, and for a moment he thought that perhaps, after all, she didn't understand.

But she only let go to leave her chair and climb into his lap. She tucked her head into the crook of his neck. He put his arms about her and nuzzled her hair and drank in her scent with silent thanks. She was alive and warm in his arms. She was his, and she understood.

"It's good to be a duke," she said softly. "It's good to have the Prince Regent's ear. With a word you can save the life of a man and a woman and give them another chance."

He lifted his head and gazed at her.

She tipped her head back and looked at him. "What?" she said.

"What you said," he said. "It's good to be a duke. Do you know, Zoe, it *is*."

It was. For the first time, and at last and thanks to her, it truly was.

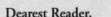

History of Passion . . .

Dearest Reader,

Don't be deceived. Behind her demure smile and guarded gaze even the most proper lady has a secret. But what happens when the sting of betrayal, ache of sacrifice, or ghosts of lovers past return, threatening to shake that Mona Lisa smile?

This summer, Avon Books presents four delicious romances about four women who are more than what they seem, and the dangerously handsome heroes who are captivated by them. From bestselling authors Elizabeth Boyle, Loretta Chase, Jeaniene Frost, and a beautifully repackaged edition by Susan Wiggs.

Twenty years ago, Pippin betrayed her heart and married another in order to save Captain Thomas Dashwell's life. Now their paths cross again and Pippin is determined not to let a second chance at love slip away. Dash's world stops when he sees her standing aboard his ship but promises himself he'll never again fall for the breathtaking beauty.

Dashwell's nostrils were filled with the scent of newly minted guineas. Enough Yellow Georges to make even the dour Mr. Hardy happy. Nodding in satisfaction, he whistled low and soft like a seabird to the men in the longboat.

They pulled up one man, then another, and cut the bindings that had their arms tied around their backs and tossed the two over the side and into the surf.

That ought to cool their heels a bit, Dashwell mused, as he watched the Englishmen splash their way to shore. His passengers had been none too pleased with him last night when he'd abandoned their delivery in favor of saving his neck and the lives of his crew.

Untying the mule, he led the beast down the shore toward the longboat. It came along well enough until it got down to the waterline, where the waves were coming in and the longboat tossed and crunched against the rocks. Then the animal showed its true nature and began to balk.

The miss who'd caught his eye earlier came over and took hold of the reins, her other hand stroking the beast's muzzle and talking softly to it until it settled down.

"You have a way about you," he said over his shoulder, as he walked back and forth, working alongside his men, who were as anxious as he was to gain their gold and be gone from this precarious rendezvous.

"Do you have a name?" he asked, when he returned for the last sack. This close he could see all too well the modest cut of her gown, her shy glances, and the way she bit her lip as if she didn't know whether to speak to him.

Suddenly it occurred to him who, or rather what she was, and he had only one thought.

What the devil was Josephine doing bringing a lady, one barely out of the schoolroom, into this shady business?

"What? No name?" he pressed, coming closer still, for he'd never met a proper lady—he certainly didn't count Josephine as one, not by the way she swore and gambled and schemed.

As he took another step closer he caught the veriest hint of roses on her. Soft and subtle, but to a man like him it sent a shock of desire through him as he'd never known.

Careful there, Dashwell, he cautioned himself. If the militia didn't shoot him, he had to imagine Josephine would. "Come sweetling, what is your name?"

There was no harm in just asking, now was there?

The wee bit of muslin pursed her lips shut, then glanced over at her companions, as if seeking their help. And when she looked back at him, he smiled at her. The grin that usually got him into trouble.

"Pippin," she whispered, again glancing back over toward where Josephine was haranguing Temple and Clifton for news from the Continent.

"Pippin, eh?" he replied softly, not wanting to frighten her, even as he found himself mesmerized by the soft, uncertain light in her eyes. "I would call you something else. Something befitting such a pretty lady." He tapped his fingers to his lips. "Circe. Yes, that's it. From now on I'll call you my Circe. For you're truly a siren to lure me ashore."

Even in the dark he could see her cheeks brighten with a blush, hear the nervous rattle to her words. "I don't think that is proper."

Proper? He'd fallen into truly deep waters now, for something devilish inside him wanted to make sure this miss never worried about such a ridiculous notion again.

But something else, something entirely foreign to him, urged him to see that she never knew anything else but a safe and proper existence.

A thought he extinguished as quickly as he could. For it was rank with strings and chains and noble notions that had no place in his world.

"Not proper?" He laughed, more to himself than

at her. "Not proper is the fact that this bag feels a bit lighter than the rest." He hoisted it up and jangled it as he turned toward the rest of the party on the beach. "My lady, don't tell me you've cheated me yet again."

For indeed, the bag did feel light.

Lady Josephine winced, but then had the nerve to deny her transgression. "Dash, I'll not pay another guinea into your dishonest hands."

No wonder she'd brought her pair of lovely doves down to the beach. A bit of distraction so he'd not realize he wasn't getting his full price.

"Then I shall take my payment otherwise," he said, and before anyone could imagine what he was about, he caught hold of this tempting little Pippin and pulled her into his arms.

She gasped as he caught hold of her, and for a moment he felt a twinge of conscience.

Thankfully he wasn't a man to stand on such notions for long.

"I've always wanted to kiss a lady," he told her, just before his lips met hers.

At first he'd been about to kiss her as he would any other girl, but there was a moment, just as he looked down at her, with only one thought—to plunder those lips—that he found himself lost.

Her eyes were blue, as azure as the sea off the West Indies, and they caught him with their wide innocence, their trust.

Trust? In him?

Foolish girl, he thought as he drew closer and then kissed her, letting his lips brush over hers. Yet instead of his usual blustering ways, he found himself reining back his desire. This was the girl's first kiss, he knew that with the same surety that he knew how many casks of brandy were in his hold, and ever-so-gently, he ventured past her lips, slowly letting his tongue sweep over hers.

She gasped again, but this time from the very intimacy of it, and Dash suddenly found himself inside a maelstrom.

He tried to stop himself from falling, for that would mean setting her aside. But he couldn't let her go.

This Pippin, this innocent lass, this very proper lady, brought him alive as no other woman ever had.

Mine, he thought, with possessiveness, with passion, with the knowledge that she was his, and always would be.

He wanted to know everything about her, her real name, her secrets, her desires . . . His hands traced her lines, the slight curve of her hips, the soft swell of her breasts.

She shivered beneath his touch, but she didn't stop him, didn't try to shy away. Instead, she kissed him back, innocently, tentatively at first, then eagerly.

Good God, he was holding an angel!

And as if the heavens themselves rang out in protest over his violation of one of their own, a rocket screeched across the sky, and when it exploded, wrenching the night into day with a shower of sparks, Dashwell pulled back from her and looked up.

As another rocket shot upward, he realized two things.

Yes, by God, her eyes were as blue as the sea.

And secondly, the militia wasn't at the local pub bragging about their recent exploits.

*L*aura seated herself, and Sandro took the opposite
chair. The fire crackled cheerily in the marble framed
grate. "Have you run afoul of the law, madonna?"

"Of course not." She folded her hands demurely in her
lap. "My lord, I have information about Daniele Moro."

Her words pounded in Sandro's head. Disbelief made
him fierce. "How do you know of Moro?"

"Well." She ran her tongue over her lips. Sandro knew
women who spent fortunes to achieve that beautiful

shade of crimson, but he saw no trace of rouge on Laura. "I have a confession to make, my lord."

A denial leapt in his throat. No. She could not be involved in the butchery of Moro. Not her. Anyone but her. "Go on," he said thickly.

"I heard you speaking of Moro to Maestro Titian." She leaned forward and hurried on. "Please forgive me, but I was so curious, I couldn't help myself. Besides, this might be for the best. I can help you solve this case, my lord."

He didn't want her help. He didn't want to think of this innocent lamb sneaking in the dark, listening at doorways, hearing of the atrocity that left even him feeling sick and soiled.

Without thinking, he jumped up, grasped her by the shoulders, and drew her to her feet. Although he sensed the silent censure of Jamal, he ignored it and sank his fingers into the soft flesh of her upper arms. He smelled her scent of sea air and jasmine, saw the firelight sparkling in her beautiful, opalescent eyes.

"Damn you for your meddlesome ways," he hissed through his teeth. "You have no business poking your nose into the affairs of the *signori di notte*."

She seemed unperturbed by his temper, unscathed by his rough embrace. She lifted her chin. "I'm well aware of that, my lord, but remember, I did warn you of my inquisitive nature."

"Then I should have warned you that I have no use for women—inquisitive or otherwise."

She lifted her hands to his chest and pressed gently. "Your fingers are bruising me, my lord."

He released her as abruptly as he had snatched her up. "My apologies."

"I wouldn't worry about it, but Maestro Titian will

question me about any bruises when I model for him."

Sandro despised the image of Laura laid out like a feast upon the artist's red couch, lissome and sensual as a goddess, while Titian rendered her beauty on canvas.

"Do you truly have no use for women, my lord?" she asked. "That's unusual, especially in so handsome a man as you."

Sandro ignored her insincere compliment and paused to consider his four mistresses. Barbara, Arnetta, Gioia, and Alicia were as different and yet as alike as the four seasons. For years they had fulfilled his needs with the discretion and decorum he required. In exchange, he housed each in her own luxurious residence.

"It's my choice," he said stuffily, settling back in his chair. He did not need to look at Jamal to know that he was grinning with glee.

"Well, I believe my information could be useful to you." She sent him a sidelong glance. Not even the demure brown dress could conceal her lush curves. "That is, if you're interested, my lord."

As she sank gracefully back into the chair, he stared at the shape of her breasts, ripe beneath their soft cloak of linen. "I'm interested."

She smiled, the open, charming expression that was fast becoming familiar to him. "I happened to mention the murder of Daniele Moro to my friend Yasmin—"

"By God," he snapped, "don't you understand? This is a sensitive matter." He gripped the chair arms to keep himself anchored to his seat. "You can't go airing police business all over the city."

"I didn't." She seemed truly bewildered. "I told only one person."

"You could endanger yourself, madonna. The killer is still at large."

"Oh. I'm not used to having someone worry about my welfare."

"It is my vocation to worry about the welfare of every citizen of the republic."

She shifted impatiently. "Never mind all that. I found someone who saw Daniele Moro on the night he was killed."

Once again, Sandro came out of his chair. *"What?"*

"I'll take you to meet this person, my lord."

"Do that, and I'll think about forgiving you."

Coming July 2009

Don't Tempt Me

by *New York Times* bestselling author
Loretta Chase

Imprisoned in a harem for twelve years, Zoe Lexham knows things no well-bred lady should . . . ruining her for society. Can the wickedly handsome Duke of Marchmont use his influence to save her from idle tongues? A simple enough task, if only he can stifle desire long enough to see his seductive charge safely into respectability . . .

Zoe went cold, then hot. She felt dizzy. But it was a wonderful dizziness, the joy of release.

Now at last she stood in the open.

Here I am, she thought. *Home at last, at last. Yes, look at me. Look your fill. I'm not invisible anymore.*

She felt his big, warm hand clasp hers. The warmth rushed into her heart and made it hurry. She was aware of her pulse jumping against her throat and against her wrist, so close to his. The heat spread into her belly and down, to melt her knees.

I'm going to faint, she thought. But she couldn't let

herself swoon merely because a man had touched her. Not now, at any rate. Not here. She made herself look up at him.

The duke wore the faintest smile—of mockery or amusement she couldn't tell. Behind his shuttered eyes she sensed rather than saw a shadow. She remembered the brief glimpse of pain he'd had when she'd mentioned his brother. It vanished in an instant, but she'd seen it in his first, surprised reaction: the darkness there, bleak and empty and unforgettable.

She gazed longer than she should have into his eyes, those sleepy green eyes that watched her so intently yet shut her out. And at last he let out a short laugh and raised her hand to his mouth, brushing her knuckles against his lips.

Had they been in the harem, she would have sunk onto the pillows and thrown her head back, inviting him. But they were not and he'd declined to make her his wife.

And she was not a man, to let her lust rule her brain. This man was not a good candidate for a spouse. There had been a bond between them once. Not a friendship, really. In childhood, the few years between them was a chasm, as was the difference in their genders. Still, he'd been fond of her once, she thought, in his own fashion. But that was before.

Now he was everything every woman could want, and he knew it.

She desired him the way every other woman desired him. Still, at least she finally felt desire, she told herself. If she could feel it with him, she'd feel it with someone else, someone who wanted her, who'd give his heart to her. For now, she was grateful to be free. She was grateful to stand on this balcony and look out upon the hundreds of people below.

She squeezed his hand in thanks and let her mouth form a slow, genuine smile of gratitude and happiness, though she couldn't help glancing up at him once from under her lashes to seek his reaction.

She glimpsed the heat flickering in the guarded green gaze.

Ah, yes. He felt it, too: the powerful physical awareness crackling between them.

He released her hand. "We've entertained the mob for long enough," he said. "Go inside."

She turned away. The crowd began to stir and people were talking again but more quietly. They'd become a murmuring sea rather than a roaring one.

"You've seen her," he said, and his deep voice easily carried over the sea. "You shall see her again from time to time. Now go away."

After a moment, they began to turn away, and by degrees they drifted out of the square.

Coming August 2009

Destined for an Early Grave

by *New York Times* bestselling author

Jeaniene Frost

Just when Cat is ready for a little rest and relaxation with her sexy vampire boyfriend Bones, she's haunted by dreams from her past—a past she doesn't remember. To unlock these secrets, Cat may have to venture all the way into the grave. But the truth could rock what she knows about herself—and her relationship with Bones.

If he catches me, I'm dead.

I ran as fast as I could, darting around trees, tangled roots, and rocks in the forest. The monster snarled as it chased me, the sound closer than before. I wasn't able to outrun it. The monster was picking up speed while I was getting tired.

The forest thinned ahead of me to reveal a blond vampire on a hill in the distance. I recognized him at once and hope surged through me. If I could reach him, I'd be okay. He loved me; he'd protect me from the monster. Yet I was still so far away.

Fog crept up the hill to surround the vampire, making him appear almost ghost-like. I screamed his name as the monster's footsteps got even closer. Panicked, I lunged forward, narrowly avoiding the grasp of bony hands that would pull me down to the grave. With renewed effort, I sprinted toward the vampire. He urged me on, snarling warnings at the monster that wouldn't stop chasing me.

"Leave me alone," I screamed as a merciless grip seized me from behind. "No!"

"Kitten!"

The shout didn't come from the vampire ahead of me; it came from the monster wrestling me to the ground. I jerked my head toward the vampire in the distance, but his features blurred into nothingness and the fog covered him. Right before he disappeared, I heard his voice.

He is not your husband, Catherine.

A hard shake evaporated the last of the dream and I woke to find Bones, my vampire lover, hovered over me.

"What is it? Are you hurt?"

An odd question, you would think, since it had only been a nightmare. But with the right power and magic, sometimes nightmares could be turned into weapons. A while back, I'd almost been killed by one. This was different, however. No matter how vivid it felt, it had just been a dream.

"I'll be fine if you quit shaking me."

Bones dropped his hands and let out a noise of relief. "You didn't wake up and you were thrashing on the bed. Brought back rotten memories."

"I'm okay. It was a . . . weird dream."

There was something about the vampire in it that nagged me. Like I should know who he was. That made no sense, however, since he was just a figment of my imagination.

"Odd that I couldn't catch any of your dream," Bones went on. "Normally your dreams are like background music to me."

Bones was a Master vampire, more powerful than most vampires I'd ever met. One of his gifts was the ability to read human minds. Even though I was half-human, half-vampire, there was enough humanity in me that Bones could hear my thoughts, unless I worked to block him. Still, this was news to me.

"You can hear my *dreams*? God, you must never get any quiet. I'd be shooting myself in the head if I were you."

Which wouldn't do much to him, actually. Only silver through the heart or decapitation was lethal to a vampire. Getting shot in the head might take care of *my* ills the permanent way, but it would just give Bones a nasty headache.

He settled himself back onto the pillows. "Don't fret, luv. I said it's like background music, so it's rather soothing. As for quiet, out here on this water, it's as quiet as I've experienced without being half-shriveled in the process."

I lay back down, a shiver going through me at the mention of his near-miss with death. Bones's hair had turned white from how close he'd come to dying, but now it was back to its usual rich brown color.

"Is that why we're drifting on a boat out in the Atlantic? So you could have some peace and quiet?"

"I wanted some time alone with you, Kitten. We've had so little of that lately."

An understatement. Even though I'd quit my job leading the secret branch of Homeland Security that hunted rogue vampires and ghouls, life hadn't been dull. First we'd had to deal with our losses from the war with another Master vampire last year. Several of Bones's friends—and my best friend Denise's husband, Randy—had been murdered. Then there had been months of hunting down the remaining perpetrators of that war so they couldn't live to plot against us another day. Then training my replacement so that my uncle Don had someone else to play bait when his operatives went after the misbehaving members of undead society. Most vampires and ghouls didn't kill when they fed, but there were those who killed for fun. Or stupidity. My uncle made sure those vampires and ghouls were taken care of—and that ordinary citizens weren't aware they existed.

So when Bones told me we were taking a boat trip, I'd assumed there must be some search-and-destroy reason behind it. Going somewhere just for relaxation hadn't happened, well, *ever*, in our relationship.

"This is a weekend getaway?" I couldn't keep the disbelief out of my voice.

He traced his finger on my lower lip. "This is our vacation, Kitten. We can go anywhere in the world and take our time getting there. So tell me, where shall we go?"

"Paris."

I surprised myself saying it. I'd never had a burning desire to visit there before, but for some reason, I did now. Maybe it was because Paris was supposed to be the city of lovers, although just looking at Bones was usually enough to get me in a romantic mood.

He must have caught my thought, because he smiled, making his face more breathtaking, in my opinion. Lying against the navy sheets, his skin almost glowed with a silky alabaster paleness that was too perfect to be human. The sheets were tangled past his stomach, giving me an uninterrupted view of his lean, taut abdomen and hard, muscled chest. Dark brown eyes began to tinge with emerald and fangs peeked under the curve of his mouth, letting me know I wasn't the only one feeling warmer all of a sudden.

"Paris it is, then," he whispered, and flung the sheets off.